THE EXPAT AFFAIR

A NOVEL

KIMBERLY BELLE

PARK ROW BOOKS

PARK
ROW
BOOKS™

Recycling programs
for this product may
not exist in your area.

ISBN-13: 978-0-7783-1094-5
ISBN-13: 978-0-7783-6015-5 (Hardcover Edition)

The Expat Affair

Park Row Books
22 Adelaide St. West, 41st Floor
Toronto, Ontario M5H 4E3, Canada
ParkRowBooks.com

Printed in U.S.A.

Praise for the novels of Kimberly Belle

"I was glued to the pages of *The Paris Widow*! I couldn't stop reading and was blown away by the twists and turns. One of my favorite reads this year!"

—Freida McFadden, *New York Times* bestselling author of *The Housemaid*

"*The Paris Widow* takes you on a twist-filled journey from the twinkling lights of the Eiffel Tower to the seedy alleyways of the 19th arrondissement and into the secrets lurking behind a seemingly idyllic marriage. You'll hold your breath as Stella Knox faces the dangers of the dark world of blood antiquities in her search for the truth about what really happened to her husband and whether her marriage and life were all a facade. Kimberly Belle has crafted the perfect thriller. *Magnifique!*"

—Alex Finlay, author of *The Night Shift* and *What Have We Done*

"*The Paris Widow* is a gripping tale that takes you on a thrilling journey through some of the most enchanting locales of Europe. This book is a must-read for those seeking an enthralling escape into a world where danger and intrigue intersect with the enduring echoes of past secrets. Belle has crafted an irresistible page-turner that keeps you hooked from the first page until the very end."

—Jean Kwok, *New York Times* bestselling author of *The Leftover Woman*

"*The Paris Widow* is irresistible from the very first page. Simultaneously glamorous and harrowing, full of danger and excitement, with a passionate love story at its heart, this is the definition of a page-turner. I devoured it and so will you."

—Michele Campbell, internationally bestselling author of *The Intern*

Also by Kimberly Belle

THE PARIS WIDOW

THE PERSONAL ASSISTANT

DESPERATE DEADLY WIDOWS

YOUNG RICH WIDOWS

MY DARLING HUSBAND

STRANGER IN THE LAKE

DEAR WIFE

THREE DAYS MISSING

THE MARRIAGE LIE

THE ONES WE TRUST

THE LAST BREATH

A THOUSAND DOORS ANTHOLOGY

For Evan and Fabienne, two of my favorite Amsterdammers

PART ONE

"A Diamond Is Forever."

—Frances Gerety of N.W. Ayer & Son for De Beers

RAYNA

My eyes snap open on a jolt, and I blink into a room that's as dark as a cave. For the first few blissful seconds, my body relaxes into a scene that feels all too familiar. The spicy scent of male on thousand-count sheets. The cushion of a criminally expensive mattress cradling my bones. A down-filled comforter skimming my naked skin like a lover.

And then I remember.

Not my bed. Not my home. Where the sheets were criminally soft but the bed cold and lonely, even though there were two people in it.

Correction: there were *three* people, though you better believe I didn't know it at the time.

Stop. Abort. This is not the time to be thinking such things, when you find yourself in another man's bed and when there's *definitely* another woman in your old one. Fourteen months and a whole ocean between me and the ashes of my old life, and that man can still muscle his way into my head when I least want him there. Despite everything that brought me here, to a new life on the other side of the planet, Barry still holds that power, dammit.

I shove him from my mind and swipe my limbs across the rumpled cotton, making an angel on the feather and foam. On the other side of the bedroom wall, water clatters onto slick marble tiles. Xander, owner of this fine bed and plush penthouse apartment, taking a shower.

Snippets of last night flash in my head, lighting up some of the darkness that's lived there since the divorce. The bar, the restaurant, the fish washed down with a bottle of perfectly chilled Chablis, champagne bubbles tickling the back of my throat, making out with Xander on the freezing terrace, our bodies tangled under his thick duvet, the sky and the stars and the glittering lights stretching into the darkness like a carpet of diamonds. My head rolls on the pillow to face the far wall, where the tiniest strip of daylight pushes through the floor-to-ceiling drapes. The fabulous but freezing terrace on the other side of that wall of windows where I stood, pressed against the glass railing, staring out at the view.

I push up onto an elbow and blink around the dim bedroom, wondering how long Xander's showers typically run. My gaze drifts to the open bedroom door, and a strip of lit-up runner in the hallway. Puffs of steam waft across the plush burgundy carpet like a nightclub fog machine. Apparently, pretty long.

"Does this hookup come with coffee? Oat milk if you've got some, and I wouldn't say no to a croissant."

This new Rayna, she's cheeky. The kind of girl who wakes up the morning after a drunken one-night stand with no regrets. Zero. Not a single one.

My phone buzzes on the nightstand, and I roll onto a hip and pluck it from the charger. My roommate, Ingrid, the gorgeous, lanky blonde I met on craigslist when I answered her ad for a spare room. Ingrid works in the city center, at a shop that doesn't open until late morning. In the few months we've lived under the same roof, I've never seen her conscious before ten.

I frown, swiping with a thumb to answer. "What's wrong?"

"Well, seeing as I'm here and you're there, I'm guessing nothing." She yawns, loud and breathy into the phone. "I take it the date was a success."

Ingrid knows all about the date because she was there, eating breakfast in the kitchen when the notification hit my phone that Xander had swiped right. She plucked my cell out of my hand to study his profile picture, a close-up of his face bathed in late-afternoon sun.

"Cute," she said, handing my phone back. "If you don't swipe right, I will. Though I'm not sure about that bio. 73% gentleman. 27% rogue. What does that even mean?"

I took in Xander's sharp jawline, wide-set eyes, crooked, close-lipped smile that made him look like he was holding on to a secret.

"I don't know, but I'm intrigued."

He was handsome enough that I swiped right, too. Almost immediately, another notification pinged my phone: *It's a match!* And two seconds after that, a message.

Hello, Rayna with the red hair. How is your day so far?

Perhaps a bit overeager but friendly enough, and not the least bit icky. The perfect first message as far as I was concerned.

After that, the day was a blur of back and forth. First via Tinder, then on WhatsApp, then through comments on my Instagram. Nice wings, he left under a shot of me last summer in Nashville, standing against a wall with a painted mural of a butterfly. Next time you go to Music City, #ImIn.

I smile into the phone. "Yes, Ingrid. The date went *very* well."

"Are you still there?" she says, her voice perkier now. "Are you with him right now?"

I wriggle higher on the pillow, listening to the water on the other side of the wall. I hadn't heard him slip out of bed, hadn't so much as stirred when the shower started up, which says a little something about the state I was in last night.

"No." There's a soft whirring and the wall to my left shifts, the blackout shades working on what I assume is a timer. They travel up a wall of steel-and-glass windows, letting in a mauve, early morning light. "He's currently in the shower."

Ingrid squeals, and the sound does something to me. My old life was filled with moments like these, early morning gossip fests about the night before, trading anecdotes about our lives and families and men. Since moving to Amsterdam, my address book has become a lot slimmer, but whoever said women in Amsterdam are notoriously difficult to befriend has never met Ingrid. From the moment I wheeled my suitcase into her apartment, she's been nothing but friendly—and Lord knows I could use a friend.

"Why did you answer the phone?" she says now. "Get your ass in there. What is it you Americans say? Do it for the team."

She hangs up before I can correct her.

I toss my phone to the bed, telling myself that Ingrid is right. I *should* get in there, mostly because it's the opposite of what the old Rayna would do. The old Rayna would be chastising herself for spending a night with a man she just met and slinking out of here in shame. The new and improved Rayna, though—Rayna 2.0—she knows how to have a good time.

On the other side of the wall, the shower is still going, the steam still creeping along the hallway runner. New city, new life, new me.

I push back the covers and slide out of bed. "Hey, lover. You got room in that fancy shower of yours for me?"

LIKE THE REST of this place, Xander's bathroom is a work of art. A great wash of veiny brown and cream marble stretched across the floors, climbing the walls, plopped onto floating cabinets and molded into sinks. LED lights blaze down from sleek spotlights in the ceiling, a light so bright it stops me in the doorway. I stand there for a minute, blinking into the steamy space.

A towel is tossed carelessly on the floor next to a bath mat.

A tube of toothpaste lies on the edge of the sink on the left wall. The shower is still going, tucked behind a marble wall and a door of steamed-up glass, a steady clattering that echoes in the room. A tiny frisson of electricity crackles under my skin. He's been in there an awfully long time.

"Xander?"

No answer.

I take a tentative step forward, and my bare foot lands in a tepid puddle. That's when I notice the rest of the floor is wet, too, big pools of water like someone sprayed the marble with a garden hose. Next to the big square tub, a dented shampoo bottle lies on its side, burping up a purple-tinged goo, thick and slimy. A good ten feet from the shower door.

"Everything okay in there?"

Everything is not okay. Of this I am certain. I know it with every ounce of my being even if I can't quite name what's wrong. An instinctual kind of alarm bell, like running up to the edge of a cliff. I know it long before I step onto the drenched bath mat and tug open the shower door.

The first thing I see is a foot, male and knobby. *Don't look don't look don't look.* It's like an out-of-body experience—me screaming the instruction at myself from above, but it's too late because I've already seen the foot and the angle is all wrong. Xander's toes are pointed to the sky. Like he fell, maybe, whacked his head on the way down. Knocked himself unconscious and landed flat on his back.

Except no. This is more than unconscious. This is utterly, horrifyingly still. Despite the steaming water beating down on his motionless body. Despite me nudging his bare foot with mine.

My gaze wanders up his body. His long, lean legs, his athletic torso. One hand is curled in a loose fist on his chest, the other arm, his right, is stretched across the floor as if he's reaching for something. For a full five seconds, I watch swirls of pretty pink spiral toward the drain before I realize what it is: blood, leaking from the stump where his pointer finger used to be.

But the finger isn't the worst, not by a long shot. Xander's eyes are open, but they're wide and red and empty. His mouth hangs in a yawn or maybe a deep breath he can't catch because his neck . . .

Oh my God. His neck. A thin band of opaque plastic is wrapped around it like a tourniquet.

It's a zip tie. A fucking *zip tie.*

I scream and lurch backward, one foot catching in the mat, the other skidding across the water-slick floor. My arms flail, and my feet fly upward. I land on a hip, hitting the marble hard enough to rattle my teeth.

Holy shit.

I scrabble forward on my hands and knees, and maybe it's all the booze, but last night's dinner comes up in a sudden and sour wave, a perfectly cooked piece of halibut on a bed of creamy peas and haricots verts. It lands on the marble with the water and the blood and the purple-tinged shampoo, splashing on my knees and thighs.

I stagger to a stand and stumble back toward the hall, but the floor is wet and the bathroom is spinning and this is really happening. Xander is really dead. Someone really killed him while I was sleeping in the next room.

Not dead. *Murdered.*

The hallway sways as I wobble my way down it, holding on to the walls, trying to comprehend what this means. That someone snuck into Xander's apartment while I was unconscious. That they either surprised him or overpowered him enough to slice off his finger, strap a zip tie around his neck, and squeeze it practically in two. That someone *murdered* him while another person lay on the other side of the bathroom wall, sleeping off last night's sex and champagne.

A man was *strangled* in the next room, and I slept through the entire thing.

In Xander's bedroom, I pace the floor by the bed, my thoughts jumbled and fuzzy. Disassociation, shock—take your pick, though somewhere in the back of my head, a voice is screaming at me to snap out of it. To call the police and report a man's murder. To get them over here so they can search for DNA and lift fingerprints before all the evidence washes down the drain—if it hasn't already. To get the fuck out of here, and to fucking hurry.

That's when I hear it—a thump coming from somewhere close, too close. I let out a shriek before I can stop myself.

I clap a hand to my mouth, my breath coming hard and hot against my fingers.

Is the killer still here? Is he still lurking somewhere in this apartment? Cleaning up his tracks, wiping down whatever evidence he might've brought inside? My eyes bulge with realization, with terror.

Run.

My head whips around in a frantic but silent search for my clothes. My jeans, tossed over a chair in the corner. My shirt, in a crumpled heap on the floor. I don't bother with my underwear, and I don't stop long enough to zip my coat. I yank it on and shove my feet in my shoes and grab my bag from where it lay, splayed open on Xander's chest of drawers.

And then I run.

Down the hall and through the living room and into Xander's gleaming foyer, where I stab the button for the elevator—not exactly a speedy exit but searching for the stairs will take too long, and what if it leads me straight to the killer? The elevator whirrs upward, and I toss panicked glances over my shoulder, bracing for an ambush by a man with a bloody knife and a zip tie, silently chanting for the thing to *hurry the hell up.* The ping when the doors slide open is loud as a gunshot, and I lurch inside.

The elevator dumps me into the lobby, and I fly through the sleek space and out the door. A row of cars is parked at the curb, where I take a hard right and sprint in the direction of the park. All those miles logged on the trails along the river back home, all the endless loops through the Vondelpark—this is what I've been training for all this time. Getting away, putting some distance between me and Xander's penthouse and whoever might still be lurking there. I run as fast as I can.

I don't slow until I come to the intersection with the Willems-parkweg, a street bustling with trams and cars and bikes, people on their way to school and work. I choose the most conspicuous spot, the busiest corner, and screech to a stop. I pat the pockets of my coat, my jeans.

That's when I realize I left my phone.

WILLOW

I'm standing with the other mothers at the edge of the Willemspark School yard, watching the kids play, when I hear the sirens. More than one, a great chorus of swooping sounds, the notes weaving and undulating in the early morning air.

It's well before the morning bell still, and the playground is packed. Kids, red-cheeked and wet-nosed from the frigid January air, hanging from the monkey bars and climbing up the slide, playing marbles and kicking around a ball. The mothers, clumped together in tight huddles by the bikes or like me, lined up along the brick railing that runs along the sidewalk. The teachers, guarding the double doors in fat coats and sensible shoes. The sirens whoop and shriek, sending a hush over the playground.

Even four-year-old Sem, my sweet, soft-hearted Sem, medically deaf until his cochlear implants at fourteen months, sits stock-still in the flat stretch of metal at the bottom of the slide. I'd sign for him to get out of the way if the little girl at the top weren't frozen by the sound, too.

Lucy, an adorable blonde in Sem's class, runs up to her mother, a Brit. "*Mama, wat is er?*"

Willemspark is a Dutch school, but because of its location in posh Amsterdam Zuid, there are plenty of students here like Lucy and Sem, with one Dutch and one expat parent. Like me, Lucy's mother has lived here long enough she doesn't need a translation.

Mama, what's wrong?

She shakes her head, answering in crisply accented English. "I don't know, sweetheart. Must be a fire or something."

It's not a fire. Lucy's mom knows it, and so does everyone else. Last month, at a popular lunch spot only a few blocks away, a man was shot in the head while sucking down a plate of spaghetti. These sirens are on that level, and they have kids tipping up their heads, their gazes searching the sky. Last month, the sirens were accompanied by helicopters.

I move through the crowd of tittering mothers on the sidewalk, divided into their usual packs. The English-speakers, pasty-skinned Brits, and big-boned Americans, the occasional Australian or Scot. Other expats, neatly divided by skin color and language. The Dutch mothers, hyperinsular and utterly unapproachable, a competitive band of school volunteers whom the teachers not-so-jokingly call the *moedermafia*. I don't really fit in with any of them, but if anyone here knows what those sirens are about, it will be one of the *moedermafia*.

I sidle up to Brigitte, the loudest of the bunch, a lean, artsy type with round eyes and porcelain skin, bare except for a lipstick so red and shiny it makes me think of blood.

"What happened? Do you know?" I ask in my best Dutch, which admittedly, isn't all that great. All the weird vowels, the harsh guttural sounds. Five years in this country, and I still can't wrap my tongue around the language.

She answers me in English, which somehow always feels like an insult. "They're going to that condo building on the Valeriusplein. You know, the new building with all the *patsers*."

Patsers are show-offs, and if she's talking about the same building that I'm thinking of, it's filled with them. Loud, blustery social climbers who live there so they can brag that they own one of the most expensive homes in all of Amsterdam. The cheapest condos in that building went for six million euros a pop, and the penthouse . . .

"Nine million, Willow." Xander's voice sounds through my head. "That's more than €20 thousand per square meter, the highest square meter price in the country. Just look at all these amenities."

This was late one evening back in the fall, halfway through a lengthy and detailed tour, and he wasn't wrong. Xander's penthouse really is something else. Bought with money he earned conquering the luxury diamond market in Asia, America, and Lord knows where else before my husband, Thomas, lured him back to Holland. This hot-shot gemologist back from abroad, here to drag House of Prins into the twenty-first century.

"Are you sure? Are you absolutely certain it's that building?"

By now, I've switched to English, too. If it's true what Brigitte says, if those sirens are indeed swirling around Xander's condo building on the Valeriusplein, I can't be bothered with the effort of translating my questions to Dutch.

"Julia and I biked by there on the way to school," Brigitte says, glancing over with a brusque nod; Julia is her daughter, a six-year-old carbon copy of her mother in more ways than one. "There were all sorts of people standing outside, waiting for the police to get there. More than one of them said the word *murder*."

The woman on the other side of her—Manon is her name—sucks in a noisy breath, while, meanwhile, the air in my lungs turns solid.

I turn in the direction of the sirens, my gaze lifting across the canal and toward the building and the park beyond, but it's too far away, with too many buildings in between. There's nothing but trees and blue sky.

Still. An ominous feeling seeps through my veins like silty Dutch soil.

"How much you want to bet it was the Rolex gang?" Manon says to Brigitte in Dutch, ignoring me completely. Manon is a former model with a tongue as sharp as her jawline, and I've never been a fan—though I'm fairly certain the feeling is mutual. "There's so much money in that building. It's Walhalla for the Rolex gang."

The Rolex gang, a group of delinquent teenagers roaming the city, trawling the shops and streets for anyone worth mugging, then following them home and robbing them blind. They especially love watches and jewelry.

"Maybe you just misheard. Surely, no one was really murdered," I say, even though what I really want to know is who? Who was murdered? *Who?*

"I know what I heard," Brigitte says with a sniff. "They said the word *murder* more than once."

On the other side of the playground, the teachers begin clapping, a signal for the kids to line up even though the bell is still a good minute or two away. My gaze tracks to Sem, already bored of the drama, watching a couple of the older boys play soccer with an empty Coke bottle. He's standing close enough to hear the clapping, but there's too much ambient noise for it to register.

"But how did they get inside?" Manon says in her native tongue. "A troop of teenagers can't sneak past a doorman. Not unless they beat him up, too."

Even if she doesn't have all the details right, she's not wrong about the building's security. The doorman is indeed a hurdle, as are the locks on every gate and door, as are the security cameras monitoring every entrance and hall and exit. Whoever did this would have had to pull a trick or two to get inside, and they'd need a fob to operate the elevator.

I tug my phone from my pocket, pull up my local news app, and scroll through this morning's headlines. There's nothing about a murder. Nothing about any sort of disturbance on the Valeriusplein.

I look up and spot Sem, watching me just outside the door. *What's wrong?* he signs.

Nothing, I sign back. I try to smile, but my lips stick to my teeth. *Have a good day.*

With a reluctant nod, Sem slips into the stream of little bodies shuffling toward the door and disappears inside. I shiver despite my fur-lined coat.

"According to what I heard, the doorman didn't even know anything was wrong. Not until one of the neighbors reported a pretty woman racing out of there. Apparently, she was frantic."

A hard knot forms in the pit of my stomach because a pretty woman also tracks. Xander has a constant parade of them going in and out of his penthouse, Amsterdam's very own version of a fuckboy. The first time I called him that, he laughed so hard he had to sit down. In the months since, it's become something of an inside joke.

And yet . . .

And yet.

"We have a problem," Xander told me only a few days ago. "I think there's someone following me."

Thomas was upstairs putting Sem to bed and it was drizzling out, but I still ducked into the backyard with my phone just in case. Xander knew better than to call during family time, but sometime in the past month or so, the rules had been tossed out the window.

"You think or you know?" I said, keeping an eye on the slice of kitchen I could see through the back door window, empty for now. Deeper into the yard, my rescue Ollie sniffed at his favorite bay laurel bush. Ollie was my excuse if and when Thomas suddenly reappeared.

"I know," Xander said that night in my ear. "I've seen him twice now. At the café across the street from the factory and just now, on the sidewalk outside my apartment. A tall guy wearing a black baseball cap."

Which could describe a million men in this country, and was

he *really* sure? Because last week, he'd called to tell me someone rummaged through his desk at the factory. The week before, someone was listening to his calls. I didn't take it very seriously because Xander is under a lot of stress. Everyone at House of Prins is. A lot is riding on the new lab-grown line, and it still isn't meeting projections.

Next to me, the *moedermafia* has grown by three more mothers, all of them still chattering away about the doorman, the woman, the *patser* dead on the floor. I listen with half an ear, thinking there are almost a million people living in Amsterdam proper. A million other people the *moedermafia* could be referring to now, in any one of dozens of other buildings backing up to the park. Just because they say it's the one on the Valeriusplein doesn't mean it's true.

"Let's go see what we can find out," Brigitte suggests, waving the other mothers toward the sidewalk and the row of bikes beyond as the last of the children shuffle into the school. "Maybe the neighbors will still be standing outside, or we can try that café on the corner. Somebody must know something." Their gazes don't so much as skim over mine.

My husband is always telling me that I should try harder, that small talk between mothers at the school fence is a beloved Dutch tradition, but Thomas is a Prins, the sixth-generation heir to a diamond dynasty who's never had to work to make friends. People gravitate to him for his money and status, but that privilege doesn't automatically extend to me just because we share the same last name. For these women, for the other mothers here at school, I'm not *really* a Prins, and I never will be.

I stand there for a long moment, alone in a lingering crowd of women making plans for workouts and boozy lunches and book clubs that don't include me, and for once, I don't feel like the last kid to get picked for a team I don't really want to be on anyway.

My head is swimming with what I just heard, the news drowning out all the rest.

A pretty woman.

A murdered man.

There are easier ways to get to the truth than asking the *moedermafia.*

ON THE SHORT bike ride home, I call Thomas.

He answers, like always, in English, because it's faster and less awkward than suffering through my clunky Dutch. "I'm in the middle of something. Can I call you back?"

No *hello, my love.* No *how's your morning going?* But at least he takes my call. Thomas *always* picks up when I call, no matter where he is or what he's doing. It's the one positive of having a medically fragile child, I suppose, that your husband never ignores your calls.

"I won't keep you long. I was just calling to see how your morning is going."

There's a long, empty pause, mostly because I *never* call to see how his morning is going. But I can't just come out and ask if Xander happens to be sitting at his desk down the hall. I can't just tell him about the sirens and the *moedermafia* and ask if the rumors are true without raising Thomas's suspicions. Voicing my worry would only raise Thomas's radar in ways I really don't want to be raising right now.

"Busy," he says. "The factory is in complete chaos."

"But no disasters?"

Thomas laughs. "Not yet, but the day is still early, so let's not jinx it. Just the normal, end-of-the-week pandemonium."

"Oh. That's good, then, I guess. Want me to swing by with lunch?"

It's what I used to do when Sem was a tiny baby, strap him to my chest and let the tram carry us across town to the Prins factory, a beautifully restored building his family has owned for five generations. This was back when Thomas and I still felt fragile and new, when both of us were still trying very hard to make it work. Maybe he thinks five years is long enough.

"Lunch?"

I laugh. "Yeah, you know, that thing people do where they eat food in the middle of the day? I could pick up sandwiches from that Italian place on the way. Or sushi if you'd prefer."

I'll need to make arrangements though; Sem's school breaks for lunch, which means I'll need to ask our housekeeper, Martina, to handle pickup.

Another quiet follows, an awkward silence that stretches a couple of beats too long. "I'd love that, Willow, but today's . . . not great. I have a meeting with the architect at the new store in a few minutes, followed by back-to-back interviews all afternoon. My father keeps trying to corner me to ask about the agenda for next week's board meeting, but I haven't had a second to think about it yet. And my inbox is a jungle."

It's such a stark difference from when we first met, when he walked into the Atlanta restaurant where I was waiting tables. A business dinner, though he told me later they got close to nothing done. Thomas was too busy coming up with excuses to call me over, chat me up, sweet-talk me into meeting him after I got off work. He was so not my type—too thin, far too bookish in those horn-rimmed glasses—but he was sweet and persistent enough that I relented. Thomas ended the meeting right then and there.

That's what I remember most about our beginnings, a blur of ditched appointments and called-in sick days, blowing off friends and work and other commitments whenever he was in town, so we could hole up in his suite at the St. Regis. Even now, the smell of freshly starched sheets will take me back there, to the sun slanting through the plate glass window onto a carpet littered with room service plates, our bare legs intertwined under seven-hundred-count Egyptian cotton while his cellphone buzzed away on the nightstand. We burned so hot and heavy in the beginning, and I know long-distance relationships come with a particular ache that dulls when you see each other every day, but still. When I think back to those early days, the gulf between then and now makes me sad.

"I hear it," I say, trying not to let the hurt seep into my tone. "You're a busy man."

"Crazy busy. Can we catch up tonight?"

"Sure. Of course. No worries."

I keep my voice breezy and bright, something that's getting harder and harder by the day. I try not to think about how long it's been since we've had one of those lunches, or even shared a quiet dinner at home. Last night, it was almost midnight before he slipped in bed, and this morning, I woke to the sound of the front door clicking shut a full two hours before my alarm. Thomas has always been a hard worker, but this doesn't feel like the schedule of a man busy with work. This feels like the schedule of a man trying very hard to avoid his wife.

In the background, a phone rings, and fingers click on a keyboard. "See you tonight," he says, and I hear in his voice that he's already moved on. His mind is already somewhere else.

"See you tonight. At dinner."

We hang up, and for a second or two, I consider a drive-by of Xander's building before I think better of it. The last thing I need is for someone to see me there, staring up at the penthouse with a horrified look on my face. I could probably explain it away to the other rubberneckers, but I know how people in this town talk. Better to monitor the news sites from the privacy of my living room.

I take a left for home, steering my cargo bike down the familiar curves of the Koningslaan, bumping over the pavers along the pond.

For well-to-do mothers in Amsterdam Zuid, bikes like mine aren't just a way to ferry kids to and from school, they're a status symbol. Sleek, electric, and stupidly expensive, but they're a hell of a lot easier to navigate the city's winding streets on than a car.

At the fork, I veer left, heading down a pretty street lined on both sides with hundred-year-old villas. Big imposing buildings of burgundy brick and bright white trim, with deep balconies and flag-topped turrets and rooftops of black slate or terracotta tile. This is the neighborhood where Amsterdam's moneyed live, including a few members of the monarchy, which is fitting, since the streets here are named after their ancestors. Sofia, Hendrik, Emma—the royal gang's all here.

And the nicest house at the far end of the street, the three-story freestanding villa with big bay windows and a deep backyard that overlooks the water—that one belongs to Thomas. The house he bought for himself long before he and I met. Thomas's home, and one day Sem's. I just happen to live there.

One of the trade-offs of marrying into old money is that all this luxury is only on loan. None of it actually belongs to me. Not the house with all the artwork and expensive furniture, not the German cars in the driveway or the walk-in closet filled with designer clothes. Definitely not the diamonds. More diamonds than I could ever wear, both a perk and a hazard of marrying a Prins. None of them are mine, not according to the air-tight prenup I signed. The second Thomas and I separate, back they go into the Prins family vault.

"Isn't it a bit . . . big?" I said after Thomas slid a six-carat flawless Prins-cut solitaire up my finger. The Rolex bandits I could handle, but what about everyone else? His overbearing father and younger sister, his mother who tolerates me but just barely. I knew how a stone this big would mark a person like me: as a social climber, as one of those people the *moedermafia* was talking about—a *patser.*

For the most part, Thomas knows about my past—my absent father, my estranged mother, my childhood marked by neglect and freebie hand-me-downs. He knows that the day after my sixteenth birthday I took off, and that it took my mom three weeks to realize I'd skipped town. He knows that while I've worked hard to reinvent myself into someone who might belong in his life, I wear the clothes and diamonds like flashy, fancy masks, covering up the parts of me I don't want others to see. My husband knows a lot about me, but he doesn't know everything.

That day, though, he brushed off my worries with a smile. "You're a Prins now, Willow. Soon you'll be telling me your diamond is too small."

But Thomas lives in Prinsland, and the too-small complaint is never going to happen.

That's what all those mothers at school don't get. The women speaking languages I don't understand, the Americans with their expensive athletic gear, the *moedermafia* who think I don't notice the way they catalogue my carats, totaling the numbers up in their head with a look of barely disguised venom. They don't get that I would trade it all, every ring and bracelet and necklace hanging from me like tinsel on a Christmas tree, pretty but temporary. They can't imagine that I'd happily give them every diamond in the vault for a husband who wants to have lunch with me.

RAYNA

I'm seated on a bar stool at the far end of a juice shop in Amsterdam Zuid, a freebie bottle of foamy green liquid clutched in a fist, waiting for the cops to arrive. The place isn't very busy, but it's the same handful of people filling the tables and lingering near the register as when I ran inside, screaming for someone to call the police. Between sips from their bottles and paper cups, they toss me noticeable, curious glances. Looks like they're waiting for the cops, too.

At the front of the shop, a man pushes through the door. He's in plain clothes, dark jeans, and a fitted gray shirt over battered Nike sneakers, but I know a cop when I see one. This one looks like the TV version of a cop, tall and a gritty kind of handsome, with a swagger and square jaw the camera loves.

He stops at the counter for a quick discussion with the girl manning the register, and she points him my way. She knows why he's here, that it's me he's here for. The cop turns, our eyes meet, and I sit up straighter on my chair.

"Arie Boomsma, detective with the Amsterdam Police," he says as soon as he's close enough, and in English, thank God. His words are heavy with a Germanic accent. "I understand you were witness to a murder."

I drop my hand in his outstretched palm, big as a dinner plate, and squeeze harder than necessary because I've lived here long enough to know that in Holland, that's how you set the tone. The one with the strongest handshake wins, and this guy just won by a mile. I slide my throbbing hand under my thigh, trying not to wince.

"Rayna Dumont. And I'm not a witness, at least not technically. When I walked into the bathroom, Xander was already dead."

I shudder as the last word leaves my mouth because I was in the same room as a fingerless corpse. I puked a puddle on the marble by his feet. My underwear is still lying somewhere on his bedroom floor. My DNA is all over the scene.

"Do you want to talk here?" He gestures vaguely to the shop behind him, to the people trying very hard not to stare. "We could go to the bureau if you prefer."

Something about the way he says it feels like a challenge, or maybe it's my history with interrogation rooms in police stations. Either way, I give an immediate shake of my head.

"Here's fine."

Detective Boomsma pats his pockets until he finds the lump he's looking for, an ancient iPhone with a scratched and cracked screen. He swipes through the apps and taps Record on Voice Memos, settling the phone, screen up, on the bar between us. "Perhaps you could start at the beginning."

So I do. I tell him about last night's drinks that turned into dinner that turned into me staying the night. I tell him about waking up this morning to the sound of the shower, and my spontaneous decision to join Xander. About the horror of finding him there—face purple, eyes bulging, tongue limp and discolored from the zip tie strapped around his neck like a tourniquet. I say these words, and it hits me all over again: Xander is dead, and I was *there*.

"You woke up to the sound of the shower," Detective Boomsma says, "but not the actual struggle?"

It's a thought that's occurred to me, as well, and more than once. A man Xander's size would have put up one hell of a fight. His fall would have shaken the floorboards. I was drunk last night, but I wasn't *that* drunk. How did I not hear anything?

At the register, an apron-clad cashier puts down the basket of oranges in her hand, watching me with undisguised curiosity. She only heard part of the story when I burst inside, the frantic bits and pieces I relayed to the 1-1-2 operator. Now she's eager for the rest.

I turn back to Detective Boomsma. "We don't know for sure that there was a struggle."

"I've been doing this job for long enough to know with absolute certainty that there was a struggle. Any man surprised by their attacker will put up a fight the second he realizes his life is in danger. And Mr. Van der Vos was a large man. Well over two meters. How much do you think he weighed, ninety kilos?"

Ninety kilos is some two hundred pounds, which seems about right. But still. The detective seems to be waiting for more from me, an estimate, maybe, or a wild guess. This feels like a test.

"Miss Dumont, how much did Mr. Van der Vos weigh?"

I clear my throat. "I couldn't say. Our activities didn't exactly include a weigh-in."

The detective quirks a brow, but he's wise enough not to touch that one.

"Regardless, it would have taken a lot of muscle to overpower a man his size, which means his attacker must have been just as large, and while the struggle might have been quick, it certainly wouldn't have been silent. There would have been shouts. Grunts. Bodies slamming against walls, falling to the floor. A fight to the death between two ninety-kilo men. You can see where I'm going with this."

Yes, I can see where he's going, and I know how this looks. A strange girl sleeping in a man's bed, oblivious while he's being tortured to death in the next room. It looks like I'm lying, or at the very least, hiding something.

I shut my eyes and try to picture how it happened. Xander's body slick with soap, his handsome face tilted up to the spray when someone came up on him from behind.

"Maybe he was washing his face," I say, opening my eyes, "or, I don't know, rinsing the shampoo from his hair. Maybe he didn't know what was happening until there was a zip tie strapped around his neck and *boom*, no more air. And you can stop looking at me like that, Detective, because I promise you there's not a woman on this planet who doesn't think someone will choose that exact moment when she's rinsing the soap from her eyes to rape or stab or strangle her."

The girl behind the register catches my eye, and I can tell she agrees.

Detective Boomsma lifts a neutral shoulder. "That is all possible, yes, but one of the bodies still crashed to the ground. It's strange that you didn't hear it."

My cheeks go hot because the detective's point is valid. It *is* strange. All those minutes I wasted pacing Xander's floor, trying to make sense of the fact that he was dead, trying to cram that awful fact into my brain, I was too stunned to think this very thing. How did I not hear his big body fall?

"I already told you we'd had a lot to drink. We went to bed really late and I'm a hard sleeper. There's a solid wall separating the bedroom from the bathroom. Whatever noise Xander made in there, I didn't hear it over the shower. Or maybe I heard *something*, because I remember startling awake. Something woke me up."

"A thud? A shout?"

"A thud, maybe. I think I would have remembered a shout. Or maybe it was a door closing, or footsteps. I wish I could be more helpful."

I hate the way my voice sounds, so desperate and unsure. I want to go back and try those words all over again, in a calm and matter-of-fact tone. The detective looks like he isn't buying it, and honestly, why should he? I don't understand how I didn't hear anything, either.

"Over the course of the evening, how much would you say you had to drink?"

I pause. I've always hated this question, the way it always comes with an undertone of judgment. I could play the number of drinks down, but there were witnesses to last night's boozing, bartenders and waiters and the people sitting all around us, and we weren't subtle about it. We were loud and having a good time.

"More than I usually do," I say, and that part at least is the truth. "We'd been out since 7:30."

"How much?"

I shrug. "A couple of drinks at the bar, a bottle of wine with dinner, champagne on Xander's terrace. But I made sure to drink lots of water, too. And I ate, so it's not like I drank all that on an empty stomach."

"Any drugs? Weed, shrooms, cocaine, pills?"

"I know what drugs are, and no." I frown. "No drugs."

He flashes what appears to be an apologetic smile. "Sorry, but you wouldn't be the first American tourist to come here for the drugs. But even without them, that's a lot of alcohol in a fairly petite frame. You must have been quite drunk."

Wasted, though I hold back on offering up that truth. Yes, I drank more than I should have, certainly more than is wise for a person my size. Yes, after midnight the edges of the evening turn slippery and vague, but are there any black holes? Any blank spots in my memory where I might not have noticed a killer tiptoeing from room to room? Also yes, as much as I'm reluctant to admit it. Everything after the champagne is a bunch of random snippets for me to puzzle together. There are plenty of blank spots.

"We were *both* drunk, yes. We passed out pretty hard. And before you ask, I don't know what time Xander was killed, or how long he'd been in the shower. I only know that when I woke up at just before eight, the water was already running. Still hot, too."

"We don't have boilers like in the States. Our water heaters are gas-fired, meaning the hot water never runs out." He pauses, regarding me. "It just seems very unlikely."

I shrug again, both shoulders hiking high enough to touch my ears. "I don't know what to tell you, Detective. I'm a really heavy sleeper."

"No. I mean it seems unlikely that someone would go to the trouble of murdering Xander and not you. Especially seeing as you are a witness."

"I just told you I was asleep. I didn't witness anything but the aftermath."

He doesn't respond to that, just sits there and watches me for so long it becomes uncomfortable. Detective Boomsma doesn't believe me. He thinks I'm lying, that I know more than I'm telling. He thinks I'm holding something back, which I suppose I am.

"Are you in the Netherlands as a tourist?" he asks. "Or are you here on a more permanent basis?"

"I have a DAFT visa, if that's what you're getting at." The Dutch American Friendship Treaty, an agreement that allows Americans to live and work in Holland as long as they remain gainfully self-employed—though so far, the *gainfully* part is up for debate. Freelancing is turning out to be a lot harder than I thought it would be.

"So you've been to the IND." The Dutch immigration services. He pauses to receive my nod. "Then we have already collected your fingerprints when you gave your biometrics. But a DNA sample would be helpful. You can give one at the station."

"I puked all over the bathroom floor, Detective. You can mop my DNA sample off the marble."

"We would still need an official swab to match with your . . . *sample*, as well as whatever other evidence we find at the scene. That way we can rule you out."

Or box me in. A cool breeze whispers up the back of my neck, a warning to tread carefully.

"And if I say no?"

"That is certainly your right. But it would be easiest for both of us if you cooperate. It will only take a few minutes."

Not a threat, exactly, but I can read between the lines. He'll visit a judge, get a subpoena—do they even call them subpoenas in the Netherlands?—and force me. Another mountain of attorney fees I can't afford, when I still haven't paid off the first pile.

Then again, surely this conversation can only have convinced this man that I *cannot* be guilty. After all, he's the one who brought up Xander's size, a good two heads taller than me, in the same breath he called me petite. I could barely reach both hands around Xander's neck without a stepladder, much less climb up his soap-slicked body and overpower him with something as flimsy as a zip tie. Giving the police my DNA will help them cross me off the list of suspects.

Still.

"I left my bike in town last night. Xander and I walked home from the restaurant."

"I'll give you a ride."

I can't imagine anything I want to do less than climb in this man's car and let him drive me to the station. I look around, and every eye in the place is on me. The girl manning the row of blenders, the apron-clad cashier, a cluster of people waiting in line. They're all looking at me. Waiting to see how I will respond.

And this is where my pride gets the better of me.

Because while it's true that I've got nothing to hide, after this past year, I have a whole hell of a lot to prove.

"Fine. Let's go." I grab my things and push to a stand, then with the entire shop watching, I follow the detective out the door.

THE POLICE STATION is bright and modern and rank with fear—or maybe that's mine, the sickly, shaky aftermath of a body depleted of adrenaline. My head throbs with it, and from what's shaping up to be an especially wicked hangover. My stomach churns as I follow the detective through the lobby and down a hallway of tired, gray linoleum, and I tell myself to breathe.

Now that he's done hurling questions at me, Detective Boomsma is a man of few words. *This way. Through here. Please have a seat.* I sink onto one of two chairs, blinking around the plain white room. A table, a door, and little else.

The detective disappears, and my mind flashes to the last time I was alone in one of these rooms, white and bare, with cameras in the corners and a steel door that locks from the outside. At least this cop said please.

Not for the first time, I wonder about the wisdom of forking over my DNA, if it will clear me like the detective insinuated or come back to haunt me later. As an American, I should know better. The right to remain silent. The right to have an attorney present. Rights that, like my green eyes and the birthmark on my right shoulder, are ingrained in my DNA, which the detective wants me to willingly let someone swab from the inside of my cheek.

The woman who steps into the room looks more like a girl, her face scrubbed clean of any makeup, her dark hair pulled into a ponytail so severe it puckers the skin of her temples. She drops a single sheet of paper on the desk along with a pen.

"Read and sign at the bottom, please."

I scan the form, a longwinded narrative in British English that the samples are mine, that I am giving them willingly. I pick up the pen and scribble my name and the date on two matching lines.

Why? Because I've lived here for all of two months. Because I don't know a single attorney, or even how to go about finding a decent one who works for peanuts, because that's about the only thing I can afford.

I tell myself I did nothing wrong. I called the police and reported the murder, as is my civic duty. I've been a willing participant in answering any questions they have. When the woman picks up the swab, I open my mouth wide. When she's done, the detective appears like magic.

"I take it we're done here?" I say, reaching for my bag, which I'd dropped on the floor. "I have to go. I have work."

This isn't exactly accurate. I have a two-thousand word fluff piece about a wellness center near Maastricht that could use some polishing and vague plans to scroll through the freelancing sites, Fiverr and Upwork and Guru and a dozen other smaller ones, praying that someone might be looking for an unknown, inexperienced travel writer willing to sling words for cheap. Other than that, and a mountain of laundry, and my afternoon run through the Vondelpark, there's not a whole lot on today's agenda.

Detective Boomsma steps aside to let the technician disappear out the door. "We're done. You're free to go."

"And my phone?"

He leans a shoulder against the wall and folds his arms across his chest, looming above me, above the table. "Your phone was found at the crime scene, which unfortunately means that it's evidence."

"For how long?"

He gives me what I've come to refer to as a Dutch shrug, a gesture that can mean anything from *I don't know* to *Who cares?*

"I need a phone, Detective. If for no other reason than to call myself an Uber."

Also, I'm not entirely sure where I am. The last thing I recognized on the drive here was a stretch of condo and office buildings that towers over the A-10, which means we're outside the ring. I'm pretty sure there's a Metro station nearby, but my pass is in the cardholder on the back of my phone, along with my debit card. Without those, I have no way to get home.

He pushes off the wall, holding out a business card he pulls from his pocket. "Please let me know if you have plans to leave Amsterdam."

"I live here, remember? I'd show you my residency permit, but it's in the card holder on the back of my phone."

And then the rest of what he said hits me, the part about not leaving Amsterdam.

"Hang on, are you telling me I'm not allowed to leave at all? For how long?"

"Until I tell you otherwise."

I think about Xander and his finger, about my DNA on his floor and headed to a petri dish somewhere at a police laboratory. About the Dutch judiciary system and the state of Dutch prisons. I hear they're a lot nicer than their American counterparts, but I still don't want to go to one.

"But I'm a travel writer. My job requires me to go to the places I'm writing about. Am I . . ." I hear it then, the catch in my voice, the way it's shaking despite my every attempt to hold it level. I pause to get myself under control. "Am I a *suspect*?"

"That's not what I said. I'm merely asking you to let me know if you need to leave the country."

"How am I supposed to let you know anything if I don't have a phone?"

"I'm sure you'll find a way." When I don't take his proffered card, he drops it to the table.

The reality of the situation settles over me again—not only that Xander is dead, but that it just as easily could have been me. That his killer could have flipped on the lights and seen me lying there, my hair spread out across Xander's pillow. Could have just as soon strangled me, too. My fingertips flutter to the side of my neck, grazing over skin that's soft and smooth.

I slide the card into my bag, and the surge of bravado I felt back in the juice shop has all but melted away. Detective Boomsma opens the door, a silent gesture that I'm free to go.

Outside, I stand in a slice of shade and stare at traffic, trying to figure out where I am. This is not the charming Amsterdam I've come to know and love, not the hodgepodge rows of gingerbread buildings lining the glittering canals. This is modern, industrial, ugly Amsterdam, a million miles away from that view from Xander's sleek penthouse and the feeling of endless possibility.

I tell myself that despite everything, I can still do this. No—not just that I can but *should*. That's what happens when you survive a terrifying brush with death, you are obliged to live the hell out of your life. I should still push forward with my *Eat, Pray, Love* era. Should still say *yes* to adventure. Reboot myself as someone who doesn't just fall into a marriage because all her friends are doing it or because her mother expects it of her; not someone clinging to her small-town, country club life because she doesn't know any better and change is terrifying. Who doesn't let life happen to her, but makes her own life happen.

A bus zooms past, stirring up a pile of trash and leaves that rain like confetti over the busy street. I turn left, then right, then left again, pointing myself toward what I think—I *hope*—is the city center.

Rayna 2.0 can find her own way home.

WILLOW

In the end, I have not one lunch date but two. Sem and his best friend, Vlinder, a stunning Dutch girl with blue eyes and blond ringlets. They sit shoulder to shoulder in the front cubby of my cargo bike, deep in conversation about Juf Addie, their teacher who's getting married in May. Apparently, she's invited the entire class.

At the end of the driveway, Sem twists around, his fingers tugging at the seat belt. "Mama, help."

Two little words, but they never fail to stir up a storm in my chest. Partly at the lack of mother I have in my own life, but mostly because I am one. Despite all the warnings doctors gave when I was pregnant. Despite all the close calls and hospital stays. Those other mothers at school, they love to complain about how motherhood is *so hard*. The endless chores, the lack of time for yourself, the constant onslaught of motherly guilt for doing too much or not enough or making some mistake that can mess your kid up forever.

But for me, the hardest part has always been the worry.

Sem, the child that almost wasn't. An accidental pregnancy in every way—only eight months into our long-distance relationship and while I was on the pill. Too soon, too unplanned, a pregnancy so precarious it felt doomed from day one. And yet from the day those two lines appeared on the test, there was nothing I wanted more.

I lean in and help him unclip the buckle to his seat belt, then drop a kiss on top of his head. His hair is the only place on him that's warm, the dark strands soaking up the January sun, and that familiar cloud settles over me like a lead blanket.

Already this has been a rough winter, filled with one long, chronic cold that's morphed into croup and spiked his fever so high it sent us to the hospital three times. He requires constant monitoring and a whole host of specialists we have on speed dial. For a medically complex kid like Sem, every bug that blows through town, every bacterium that sneaks onto every surface is a danger.

But scariest of all are the ear infections—what might be mild for most kids could be deadly for Sem. Too close to his cochlear implants, too dangerously close to his brain, which could mean yet another operation to place ventilation tubes, explantation of his cochlear implants, meningitis, death. Every hurdle we make it past feels like a miracle.

I press the back of my fingers to his forehead. As usual, he bats my hand away.

"Okay, my love. You're free. Now help Vlinder."

As soon as she's loose, the two of them clamber over the sides and race on skinny legs to the side door, eight centimeters of solid, fortified wood too thick for even the Nazis to bust through once upon a time. According to Thomas, they came through the front room's stained glass windows instead, now a sheet of bulletproof glass.

This is the cost of being a Prins, we live in a freaking bunker.

Inside the house, Vlinder and Sem shrug off their coats, dropping their backpacks like sacks of cement to the well-worn marble floor. They take off down the hall as Ollie comes racing the other way, his tail and tongue wagging in his hurry to get to me, even though it's only been fifteen minutes since the last time I saw him.

I scratch him behind a scruffy ear. "I know, I know. I missed you, too."

I dump my keys in the bowl on the hallway table, patting down my windblown hair in the mirror, an eighteenth-century masterpiece of smoky glass and gilded wood and plaster, with an ornate frame of swirling ivy and flowers and shells. Of all the fabulous pieces in this house, the imported furniture and the artwork decorating the walls, the silverware and the chinaware and the safe full of jewelry upstairs, this mirror is by far my favorite—a Christmas gift from Thomas's father from a restoration shop in the city center. He bought two more just like it, one for himself and the other for Thomas's sister, Fleur.

"I hope you don't mind, Martina," I say, coming into the kitchen where she stands at the counter, slicing wild radishes for garnish. I snag one and drag it through a plate of softened, salty butter. "We have an extra mouth to feed for lunch. I hear she's hungry."

Vlinder and Sem give each other matching smiles. They're an island unto themselves, those two, like Thomas and I once were. Twin flames, I used to call them. Soulmates. Now the only thing I can think is *Just wait. Give it enough time, and she'll lose interest in you, too.*

Martina is my mother's age, somewhere in her early sixties, but that's where the similarities stop. Where my own mother is bleached blonde and perpetually bronzed from the tanning salon, Martina's look is au naturel. She's also scrupulously loyal to Thomas and thus to me, and she loves on Sem like he's her grandson—a welcome bond since I haven't spoken to my mother since I was sixteen.

"I hope so," Martina says. "We certainly have plenty."

I eye the platter Martina has prepared, piled high with every meat imaginable. Juicy slices of roast beef and fat sausages and multiple kinds of salt-cured hams, more food than three people can eat in a week. Which in the Prinses' world, is also the point. Do you want roast beef? We've got four kinds. Pâté? Which do you prefer: duck or goose? For families like the one I married into, it's not about the excess but about options. Getting exactly what you want when you want it is the ultimate privilege.

She tips her knife at the sink, an order for the kids to wash their hands, and they obey because this is *her* kitchen. Martina is cook, maid, grocery shopper, dog walker, organizer of repairmen and gardeners, occasional babysitter, and overall master of this domain. Thomas, Sem, and I only live here.

"I hope you didn't get stuck in all the commotion near the park." Martina's gaze flits meaningfully to the kids, but they're oblivious, chattering away at the sink.

I shake my head, reach for another radish. "No, but I heard all the sirens. They were a hot topic this morning during drop-off."

"Someone was—" Martina swipes a finger across her throat while making a clicking noise with her tongue.

"That's what I heard, too. Do you know any details?"

I certainly don't. I spent most of the morning hitting Refresh on the various news apps, but there wasn't much. Just a one-sentence bulletin in *Het Parool*, Amsterdam's main newspaper. *Man (44) dood gevonden in eigen woning.* Forty-four-year-old man found dead in own home. No mention of what part of town he lived in, or how the man died, or that he may or may not have been murdered. Only that he's dead.

Martina, however, might. She grew up in a tiny town in the south of Holland, but she's lived in Amsterdam for ages, and she's worked for Thomas's family almost as long. She knows everybody in this part of town. There's a good chance she knows more than what they've reported on the news.

"I ran into Dirk at the market this morning, you know, the Akkermans' chef, and he told me the man was strangled. In the shower, apparently." She pulls a jug from the fridge and moves to the other side of the island, waving a hand in Sem's line of sight until he looks up. "*Jongens, wie wil d'r een kopje melk*?"

Guys, who wants a cup of milk? It's a rhetorical question, as Martina is already pouring.

Strangled, though, and in the shower. I shudder as the image comes to me, a dead and naked Xander sprawled on all that expensive marble.

And the pretty woman—where was she when this happened? Sitting on his chest with her hands around his neck? Hiding in a closet or under a bed? I try to picture it, but the image won't form. The woman is a mystery.

I get the kids settled at the table, then pluck my iPad from the charger. "Martina, I need to answer a couple of emails. Do you mind keeping an eye on the kids?"

If it were Thomas or his parents, they'd phrase it differently. *Keep an eye on the kids, would you, Martina, while I tend to my email.* Polite, but still technically an order. Thomas grew up with a whole team of Martinas, hired hands to do the cleaning, the cooking, the laundry and the yard work, who cater to his every whim. He's used to doling out demands for things he's perfectly capable of doing himself, while I spent most of my adult life like Martina, on the receiving end.

She wipes her hands on her frilly apron and shoos me toward the door. "Of course, of course. You go. I'll handle things here."

Ollie trails me into the solarium, a sunny room that juts into a deep backyard. I dig my cell from my pants pocket and toss it onto the couch, then sink onto the cushion beside it. *Het Parool* has added a few more details under the headline I spotted earlier, only a couple of paragraphs, but they push the boundaries of my Dutch vocabulary just the same. The man was found this morning in his luxury apartment in Amsterdam Zuid by a female guest, the same woman who police carted in for questioning. The piece summons up more questions than it gives answers.

I'm about to back out of it when I spot a graphic at the bottom, one with the paper's headline in tweet form. And underneath, two little words: 47 Replies. I click it and the screen flips me to X.

The comments are all in Dutch, and most of them seem like what I overheard from the *moedermafia*—light on facts and heavy on conjecture. I'm almost to the bottom when one little word stops my scrolling.

> **@j_sperd__rcks47** I hear the dead guy worked in diamonds. The killer hit the jackpot. A killer and a diamond thief.

Diamonds. The dead guy worked in diamonds. He lived in the building on the Valeriusplein. There was a pretty woman. It's too much. The connections churn like acid in my stomach.

Now that the news is out there, I scramble for my phone and fire off a text to Thomas. Maybe a weird question, but is Xander at work? I just heard some concerning news.

The message lands as delivered, but not read.

I picture Thomas in his sleek office overlooking the factory floor, typing away at his laptop. I see his look of confusion as police officers march across the catwalk to deliver the news, the cutters down on the floor putting down their tools in confusion, in distress. A House of Prins executive murdered in his own home. It's a shock that will shut down the factory for days.

"Sem wanted to show Vlinder his new train set," Martina says, coming into the room with a glass and a plate, "so I let them go upstairs. I hope that's okay." She slides my lunch onto a side table, two slices of seedy brown bread topped with a generous layer of ricotta and prosciutto, and a glass of fizzy water, doing a double take at the look on my face. "What? What happened? What's the matter?"

I shake my head, pointing at my screen. "I just . . . I don't know if it's true, but this person on X is calling the murderer a diamond thief."

Martina tuts, shaking her head with a frown. "Not the Rolex gang again."

"No, listen." I read the post out loud, my tongue twisting around the Dutch. "The dead guy worked in diamonds, Martina. This makes it sound like his death was a robbery gone wrong."

"You think it was someone you know." Not a question. A statement.

I nod. "One of the mothers at school said this happened in that new building on the Valeriusplein. Apparently, there were all sorts of people standing around outside, tons of police cars. You know who lives there, right? Xander owns the penthouse."

The gleaming apartment plopped onto the building like the fancy top layer of a cake. An architectural masterpiece of steel and stone and sliding glass, surrounded on all sides by a lush terrace.

"Did you talk to Thomas?" Martina says, the blood draining from her ruddy cheeks. "Thomas will know."

I tap my phone to awaken the screen, but the text status hasn't changed. Thomas still hasn't read my text, which is not a good sign. I flip to his contact card and hit Call, but his cell doesn't even ring. It kicks me straight to voicemail.

"Voicemail," I say, and my stomach twists. The voicemail is another tick in the Xander column. It means Thomas is busy, and with something pressing. He *always* answers my calls. The thought sits like a hot ember, sizzling in my stomach.

"I'll go make some calls. See what I can find out. I'm sure it's nothing, but . . ." Martina doesn't finish, just pats me on the shoulder and hustles back to the kitchen.

I scroll a bit, but there's nothing more. Only the most basic of facts amplified with rumor and conjecture. I toss my iPad to the couch cushion and listen to Martina loading the dishes into the dishwasher, waiting until she's good and busy. And then I push off the couch and step to the built-ins by the window.

There, on the bottom shelf, at the bottom of an old, dusty box shoved to the very back, is a phone. One that no one knows about because nobody digs through this box but me, filled with a messy jumble of toys Sem outgrew ages ago, rattles and wobble balls and loud, flashy, torture devices Thomas was constantly pulling the batteries out of because the noise drove him to madness. I push them aside and my fingers connect with the used Samsung I bought at the market with cash. Before today, I've only used it twice.

With one ear on Martina banging around the kitchen, I power the burner up—still at 49%, thank God—and navigate to the messaging app, which is empty. Nothing. Not a single peep. I don't know if it's good news or bad.

My heart gives a kick at sudden movement in my periphery, and I slide the phone into my pocket and sink onto the couch. Sem and Vlinder watch from the doorway, already bundled in their winter coats. She's such a pretty little girl, all big eyes and flouncy sleeves. Her name is the Dutch word for butterfly, and I kind of see the resemblance.

Sem's fingers close around hers. "Vlinder wants to play outside."

"Okay, but you know the rules. Stay in the yard, and don't go near the water." I sign it, too, just to be sure.

In unison, they give a solemn nod and turn, hand in hand, for the back door. I sit for another long moment, giving my heart time to settle while I watch them kick a ball around the grass.

What's next? An investigation, for sure. An army of police marching through the factory and the neighborhood and the house, gathering evidence, questioning witnesses. A media frenzy, reporters and cameras everywhere, a perverse sort of entertainment that will fall back on the already struggling House of Prins. I tell myself to stop catastrophizing. We don't know who the dead man is yet. Now is not the time to panic.

My mind drags back to a night this past November, that first, fateful step down a road filled with burner phones and this slow, steady drip of dread. Surely this isn't what I think it is. Surely it's not Xander but another man murdered on his shower floor. One big, weird coincidence he and I can laugh about later. Much, much, *much* later.

My phone buzzes—not the one buried in the couch but my regular cellphone. I pick it up off the table.

Diamond exec Xander van der Vos murdered in Amsterdam Zuid. Millions of euros worth of diamonds missing.

Now.

Now is the time to panic.

RAYNA

My hangover evaporates on the long trek home, thanks to an unexpected drizzle in the frigid January air, a chicken and avocado sandwich I scarf down on my shortcut through the Vondelpark, and the climb to my apartment at the top of four flights of the steepest stairs known to man. By the time I finally push through my front door, I'm panting, but feeling much more like myself.

My room is at the end of a short hall, a cramped space with slanted walls and a tiny window that leaks when it rains, but for €500 a month, the price is right. I step over the clothes and shoes littering the floor, pluck my laptop from the charger, and collapse with it on the bed.

All morning long, the questions went round and round in my head. Who killed Xander? Why him and not me? How am I still alive?

That last one, especially. I try not to think about it too hard, but it's impossible. A man was murdered while I slept in the next room. He took his last breath while I snored away in his bed, oblivious. It's a miracle I'm not in the drawer next to Xander at the morgue.

I shove the morbid thoughts away and wriggle the mouse, and my eyes bulge at the number sitting at the top of my text app. More messages than people in my address book, which since the divorce, has become paper thin.

Most are from my sister, Addison, and my heart clangs with

alarm. Automatically, my thoughts go to my father and his affinity for fried foods despite his dangerously high cholesterol, my mother who climbs behind the wheel at all hours of the day and night even though she can't see a lick in the dark, my sister, Addison, and her two small kids including my daredevil nephew with his predilection for diving headfirst off couches and beds.

Or maybe Barry finally drove off that cliff.

I point the mouse at the top message and give it a tap.

Niiiiiice, sis. But imma need details, pronto.

Where are you? Whose bling?

Seriously, Ray, stop ignoring me and call me back.

WHY AREN'T YOU ANSWERING ME???

The rest are more of the same, urgent and insistent cries for me to respond or else, typical fare for my bossy older sister. I back out of the string as a memory pulses, the image of Xander with my phone, grinning at me from above. Were we at his house? In his bed? I blink, and the vision is gone, as insubstantial as smoke.

The next message is from a phone number not labeled with a name, though I recognize it as belonging to a former friend, one who told me secretly that she hated Barry for what he did, but not enough to rock the boat in our tiny Louisiana town. It's shocking, actually, how many people did that—worked themselves into knots flip-flopping from lame excuse to lame excuse. Their husbands worked with Barry. They were neighbors, friends, members of the same country club. In the end, Barry's money and status eclipsed his misdeeds.

Or maybe it's just that my own misdeeds loomed so much larger.

Yes, it does. Don't tell you-know-who I said so but good for you.

I frown. The message doesn't make much sense, and neither do any of the others further down.

Hahaha looks like you're settling in just fine.

Whoa, maybe I should come for a visit. You can introduce me to your new friends.

As grasping as ever, I see. IDK what you're trying to prove with that picture but honey this isn't it.

I lurch upright in bed, the memory thudding in my temples.

The picture. Oh, shit, the *picture*.

I flip to Instagram, where things are even worse. DMs and comments in the high double digits, along with a picture me in my full, sexed-up glory. My hair, big and pillow-mussed. My lips, swollen from his kisses. My half-mast eyes, smiling at the camera like I'm not completely naked.

Or—*almost* naked. One hand clutches Xander's duvet to my chest, fluffy white fabric that provides some cover, but not nearly enough. The left side dips dangerously low, exposing a generous slice of waist and . . . I gasp, leaning in for a closer look. Is that a *nipple*?

Oh, God. Let's just pray my mother is still asleep.

I cringe at the caption—Amsterdam looks good on me, don't you think? ☺

It wasn't the city I was referring to but the spectacular jewels Xander had just hung from my neck, a complicated collar of hundreds of white and yellow stones. I can still feel the weight of the piece, the chill of the cool metal and rocks against my skin. A prototype he'd been working on, Xander had told me when I'd asked if it was real. His comment is pinned to the top of the string.

Like a Cullinan, all sparkle and fire.

Whatever that means.

In the few hours it's been up, the post generated a flurry of likes and comments from handles I don't know and have never heard of, but also from Ingrid, three fire emojis followed by a somewhat perplexing #readywhenyouare. As generous as my roommate is with her comments, they don't always make much sense. Her English is good but apparently not *that* good.

And that brown smudge just below the biggest stone, a cushion-cut whopper the size of a small plum, is definitely a nipple, dammit.

I tap View Insights, and my eyes bug. Three thousand accounts reached *how*? I don't have three hundred followers. I don't have anywhere close. I delete the picture, even though I'm pretty sure that won't be the end of it. Those people in my DMs and text app? They're the kind of assholes who take screenshots.

There's a sudden pattering above my head, a mixture of rain and sleet pinging against the window high on the slanted wall. On the other side of the glass, the weather has turned, a ceiling of low-hanging clouds that match my mood. Detective Boomsma with all his judgmental questions and blank stares was right to drop one thought in my head: I know very little about the man whose bed I spent most of last night in.

A gemologist—a successful one with plenty of money to burn. I know that from the obligatory scroll I did through his Instagram after his first DM hit my inbox. Pictures of fast cars, cityscape views from his penthouse, dinners in fancy restaurants or crowded VIP tables at nightclubs, big jets that carted him off to foreign cities or windswept beaches. His page was like an advertisement for the American Express black card, filled with exotic places and gorgeous, glamorous people. I tried not to think too hard about why that made me say yes to a dinner date with him, or what he might possibly see in me.

I spend the next few hours on Google, combing through every single link the internet has to offer about Xander van der Vos, following every sticky fingerprint he left on the World Wide Web, and there are a *lot*. Social media hits and news reports and prime-time television interviews and profile articles printed in glossy magazines. They're not all in English but there are enough for me to get the gist. Xander wasn't just some handsome, wealthy Tinder date I found dead on the floor of his shower. Here in Amsterdam, in the international world of diamonds and jewelry design, Xander was a big fucking deal.

Paris Hilton. Eva Longoria. Amy Adams. A whole slew of Kardashians. I guess he forgot to mention he has some of the world's biggest celebrities on speed dial, or that those are his custom designs weighing down their wrists and ring fingers.

He also failed to mention he worked for one of the oldest and most respected diamond houses in all of Europe, or that he headed up the house's latest venture, a bespoke line of luxury jewelry featuring lab-grown diamonds. Tennis necklaces of fifty-plus carats and marble-sized solitaires that go for a hundred grand a pop. A tenth of what a mined diamond would cost, but still more than most people can afford. Big Diamond Energy, he called it, and it came with an even bigger price tag.

Is that what that necklace was—lab-grown diamonds? According to everything I've read, still valuable. Is that why Xander is dead, because he was hawking diamonds with six-digit price tags? Like the necklace I took off and carefully handed back, only for Xander to chuck it in a drawer. As charming as he was with me, as impressive as his internet footprint is, he was also known in the industry as something of a villain.

I flip back to one of the longer articles I came across, an in-depth profile of Xander after House of Prins announced the plans for a lab-grown line. The author positions him as a visionary in the same paragraph they call him a disruptor. They say his lab-grown line is taking a wrecking ball to the market for mined stones, that it will tank their prices. They say by horning in on the mined diamond market, Xander is a traitor to the entire industry.

"I prefer to see myself as a pioneer," the author quotes him as saying. "The diamond industry is going through an existential crisis. Lab-grown diamonds are without a doubt the biggest innovation the jewelry industry has ever seen. We can scale them, grade them, set them just like mined stones to create high jewelry, but at a fraction of the cost. A new influx of customers who can suddenly afford to purchase a flawless House of Prins diamond. I've spent the past decade studying the world's most powerful consumers—the American Affluent—and where America goes, the rest of the world follows."

I snort—the American Affluent. Makes me wonder what on earth Xander saw in me. My nipple, probably.

I land on a photograph of Xander with another man. Tall, six-feet plus, and lean like Xander, with horn-rimmed glasses and a thatch of dark brown hair. The caption is in Dutch, but I hit Translate and it reads, "Rocking the industry: House of Prins launches luxury line of lab-grown diamonds." The man's name is Thomas Prins, and he's holding a lab-grown whopper in the palm of his hand, a diamond so big, I'd have to sell an organ on the black market to be able to afford it. A double row of pave diamonds serves as its band, and tucked under a hidden halo of diamonds below the solitaire? A secret, custom stone "for her eyes only."

What kind of buyer wants to hide their diamonds? One who

can afford to drop a hundred grand on a ring, I suppose. One who chucks priceless necklaces in the nightstand drawer.

"There you are," Ingrid says from just behind me. "I've only been calling you for the past hour."

I twist around, taking in her pretty face framed by long blond curls, windswept and damp from the rain. Her winter coat a painfully fashionable beige and brown thing that's normally fluffy, now looks like it's made of wet teddy bear.

I tip the laptop closed. "Ingrid, did you hear about the man who was found dead in his shower?"

Ingrid grew up in Amsterdam. Her family lives here, in a city where news travels fast, especially bad news. If Xander's death isn't plastered on the front page of every news site in town by now, it will be soon.

"The guy with the *ritssluiting*?" She mimes threading a zip tie with her hands, her keys jangling from a pinkie. "Sorry, I don't know the word in English."

"Zip tie." I shudder at the memory of Xander's empty eyes, his lolling tongue, the claw marks at the thin band of plastic squeezing his neck, the red swirls in the water where a finger was supposed to be. "That was him, Ingrid. That was Xander. I found him right after I got off the phone with you."

Her shock is almost comical. She stumbles, catching herself in the doorway as a hand flies to her mouth. Her eyes growing wide above her fingers. "Wait. Xander is *dead*?"

I nod. "It was awful. He was just lying there, and it was obvious he was . . . His throat. His eyes." I shudder, the memories coming back in terrible flashes. "I got out of there as fast as I could, and then I called the police."

"Oh my God, Rayna. Oh my *God*. I—I can't believe this." She steps into the room, shoving some clothes from a wooden chair before collapsing onto it. "What did the police say? Do they know who did this? Did you see?"

"No. Apparently, I slept through the whole thing, which I'm kind of assuming is what saved me. The room was dark. It's possible the killer didn't know I was in there. I don't know. I have no idea why I'm still alive."

I watch an angry patch of clouds chug by the window above my head and picture Detective Boomsma's face, the heat of his gaze as he peppered me with questions I couldn't quite answer, the way he tried very hard not to frown when I kept circling around the same answers. *I don't know. I was asleep. I was drunk.*

Ingrid blows out a loud, hard breath. "Wow, Rayna. This is just . . . Wow. Did you . . . Do you have a lawyer?"

"You think I need a lawyer?"

"Yes, Rayna, I think you need a lawyer. A man is dead, and you were there when it happened. You don't know what the police are thinking, what kind of evidence they've got, how much of it points to you. What if they don't find someone else to point a finger at? You could be the only viable suspect."

"Except I didn't do it. And think about it, Ingrid: little me, in a hand-to-hand fight to the death with a man as large as Xander. Physically, it's impossible. And what possible motive do I have? I actually liked the guy."

"That necklace in the picture is a pretty big motive."

"That necklace wasn't real. I'm pretty sure he said it was a prototype."

"A prototype that looks like it costs a fortune."

"If that's true, then why did he just . . . hang it on my neck like it was a toy? Why would he chuck it in the drawer? Shouldn't he have been more careful? Shouldn't he have, I don't know, locked it away in a safe?"

I say the words with more conviction than I feel. Even if the diamonds in that necklace were lab grown, they would have been worth a shit-ton of money.

"Is that where he got it, out of his safe?"

I squeeze my eyes shut and try to remember what came before he hung it on my neck, but my memories are fuzzy at best. Champagne, music, laughter, sex. They're all running together in a twisting, spiraling loop.

"I have no idea. The necklace just . . . appeared. I wouldn't have remembered it at all if it weren't for that stupid picture. What happened before and after is just snippets."

Ingrid doesn't respond. She just stares at me like the detective did, like she's not entirely sure of my answers, either.

"Anyway, I've been doing some digging, and this company Xander worked for sells lab diamonds." I peel open the laptop, unlocking the screen with my fingerprint. "The same chemical makeup as mined diamonds, same brilliance and shine, but for a fraction of the price, which a lot of people in the industry aren't happy about. From everything I've read, there are dozens of people who might want him dead."

"So what, you think his murder had something to do with the fake diamonds he was selling?"

"They're not fakes. Lab-grown diamonds look, feel, and sparkle just like mined diamonds. Not even a jeweler can tell the difference between the two, not without a special machine that measures things like luminescence and fluorescence and some other complicated shit I don't know anything about. Something to do with the stone's growth structure."

Ingrid tilts her head, frowning as she studies me. "You know an awful lot about this stuff."

"I'm good at research." It's one of the few perks of my English Lit degree from LSU, that I can retain long passages, analyze them down to a sentence or two. I tap a finger to my laptop screen, bright with the House of Prins homepage. "Honestly, I don't understand all the science, but what I do know is that lab-growns are still super expensive."

Ingrid lifts a shoulder. "And money *is* a big motivator. It makes sense the killer was there for diamonds, I guess. People have certainly killed for less."

I sit back on the bed, and the tight knot I've been carrying around between my shoulders loosens just a tad. Most likely the killer is someone from the diamond world, or someone who knew Xander and knew the value of the stones he dealt with every day. A neighbor, perhaps, or even a friend. Maybe they thought Xander brought some of these big rocks home and wanted them for themselves. Or maybe it's a revenge killing, one of the dozens of people calling Xander a traitor online.

"Did he get any?" Ingrid says, and I frown. "Diamonds, I mean. That necklace couldn't have been the only piece Xander had lying around. Did the killer get more?"

"I don't know. I ran out of there so fast, I didn't see anything other than the bedroom and the hall to the elevator. It's possible, I guess."

Still, it doesn't make any sense. If the killer was there for the diamonds, then why murder the guy? It's not like Xander had diamonds on him in the shower. And what kind of diamond thief carries around a zip tie? This feels like more than a robbery gone wrong.

She leans back in my chair, blowing out a long breath. "Jesus, Rayna. This is some serious shit."

I nod. The understatement of the century.

I think of Xander on his shower floor, the water washing away the blood and whatever evidence might have been sitting on his skin or under his nails. Is that why they took his finger, because it clawed into the killer's skin? I think of my DNA lying in a puddle on the floor or in a laboratory somewhere, and my legs grow wobbly all over again. When I let that detective drive me to the station, it was because I was convinced that guiltlessness is on my side. That sometime very soon the cops would find a speck of evidence the killer left behind, a clue that will lead them away from me.

But what if that's why the killer chose that very moment, when Xander was in the shower, because it was a convenient spot to wash away his DNA? What if the only foreign DNA in Xander's apartment is mine?

My heart gives a hard kick. "You know how these things work in this country, Ingrid. What would you do if you were me?"

"That's easy." She blows out another breath as she pushes up off the chair, pointing at the laptop with the end of a sharp key. "First I'd call a lawyer, and then I'd wipe the internet clean of the picture of you in that necklace. Because if the killer sees you in that necklace, he'll know he left behind a witness."

WILLOW

I'm sitting at the kitchen table with my iPad, deep in a comment thread on X when I find her. The pretty woman who was with Xander when he died, posted to the checkmarked account of someone claiming to be a Dutch journalist.

> The Expat Affair: American expat Rayna D. questioned for role in Van der Vos murder & theft, millions of euros in diamonds missing #blooddiamonds #houseofprins #theexpataffair

An American expat, like me. That little tidbit gives me pause, a shiver of kinship with this woman I don't know and have never met.

Already, the post has racked up a flurry of responses and retweets, dated only seconds ago, and I click to expand the comments. I spot a bunch of screenshots of the same picture, one pilfered from Rayna's Instagram page, a shot of her seated at the foot end of Xander's bed, naked but for a collar of yellow and white diamonds and a strategically placed strip of fluffy white duvet. It's staggering how many people are posting this same picture, how quickly the likes and comments are ticking up, up, upward. It occurs to me then: I'm watching this woman go viral.

The caption reads, Amsterdam looks good on me, don't you think? ☺

Brigitte was wrong, though, when she called this woman pretty.

Rayna is *stunning*. Big doe eyes and generous lips. Messy, pillow-mussed curls. I take in the slope of her freckled shoulder, the slice of lean waist, the barely-there peek of a nipple underneath a complicated necklace of marquis and pear-shaped diamonds, 196 of them in total. I know, because it's a copy of the most iconic House of Prins design.

I wonder if she has any idea of the significance of the piece sitting on her chest, glittering there for all the world to see, if she has an inkling of its value. The centerpiece stone alone is worth more than €100,000—and that's assuming it's lab-grown, which I am, because this copy is Xander's. A flawless, colorless, fourteen-carat pear is not as valuable as the mined version, but still. The necklace is probably worth five times that.

My attention returns to the comments, rolling in faster than I can read them.

If this woman had any brains, she would have broken some things in the house. Roughed herself up some. Given herself a black eye or knocked herself out for a minute or two. At least then her story would be semi believable.

Rayna was there, in the penthouse, when a man was murdered in the shower. And now there are diamonds missing? Of COURSE she has them

WTF!!! SEND HER ASS TO JAIL!

I try to imagine it, tiny little Rayna climbing a naked and soaped-up Xander, managing to hold him still enough to strap a zip tie around his neck and pull it tight so she could make off with the diamonds. If that's what happened, then why call the police afterward? Why not scrub the place of evidence and disappear without a trace? No criminal with any sort of brains would upload a photograph putting her in the victim's apartment the night he was murdered. I don't know Rayna, but I find it hard to believe she's that careless.

Also, there's this: I happen to know that Xander was a difficult sleeper. He told me that once, in the same breath he pointed out all the devices in his bedroom designed around a good night's sleep. Triple-glazed windows to keep out any street noise. Blackout curtains pulled tight so they don't let in even a pinprick of light. Air conditioner he sleeps with on high because it fills the room with a frigid wind and a constant, breathy hiss of white noise.

An air conditioner that works on a timer.

I look up from the iPad and into the backyard, going very still as a wind shear rattles the trees. Surely, Rayna knows about the timer. Surely by now she's realized that whatever death-throe sounds Xander might have made would have been muffled by a wall of solid concrete and the steady static coming from a machine high on the wall, one designed to mask any background noise. Especially if his killer was worried about the people on the floor below and lowered him gently to the floor, it's conceivable she could have slept through the whole thing. I can't be the only person with this knowledge.

And yet, what if I am? Then what?

My attention drags to the iPad screen, to the comments rolling in faster than I can scroll.

IDK who this #hobag is, but she is what's wrong with the world today. Keep your legs closed on the first date, ladies, otherwise karma will come for you.

This girl is pretty, but how old is she? And why do the guys in the diamond industry always go for the barely legal types?

Barely legal. I have to sit with that for a minute. It's true that I'm younger than Thomas by a whole sixteen years. A big enough age gap that, for many months, I wondered what a forty-four-year-old heir to a diamond fortune could possibly see in me, the uneducated twenty-something waitress who ran away from home when she was sixteen.

Before I came along, though, there were others. Of course there were. Blue-eyed beauties with blond hair and patrician noses, leggy brunettes with thin lips and serious eyes. They were nothing like me, and far better suited for life as a Prins than I am, but they weren't young. Thomas didn't have a constant parade of pretty young things he collected in bars and on dating apps like Xander, and they stuck around for a lot longer than just one night. Thomas is very different from Xander in that way. In a lot of ways, actually.

I see what Xander saw in Rayna, though. She's exactly his type.

The online gossips are right about another thing. The necklace is not a good look for her. Especially now that Xander's dead and there are reports of diamonds missing—not from the police, at least not that I've seen, but that doesn't stop the trolls from shouting fully formed opinions of guilt in the comment sections, ticking up likes and views on every social media platform. #americandiamondthief #theexpataffair #blooddiamonds. Everywhere I look, Rayna is trending.

My phone buzzes on the table, an incoming text from Thomas.

Dreadful news. Don't wait up.

I follow the link to a news site, a brief report that tells me absolutely nothing new. Xander is dead. Diamonds are missing. An American expat is involved. The story is developing.

I fire off a reply that's filled with platitudes. I'm so sorry. Here for you however you need.

But I don't ask if he's seen the picture of Rayna in that necklace. If he hasn't, he will soon enough.

I cringe when I think of what his sister, Fleur, will say, their father, Willem. Neither is completely on board with the lab-grown line—or rather, they're on board, but only if the line rakes in the projected profits, which so far it hasn't done. Thomas is the one who championed the new line. He's the one who swore it would save the House. He's been working his ass off for more than a year now, but he hasn't quite managed to deliver.

One of Willem and Fleur's stipulations from the very beginning, though, was that the lab-grown pieces have a drastically different look and style, so there's no crossover with the natural diamond line. No one wants to drop a hundred thousand on a piece of jewelry featuring mined stones only to learn that there's a lab-grown equivalent for one-tenth of the price. That necklace hanging on Rayna's neck, the lab-grown twin to the House's most famous design? Willem and Fleur will see it for what it is: a giant middle finger from Xander.

What the hell was he thinking? Not just that he let Rayna upload that picture to Instagram but that he made the necklace in the first place, that he had it just . . . lying around his apartment. It was a foolish, cocky move—which now that I think about it, was exactly Xander's problem. He was always too damn cocky.

For Rayna, though, that necklace is a real problem. That picture of her is still gaining speed on social media, still chugging closer and closer to the wrong screen. If the killer has that necklace, he'll see her as a witness. If he doesn't, he'll see her as a target. Neither scenario is good news for Rayna.

A travel writer, according to a link I find buried in the comment section. I follow the link to her website, a landing page filled with pictures, links to articles she's written (only a couple dozen at most), invitations to connect on her socials (which she's since set to private), but it's too late. Whether she meant to be or not, Rayna is already *Out There*, a bell that can't be unrung.

My iPad buzzes with an incoming text, and I flip from the news app to the message string. The unread text at the top is from a Dutch cell, a string of numbers my phone doesn't recognize. I tap the message with a finger.

Where are the diamonds? You promised.

My head whips up, and I look around the empty kitchen, half expecting the sender to be standing on the other side of the steel and glass windows. But except for the swaying trees, the backyard is empty.

I don't think too long or hard about it. I tick out a reply.

Who is this?

The dots bounce around almost immediately. Two seconds later, a reply hits my phone.

Don't fuck with me, Willow. I can bury you. And if you don't bring the diamonds to me, I will.

A tingling spreads through my body, visceral and intense, not just at the threat, but at the fact it was sent to this number. To this device—an iPad stuffed with Sem's games and that everyone in the house knows the passcode to. Ditto for my phone, and as the two devices are synced, I'm guessing the messages landed there, too. This is why people have burner phones, to intercept messages like these.

I think about my next move. Play dumb? Delete the text string, block the number, wipe both from my memory banks? Then again, what will that accomplish? And while we're at it, *which* diamonds? The ones dangling from my neck and ears? The ones upstairs in the vault? He's already got plenty of diamonds, and now he wants more? After Xander, I know what he'll do to me if I don't deliver.

The front door swings open, ushering in Martina on a gust of frigid wind. I flip the iPad cover closed and try to adopt the pose of someone who isn't losing her shit, someone who doesn't have tension rolling off her like an electrical field, but my muscles are steel under my skin. I stare at a couple of pigeons huddled on a branch outside the kitchen window and force myself to breathe.

Martina bustles down the hallway, a commotion of squeaky shoes and crinkling shopping bags. "I picked up a lovely piece of halibut for dinner. I hope that's okay."

I twist around in my chair. "Halibut sounds delicious. Thank you."

"I thought I'd make that Jamie Oliver recipe that—" She stops at the island, her gaze sticking to my face. "What's wrong? What happened?"

I wave a hand in the general direction of my iPad and sigh. "I was reading the news about Xander. It's just so awful. I can't stop picturing him."

She heaves the bags on the marble with a commiserating sigh. "I talked to some of the neighbors earlier, and everybody's spooked. Let's just hope the police do their job and find the person who did this. We'll all feel better when that monster is behind bars."

"I know I will." I push up from the chair and do my best to shake it off—a problem to deal with later, when I'm alone. "Here, let me help you unpack the groceries."

November 17th, 10:27 p.m.

"MADAME."

I stare up at Xander standing in the open passenger's door, and he really is handsome. Backlit from above, the overhead lights hitting his thick hair, broad grin, sparkling brown eyes fringed with impossibly long lashes. He wriggles the fingers on the outstretched arm like he's an actual gentleman, when we both know he's anything but.

I drop my hand into his and let him haul me out of the cocoon of his Bentley and into the cool parking garage under his building. A smelly space of cement and fluorescent lighting that, as far as I can tell, seems to be devoid of humans, which is good. The last thing we need is for someone to spot me here.

"This way," Xander says as soon as I'm upright. He takes off toward a set of double glass doors at the far end. A man on a mission.

I follow behind as quickly as I can in this pencil skirt and five-inch heels, my soles clicking on the cold concrete floor. I catch up to him at the bank of elevators, one of them waiting to whisk us upstairs.

"I have a wine cellar in the basement." Xander searches through his keys for a fob, a round gray thing he holds against a sensor by the buttons. It beeps once, and the top button lights up. *PH*, for penthouse floor. "I could send down for a bottle of Cristal if you'd like."

"A wine cellar, huh? Sounds fancy."

"There's also a catering kitchen for whenever I need a private chef. I'll have to have you and Thomas over sometime."

"Do you even hear yourself? No one *needs* a private chef, Xander, or a wine cellar for that matter. When did you become so bougie?"

"Twenty years ago, when I made my first million. And you're one to talk. Isn't your chef named Marina?"

"It's Martina, and she works for Thomas, not me."

He cocks a *sure she does* brow, and I laugh and lean a hip against the side wall. Xander and I only talk like this when it's just us two, and always out of earshot of a Prins. Even Thomas. Especially him. For Thomas, my and Xander's mutual climb out of poverty puts us on the same team, makes us co-conspirators in a game Thomas doesn't want or know how to play. He'd see our back and forth as, at best, shutting him out, and at worst, flirting, but Thomas would only be partially right.

Yes, Xander and I have a lot in common. Yes, we both clawed our way into a life most people dream about. But mostly, what we like to do is push each other's buttons. Depending on the day, our exchanges are a volley of either affectionate teasing or snarky exasperation.

I jut my chin at a round object in the corner of the ceiling. "Is that what I think it is?"

"Yeah, but it doesn't work. Well, the camera works, but the footage isn't saved, just streamed to a screen behind the concierge desk downstairs. Joop sees it, but Joop is cool." Xander waves at the camera. "Trained in the art of discretion."

"In other words, Joop is used to watching you sneak strange women up to your apartment every night."

"Not *every* night. But he might have seen it once or twice."

The doors ping open, and the lights in the foyer turn on, almost as if by magic. He sweeps an arm at the gleaming space.

"After you, gorgeous."

RAYNA

On Sunday afternoon, the stress finally catches up to me. I fall asleep hard, but my dreams are like shallow puddles, the images so sharp and vivid that they feel almost tangible.

Me, standing alone on Xander's terrace. The wind has picked up, the icy gusts whipping my hair and the duvet all around, raising chill bumps wherever it touches my naked skin.

And on its tail, Xander's voice, speaking in Dutch.

I follow the sound inside, chasing the guttural gibberish through the empty bedroom and down a long, art-lined hallway, black-and-white framed photographs of faces I recognize, models and actors and rock stars. Xander's voice grows louder, more heated, until suddenly, there he is, standing between his desk and the far wall of his study, talking on the phone.

No, not talking. Screaming. Under the buttery terry cloth of his robe, his back is rigid with fury. I don't understand any of what he says, but I know instinctively that it's not pleasant.

And all around him are diamonds. In giant piles on the floor, spread in glittering heaps on his desk, spilling over from his fist and a safe cracked open on the wall. Massive mounds of diamonds everywhere.

Suddenly, he turns. His eyes meet mine, and he mouths one word.

Run.

I lurch upright on a gasp, blinking into my dim beige bedroom.

The metal table lamp on the dresser is still glowing, sending up a halo of dirt-tinted light. I fish around in the bedding for my laptop and check the time: 8:17 p.m. Outside my little window, the sky is black with night.

That one word echoes through my brain: *Run*. Did Xander try to warn me? Did he know he was in danger that night? That I was?

I fall back onto the bed and replay my memories for the millionth time. I squeeze my eyes shut and poke around the edges of what I can summon up, playing back the snippets over and over in my mind, trying to connect them, to line them up in chronological order. The booze, the terrace, the sex, the bed, the shades that peeled up the terrace windows unprompted like they worked on a timer.

But anywhere during those however many hours, did I follow his voice to the study? Was there really a phone call and piles and piles of diamonds? The dream felt so palpable. The smell of night jasmine on the wind, the feel of the hallway runner under my bare feet. Xander's dismissive tone, the sharp blade of anger behind every word. I can't tell what's real and what is my mind playing tricks. Did Xander even have a study?

My heart won't stop thudding, because I feel like he did. That bit about following his voice, the art-lined hallway . . . An image pops in my mind of a giant box of bonbons, colorful chocolates in all shapes and sizes cushioned in shiny, pleated cups. Not a painting but a sculpture, hung on the wall at the very end of the hall. I see it, lit up with a spotlight from above, and another memory comes to me in flashes.

Getting turned around on the way back from the bathroom, taking a left when I should have taken a right. A room with a big desk parked before the window. Xander was there, and the phone call, that part was real, too. I backed out of the room before he could catch me eavesdropping on what was clearly drama because I thought it was a former girlfriend, or maybe an ex-wife.

Later, when Xander joined me in the bedroom, I didn't mention the call, and neither did he.

Still. This seems significant.

I swing my legs out of bed and push to stand, rummaging through my bag for Detective Boomsma's business card. I find it tucked in the side pocket, and I'm looking for my phone before remembering I no longer have one. The detective confiscated it, which means it's in an evidence drawer somewhere, along with my most important cards sitting in the holder on the back. If I don't get them back soon, I'm going to have to start chasing down replacements.

I awaken my laptop and pull up Google Voice, plugging in the number on the card. A few seconds later, the detective's voice crackles in my speakers.

"Arie Boomsma."

The name pushes through an uproar of background noise, house music blaring over a loudspeaker that sounds like it's positioned directly above his head in a room packed full of people, great swells of animated voices and laughter. If it weren't for the hour and the delighted squeals of what can only be kids, I'd think he was in a nightclub.

I lean in to the laptop, putting my lips close to the speaker. "Hi, Detective, this is Rayna Dumont. Sorry to call on a Sunday evening, but I just remembered something that might be pertinent to the investigation. Do you have a minute?"

He pauses, but he must have caught at least some of what I said, because his next words are in English. "What? Who is this?"

"Rayna Dumont," I shout back, overenunciating my words. "I'm calling about Xander van der Vos."

"Hang on, give me a second. I can't hear a thing." He says something in rapid-fire Dutch, then he must step outside because suddenly, the racket dies away. "Okay. Say all that again."

"This is Rayna Dumont. I just remembered something that might be pertinent to the Xander van der Vos investigation."

"My phone didn't recognize your number."

"Because I'm calling on Google Voice. You still have my cellphone, remember?" I pause to give him room to respond, but he doesn't bite. "Speaking of, when do you think I could get my cellphone back?"

"We will release it when we are done with it."

"Do you have any idea when that will be?"

"Like I said, when we are done."

I can't get a read on this guy, can't figure out if he's being difficult on purpose, or if he's just grumpy because I interrupted him in the middle of what's obviously a social event.

"Okay, then. What about the cards on the back? My tram card, debit card, and residence permit. It's illegal to just walk around this country without an ID, you know."

A weird little tidbit I learned about this country from the lady at the IND. You must be able to show proof of identification always, at all times, or risk arrest. I could use my American driver's license as ID, I suppose, but all those other cards in the holder—I want those back, too.

"I'll see what I can do. Is that all?"

"No. I called to tell you—" There's another wave of noise, music, and squealing kids, like someone opened the door. I picture him standing on a sidewalk somewhere. "Where are you, at a rave?"

A puff of air into the phone, not quite a laugh. "Close. It's my niece's birthday party, and they're about to bring out the cake, so perhaps you could hurry this along."

An order, not a request.

"I'm calling because I remembered something. I was coming back from the bathroom when I heard Xander talking to someone in the study. He was on the phone. The conversation was in Dutch, but I understood the tone. It was an argument, a pretty heated one."

"I see. Was the call on the house line or his mobile?"

"His iPhone. I remember that part clearly."

"Did he tell you who it was?"

"No, and I didn't ask. I was worried he'd think I was eavesdropping, which I guess I kind of was. I thought maybe I'd stepped into some kind of past relationship drama, so I cleared out of there before he saw me. Neither of us talked about the call afterward, not that I recall." I pause, turning over the memories in my mind. Xander returning to the bedroom and shucking his robe, crawling up the bed with a grin. "At least, I'm pretty sure. Almost positive."

"You're almost positive."

"Yes." I frown because I know what the detective is getting at, and I don't need his judgment. "I already told you we drank a lot, Detective. The end of the night is a little spotty."

"Okay, well, do you remember who called who, or what time this phone call occurred?"

I pause, considering the question. "I remember hearing his voice and following it down the hallway, so no. I don't know who initiated contact. The conversation was already underway when I got there."

"And the time?"

"I didn't look at the clock, but I . . ." I trail off, about to say I was already naked when this all went down, which means it was late. "After midnight, certainly. Can't you pull up his phone records to check?"

"We'll take a look at his call logs. Anything else?"

His voice is brusque, clearly in a hurry to get back to his party, his people, his life, and honestly, who can blame him? Detectives need days off, too.

Still, though. I can't let him go just yet.

"Actually, yes. Did Xander have a safe?"

There's a stretch of silence so long I'm about to wriggle my mouse to check the connection when finally, he clears his throat. "What makes you ask about a safe?"

"I had a dream that he had one, and that it was filled with diamonds. But I don't remember seeing it when I was there, so now I'm wondering if the dream is my mind's way of telling me something I've forgotten or if I just made it up."

"I see. And in your dream, where was this safe?"

"In the study, hidden behind a painting in the wall."

"Which wall? Do you remember the painting?"

"In my dream, the safe was already open, which means the face of the painting was facing the wall. But it was in the wall behind his desk, kind of to the left, between the desk and the window." Another long spell of empty air, which I fill with, "That's where it is, isn't it? I wasn't making it up."

He doesn't answer, but his silence seems like a pretty firm yes to me, and I feel a warm rush of heat, my breath catching in the back of my throat. My dream wasn't entirely fiction, wasn't just my mind making up a story around the trauma I've been carrying around for two days now. Suddenly, I'm wondering what else I've forgotten. What else happened while my brain was too booze soaked to think clearly? What else did I miss while I was in Xander's bed?

"Was the safe filled with diamonds like in my dream?" I ask. "Because I know about Xander's job. I know he worked for a diamond house and that he ran their line of lab-grown diamonds, big ones that go for a hundred thousand a pop."

"Like the necklace you were wearing in that picture."

An elevator plunges down the center of my chest and lands in my stomach with a thud. And here I thought it was the people back home I had to worry about, their gossip and screenshots and shares. The detective saw the picture of me in that necklace.

"That picture was a joke. I already took it down." Though apparently, not quickly enough.

"Ms. Dumont, I don't know if you're aware, but Xander van der Vos was something of a celebrity here in Amsterdam. His death is all over the news, and so is that picture of you wearing his necklace. The legitimate news sites are one thing, but people are posting to X and Reddit and TikTok, and they're jumping to their own conclusions. I'd advise you not to go searching for those comment threads, but here's the basic gist: they say as the last person to see Xander alive—"

"I'm pretty sure the last person to see him alive was his killer."

"Exactly my point. People are talking about you. They're identifying you by name, and they're wondering if you took that necklace. If you have it in your possession right now."

"The answer, for the record, is no. The last time I saw the necklace, Xander was dropping it in the nightstand drawer."

"It's not just the necklace. My colleagues and I are still trying to determine what was in Mr. Van der Vos's safe, which is exactly where you said it was, by the way, except there was nothing in it. By the time we got there, it had been emptied out. The nightstand drawer, too."

"So what are you saying? The necklace is missing?"

"Yes. The necklace is missing."

My body goes hot and then cold, and I think about what this could mean. Maybe Xander moved the necklace after I fell asleep. Maybe he put it back in the safe for the killer to clean out later.

But what if he didn't?

The thought drops into my head fully formed. What if the necklace was still in the nightstand when Xander got out of bed, when he flipped on the shower and stepped into the stream? What if the killer was *right there*, opening and closing that nightstand drawer while I snored away, oblivious?

I hear the thump that sent me racing out of the penthouse, picture a nameless, faceless killer fetching another zip tie in another room so he can wrap it around my neck and silence me, too. A shiver goes down the skin of my back, a feverish kind of panic that feels like the start of the flu.

"What about the building's security cameras? Did you see anyone on the footage?"

Because I was lucid enough when we got there to remember that Xander's building had dozens of them. That he used a fob to operate the elevator, and it opened straight into his apartment. There's no way the killer could have gotten inside without passing multiple cameras, not unless he scaled the outside of the building like Spiderman, and even then, a building like Xander's would likely have outdoor cameras, too.

"How do you know Xander didn't buzz his killer up?"

"Excuse me?"

"If you slept through a fight to the death between two large men and possibly a killer emptying out the drawer next to your head, then how do you know you didn't miss something else? How do you know Xander didn't invite his own killer upstairs?"

I don't answer, because I *don't* know. I have no idea what else I might have slept through. Is that what happened? The killer was someone Xander knew? Or is the detective implying that he thinks *I'm* the killer Xander invited upstairs?

"Is that an accusation? You don't really think I had anything to do with his murder, do you?"

"I'm simply trying to put together the chain of events that ended in a man's death. And now there's this picture of you in a priceless necklace floating around the internet, one someone was presumably willing to kill for once. All those people on Reddit right now, all the people on the other sites? If one of them wants that necklace just as badly as the killer did, where do you think they'll look first?"

To me. They'll assume that *I* have the necklace.

"But I don't have it," I say, as emphatically as I know how, even though a smarter part of me says it's not the detective who needs the most convincing. "I don't have the necklace."

"Thanks for calling, Ms. Dumont. I'll be in touch."

There are two quick beeps, then nothing. I wriggle the mouse, and he's ended the call.

WILLOW

"Oh, look," Fleur says as we come into their parents' living room. "It's darling baby brother here to save us from ourselves." She's immaculate as usual, in monochromatic burgundy down to her shoes and nail polish. Even the lipstick lining the edge of her wineglass matches—and by the looks of things, it's not her first.

I shoot Thomas a commiserating look. There was a time when we could laugh about his sister's backhanded digs, but those days are in the past. His eyes look everywhere but at mine lately, and there's a rigid politeness to his posture that I haven't seen since that first day at the restaurant. I don't know when this happened, exactly, or how, but it's been this way for longer than I'd care to admit.

We start with his mother standing by the windows, the glass lit up with a view of the glittering Amstel canal. Uniformed servers skim the edges of the room, offering up complicated hors d'oeuvres from silver trays: tiny bite-sized quiches filled with leek and Italian ham, ornate cucumber slices topped with crème fraîche and beluga caviar. Sem turns up his nose at the food, flopping instead onto a chaise with my iPad—minus the messaging app.

Not that there have been any new messages, not on my cellphone and not on the burner, either. Even worse, when I copied the number into the burner and hit Call, I was greeted by a recording: *Dit nummer is niet in gebruik.*

This number has been disconnected.

I'm not foolish enough, though, to think that's the end of things. The person behind those texts knows my cellphone number. He thinks I owe him diamonds. This is like the quiet hours after a devastating earthquake. You just know there will be aftershocks.

"Hello, Mama," Thomas says, giving his perfectly coiffed mother the standard Dutch greeting, three kisses to the cheeks. "You're looking particularly lovely tonight."

Anna bats away the compliment with a tut, even though everybody here knows she's never looked anything short of immaculate. Tweed Chanel hanging from birdlike shoulders. Flawless makeup. Hair like she spent the entire afternoon in a salon, which she does every two weeks to ensure her highlights stay fresh, four different shades of blond that curl perfectly around her face. She pats him on the cheek and turns to me.

"Willow, darling." It's *darling* now, but it only took forever and I'm still not convinced she means it. Anna only tolerates me because I gave her a grandchild. "I'm so glad you and the boys could make it."

Her Dutch is slow and perfectly enunciated, but I still need a second or two of processing time to translate her words in my head. Even in a foreign language, though, I know a dig when I hear one.

I smile and respond in my best Dutch. "Thank you for having us. Everything smells delicious."

She gives a nod of approval at my correct grammar, and then another as her gaze wanders down my outfit, a burgundy cashmere sweater over tan suede pants she recognizes from a boutique on the Beethovenstraat. The smile sticks to her cheeks, though, when she gets to my shoes, clunky brown combat boots that squeak when I walk. Dior makes a similar pair, but these are knockoffs, and a million times more comfortable. Anna sees them for what they are, a clear sign that while I'm able to mostly look the part, I'm not quite willing to commit.

I excuse myself and make the rounds, doling out hellos to

Thomas's sister and her husband, Roland, their preteen twin girls, Yara and Esmée, ending with the most important stop, at Willem's wingback chair under the antique mirror, a twin to ours. *Kissing the ring*, I once called it, but Thomas didn't share in the humor. For a Prins, there's nothing funny about these Sunday suppers.

By the time I make it back around to Anna, she's sidling up to Sem. "Sem, *lieverd*, the girls are putting together a puzzle in the upstairs study. Wouldn't you prefer to play with them?"

The girls are a good eight years older than Sem, who isn't crazy about either of them. He says they treat him like a baby.

Sem doesn't lift his gaze from his iPad. *BrainCraft*, by the looks of things.

Anna turns to me with a frown. "Does he do this at home, too?"

This, as in ignore when people are talking to him.

If I had the patience and the vocabulary, I'd explain for the millionth time that Sem isn't like her other grandkids, that while his cochlear implants have helped significantly, he still can't always distinguish Anna's voice from all the other noises. The cooks banging around in the kitchen. The living room filled with six adults, their words tumbling over each other in a competition to be Loudest Prins. Gregory Porter playing on the Sonos speakers, a music choice that Anna thinks makes her painfully hip. In order to respond, Sem needs to know that someone is talking to him. He needs eye contact and visual cues, facial expressions and body language, and an unobstructed view of their lips. Anna knows this, but for some reason, she refuses to remember.

Thomas appears at my side just then. He drapes a hand over Sem's shoulder, waiting until he looks up. "I hear the cookies are ready for decorating. Want to see if the chef needs some help?"

Sem might have not gotten all of that, but he definitely got the word *cookies*. His face brightens, and he tosses the iPad to the couch.

Anna gestures the server over, ordering her to leave the tray and take Sem from the room. I don't stop either of them, even though I know there'll be more icing in my son's belly than on the cookies, that the sugar will keep him hyped up until well past his bedtime. I let him go because I understand what Thomas and Anna are doing: clearing the room of child-sized ears, even ones that don't pick up on every conversation.

As soon as they're gone, my father-in-law, Willem, clears his throat, a dramatic gesture that calls this meeting to order. "I spoke to Arthur this afternoon. He gave me an update."

I frown, trying to place the name. Thomas sinks onto one of the plush velvet couches, and I claim the spot next to him.

Willem is back in his usual chair, a modern wingback of wine-colored velvet, one liver-spotted hand clutching his glass. He rolls his drink around a solitary ice cube, one of the cylindrical ones his staff makes from imported mineral water.

"Arthur says the building's security cameras are useless. They were set up to be live stream only, meaning the doorman can watch things as they happen on the screen behind the reception desk, but the cameras don't feed to a computer. There's no hard drive where the footage is saved. Apparently, the company that installed the system never finished the job. They've been trying to get them to come back for months now."

At least I *think* that's what he says. My brain stumbled on a couple of the words, but I'm pretty sure I got the full picture. When it comes to Dutch, I understand a lot more than I can say.

"Typical." Anna rolls her eyes. "People in this country don't want to work these days. They just want things handed to them."

She says this despite a house filled with an army of staff, or the fact that she's never lifted even one of her manicured fingers to hold down a job herself. It's a common refrain from the Dutch privileged class, especially since the pandemic. Taxes are too high. People are too lazy. Stop using my money to pay them to stay home. The first time I heard it roll off her lips, I wanted to scream.

"What about the doorman, didn't he see anything? Is he a potential witness?" Fleur, God bless, keeping the conversation on point.

Willem shakes his head. "Not the doorman, not any of the building's staff. None of the neighbors noticed anything out of the ordinary that night. Except for the woman who reported him dead, the police have zero witnesses."

Fleur throws her hands up in disgust. "Why have cameras if they don't record? Why have a doorman if he's going to sleep on the job? At this rate, it could be anybody who took those stones. It could have been a junkie off the street."

We're talking about the missing diamonds again, and not the fact that a man was murdered. I tip up my wine, an ice-cold Sancerre that feels so good hitting my system it's a little frightening.

Next to Fleur on the loveseat, her husband, Roland, mirrors her exasperated expression. He's not the type of man I would have put with a woman like her, a bombshell heiress who'd look more at home next to a billionaire businessman, or maybe a professional footballer. Roland is the exact opposite, a spindly guy with thinning hair and cheekbones so sharp they look carved from stone. He doesn't say much, but then again, he doesn't have to. Roland is a baron, and his family owns half the countryside in Limburg.

Willem takes a pull from his drink, then puts the glass down carefully. "Arthur is investigating everyone connected with both the security company and the building, and he'll let me know the second his background checks produce anything suspicious."

"I'm sorry," I say, glancing back and forth between Thomas and his father. "Who is Arthur?"

"Arthur Pronk, head of police for Amsterdam. We were in the corps together."

Of course they were. Every Prins going back generations was a member of the *Studentencorps*, the oldest fraternity in Holland and a veritable network of who's who in business and politics. Willem is a member. Fleur and Roland are members. Only Thomas is not.

"What about police cameras on nearby streets?" Fleur says, moving things along. "I assume they've looked at those, too?"

She looks at Thomas as she says it, even though the question is clearly meant for their father. It's him she's always trying to impress, his footsteps she's always trying so hard to step in—the corps, an MBA from Erasmus in Rotterdam, a newly renovated villa in nearby Blaricum that's been featured in international design magazines. And three years ago, as thanks for her efforts, Willem bypassed Fleur to appoint the younger Thomas CEO of House of Prins. Why? Who the hell knows. Thomas was as surprised as anyone.

Thomas leans forward on the couch, shifting to face his sister. "My understanding is that most police cameras are in the center of the city, in Oost and De Pijp, where crime is more concentrated. Not in Zuid, at least not further south than the Van Baerlestraat. There's a map of the cameras on the city website."

Fleur huffs a frustrated sigh. "Neighbors, then. Local shops. Plenty of people and businesses allow police to look at their camera feeds. Somebody must have seen something."

"What about the woman?" I say, and every head swivels to me. The sudden attention, all those probing Prins eyes, makes me stumble over my words. "There was a woman. In Xander's apartment when he was killed. An American expat. She found him."

Willem sets his glass onto the side table with a thunk. "Yes, the whole world has seen the picture of her in that necklace, and if Xander were here, I'd fire him for a second time, but Arthur's men will deal with that girl. Until they come up with enough evidence to make an arrest, though, we can't sit still."

An electrical current zaps through me, shooting my back straighter. Fire Xander for a second time, and which *we* is he referring to? The Prins family? The House of Prins? Both, probably.

But more importantly: "Deal with her how?" I say it in clear, full-throated Dutch, but Willem ignores me.

"We need to be very clear about what happened here. Where is the statement, Thomas? Where are the talking points? We should have had both these things days ago."

My chest gives a little quake and I try again, directing my question this time at my husband. "Thomas, how will Arthur deal with her?"

He taps my knee, a silent signal we'll talk about it later. "I'll write up both tonight," he says to Willem, his marching orders clear. "As soon as we leave here, I'll do it immediately."

Fleur whips out her iPhone, tapping at the screen with her thumbs, holding the mic up to her mouth. "It is with great sadness and a heavy heart that we announce the untimely passing of one of our esteemed employees, Xander van der Vos. The House of Prins is deeply saddened by his tragic death. Our thoughts and prayers go out to his family and friends." She smiles at her father, then Thomas. "If you want, I can email you a copy."

Roland looks impressed. Thomas tosses back his wine. In the Prins family, sibling rivalry runs deep.

"Shouldn't we also say something about the Cullinans?" Thomas says, plunking down his empty glass. A server scurries forward to refill it.

The Cullinans, ten flawless diamonds cut from a stone that Willem's great-great-grandfather once pilfered from a Praetorian mine. Hendrik Prins, the original diamond thief, smuggled the rock back to Amsterdam and cut it to chunks of what's now known as the Prins cut, then used his booty to position himself as the city's premier diamond house.

And now, nine of them are missing, vanished last summer from the Prins vault in what police are calling the heist of the century. How? Nobody knows. Even now, police are stumped.

"What about them?" Fleur asks, at the same time Willem barks, "Absolutely not."

"I think we have to," Thomas says, throwing up his hands. "The media can't get enough of the missing Cullinans, and now there's that necklace floating around the internet and reports of diamonds missing from Xander's apartment. They're going to link the stories, especially if they find out I fired him."

At that, my head whips to Thomas. "*You* fired Xander? Why? When?"

"Three days ago, and for theft, essentially." Thomas pushes his glasses up with a knuckle, and I don't have to count back on my fingers to know that three days ago is the same night Xander was killed. Looks like I'm not the only one in this relationship with secrets. "I found extra diamonds in the shipments from our Asian lab, way more than Xander had officially sourced and not listed on any of the waybills. I'm pretty sure he was selling them under the table."

Thomas's tone is calm, but for a company like Prins, where every diamond, no matter the quality or the size, goes through multiple levels of security, a situation like the one he's describing is a five-alarm fire. Prins stones do not go unaccounted for on a waybill. A shipment doesn't arrive with more diamonds than on the order. When Thomas discovered that discrepancy, he would have lost his mind.

But more to the point, selling siphoned diamonds under the table sounds very much like something Xander would do.

"So make sure the press doesn't find out, then," Willem says, in a tone I've heard him use on chauffeurs and household staff and now on his son. "And while you're at it, make sure they don't link the stories."

"How? People are going to hear the words *missing diamonds* and automatically think of the Cullinans."

Thomas is not wrong. The Cullinans are iconic, the House's flagship stones carted out only for the most special occasions. Even now, almost seven months later, the tiniest updates on their whereabouts still make the front page of every newspaper, and rumors are still flying on every tabloid and social media site. It was Frederik Albers, the diamond trader Thomas fired last fall. Or an Italian jeweler who was either pushed or leapt from a hotel rooftop the day before Christmas, depending on who you want to believe. Xander had been at House of Prins for only six months before they vanished from the vault. No way he's going to escape the scrutiny.

Still. The Prins vault isn't some muddy river in the middle of nowhere, where you can drop a gigantic rock in your pocket and wander off like Hendrik once did. There are rules and regulations around handling stones, protocols to track them whenever they're removed from their drawer in the vault, which you can't open without a Prins. Willem. Thomas. Fleur. They're the only ones who know the code.

Willem takes a pull from his drink, then puts the glass down carefully. "Whatever diamonds Xander had in his apartment, whatever the killer managed to take on his way out the door, they were not stones from the Prins vault, and they most certainly were not the Cullinans. I need you to make that very clear."

"How do I do that?"

"By spinning the story. By distracting them with another one. The insurance company is already being difficult enough. The last thing we need is another reason for them to delay the payout."

Diamonds pulled from African dirt. Diamonds grown in a sterile lab. Diamonds cut from the Cullinan stone and vanished into thin air. A man can be killed with a zip tie in his own shower, and every conversation still revolves around diamonds.

"And for God's sake," Willem says, picking up his glass, "do not let anyone find out that you fired Xander."

Thomas leans forward on the couch, directing his next words at his father. "I'm telling you, Xander didn't get his hands on any of the mined stones. The mined stones are all accounted for. Every single one."

"Except for nine of the Cullinans," Fleur reminds him, her words a projectile, a reminder of everything they've lost.

He sighs, long and stoic. "Xander is gone, Fleur. Can we leave the I-told-you-sos alone now?"

I'm unsure if *gone* means *dead* or *fired*, though it's probably not relevant here. What's relevant is that Thomas fired Xander for theft hours before a killer snuck into his penthouse and strangled him with a zip tie. I wonder if the police know any of this.

"I told you hiring that man was a mistake," Fleur says. "I told you a lab-grown line would devalue the House of Prins."

Roland dips his head in agreement. Fleur could have said anything—that Xander was a luminary, that he was a scoundrel and a thief, that unicorns exist and the earth is flat—and Roland would back her up on it. It's why she's stayed married to him all this time, because the man is like a mime, mirroring her moods and gestures and facial expressions. He's basically her, which is why she keeps him around. With them, it's always two against one.

A muscle works in Thomas's jaw, but he manages to keep his cool. "The House was already in free fall, Fleur, long before I took charge. You've seen the balance sheets. We need the customers the lab-grown line is bringing in or we will die."

"Fake stones are not the answer," Fleur says, her voice rising in a common refrain. "Lab diamonds are poisoning the mined diamond supply. By capitulating, we are essentially shooting ourselves in the foot."

Thomas gives an emphatic shake of his head. "They're not fake, and we're not capitulating, we're being smart. Income from lab-growns has grown more than four hundred percent in the past year alone across the board, in every country including the Netherlands. How is it capitulating for us to benefit from that trend?"

"Income is not the same as profit, Thomas. Surely your precious Nyenrode taught you that."

Nyenrode, one of the best business schools in Holland, but a constant source of tension between Thomas and Fleur. Thomas was expected to follow in Willem and Fleur's footsteps at Erasmus, but he chose Nyenrode. His last little protest before falling in line for the Prins baton.

"Children, please," Anna huffs, holding up a perfectly manicured hand, her nails painted the exact same shade of dusty pink as her lipstick. "Can we not do this again? Think of your father's heart."

At that, all eyes go to Willem, who since retirement has gained a few extra kilos around his middle, sure, but is otherwise perfectly healthy. He brushes off her words with an animated grunt.

"Whatever happens, Xander's death must not reflect badly on the House," Willem says, picking a nonexistent piece of lint from the chair's armrest. "I need you to make sure our hands stay clean. And if Xander's death has anything to do with Prins or the lab-grown line . . ."

Willem doesn't finish, but the message is clear.

Fix it, Thomas. Fix what you broke.

"Dinner is served," the chef says, appearing like magic in the doorway to save us from ourselves. Next to her, a hyped-up Sem bounces on his toes. There's a streak of blue icing on his ear, a blob of something yellow and shiny in his hair. He clings to her with a sticky hand.

Silently, we file into the dining room and to our regular seats, Anna and Willem at the heads, Thomas and Fleur each at their father's elbows, their spouses on the other side. I help Sem onto his chair before sinking into mine across from Roland and the girls, and it occurs to me I should probably be appalled at my in-laws' callous response to a man's brutal death, but I'm not.

For a Prins, diamonds always come first.

RAYNA

On Monday afternoon, I step out of the PrimeFone store into a horde of tourists, a whole five hundred euros lighter thanks to my brand-new replacement debit card, still smoking in my pocket. Five hundred euros I don't have and can't really afford for a dinky, refurbished iPhone, which I'll need to call the police if someone's chasing me.

Last night after the detective and I hung up, I lay in bed, staring at the clouds trailing past my little window while his ominous words drew tight around my neck like a noose—or a zip tie. Every time I closed my eyes, it wasn't Xander I saw lying sprawled on the shower floor, not his neck or his finger . . . but mine. The detective thinks someone is coming after me, and now, so do I.

At least the Leidsestraat is bustling, a wall-to-wall sea of people crowding the pavement. I find a quiet-ish spot by a corner and scroll through the messages on my new cell. The second the salesman helped me connect it to my iCloud, the notifications started rolling in, a series of missives that got progressively longer and more urgent in tone. I pause on one from my sister—better watch out mom saw the nip-pic—followed by one from my mother: CALL ME OR ELSE!

I haul a breath, pull up FaceTime, and hit Call. The line connects, and the screen goes in and out of focus on something white and fuzzy.

"Mom. This is FaceTime. Take the phone off your ear. Look at the screen."

More jumbling. More images from a camera lens that can't quite get a grip on anything solid. And then, there it is: my mother's face.

And she doesn't look happy. "Well, *finally*. I've only been calling you all weekend. I was starting to get worried."

She uses her librarian voice, terse and highly annoyed, mostly because my mother is always worried about something. The way my dad works too hard and eats too much red meat. My sister's daughter still not walking at thirteen months and how it's a sign of something awful. Fentanyl finding its way into the Halloween candy supply and China listening in on her calls. The state of the world in general.

And me. These days, most of her worries seem to center around me.

"Everything's fine. I just lost my phone, that's all."

If the news of Xander hasn't made it across the Atlantic yet, I'm not going to be the one who brings it up. Maybe I deleted the picture before someone could connect it with his death, or maybe it's just that a dead Dutchman doesn't make a big enough wave to make a splash on American news sites, I don't know. What I do know is that for my mother, the nip-pic will be the real story.

I slip back into the crowd of tourists and follow the tram line south. "Before you start, yes, I know that picture was ill-advised, but it was only up for a couple of hours. I took it down as soon as I realized."

"Realized what, that the entire world had seen your lady parts?"

I wince. "You don't have to fuss. I've already gotten an earful from all sorts of people I was really hoping never to hear from again. Also, while we're at it, how did everybody in St. Francisville jump on that post so quickly? It was only up a couple of hours and it was the middle of the night. What are they, vampires?"

"You know how people here love to talk."

Why, yes. Yes, Mom, I *do* know. It's a big part of why I left. The other part is Barry.

"Did he see, you think?" I ask.

"Oh, Rayna . . ."

I hate the pity I hear in my mother's voice, but mostly I hate how much I care about the answer. Of course I wanted Barry to see that picture. He's the real reason I posted the damn thing, so he would see that sultry, sexy version of me and feel . . . what? Sorrow? Remorse? It was a stupid, vengeful move that resulted in three thousand people seeing my nipple.

"Never mind. Do *not* answer that." I muscle my way down the busy street. "How are you? How's Dad?"

"Oh, you know. Same old, same old. The well has been acting up again, and now they're saying we'll probably have to dig a new one. Your father about keeled over when he heard how much that's going to cost. It's why he couldn't say no."

"Couldn't say no to what?"

Dad is an electrician, a one-man shop he advertises on the side of his van with an orange cartoon man holding a light bulb, lit up in an orange glow. *Ted Dumont, For All Your Electrical Needs.* Dad does okay, but St. Francisville isn't exactly a booming metropolis, and the client pool is the size of a rain puddle.

Mom fills the silence with one of her sighs, and in it, I hear the answer. I lurch to a stop in the middle of the sidewalk.

"Mother, you can't be serious."

A cluster of Italian teenagers come tumbling out of the pharmacy and ram me from the side, nearly knocking me into the tram tracks. "*Scuzi*!" one of them shouts as they skitter past, but I don't acknowledge any of it because I know what my mother is working very hard not to tell me. I know why Dad couldn't say no.

"Your father said you'd be angry, but sweetie, please don't blame him. That PPP money wasn't nearly enough to keep us afloat, and we're still digging ourselves out of that hole in a market that isn't the greatest. Barry's the only developer in town who's not slowing down. If anything, he's busier than ever."

I grit my teeth, clamping down hard to hold back a scream. Never, not once in our eight-plus years together would it have ever occurred to Barry to hire my father for one of his builds. He always chooses a firm from Baton Rouge, the biggest and the best with a CEO that kisses his ass and steers a whole slew of qualified electricians. There's only one reason Barry hired my father, and that's to mess with me.

"I'm not mad at Dad but Barry. No—I'm mad at *myself*, because this is why you don't drunk post. Because alcohol makes you think it's okay to upload a picture of your nipple for all the world to see, except it wasn't all the world I was going for. You know that, right? It was one person. One idiot asshole ex who I hoped would see it and say, *Whoa. What kind of loser lets a woman like this get away? What kind of dumb fuck am I?*"

"Sweetheart, you know how I hate the f-word."

"And now that picture is out there in a big way, stirring up a shitstorm of epic proportions and constantly bringing me back to what ended up being a seriously traumatic night. All because in a moment of drunken delusion, I was hoping to summon up guilt or remorse or shame when Barry has given me zero indication he's capable of feeling any of those things. God! I'm so stupid. And petty, too, apparently."

"Oh, Rayna Jo . . ." Mom heaves another sigh. "Honey, you're not stupid. What you are is *human*, so please stop beating yourself up. I hate what that man did to you, but mostly I hate how it's made you want to put a whole ocean between you and your home. Your father and I miss you so much."

"I miss you, too." My throat goes tight around the words.

"And he did see the picture, by the way. His receptionist told your father he's been impossible ever since."

I don't want to love the image of Barry stomping around his office as much as I do, but there it is. The one bright spot in a couple of really shitty days.

The ground under my sneakers begins to vibrate, the tram scattering tourists as it comes clanging down the center of the street. I shoulder my way through the crowd, trying to beat it to the stop on the next bridge.

"Mom, I gotta run. This is my tram. Give Dad my love, okay? And tell him I said congrats on the big job. Love to you both!"

We hang up, and I drop my phone into my bag.

I bulldoze my way through the tourists to the bridge just in time. The tram doors slide open, burping out a thick cluster of tourists, their faces flushed with cold and excitement. They push past me with bright cheeks and windblown hair.

I collapse onto an empty seat by the window and let the tram carry me away from the noise and the crowd, still breathing hard as I stare at the scenery flashing by on the other side of the glass. The tunnel of ancient gingerbread buildings gives way to the Leidseplein with its street artists and terraces, the Bulldog with its striped awnings and neon signs, the Municipal Theater of orange and white brick that dominates a whole corner. The familiar sights bring me back a little, and I tell myself to let it go. Barry saw the picture of the nipple he'll never touch again as long as he lives, and I have bigger problems to worry about than a manipulative ex.

Like dead Tinder dates, for example. Like killer diamond thieves.

I'm digging in my bag when my fingers make contact with something foreign at the bottom. Something white and round and smooth and definitely not mine. I pull it out, hold it in a palm. It looks suspiciously like an AirTag.

Except it's not. The Find My app on my phone shows Rayna's Luggage exactly where it should be, in the suitcase I shoved under my bed on the P.C. Hooftstraat. According to the app, no other devices are near me.

If not an AirTag, then what?

I flip the thing over, study it from both sides. There's no Apple logo, no logo on it at all. I inspect the smooth metal rim, turning it every which way, but there's nothing there, either, no words or writing to identify it, but I know instinctively it's some kind of tracker.

Fear rises in my belly, and I slap my bag onto the empty seat beside me and sort through the contents. I take everything out, feeling in the side pockets and poking through every compartment in my makeup bag and wallet. I turn my bag upside down and give it a good shake, until nothing falls out but crumbs. The tracker in my hand is the only one like it in my things.

A fluke? A random stalker following me through the Leidsestraat?

I think about whoever's out there, sitting in a coffee shop somewhere or maybe even here in this tram, watching my little blue dot dance across their screen. My heart thuds at the thought, my gaze panning over the people near me. Two women sitting close, their heads pressed together as they talk in a language I can't understand. A trio of teenagers, passing around a Starbucks cup. A mother trying to wrangle her overactive preschooler, hyped up on the half-eaten cookie in his hand. A man in a red shirt and a battered ball cap staring at his phone. I'm pretty sure he got on when I did, and now he's standing by that same door, his body positioned so that if he raises his gaze even a little, we'd be eye to eye. I watch him, and panic zings through my veins. Is he *following* me?

The tram rolls to a stop, and I shove my things back in my bag and strap it across my chest, my muscles jumping out of my skin.

The doors ding open, and I force myself to sit still, waiting as people filter in and out, pretending to adjust my shoe as I drop the tracker to the floor and shove it under the seat as far back as it will go.

And the whole time, I watch the man in the ball cap the same way my father taught me to ride a horse once upon a time, with eyes that focus on nothing and everything. The second you turn your head, your body moves and you confuse the animal. I watch the man in the ball cap without looking at him, without moving a single muscle. He doesn't move, either. Not even to look up from his phone.

By now, the last stragglers have boarded the tram, and the doors are ready to close. I wait until the very last second and lunge for them, landing on the sidewalk right as the doors slide shut behind me. The tram clangs, the signal it's about to pull away.

Triumphant, I whirl around, my gaze searching out the man behind the glass. He's still standing in that same spot by the door, still clutching his phone, only now his head is raised. He sees me watching and smiles, right before the tram slides away.

WILLOW

Tuesday blooms bright and sunny, a blessing after what feels like months of rain. Thomas left this morning before the sun came up for Antwerp, where he's tonight's keynote speaker at the World Diamond Centre's annual conference. Sem and I have the house to ourselves. The whole entire giant house with all its walls and its rooms and my phone that still hasn't buzzed with a follow-up threat. I told Martina we'd be eating out tonight and sent her home early.

At just before three, I leash Ollie, heave him into the front of my cargo bike, and pedal through the lingering puddles to school. Sem spots us and skids to a stop, frowning across the pavers.

The park I sign.

His face breaks into a grin.

For days now, Sem has been a bear, whining about the tag on his sweater that was scratching his neck, about the milk that tasted funny so I'd squirt in some extra chocolate, about Ollie knocking over the Lego tower he'd spent all of five seconds building. He's a sensitive kid, and not just because he's overly attuned to nonverbal cues, facial expressions and body language and eye contact. Ever since Xander, his radar has been going full tilt. This park outing is as much for him as it is for me, to allow both of us to blow off some steam.

"What do you want for dinner, my love?" I say once he's close enough, pulling his beanie down over his ears. It may be sunny but it's bitterly cold, and the icy wind isn't helping any.

Sem throws up both arms, two little fists punching the air. "*Pannenkoeken*!"

There's not a kid in this country who doesn't beg for pancakes for supper, and in Holland it's a real thing, though the Dutch version is more crêpe than fluffy pancake. Sem likes his with ham and cheese and topped with powdered sugar and *stroop*, a syrup made from sugar beets.

And why the hell not? Thomas is in Antwerp, and Sem and I are on our own for dinner more often than not these days.

I get him settled with Ollie in the front of the bike and pedal the short distance to the park. It's only a few blocks from the school, and both Sem and Ollie know the drill. Through the gates of the Emmastraat entrance, dodge the chaotic flow of people and dogs coming from town, slow at the wide stretch of grass across from the fountain. That's our spot. Ollie sees it up ahead and lets loose one excited bark. Like Sem, he's eager to stretch his legs.

I park at the edge of the grass, then help them both out and unclip Ollie from his leash. For Sem, I produce a grubby tennis ball from my coat pocket. "You want to practice your throws?"

With a squeal, Sem snatches the ball from my fingers and takes off across the grass, Ollie sticking close to his heels. The ground is still drenched from the week's rain, scarring the field with a mix of muddy grass and half-frozen puddles. We've been here all of five seconds and already Sem and Ollie are filthy, but again: Who cares? It's not like Thomas is home to complain.

I buy a cup of coffee from the vendor's cart on the path, sink onto a bench at the edge of the field, and keep an eye on my son while I watch the path. The park is packed, the Dutch as a whole well used to braving the cold. Runners and walkers and commuters whizzing by on bikes, mothers like me getting dragged by kids and dogs, the occasional stoner sucking a fat joint on a park bench. I clock every face that passes by.

Fifteen minutes later, I spot her up ahead, a runner with a red ponytail swaying in time with her stride. Rayna on her first of two loops around the park—a runner's paradise that, considering she lives only a few blocks from here, might as well be her backyard. And unfortunately for her, she was far too easy to find.

For months now, Rayna has been cataloguing her life on Instagram and TikTok, and though since Xander she's set her pages to private, there are still plenty of pictures floating around online, most of the images easy to place. There were the typical touristy shots of canals or other picturesque spots, flower markets and famous buildings in the city center, must-see spots listed on every tourist's guide. I concentrated instead on the ones in the museum quarter, the shopping streets and cafés clustered around a few square blocks. And tons of the P.C. Hooftstraat—thanks to all the designer boutiques, one of the most recognizable streets in all of Holland.

And all those snapshots of her working or lounging or drinking tea in a sad beige room? Enough of them were geotagged on a building smack in the middle, a block of rent-controlled apartments above the Mont Blanc store.

Rayna shops at the Albert Heijn under the museums. She spends the mornings with her laptop at Joe & the Juice the next block over. She buys flowers at the stall across from the tram stop, and for the past three afternoons at around this time, she's made two clockwise loops through the Vondelpark.

And if I can do it—find her, watch her, learn her habits and patterns—then so could anyone else.

I watch her head bobbing in the crowd on the path, and I'm not quite sure how to play this. It's not like I can just walk up to her and introduce myself. What would I say? *Hey girl, I know you don't know me, but you're in danger.* She'd think I'm insane. She'd think she was in danger from *me*.

Maybe I could toss Ollie's ball her way, let my overly enthusiastic dog make the introductions. If I can manage to chuck the ball close enough for her to stumble over or even bend down and pick up, Ollie will be impossible to ignore. Or maybe I should go get another coffee. If I time my trip across the path just right, I could accidentally on purpose bump into her.

"*Mama, kijk*!"

I turn back to Sem, holding both hands high in the air, his palms and fingers dark with dirt. He might be half American, but he's a Dutch kid on Dutch soil, which means my attempts to make English his preferred language are a lost battle. He's telling me to look at his filthy hands.

I wrinkle my nose. "Is that dirt or poop?"

His adorable face splits in a wide grin. "It's dirt! Ollie gave it to me."

By the time I turn back to the path, she's gone. I push off the bench and hurry into the stream of people, searching for a streak of red hair in the crowd of runners and walkers. I look one way, then the other, then back again. *Shit.* I've lost her.

And then I spot a flash of red ponytail at the edge of the grass field, *my* grass field. Rayna leans against the back of a bench, stretching out her calves.

"Hey, did you happen to see a tennis ball?"

Rayna looks over, and she's as pretty in person as she is online. Prettier, even. Big eyes, cheeks flushed from exertion and cold, skin so porcelain it's almost see-through.

She shakes her head, looks about on the grass. "No, I don't think so. Sorry."

I point my face at Sem, chasing Ollie along the bushes at the back end. "It's not here. Keep looking." I shout the words even though

I know they won't reach Sem's ears. My son is running the other way, and the only way to get his attention short of running after him, is by whistling for Ollie. Where the dog goes, Sem follows.

"Cute kid." Rayna straightens, her gaze going to Ollie, streaking like a demon across the grass, a blur of fur and mud splatters. "Is that your dog?"

I nod. "Ollie. He's a rescue."

"He's cute, too," she says, but with a lot less enthusiasm than the first time. Ollie's fur is patchy. His ears are too small and his legs are too short and his underbite gives him a hilarious snaggletooth. Even when Ollie is clean, nobody would ever describe him as cute.

"Liar." I laugh. "Ollie won't be winning any ribbons anytime soon, but he's the sweetest."

"Rescues always are." She smiles.

"You have a dog?"

Rayna doesn't have a dog, at least not one in any of the pictures I've found of her online. She's the type, though, prim and deeply Southern, though hers would be a hunting Labrador, or maybe one of those bulldogs with the squished snouts. Not a mutt like Ollie. This woman is too pretty for a mutt.

She shakes her head, shiny ponytail swinging against her shoulder. "I used to. My ex has him now."

Just this morning, deep in one of the comment sections on X, I landed on a post from a woman claiming to be from Rayna's hometown. She spilled all sorts of dirt—about Rayna's ex, a real-estate developer named Barry Broderick, about their talk-of-the-town divorce and the way it shot Rayna so far off the deep end that she drove Barry and his fiancée off the road. Apparently, she caught him in bed with her best friend.

Sorry—*former* best friend.

"He sounds like a real snake."

She barks a laugh. "Taking my dog isn't the worst thing he's done, not by a long shot." She bounces on her toes, either because she's cold or eager to get back to her run. Maybe both. "Anyway, good luck finding your ball."

She takes off with a little wave, and that's that. Conversation over. No, she didn't confess where she stashed the necklace or give me a description of Xander's killer, but my gut says she's an innocent bystander in all this. An accidental victim who got swept up in a spectacular string of wrong-place, wrong-time bad luck.

I also learned that this girl is too easy to find, too trusting of strangers who chat her up in the park. I watch her body get swept into the throng of tourists and runners on the path, and worry pings me in the chest. I need to find a way to warn her.

"Mama, I'm *starving.*"

I whirl around to find Sem, standing at the edge of the grass, covered from head to toe in mud. He wipes his hands down his clothes, leaving twin streaks of mud on his coat, his pants, across one grubby cheek. There's not a restaurant in the city that would let us inside.

"Change of plans, big guy: I'm cooking." I whistle for Ollie, and he gives a great shake, spraying some poor girl with grass and mud and water. "Looks like you two worked up an appetite."

He gives me a solemn nod. "I'm gonna eat four *pannenkoeken.* No, *twenty*-four."

I smile. Sem, my sweet, fragile, *skinny* Sem. I'll be lucky if he eats just one.

I fish around my pocket for the bike key, then help them into the bike. On the other side of the pond, the wind is picking up, and dark, bloated clouds are gathering just above the tree line. Those are rain clouds rolling in. If I hurry, we can beat them home.

"Let's go. I'm starving, too."

Once everyone is settled and Sem buckled in, I pedal for the exit on the north end of the park, a little longer in terms of kilometers but an easier route to navigate at this time of day—rush hour. The path spits me out onto the busy Van Baerlestraat, and I merge into the thick stream of bikes and follow the horde south.

I'm passing a couple of slow-moving tourists when something catches my eye across the street. I see the elegant set of a man's shoulders as he comes out the door of the Conservatorium Hotel, the dark smudge of his glasses and the swing of his arms as he jogs down the steps. As the crow flies, no more than thirty feet away.

Not eighty kilometers away at a conference in Antwerp. Thomas is here, at a hotel in Amsterdam, wearing the sweater I gave him for Christmas, his favorite camel coat, and a smile I haven't seen in ages.

My skin goes hot, my body practically sizzling in the frigid wind as I pedal by in the sea of bikes, and I can't stop staring. Leaning back in my seat so I don't lose him in the crowd, craning my neck to scan the rest of the faces on the sidewalk. Is he *with* someone?

"*Kijk uit*!" someone yells—watch out!

I slam the brakes just in time, screeching to a stop behind a cluster of bikes waiting at the light. Sem's body strains against the belt, but Ollie tumbles and rolls, yelping as his body hits the front of the carrier. He scrambles upright and shakes it off with what looks suspiciously like a side-eye.

I lean forward to run a shaking hand over Sem's head. "You okay?"

As usual, he bats my hand away.

By the time I turn back, Thomas is gone, almost like he was a mirage.

Except I saw him. I *saw* him. At a hotel in Amsterdam when he's supposed to be in Antwerp.

All those late-night "meetings" and "business dinners," all the mysterious phone calls in his study, the door tightly closed. All those times he's come to bed late and left early, so he doesn't have to make excuses for why he hasn't touched me in ages, when I ask him what's wrong and he can't quite look me in the eye when he assures me that it's nothing.

And the Conservatorium is not just any hotel. It's one of the busiest in this part of town, located on one of the busiest corners. Where hundreds of possible witnesses could be biking or driving or tramming by at any given moment. What if someone besides me saw him? What if *Sem* had seen?

The light flips to green and the mass of bikes take off. I lean into the wind and pedal like a fiend, a new sense of urgency beating in my chest. All this time, I thought *my* betrayal would be the end of me and Thomas. I thought it would be *my* sins that unraveled the bonds between us, not his. It never occurred to me that I should be watching out for his. But I was wrong.

My eyes are open now.

November 17th, 10:39 p.m.

I STEP INTO Xander's foyer, a muted expanse of sand-colored marble that smells of lemons and something darker, something spicier. Patchouli and cloves, maybe. The speakers above my head flip on, too, Amy Winehouse crooning about love being a losing game. Appropriate, considering tonight is my fifth anniversary and I'm here, staring down the hallway of Xander's penthouse at almost eleven at night, while Thomas is at work.

"Swanky," I say, peeling off my coat.

Xander takes it from me and drapes it over a corner chair. "Come. I'll give you a tour."

He leads me from room to fabulous room, and I nod and hum as he points out all the amenities. Oversized Italian furniture sitting atop shaggy wool carpets. Solar shades that filter light and offer privacy without obscuring the spectacular views. Floor cooling—

a real luxury here in Holland—for those three weeks in the summer when the sun heats up his penthouse like one of the many greenhouses jutting up from Dutch fields. Pads on the wall of every room that control every tiny thing, from the electronics to the lighting to the music and temperature, all of which can also be controlled from his phone. The blackout shades in his bedroom that work on the same timer as a sleek contraption high upon a wall, a white noise machine and air conditioner in one.

"I sleep like a baby with that thing," he says. "From midnight until 8:00 a.m. on the dot. I don't hear or see a thing."

"Must be nice. Last night I was up four times checking on Sem. Bronchitis."

I leave off the *again*, or the fact that Sem's viruses are often coupled with a scary fever that spikes in the middle of the night. Xander is not the fatherly type, though he once told me it's not the physical well-being of a potential child he's so worried about, but the mental. He doesn't want to mess up his kid like his own father did with him.

"Wait'll you see the master bath," he says, motioning for me to follow.

My heels tangle in the terry loops of his bath mat as he points out the Italian marble, the porcelain tub big enough for two, the floating double vanities, the tower of towel warmers, and the giant glass-enclosed shower. It feels intimate to be standing here, in the place where a naked Xander showers and shaves, alone with him this late at night. It feels illicit.

"Do you do this with all your female guests?" I say, interrupting him mid sales spiel on the health benefits of a steam shower.

"Do what?"

"Brag. Tick off your home's luxuries like you're trying to sell them the place. Girls don't like that, you know."

"Some girls do."

"Yeah, well, stay away from those ones. They're here for all the wrong reasons."

He gives me a smile that tells me that as far as he's concerned, they're here for all the *right* reasons.

I laugh and slap him on the chest. "Come on, fuckboy. Let's get this over with. I want to get home before Thomas does."

RAYNA

I've just turned up my street when a text hits my new phone, a message from the detective asking how I'm doing and if I've found any more trackers. When two days ago I told him I'd left the first one on the tram, he made me promise to bring any others I might find straight to the police station. He says it's the only way to trace them to the owner.

As much as I appreciate the detective's check-in, I don't love the thought of holding on to the next tracker long enough for my stalker to grab me on the way to the police station. The idea terrifies me, even more so when I think how close that asshole had to get in order to drop a tracker in my bag.

I dodge shoppers as I pound out a reply. All quiet for now. Will keep you posted.

I slip the phone in my pocket, adding a new item to my to-do list: research trackers so that next time—and it seems like Detective Boomsma assumes there will be a next time—I know how to disarm the little fucker.

I'm almost home when I pause in front of the Chanel store, eyeing a thick cluster of bodies across the street. At least a dozen of them, parked between Ferragamo and the Mont Blanc store, and not a single shopping bag among them. Weird, since this is the P.C. Hooftstraat, the poshest of Amsterdam's shopping streets, where stores like to line people up on the street while they wait for entry.

But these people aren't lingering behind a red velvet rope. They're not standing by a storefront but next to a plain brown door.

My door.

Damn reporters. I duck behind a group of tourists before they see me. With that nipple picture still making the rounds on social media and the threads doxing me by name, I suppose it was only a matter of time before they found me.

Dutch reporters, I can tell by their height and their clothing. Dark, slim-cut denim and coats made for Holland's sea climate, thick and waterproof. Sturdy shoes for walking on ancient cobblestones. Windswept hair and foreheads that have never seen a spot of Botox.

One of them, an older blonde with glasses and cheeks ruddy from the cold, peels off from the group. She marches to the brown door and leans in to read the names by the bells. Five floors, five apartments, five names written in neat block letters. She turns back to the group and shakes her head.

As one, the group tips their heads back and look up the face of the building—and I think back to a picture further down on my Instagram, a grinning me with my arms spread wide, standing before the same brick facade, the same brown door. I follow their gazes to the very top, to the window just under a hoisting hook strong enough to haul up a piano. Behind that window is a drafty, cramped living room, with beige walls and creaky floors and a narrow hallway that leads to the back of the building and my tiny beige room.

Not that any of them would know from the bell that I live here. I rent my room from Ingrid. It's her name next to the buttons.

Down here on the ground, the crowd is regrouping. I'm too far away to hear what they're saying, and I may not understand Dutch, but I understand facial expressions and body language.

They're discussing their next moves, spitballing ideas, negotiating who does what.

Shit. Now what? Do I keep walking? Find a café quiet enough to make my phone calls and wait these people out? Or do I put my head down and muscle my way to the door? By the looks of things, these people are not leaving anytime soon.

And then it happens. The decision is made for me. The blonde turns my way. Our eyes meet across the sea of shoppers and a row of parked bikes. Hers widen in surprise.

"Rayna!" she shouts.

One by one, their heads turn. People start peeling away from the crowd, slowly at first, skirting around each other and oncoming traffic in the street, falling over each other in a race to get to me. They barrel across the street, a red rover line of bodies racing my way, whipping iPhones from pockets and aiming them at my face. Peppering me with questions in English.

What was your relationship with Xander van der Vos? Were you his girlfriend?

Where's the necklace, Rayna? Did you take it?

Did Xander mention the Cullinans to you? Did he tell you where they are?

What about all the other missing diamonds? How many were in his safe?

Where are the diamonds, Rayna?

The shoppers hear *diamonds*, and they perk, but I'm more focused on Detective Boomsma's words, ringing in my head: *If someone wants that necklace as badly as the killer did, where do you think they'll look first?*

Xander had a safe, it was cleaned out, and now these reporters have connected me to the missing diamonds.

I duck my head, letting my hair fall across my face. "Excuse me, please. Let me through."

My politeness gets me exactly nowhere. The reporters release another onslaught of questions, a claustrophobic mob of bodies that are so much bigger than mine. Holland is the land of giants, and these journalists are too tall, and there are far too many of them for me to just barrel through. I stare at their chests, their jostling elbows and thrusted microphones, their mouths as they bite off a string of razor-edged questions.

What do you hear from police, Rayna?

Do you think they'll make an arrest soon?

Are you a diamond thief? A murderer?

What do you say to the people on X calling you the Tinder Terminator?

If the moniker hadn't come on the tail of words like *thief* and *murderer*, I might have laughed. Tinder Terminator. Give me a break. I hold up a hand and bark, "No comment."

I have no idea if that's even a thing here in Holland, and I know from experience that even if it is, there are no words magical enough to shut down a jacked-up reporter on a deadline.

"Seriously, guys, back up. I—I can't breathe."

They don't back up. If anything, the huddle around me tightens.

I'm filling my lungs for a scream when suddenly, the sidewalk tilts. I squeal and lurch to the right, falling through a gap in the crowd.

Or no—not a gap. An empty spot that someone has elbowed their way into making, the same someone who now has a hold of my arm, long fingers clamped down on my wrist like a vise.

"Hey, let go!" I shout, right as the fist gives a hard yank.

I'm heaved straight at one of the journalists, at close to seven feet a mountain of a man. He pivots right before I crash into his chest, allowing a sliver of space just big enough for me to squeeze through. My bag gets caught on something, a belt buckle, a fist, before it releases with a thud against my hip.

And then, suddenly, air. Freedom.

Ingrid, my savior in a teddy bear coat and red lipstick.

She barks something in vicious Dutch at the reporters, not vicious enough to make them back up, but at least they stop swarming long enough for her to hustle me across the street. A bike whizzes by, barely missing us as the biker leans on the bell. As soon as it's gone, we break into a jog.

At the door, Ingrid digs through her keys for the right one, and I bounce on my toes. I can hear them behind us, clunky Dutch shoes coming across the pavement. I lean in and whisper, "You should hurry."

Ingrid nods because she hears them, too. "I know."

"They're almost here."

"I *know.*" I'm bracing for another ambush when she shoves in the key, gives the doorknob a twist, and the two of us tumble inside. "*Flikker op,*" she shouts, and I laugh because I know that one—the Dutch version of *fuck off.* She slams the door in their faces.

I'm about to thank her for a second time when another question worms its way through the wood, smacking me on the back of my skull, a direct hit.

Rayna, how do you respond to police naming you the lead suspect?

WILLOW

The Nine Streets are three square blocks lined with boutiques and cafés smack in the city center. The sidewalks are packed despite the cold, with people jamming the doorways and in snaking lines outside of specialty food shops offering up everything from bubble tea to hand-dipped *stroopwafels* to overpriced french fries smothered with Parmesan.

I'm seated away from the fray, wedged between a giant potted Buxus and a chalkboard sign on a sidewalk terrace, freezing my ass off and trying not to think about how, yet again, I'm trailing another human around town.

Not Rayna this time but Thomas, who's been in the store across the street for—I check my phone—going on twelve minutes now. Rive Gauche, according to the sign painted on the window, which sells a mix of heavily curated clothing and trendy home decor, candles and vases and lacquered trays topped with vintage carafes and hung with cheap jewelry. Gold-plated chains, bracelets made with colorful beads, fake pearls of every shape and color. The best thing I can say about it is at least it's not lingerie.

Not that Thomas would ever be so cliché, but I also never thought he'd be the type to have an affair. I've thought about it a lot since seeing him outside that hotel, and really, I can't come up with another explanation. Especially since he turned off location sharing for the twenty-four hours he was supposedly in Antwerp, and when yesterday I texted to ask how things were going at the conference, he said that everyone loved his speech. And then suddenly this morning, his dot reappeared, which is why I'm sitting here now.

Also suspicious is the way he's dressed, in a sweater and faded jeans he must have dragged from the very back of his closet, under a peacoat I thought he threw away ages ago. Definitely not what he had on when he left the house this morning. A disguise, then, a ploy to make him look very much not like himself.

Meanwhile, I'm dressed like everyone else in this part of town, in generic jeans and a dark puffy coat, a new pair of sunglasses covering my face. They're much like the kind of plastic things I used to own, purchased at a discount store between Sem's school and here for a whole five euros. The glasses sit crooked on my nose, and it feels silly to be wearing shades on a day when the sun is muted at best, but I need a disguise and Gucci would never make a pair this tacky.

A woman's voice floats from across the street. "Willow? I thought that was you."

Shit. Not that good of a disguise after all, and what are the chances? Running into a neighbor all the way here, a good dozen tram stops into the thickest part of the city. Especially this neighbor, the neighbor Thomas refers to as *de prater*—the talker—because neither of us can ever remember her name. Vittoria? Francesca? Giada? The only thing I know for sure it that it's very Italian, and this is hitting too close to home.

I look up with a smile, my voice going unnaturally bright. "Hi! What are you doing all the way over here?"

"Oh, just a bit of shopping. It's Matteo's birthday next week, and he's *so* impossible to shop for. I bought him a pair of shoes, which more likely than not he'll take back." She holds up a bag from a department store nearby, hooked over a manicured finger. "You?"

Her gaze dips to the empty chair next to me, and I scramble for an excuse that won't prompt her to sink onto it.

"I'm shopping, too, but for a new speech therapist for Semmy since his is retiring. I've got a meeting in twenty minutes with someone who comes highly recommended, but she's all the way over in the Red Light, and I'm really not looking to make that trek every week. I'd prefer to stay closer to home."

Immediately, I regret involving my son in the lie. Sem's speech pathologist is fantastic, and nowhere near retirement age. What if this woman runs into Thomas or Martina? She'll definitely bring it up, and I'll have to come up with a cover. I should have just told her I was shopping, too, and left it at that.

De prater launches a long-winded comparison of the shopping in Amsterdam versus her beloved Milan, living up to her nickname. I smile and nod and pretend to listen, but I'm distracted by sudden movement across the street. A flock of noisy females bursts out the door of Rive Gauche, filing down the sidewalk with a flurry of excited chatter, and thanks to nosy neighbor here, I don't get a good look at any of them.

At least it's not Thomas who makes his escape. I spot him through the front window, lingering behind a pretty sales associate reaching into the display. She untangles a jumble of necklaces on a padded bust, then pulls out a single chain, long and delicate and shiny. She holds it up for him to see, and he cradles the charm in his palm, leaning in to inspect it. He says something to the woman and she laughs. He hands the necklace back, and they disappear deeper into the store.

". . . is really getting hit hard lately."

There's an awkward silence as Bianca—her name comes to me in a flash—waits for me to jump in on whatever she just said. She raises her brows, and her perfectly painted lips spread into an awkward smile.

"I'm sorry," I say, shaking my head. "I think I missed the first part."

"I said, the news I read this morning said the police are no closer to finding the killer than they were days ago, and now they're saying more diamonds are missing. Millions of dollars' worth. Poor Thomas, he's really getting hit hard lately, isn't he?"

My gaze flits to the glass door across the street. If he comes out now, my entire cover will be blown.

And yet I can't help but ask, "Hit hard how?"

"The news made it sound like this dead employee was involved in last summer's theft. Those big stones that were taken from the vault, I mean. I can't remember what they were called."

"The Cullinans."

"That's right, the Cullinans. Is that why that man is dead, because the killer wanted them?"

I think about how to answer this, because Thomas was right. Even if he can manage to spin another believable story, it's already too late for people like *de prater.* She's already connected the theft of the Cullinans to Xander and the missing diamonds. She already thinks they're the same stones, which . . . could it be possible? Thomas fired Xander. He accused him of theft. It's not inconceivable to think Xander stole more than just some extra stones tossed in the Asian shipments. I happen to know he wasn't exactly the most trustworthy person.

Out of the corner of my eye, I spot movement behind the glass. I tap my phone to check the time. "Oh, shoot. Lovely running into you, but I've got to run. I'm about to be late for my appointment."

"Want to grab lunch sometime soon? I could do next week."

"Sure. Next week works." I pull a ten from my bag and wedge it under my empty coffee cup, pushing to a stand.

"I'll call you," Bianca says, and with a quick hug goodbye, continues on down the street.

As soon as she's gone, I fall back onto my chair, my gaze glued to the door. I don't care about the Cullinans or any other missing diamonds. I give zero shits about whatever story Thomas has spun to differentiate between the two. I only care about what my husband is doing in a store like Rive Gauche. I'll sit here all day if I have to. I have absolutely nothing better to do.

It's ironic, really. The kind of woman who stays in a €1000 room at the Conservatorium Hotel would expect more from a Prins than a cheap trinket of plated gold, and Thomas would give it to her, I know this for a fact. I'd known him for all of five minutes before he started tossing diamonds my way. Solitaire studs, a chain set with dozens of bezel-set stones, blingy bracelets and dangly earrings and diamond-encrusted pendants big as a silver dollar. Rive Gauche is no House of Prins, for crap's sake. Whoever this woman is, I hope that necklace turns her skin green.

A few minutes later, he steps out the door, a tiny bag clutched in a fist. I hold my breath as he pauses on the sidewalk, turning left, then right, then left again. This is a man who grew up in this city, who except for the time he spent in boarding schools and business schools and in California getting his gemology degree, has lived here all his life. He's roamed these streets since he was a child and *still* he gets turned around. Normally, this would make me laugh, but not today. Today I shrink behind the Buxus bush and pray he doesn't spot me sitting here, watching him.

He settles on a direction and takes off down the sidewalk, and I wait until he's turned the corner onto the Prinsengracht before I push to a stand. Thomas is headed in the direction of the Westermarkt; I'm guessing either to the tram stops or the taxi stand. I hurry down the sidewalk, determined not to lose him.

Just past the Pulitzer Hotel, he stops dead. He whirls around and I freeze, but he's not looking at me, standing half a football field away. He's checking for traffic on the road. He waits to let a car pass then jogs across the street to a row of parked bikes at the water's edge, stopping at one that looks like it's been there awhile.

I frown, pressing my body to the building.

He hangs the bag on a handlebar of an old, rusty Gazelle, then keeps moving up the street, and now I'm more confused than ever. What kind of woman stays at the Conservatorium but rides an old, rusty Gazelle? I look back up the street, watching that ugly peacoat disappear into the crowd, a swarm of pedestrians and tourists heading to the Anne Frank House further up the street.

As soon as he's out of sight, I jog across the street and pluck the bag from the bike.

It's the necklace I watched him pick out through the glass, an upside-down heart decorated with tiny white stones dangling from a paperclip chain. Stones that are paste, and not even good paste. This is the type of necklace you'd give to a child—though the twins wouldn't be caught dead in this cheap trinket. According to the receipt, Thomas paid a whopping €28.

I turn and stare up the street, the necklace still tangled around my fingers, half expecting to see . . . what? The owner of this bike? Why leave the necklace, even a cheap one, hanging on a bike for anyone to swipe? None of this makes any sense.

An icy wind sweeps up the canal, tingling the tips of my ears and fingers. Whatever the answers are, I'm not going to find them here, freezing my ass off on the side of the street. It's a mystery to solve later, at home, when Sem is at school or playing outside, when Thomas is at work and Martina at the market, shopping for ingredients for dinner.

Because this necklace can't be the only clue. There's got to be more hiding in his desk, maybe, or tucked somewhere deep in a pocket. Maybe it's a mistake, but I can't bear staring down the evidence of my husband's betrayal for another second. I toss it all—the box, the bag, the cheap costume necklace, and those ridiculous sunglasses—into the canal.

All I need is a few moments in the house alone.

RAYNA

I stare at Ingrid, half expecting her to open the plain brown door and shove me back outside. The journalists are still out there, shouting their awful questions through the wood, though there are fewer of them and a lot less venom in their voices now that I'm gone. Their last little bombshell rings in my ears, snuffing out all the street noise.

Rayna, how do you respond to police naming you the lead suspect?

"You're the lead suspect?" Ingrid says, her pretty face crumpled into a frown. Light filters through the frosted glass window at the top of the door, glowing like highlighter along the tops of her cheekbones.

I shrug. Shake my head. "No idea. That's the first I've heard of it."

Ingrid waves a dismissive hand, swiping a pile of mail from the stairs and flipping through it. "Don't believe it, then. If you were the lead suspect, you would have heard it from the police, not a bunch of pesky journalists."

I blow out a sigh of relief, though the worry isn't gone, just . . . delayed somehow. Or maybe insignificant compared to those reporters out there. They pointed a camera at my head. They put a target on my building, my front door, my back. All those people tearing up the comment threads on Reddit and X and wherever else about me and the missing diamonds—they now know where I live.

"Thanks for saving me out there. Dutch reporters are hard-core."

"Eh, they're just doing their jobs. Here—this one's for you." She shoves an envelope at my chest and grins. "I was thinking of staying in tonight anyway. How do we feel about sushi and Netflix?"

A wave of gratitude washes over me. After the ambush on the stoop, the last thing I'd want to do is spend the evening alone. "We love them."

The two of us start the long, steep climb up the stairs, Ingrid chattering away about her day. She tells me about the new technique she's learning from the antique restorer she works for, how to make a bolus of animal glue and soft clay and shape it with her fingers to recreate the ornaments on the wood. I have no idea what a bolus is or if that's even an English word, but I feign interest whenever she pauses for my response, which is often.

I interrupt her midstream: "Ingrid, what's a Cullinan?" Xander's comment—*like a Cullinan, all sparkle and fire*—was the first time I heard the term, and now from those reporters down on the street.

"Xander didn't tell you?" She pauses just long enough for me to shake my head—at least I don't *think* he told me. Or maybe I was already too far gone. "Ten of the most spectacular natural diamonds that have ever been found. Flawless, colorless, irreplaceable. They're also gone. Disappeared from the House of Prins vault early last year."

"The reporters out there asked me if I knew where they were. Why would they think that?"

"Because they know you were in bed with Xander, literally. He worked for the House when the Cullinans disappeared, and the police can't figure out how the thief got in the vault or how they got the diamonds out, so it's not all that much of a leap to think it might have been an inside job. And since Xander was Xander and he worked there at the time . . ."

She doesn't finish, but she also doesn't have to. A giant, invisible ellipsis that I can fill in myself. Since he worked there, since he was known in the diamond world as a villain, since he seemed to be coveted by plenty of people but not all that well liked. All those things make him an easy and logical scapegoat, especially now that he's not here to defend himself.

"Do you really think—" I stop short at the top of the last staircase, the envelope crinkling in my fist. My skin prickles in alarm.

"Do I think what?" Ingrid keeps clunking up the stairs.

I shush her, and she stops, too.

"What? Why are we stopping?"

I fist a railing spoke with one hand, pointing with my other at the door. Our door. Light filters through the bottom, lighting up dust bunnies on the hallway floor, a thin slice of scuffed buttercream wall.

The door is cracked open by a good two inches.

Ingrid lurches forward, taking the last steps in one giant leap for the door.

"*Wait.* What if he's still in there?"

It's too late. Ingrid has already disappeared inside the apartment.

I step onto the top landing, unsure of my next move. If the intruder is still inside, if we've surprised him, then he would have heard us by now. We weren't the least bit subtle as we clomped up the stairs, and Ingrid is even louder now, by the sounds of things, tossing her room. I picture someone else in there, lurking behind a door or under a bed as Ingrid lets out a shriek loud enough to shake the walls.

I exchange the envelope for my phone, tucked in the inside pocket of my bag, and tap the number for the detective's cell.

"Arie Boomsma."

"Detective Boomsma, it's Rayna Dumont."

"I know," he says dryly. "Your name came up on my screen."

"There's been a break-in at my apartment. My roommate and I just got home to an open door."

Had I locked it when I left? This building is literally ancient, and it hasn't been renovated since sometime in the last century. The doorknobs are old-school, the kind you have to secure with a key from the outside. It's a system that makes it impossible to lock yourself in the house, and why I never forget my keys. But did I actually lock the door, or did I just pull it closed?

"Is anything missing?"

There's a loud thump from inside the apartment, followed by a stream of the most colorful Dutch cuss words. "*Kut. Godverdomme. Fuck.*" The last one is apparently universal.

I nod into the phone. "Sounds like it, yeah."

"I'm nearby. Wait outside."

The line goes dead before I can tell him it's too late. Ingrid is already inside.

I pocket my phone and peek into the apartment. The hallway is empty and still, and so is what I can see of the living room, a flat-screen hanging above a console shoved against the wall, a fiddle leaf fig in a pot in the corner, its leaves brown edged and dusty.

"Everything okay in here?"

Ingrid's voice comes from the opposite direction, her bedroom down a tiny hallway. "No. It's gone. It's all gone!"

"What's gone?"

"*Kuuuuuuuut.*"

I creep into the hallway and hang my head around her open door, taking in the mess. Her mattress, hanging off the bed. The chest of drawers, open and emptied out. The clothes and the bedding and her teddy bear coat, now lying inside-out where she dumped it on the floor. She steps to the wardrobe and heaves the double doors wide, shoving the hangers and clothing aside.

"Did you make this mess, or did he?"

"I did." She reaches an arm into the back right corner of the wardrobe, behind a jumble of fabric and a messy pile of shoes, grubby sneakers, and floppy boots, what looks like the entire collection of Havaiana sandals, well-worn and in need of a bath. When she doesn't find what she's looking for, she falls backward onto the floor, tilting her head back to shout at the ceiling, "*Neeeeeeeee.*"

A long, defeated *no.*

"What did they take?"

She drops her head in her hands, her hair falling across her face. "Cash."

I wince. "How much?"

"Lots." She looks up from between her fingers, and her eyes are wet. She's trying very hard not to cry. "*So* much."

"How much?" I ask again, guilt pushing up in a sour surge. I think of the door I may or may not have locked, the tracker I shoved under the seat on the tram, the detective's warning that whoever might be looking for the diamonds would be coming to me first. Is that what this is? Did I leave the door open for a thief and a killer? Is this *my* fault?

She shoves her fingers into her hair and makes two tight fists, yanking big chunks at the temples. "All of it. *Verdomme.*" *Dammit.* She says more, a stream of fiery, feverish Dutch.

"Shit, Ingrid. I'm . . . I'm so, so sorry. Is it . . . Are you insured?"

Her head whips up, her eyes squinting. "It's *cash.* Of course I'm not insured." She makes a sound deep in her throat and pushes herself off the floor.

I watch her shove everything back in the wardrobe, telling myself this is just her anger talking. And I don't blame her for being pissed. Someone was here, in her things, taking her cash, all of it. I'd be furious and heartbroken, too.

I think of the twenty-euro bill I left on my nightstand, the jar of coins on my dresser. Neither of them are worth crying over, but my laptop is. My passport, too. A fully loaded Kindle my sister shoved in my carry-on as I was leaving for the airport. I'm not insured for any of those things, either.

I look over my shoulder, peering down the hallway toward my bedroom, wondering if there's someone in there with a knife or a zip tie, just waiting for me to get close enough to ambush me. Late afternoon sunlight filters through the window high on the slanted wall, casting a yellow glow on the hallway floor. Did I leave that door open, too? Honestly, I can't remember.

"What if they're still here?" I whisper, turning back to Ingrid. "Detective Boomsma said to wait outside."

"You have a detective on speed dial?" She uses her normal voice, at normal volume, and I cringe, casting another panicked glance down the hallway—still empty. "Jesus, Rayna. I can't believe this."

"He said he was nearby." I say it loudly, too, just in case someone's down there, listening.

A buzzer rips the air just then, startling me hard enough that I catch air. I step to the intercom system, hitting the button to speak to whoever's downstairs. "Hello?"

"I thought I told you to wait outside." The detective, thank God. If the intruder is still here, he's about to wish he wasn't.

I press the button to let him in. A minute later, the place is crawling with cops.

Two of them go room to room, hands draped loosely over their guns but trigger fingers poised and ready, while the others wait outside on the landing, nodding at whatever Detective Boomsma is saying—orders, by the sound of things. He points to the front door, to the stairwell behind them, to the hallway and beyond, to Ingrid and me watching from her bedroom doorway.

"I thought I told you to wait outside," he repeats, not willing to let it go.

"We were already here," I say, hooking a thumb at Ingrid. "She was already in her room. They took her cash."

"How much?"

"I'm not sure," she says, and either she's in shock or intimidated by an apartment full of uniformed cops. She eyes them as they clomp inside, dropping their big bags of supplies. Her voice is a lot less adamant than it was just a minute ago, with me. She says something to him in Dutch, and he nods.

The detective turns back to me. "What else did they take?"

"I don't know. I haven't checked the other rooms yet."

By now, the cops have declared the apartment empty of anyone but us, and I make a beeline to my room, my eyes darting left and right as if half expecting someone to leap out of an open doorway.

At my bedroom, I pause just inside the door, cringing at the unmade bed, the strip of black lace peeking out from a pile of dirty laundry in the corner, the bra hanging from a doorknob on the chest of drawers. My bedroom feels too hot, too beige, far too small for two people, especially someone as large as Detective Boomsma. He steps inside and gives me an expectant look.

I open the top drawer on the dresser and slide the bra in, feeling under a stack of folded T-shirts. "My passport is still here, and so is my Kindle." I point to it, charging on the nightstand, then fish my laptop from where it's tangled in the duvet. "Everything is here, except . . ." I drop the laptop to the bed like it's sizzling.

From the other side of the apartment, Ingrid says something in emphatic Dutch.

"My laptop was open when I left. I was on FaceTime with my sister. I put on my coat and shoes while we talked. I remember waving to her from the doorway, and then she's the one who hung up, not me. I didn't close the laptop when we were done. I just . . . left."

"So you're saying whoever was here shut your laptop and moved it to under the duvet."

I nod. "That's exactly what I'm saying."

The detective leans his head into the hallway, calling out something in Dutch. "Don't touch anything, not until we dust the room for prints. What else?"

I point to the drawer containing my passport, still sitting open. "See that stack of T-shirts? It's messier than it was when I left, and my Kindle was wedged in the drawer on my nightstand, not on top with that pile of books. Someone was definitely here. They went through my stuff."

"They went through it, but they didn't take anything."

I look around the room, doing a quick inventory of my meager belongings, but it doesn't take me long. There's not much here to steal, and the MacBook is by far the most valuable thing that I own, a holdover from when I was married. For some reason they left it, along with the TV on the living room wall. Along with the crumpled twenty on the nightstand.

"Why would they steal Ingrid's cash but not mine?"

The detective shakes his head, and he's nice enough not to mention that a twenty is hardly worth taking. "What about any other valuables? Medicine, electronics, jewelry?"

"I already told you. The last time I saw the necklace was when Xander tossed it in the drawer."

"I meant *other* jewelry."

A fresh surge of something unpleasant rises in my chest, though a wiser part of me knows the detective can't possibly realize the landmine he's stepped on. That all those pieces I used to place so much importance on—the six-carat engagement ring, the tennis bracelet, and the Cartier Love bangles, the gold chains and diamond-encrusted pendants—are decorating somebody else's body now. That even *thinking* that enrages me—not because I want them back, but because of who I lost them to.

"No, there's nothing else. Everything I own is here." Downstairs on the street, a horn honks, and I think of the reporters. "Did you ask the reporters? They must have seen something."

"They didn't. Not anyone out of the ordinary, at least. We'll talk to the neighbors, though. Maybe they let somebody in, a delivery person or a cleaner."

"That's it. You'll talk to the reporters and neighbors. What about protection? What about someone guarding my door?"

"We don't have the funds or the manpower, unfortunately, but the reporters are doing a decent job of watching your door. All those stores out there—they have security guards and multiple cameras. I'll talk to them, too, and arrange some extra patrols of your street. Speaking of cameras, I don't suppose you have any of your own?"

I give him a look. "For what, my thrift-store clothing and IKEA furniture? Other than Ingrid's cash, there's nothing else. He couldn't even be bothered with my laptop. There's nothing here worth stealing."

"Maybe because the thief was looking for something else."

I don't have to think about it, not even for a split second. "Like diamonds."

The detective puffs a breath through his nose, sharp and loud. "Like diamonds."

WILLOW

That same night, Thomas and I are seated at a table at Willem's business club on Dam Square when his finger taps my knee, a silent signal to stop my bobbing leg from rattling the table and his nerves. The board room is far too big for just us four—Fleur and a bored-looking Roland sit in the chairs across from us—but at least the decor snuffs out the noise from the bustling Dam, the navy silks and wood paneling sucking up most of the street sounds. I shove both heels into the thick carpet and clamp my teeth together to hold back a scream.

How do people do this? Smile and kiss their husband when he returns from the business trip that wasn't? Live with someone who's lying about where he is, who he's with, acting like there's not another woman banging around his brain but who's sneaky enough to not leave any clues?

Because I spent the entire afternoon searching the house. I turned the place upside down, and there's nothing there. No more ugly necklaces tucked away in a drawer, no notes or crumpled receipts in his pockets from stores or romantic restaurants, nothing at all to indicate Thomas has been unfaithful or even dishonest.

I glance at him now, his handsome profile as he downloads the newspaper on his phone, his body as relaxed as if he's lounging on the couch at home. Whatever Thomas's secrets are, he's obviously skilled at hiding them.

Roland pushes back his chair, patting his jacket pockets for his pack of cigarettes and a lighter, and Fleur shoots him a look that says *don't you dare.*

"What? I'll step outside."

She shakes her head. "You can't miss Papa. He'll be here any second."

Will he, though? I check the time on my cell, 7:49, which means we've been sitting here for a good twenty minutes. It's just like Willem to do this, too: summon us here with a *come immediately* text smack in the middle of dinner, then once we arrive, making us wait.

I stare out the wall of windows at the Royal Palace, lit up and looming over the square, and I wish I was one of those tourists outside, tipping their heads up at the imposing architecture and wondering what kind of shiny, happy people are sitting inside. I look at Fleur and Roland studiously ignoring each other, at Thomas pretending to be engrossed in the news. They're certainly shiny, but are they happy? Am I?

"A bunch of dusty old rocks." Xander's voice fills my head. We were at some stuffy diamond function, crowded like sardines in a hotel ballroom filled with old-money types, when he shout-whispered the comment in my ear.

He wasn't referring to the diamonds.

The door swings open and in breezes Willem, Anna close on his heels. They're dressed for the club in custom silks and designer tweeds, both of them holding fresh drinks because this is cocktail hour and heaven forbid their glasses run dry.

Willem catches Anna's eye, and she doubles back and shuts the door. The noise from the club below and the square outside dampens to a low murmur, like a faint and distant humming of bees.

"I spoke with Arthur tonight," he says as soon as we're alone.

"A security company in Munich specializing in low-light video surveillance systems received an order last spring for a system that's essentially a carbon copy of the one in the vault."

At that, Thomas tosses his cell to the table and sits up straighter in his chair, and so does everybody else. The vault means we're talking about the Cullinans. Willem has our full attention now.

He stretches the moment with a slow sip of his drink, ice chinking in the crystal glass. Without warning, Patrick says to SpongeBob in my head, *pinky up!*

Willem puts down his glass and leans with both hands on the table, polished to a shine so glossy there are two of him as he stares us down from the head. "The buyer was a front, a fake name attached to a shell corporation, with a PO box address here in Amsterdam. Guess who owns that PO box."

"Xander," Thomas says, and it's the first name I thought of, too. Across from us, Fleur looks like she agrees. Roland just looks bored.

But Willem shakes his head. "No, it was Frederik Albers. Police found the surveillance system invoice when they searched his house."

Frederik Albers, the trader Thomas fired after a security guard caught him smuggling in a thumb drive—an unforgivable offense in a company where computers are bolted to the desks. Where no one is permitted to work from home after hours, where there's a fully stocked cafeteria so that no Prins employee has to worry about a lunch bag. They don't want employees to bring anything in, mostly so they can forbid them from taking anything out. The drive was empty, but it was hidden in a secret compartment in his water bottle. Thomas fired him on the spot.

Now his face brightens in a way I haven't seen since the Cullinans disappeared on his watch. "This is excellent news. What did Frederik say? I assume police also questioned him."

Fleur snorts. "From a jail cell, I hope."

"They'll have to find him first." Willem sinks into the chair at the head of the table, folding his hands on the table. "Apparently, Frederik has gone underground."

Thomas frowns. "Since when?"

"Since around the time Xander was killed."

The board room falls into silence, hot and meaningful. Police have evidence connecting Frederik to the Cullinan theft, but no Frederik. He's been in hiding since Xander was killed. A diamond trader and a gemologist with a sneaky supply of lab-growns. It wouldn't take a genius to figure out the two were connected by more than just their employment history.

"They were working together," Fleur says, getting there quicker than her brother. "If Frederik is spooked enough by Xander's murder to go into hiding, then that means they were partners somehow. Moving lab-growns, I bet."

Willem gives her a good-girl nod. "It seems likely, yes. But Arthur also told me something else. A few weeks ago, a woman in Blaricum took a ten-carat solitaire ring her husband gave her for their anniversary in for an appraisal. Apparently, their insurance company required a second assessment for any piece valued at over a million euros. Her husband paid one point four."

Thomas leans onto an elbow. "I remember that stone. Internally flawless, D color. One of the finest stones I've seen in a while."

"Do you remember who sourced it?"

Thomas frowns, shakes his head. "I only ever spoke to the jeweler."

"The jeweler who sourced the stone via a trader."

Willem doesn't say who, but we all know: Frederik. Frederik was the trader.

"The jeweler did everything right. He tested the stone, had it independently certified, put it through all the correct verification processes. But somewhere between the purchasing of the diamond and getting the ring on the customer's finger, the stones got switched.

The one in the ring the customer received was lab grown, but to the specifics of the original mined stone. Same size, same cut and color, same GIA certification number engraved on the girdle. An identical twin."

He gives us a moment to process the news. A lab-grown diamond. An exact match to a certified Prins stone including the certification number, a phony copy grown with the intention of fooling the customer and making off with the original diamond. If the insurance company hadn't insisted on the second appraisal, no one would have ever known.

I have to admit, it's a pretty brilliant scheme. By the time a stone lands on the consumer's finger, it's been touched by dozens of people. The traders, the polishers, the jewelers and who knows how many of their employees. Try proving which one of them made this switch.

And more to the point, this has Xander written all over it.

Thomas blinks. "So where's the original stone?"

Willem lifts his hands in a silent shrug, but I'm pretty sure he's thinking the same thing I am: lining the pockets of Xander's killer. Millions of euros of diamonds missing, and this ten-carat flawless Prins diamond is one of them.

And it won't be the only one. There would have been a bunch more just like it, mined stones switched out for a lab-grown copy while the customer remains clueless, the stolen stones stuffed in Xander's safe.

My phone buzzes with an incoming text, and I dig it out of my bag, a familiar worry gathering in my chest. This afternoon, the school sent out an alert that a boy a few years ahead of Sem was diagnosed with fifth disease, a virus that's not serious unless your name is Sem.

It's not Martina on the other end, but an unfamiliar number.

That necklace I've been seeing all over the news. I want those diamonds too.

And then, right on its heels.

Or would you prefer I ask Thomas?

My skin goes hot then icy cold, and I drop the phone in my bag like it sizzled my fingers. I knew that asshole would be back.

Next to me, Thomas's breath is sharp and loud, and his hands curl into tight fists on the table. "For Frederik's sake, he better be deep, deep underground. When I find him, I'm going to murder him."

LATER, MUCH LATER, I carry my phone into the hallway bathroom and flip the lock, then awaken the screen. The two texts are still sitting at the top of the string.

That necklace I've been seeing all over the news. I want those diamonds too.

Or would you prefer I ask Thomas?

For the past couple days, I've managed to distract myself with thinking Thomas's secret was more scandalous than mine. I focused all my energy on his betrayal because it was easier than thinking about how mine came first. I pretended by ignoring the threats and the demands, convincing myself they were finished, even though I've always known there would be more coming down the line.

And now, here he is.

My thumbs tap out a reply.

I don't know what you're playing at, but I've already given you everything we agreed on. I don't have the necklace, and I can't get you more diamonds. Stop contacting me on this number.

I hit Block and delete the string, even though the same applies here: I'm well aware it won't be the end. This man is not going to stop firing off texts just because I tell him to, and I can't block what seems to be an endless supply of burner numbers. I'm going to have to come up with another way to appease him, and quickly.

He's already killed for Xander's diamonds. I have zero doubts he'd do the same to me.

November 17th, 10:54 p.m.

THE TOUR ENDS in Xander's study, a dark and moody man cave decorated within an inch of its life. He points me to his sleek desk and I step to one of the chairs, but I don't sit down. Not yet. The bracelet Thomas gave me weighs heavy on my arm.

Nice bling—that's what Xander said when he slid into Thomas's chair at Ciel Bleu, the restaurant on the top floor of the Hotel Okura. Thomas and I were halfway through the fish course when the call came in—yet another after-hours summons from the factory, yet another diamond emergency that no one could handle but him. As usual, Thomas obliged, but not before clasping on my anniversary gift, a platinum cuff smothered in diamonds, including the last surviving Cullinan.

Two minutes later, in walked Xander. Almost like it was planned.

Which it was, of course. I knew it the second his gaze zeroed in on the bracelet.

"It's the first time I've seen one of them in person," he said.

Them, as in a Cullinan, the eleven-carat whopper that served as the bracelet's centerpiece. It was like one of those rotating spirals, hypnotizing him, drawing him in. Xander couldn't keep his eyes off it. He still can't. All the friendly chitchat, all the flirting and teasing—it was leading to this, to getting the bracelet off my arm.

I cover the bracelet with a palm. "You could have just asked Thomas. I assume he's been working with the stone for weeks now."

Not one of the House's designers. Thomas. He made the bracelet himself, with his own hands. A labor of love. His words, not mine, and a fifth anniversary calls for something special. Inscribed in his handwriting on the inside. *For my wife on the occasion of our fifth anniversary.*

All that effort, and the best he could do was *for my wife*. Not *for the woman of my dreams*. Not *for the woman who holds my heart*. Not even *for Willow*. *For my wife*, which I can't help but assume he thought would be mighty convenient if he ever wants to find a different one.

Xander shrugs. "The Cullinans are a bit of a sensitive topic with the Prinses these days. No one who isn't a Prins is allowed within fifty feet."

An exaggeration, maybe, but he's probably not all that far off base. Now that the other Cullinans are gone, the value of the one on my wrist has quadrupled. Even here, in the safety of Xander's penthouse at the top of a well-secured building, the thought makes me jumpy.

"I want to feel the weight of the stone, to look at it under a scope with lights, optical scanners."

"You gemologists and your rocks," I say now with a roll of my eyes. It's a fascination I will never understand. "And here I thought your thing was lab-growns."

"It is. They are. I want to lab-grow the shit out of that Cullinan." He settles onto the chair across the desk, quirking a brow. "Are you going to sit down?"

I ignore his question, answering with some of my own. "Can you do that? Grow a close copy?"

"No. I can grow an *exact* one. Exact same weight, exact same cut and color, exact same microscopic occlusions. If I engrave the Cullinan's cert number on the girdle, not even your husband would be able to tell the difference, not unless he put the stone through a diamond detector, and even then . . ." He trails off, bobbing a shoulder.

It's one of the industry's dirty little secrets, that despite machines meant to identify the origins of the stone, lab-growns still slip into the mined supply all the time. Depending on who you believe, as much as thirty percent. That's one third of all those buyers shelling out two months of their hard-earned salary for what they *think* are mined diamonds, getting duped with rocks grown in a lab.

"You don't have to take the bracelet off, Willow, but do sit down. You're making me nervous."

In hindsight, this is the moment that could've changed so much. Before all the craziness started, before I added yet another secret to the stockpile. Before I took a step down a road I couldn't return back from.

But then I think about the phone call that interrupted our anniversary dinner, of Thomas running off and leaving me all alone, of him choosing diamonds yet again over me, of the hurt and the champagne still bubbling around in my veins.

Of Xander, a man on a mission that could complement mine.

I sink onto the chair.

RAYNA

I spend the rest of Wednesday tiptoeing around the apartment and Ingrid. I help her right her room, stuffing her duvet into a freshly washed cover and offering to fold her laundry. I wipe dark smudges of fingerprint dust from her doorknob, her wardrobe, her chest of drawers, and her walls. I suggest we order the sushi neither of us had the stomach for the night before, my treat.

For Ingrid, it's the last straw. "Stop looking at me like that."

"How am I looking at you?"

She sighs, stuffing her arms into her coat, and her makeup can't disguise the shadows under her eyes. Neither one of us got much sleep last night.

"Like this is somehow your fault, because it's not. My hiding spots weren't all that original. The thief didn't have to look that hard."

"Yeah, but—"

"*No*, Rayna. I'm not mad at you. I'm mad at myself for not putting my money in the bank like a normal person, so please. Stop thinking this is on you."

It *is* on me, though, and we both know it. The thief came here for me, for the necklace he thought I had stashed somewhere in the house. Ingrid's cash was simply a consolation prize, and in the end, it wasn't all that much. Less than a thousand euros—or so she said. Because now I'm wondering if she didn't lowball that number because she didn't want to admit to the detective where she got it, or that she wasn't planning to include it on her tax forms. There's a lot of black cash floating around in the antiques business, apparently.

Ingrid heads out, leaving me to spend the evening alone with my regrets . . . and my worries. I worry about the reporters downstairs, clogging the sidewalk in front of my door. I worry about whoever broke in here, and when, not if, they're coming back. I worry about taking my chances out in the streets, if there's a man in a ball cap waiting for his chance to drag me into a dark alleyway. I'm like my mother that way, my head rowdy with worry.

I decide to distract myself with work, with developing the pitch that's been beating around my brain since walking in on Xander's dead body—*When Disaster Strikes Abroad.* With my experience, an easy sell, at least.

I'm fetching my notebook from my bag when I find it, the envelope Ingrid plucked from the steps yesterday on our way upstairs. After the break-in, I'd forgotten all about it. I tug it from my bag and study the front. My name is slashed across the page in neat but unfamiliar handwriting. No address, no stamp. A hand delivery, then. I poke a finger under the seal and pry it open.

It's a note, written on a sheet of paper that's been hastily folded in thirds.

If I can find you this easily then so can he, and he wants that necklace. I hope for your sake that you have it. Either way, watch your back. You're not safe.

Adrenaline shoots through me, my heart thudding so hard I can practically see it through the wool of my sweater. I flip the paper over, check the back. Blank.

The apartment spins, and I can't stay here. At the scene of the crime, trapped in an apartment at the tippy-top of a four-story building where a narrow stairwell is the only way in or out. Alone, jumping out of my skin at every footstep and door slam coming from the floors underneath me, staring at my own front doorknob and waiting for it to turn. When Detective Boomsma said he'd put us on the watch list and send a patrol car by every hour to keep an eye on things, I tried very hard not to roll my eyes. If all the security at Xander's building couldn't stop a diamond thief with a pocket full of zip ties, why would a scheduled drive-by?

I can't stay. I can't stay. I can't stay.

I grab my keys and my coat and take off down the stairs.

By now, it's past ten, and the reporters are gone, wandered off to their families and homes. I skirt up a mostly empty street in the direction of the city center, trailing a pack of noisy partygoers to a crowded bar on the edge of the museum quarter. I find a seat near the door and keep a careful watch on the crowd, searching their faces, taking note of their clothes and their hair and their height, filing the details away in case I see any of them again—either in a lineup or trailing me around town. When the partygoers pay their tab and move on to the next place, so do I.

We end up in a dingy basement club in De Pijp, a neighborhood on the southeast side of the city. It's as good a place as any to pass a few hours, and the music isn't bad, either. The DJ, a pimply-faced kid who's barely tall enough to see over the edges of the raised booth on the far wall, spins old-school EDM I'm guessing he picked up from his parents, classics from Armin and Tiësto and Hardwell. I stand in the center of the crowd, sipping cheap vodka from a plastic cup and swaying to the beat like I'm not old enough to be his mom, like I'm not old enough to have mothered half the kids in this place. The club is hot and the floor is sticky, but the booze and the lack of men in ball caps is helping me not care.

A guy dances up to me, a cup of amber liquid clutched in a fist. He's tall, thin, nondescript in a plain T-shirt and jeans. His body moves with the music, but he sticks close to mine, so close his arms brush my hair. I meet his gaze, and his expression doesn't change. Heavy lids, blissful smile, the sappy kind that comes from narcotics. I don't think he wants anything from me but a dance, but after the break-in, I'm not taking any chances. I duck under his arm and move away, chasing a gust of cooler air to an empty space at the bar.

A bartender stands at the far end, a rail-thin woman in a tube top working the beer tap. Dozens of people vie for her attention, waving euro bills like colorful flags in the space over the bar. This is going to take forever.

A stream of Dutch comes from my right, a man with smiling eyes and Jason Momoa hair. Like the rest of the people in this place, he's young, somewhere in his midtwenties, I'm guessing.

I point to the speaker above my head, blasting music that thrums deep inside my bones like a jet engine, and shake my head. "I didn't catch a single word of that."

He leans in and shouts in my ear. "I said, good luck getting a drink. I've been waving this twenty around for the past ten minutes." He slaps it to the bar and pushes up on both hands, raising himself up above the crowd. "Yo," he yells in her direction, along with more Dutch words I don't understand. The woman catches his eye and rolls hers.

"You're American," he says, landing back on his feet.

Americans abroad learn pretty quickly their nationality isn't always a good thing in the eyes of the rest of the world. Americans are loud, they're rude and demanding, they wear running shoes and baggy jeans and don't bother to learn the customs or languages of their host country. But this guy doesn't say it like it's an insult, so I nod.

"Cool," he says. "Where from?"

"A teeny tiny town called St. Francisville, Louisiana. Blink and you'll miss it."

"What brings you to Amsterdam?"

I chew on a corner of my lip, lolling in the heaviness of a vodka buzz, considering how much to tell him. That *home* is a place with too many triggers—the house Barry and I lovingly restored and the gazebo where he dropped to one knee, the church where we said our vows in front of two hundred of our closest family and friends, only for him to break them in such a horrible, awful way six years later. That town belongs to Barry now.

I lift both hands in a full-body shrug. "It was time for me to move on. Amsterdam seemed as good a place as any to do it."

"Nice. And how's that working out for you?"

I wince. "Honestly? So far, it's been a bit too adventurous for my liking."

"Uh-oh. Anything I can do to help?"

I look down at the plastic cup in my hand, empty but for the lone lime slice stuck to the side. "I suppose a drink anytime soon is out of the question."

"Not unless you want to go back there and pour it yourself." He glances down the length of the bar, to the bartender with her back turned, her shoulder blades sharp enough to slice the fabric of her top as she punches in something on the register. "There's another place across the street, though. A bar, not a club. It'll be a lot less crowded and loud."

I stare up at this man, taking in all that hair, all those beaded necklaces and chains. I should thank him for the offer and drag my ass home, but the truth is, I don't want to. I don't want to go back to my tiny bedroom with its sad, single bed. I want to be out. I want to forget. I want to flirt with a handsome man I have no plans of ever seeing again.

And this guy has one big plus in his corner: he is the exact opposite of the men I've chosen in the past. Barry with his blazers and chinos, Xander with his fancy watch and designer-decorated apartment. This man in his faded jeans and tangle of beads and chains, all that fabulous hair . . . he's absolutely nothing like them.

I stick out a hand. "Rayna."

"Nice to meet you, Rayna. I'm Lars."

"Take me across the street, Lars, but don't give me any more vodka. Vodka is the last thing I need."

"What *do* you need?"

Suddenly, I'm thinking about the burger bar up the street, the french fry place around the corner that's open until three.

"I need food," I say. "The greasy, carby kind."

He plucks the empty cup from my fingers, tosses it to the bar, and wraps his fingers around mine, tugging me toward the stairs. "I know just the place."

"JUST THE PLACE" is Sevil Ali Baba, a late-night Turkish grill room on the next block. A long, brightly lit space lined with booths on one side and a kitchen that runs the entire length of the other, a mix of griddles and deep fryers and giant spits stacked with slices of gleaming meat, chicken and lamb and pork. My mouth waters at the smell.

A man in an apron and an enormous knife looks up when we come inside, his face splitting into a wide grin. He says something to Lars in a language I don't recognize, then points us to a booth at the back.

"Best shawarma in all of Amsterdam," Lars says, sinking onto the bench across from me. "That guy up there is my cousin."

"So you're biased." He frowns, and I clarify. "Inclined to believe your cousin when he says his shawarma is the best."

"Oh, I believe him, because it's not just him. It's Yelp and Tripadvisor, too. Voted the best in the city, four years in a row."

He calls out something to his cousin—our order, I'm guessing, because two seconds later, he appears with two bottles of Coke. "This is Rayna," Lars tells him in English. "She's a shawarma virgin."

The cousin's eyes go wide, and he tells me that late-night shawarmas are an institution in Holland, a well-loved stop on the way home from the bars, much like Waffle House is back home. The Dutch version of a hangover helper, the holy, booze-sopping grail: meat and salt and carbs.

"Prepare to be amazed," the cousin says, then heads back to the meat station.

"So you speak Dutch, English, and . . . Turkish?" I say, ticking the languages off on my fingers, feeling almost embarrassed that I know only one.

Lars nods. "My father lives in Bursa, a city on the Asian side."

"And your mother?"

"Dutch, born and bred. They met when she was vacationing in Turkey. The love of her life, or so she says, even though their relationship crashed and burned pretty quickly. He couldn't stand it here in Holland, apparently. Too cold. Too wet. I barely remember him."

"That's so sad. You don't see your father at all?"

Lars shakes his head. "Not really. My mom used to send me there on holiday a couple times a year, but the older I got, the more I pushed back. My friends are all here, and the cultural divide is so big. My dad doesn't understand my life here, and I can't fathom his. We have very little in common."

"And what about your mom? Did she ever consider moving to Turkey?"

He laughs, a warm, rich sound that makes me smile. "That would've been an even worse disaster. My mother is as Dutch as they come, which means she's fiercely independent and says whatever is going through her head, which is a *lot*, and it's far too progressive to survive in a country like Turkey. Also, she's like me. An artist, except she specializes in nudes. In Turkey, her work would get her arrested."

There's so much to absorb here. That Lars is the product of a relationship that was destined for doom. That the way he talks about his mother, with affection and obvious pride, makes me like him a little more. That he's an artist, that he inherited his mother's creativity.

Never, not in a million trillion years, would the old Rayna be sitting in a greasy diner in the middle of the night, sharing shawarmas with a random Dutch artist she met in a bar. She would have been concerned about the optics of being seen at this hour with a man who was not her husband, or what in the world the two of them would have to talk about, or the likelihood of getting mugged in a somewhat sketchy neighborhood at going on 2:00 a.m.

But Rayna 2.0 gives zero shits for optics, and she wants to stay. Mostly because Rayna 2.0 is ravenous.

The food arrives, two giant mounds of steaming sliced lamb wrapped in warm pita bread, a mountain of french fries, and little plastic bowls filled with what looks like mayonnaise and ketchup. Lars grabs a squirt bottle from the holder on the table and douses his meat, then does the same with mine.

"The moment of truth," he says with a grin.

I pick up my sandwich and take a bite, grinning when it tastes as good as it smells. I don't know if this is the best shawarma in Amsterdam, I just know that this one is damn good.

"Delicious," I say, and Lars and his cousin give a little cheer. I put the sandwich down, exchanging it for a couple of fries I dip in the bowl of mayonnaise. "So what kind of artist are you?"

Lars hikes up on a hip, pulling his cellphone from a pocket. He scrolls through the pictures, colorful drawings of people dressed in bright colors. Finally, he stops on one and flips his phone around. Three kids in orange shirts and green pants, their heads tilted together, arms slung around each other and a pink and blue LOVE sign. The background is a sea of yellow and purple flowers.

I lean in closer and zoom in on their faces, smooth swipes of dusty blue with no depth to depict the features, but the hair is like his, long and dark. I don't miss that Lars has drawn the most beautiful family, even though he grew up without one.

"This is fantastic," I say, handing him back his phone. "You're very talented."

"You really think so?"

"I do. I really think so."

He grins, a childlike smile that matches his impish eyes, so brown they're almost black. He slides the phone back into his pocket. "What do you do?"

I feel myself deflate a little at his question. "Oh, nothing nearly as interesting. I'm a travel writer. Destination itineraries, insider guides, adventures and getaways. "Twenty-Four Hours in Prague" or "Walking the Camino del Norte." Things like that."

"Have you?"

"Walked the Camino del Norte?" I shake my head. "No, but by the time I finished that article, I felt like I had. I'm pretty sure I had phantom blisters."

"You don't have to actually travel to the places you write about?"

Automatically, my brain flits to the detective, his warning words ringing through my head like a scream. *Let me know if you plan to leave town.* I think of the article I was working on in my tiny, beige room before what happened with Xander grounded me. "Top Tips for Tipping Around the World." Now the words assault me with their stupidity.

"Normally I do, at least, I'm supposed to. But the magazine gave me less than a week to write that Camino article when it takes five to walk the trail. They also gave me zero travel budget and basically asked me to write it for free, so any inaccuracies are their own damn fault."

These are common issues I run up against. Most companies need the story yesterday, and they'd rather pay in comped hotel rooms than actual cash. The ones that *do* pay, pay for shit. I have to fight for every euro, and even then, it's barely enough to get by. I don't know how writers do it. For me, this is not a long-term career.

Lars plucks a couple of napkins from the holder and wipes sauce from his hands. "Every artist's struggle. You've got to demand your own worth. Don't be giving away your art for free."

"Easy for you to say. How much do your pieces go for?"

"The one I just showed you? That one's a gift, but normally somewhere around €2000."

My eyes bulge at the number. "If I get offered a quarter of that, the magazine acts like they own me. The problem is there are so many of us out there, all fighting for the same collaborations and campaigns, which means we're all desperate enough to work for peanuts. The magazines have us by the balls and they know it."

"No offense, but it doesn't sound like you like your job very much."

I nibble on a fry, taking the time to think. "I guess I just thought it would be different, you know? That travel writing would be an easy way of going to all these exotic, faraway places, to really spend time there and experience how it feels to live in that place, even if only for a week or two. I thought it meant fun and adventure and me figuring my shit out. My sister calls it my *Eat, Pray, Love* era—not that I have those kinds of funds or am particularly interested in promoting some quasi-spiritual soul-searching manifesto to a bunch of white women in the same sorry, sad boat as I am, but I would like to experience those things for *me*. To get some sense of what my future could look like, so I can let go of the past."

It's the first time I've verbalized these thoughts out loud to anyone, let alone myself, and it's kind of a revelation. I don't want to write that article about tipping or the ten cheapest European cities. I don't want to submit another pitch only to get rejected, don't want to slave over another five thousand words only for them to end up as digital dust. I want to get paid for my work, but even more so, I want to write something I care about. Something people want to actually *read*.

Lars picks up his sandwich, shaking off a drizzle of sauce. "So write about that. Well, maybe not the quasi-spiritual manifesto stuff, but the part about leaving behind the past to find your future was good. I'd read a story about that."

He says it so sincerely, as if it would be the easiest thing in the world for me to just . . . put myself out there like that, especially when I'm nowhere near done working it out in my own head. I left St. Francisville . . . not on a whim, not exactly, but the move wasn't all that well thought out, either. More like, *screw it, I'm out*. A last-ditch Hail Mary to remove myself from a place I could no longer stay. Get up and go. See where life takes you. *That* was the plan.

My Year of Adventure, hijacked by tragedy and terror. I think about Xander, the break-in, the tracker. I think about the hope I felt that night on Xander's terrace, the excited tingle that anything was possible, and I want that feeling back. I just . . . I want it back.

The door bursts open, blowing in a swarm of college kids on an icy wind. They're loud and obviously drunk, but the sight of them is like a warning shot of adrenaline direct to the vein. One of them, a man in a beanie and a shearling coat is a good deal older than the rest, and something about him prickles the hairs on the back of my neck. I've seen this guy somewhere. In the club, maybe? Instantly, I'm sober.

"What's wrong?" Lars says. "Did you lose something?"

I slide my bag onto my lap and rummage through it, one eye

on the man as he taps his card to the register. "That guy up there, the one in the beanie. I'm pretty sure he's following me."

My fingers don't make contact with anything foreign, no smooth, round objects along the bottom of my bag. I unzip the inside pocket and shove my hand inside. Nothing in the outside pocket, either.

Lars leans into the table, lowering his voice, casting glances at the guy in the beanie. "Why would he be following you?"

I make a sound in my throat, not a laugh, exactly, but also not an answer.

The man looks over. Our eyes meet, and his are surprisingly sharp, surprisingly alert. His gaze slides quickly away, but it's too late. I've already seen it. This man is not drunk like the rest of his group. He's not here by accident. And I've definitely seen him before, but at the time, he wasn't wearing a beanie. He was wearing a ball cap. It's the man from the number twelve tram, the one who smiled at me through the window.

I scoot to the end of the booth. "Thanks for the shawarma, Lars, but I gotta go."

"Then let's go." Lars pulls a wrinkled twenty from his wallet and tosses it on the table, and I'm not opposed to him escorting me out of here. The man in the beanie is no longer pretending not to watch me. He's planted himself between me and the front door.

Lars tugs me the other way, leading me out a back door and into a dim alley that reeks of garbage. Trash rolls by on an icy wind, empty Coke bottles tangled with cigarette butts and hamburger wrappers. I have no idea where I am, and I'm too panicked to think straight. When Lars takes a sharp left, I don't hesitate; I follow.

The alley dumps us out on a cross street lit up with late-night snack bars and traffic, bikers headed home from the bars in thick coats and wool hats pulled down over their ears. I watch a cluster of them pedal past, trying to catch a glimpse of their faces, but they're bundled up and flying by too fast. And there are beanies *everywhere.*

"Which way is the Rijks?" I ask, the museum an important landmark around the corner from my apartment. Once I spot its twin pointy steeples, I'll know the way home—not the safest spot, admittedly, but the only one I've got. Hopefully by now, Ingrid will be home, and I won't have to stay there alone.

"Too far to walk." He shoves a hand in his pocket, and two quick beeps sound from a silver Vespa parked at the corner. "Come on. I'll give you a ride."

I think of finding my way through streets that are quickly emptying of people, all the deserted sidewalks and dark corners between here and home where beanie man could snatch me off the street and throw me into a van, and my skin goes tight with fear. He's found me twice now. Clearly, he's skilled at this.

"Fine, but for the record, you're not invited inside." I clamber on to the back of his bike, winding my arms around Lars's torso. "My last one-night stand didn't end on the best note."

WILLOW

I'm winding my way through the packed tables at Firelli's, still a popular lunch spot despite the bullet that not all that long ago sailed through the front window and into a mobster's head, when Fleur's peal of delighted laughter rips the air.

"Good Lord, Willow. Did you *bike* here? You're more Dutch than I am."

"What gave it away?" I flap my drenched hands, sending icy drops of water flying. "My hair? My sweater?"

Bad weather doesn't exist, people here are so fond of saying, *only bad clothing*. Within seconds, mine was soaked to the skin.

Meanwhile, Fleur is a vision in a silky white blouse. Flawless hair and makeup, a cluster of diamonds glittering at the base of her throat. I see my reflection in the mirror above her head, swiping away a dirty trail of mascara with a knuckle.

"Sit down, sit down." She motions for me to scoot into the round velvet booth, her voice peppy and bright. "I ordered us some wine. I hope Sancerre's okay."

Wine on a workday, I'm intrigued. I toss my bag on the booth and slide in after it. "Sancerre sounds perfect. I love a boozy lunch."

Normally, Fleur would turn up her nose at the thought of skipping out on a Thursday to socialize with anyone, much less her barely tolerable sister-in-law. She and I see each other all the time, but it's always at family or work events, and we never go much deeper than a polite *how are the kids?* She doesn't suggest we meet up for happy hours or call me to gossip about the latest couples drama at the golf club. When she called with the invitation to join her for lunch, I couldn't help but ask, "What's the occasion?"

"Because you and I never get any one-on-one time," she said, her voice playful in a way I rarely hear. "There are always so many other people around."

Fleur wanted something from me; that much was clear. This is a woman who doesn't make a move without an agenda, and the fact she wanted to sneak away from the office smack in the middle of a workday said that whatever that agenda was, it was an important one.

"Please?" she said, turning up the heat. "I really need to talk to you about something, and I can't do it over the phone. And please don't mention this to Thomas, by the way. It would turn into a whole big thing."

My sneaky sister-in-law knew what she was doing by dangling that little carrot. My curiosity wouldn't let me say no.

She plucks the bottle from the cooler and pours two generous glasses. "Thanks for giving me an excuse to get out of the office. Ever since the mess with Xander, Papa has been in the office every single day, and between you and me, he's not the easiest person to work for. Or to even be around lately." She leans in close like she's sharing a secret. "Papa can be so difficult."

I lift a brow. Fleur has spent every family get-together I've ever been a part of sucking up to her father, so to hear her speak this way about him now is more than a little surprising. "Imagine what it's like for people who *aren't* named Prins."

She laughs. "Oh, believe me, I know. When Papa was still CEO, we were losing employees at the rate of one a week. One a week, Willow! At every level of staff including the polishers, who are so hard to find, and even the best ones need training before we let them loose on the Prins cut. Now people are starting to remember they didn't have it so bad with the older Prins in charge. But enough about work . . ." She picks up a glass, taps it against mine. "Cheers."

I sip the Sancerre, cold and fruity and delicious, thinking about not just what she said, but how she said it, a backhanded way of telling me the staff doesn't love working for Thomas. Is this why she called me here, to complain about her brother's management style?

"So what do you usually eat here?" I say, nonchalant, trading my glass for the menu. The tangy wine, the smell of garlic and pasta, Fleur's agenda of subterfuge. Suddenly, I'm starving.

"Oh, a salad or something, I don't know." Fleur plunks her glass onto the table with a soft sigh, her fingers twisting the stem. "Look, I know it's no secret that I don't agree with Papa appointing Thomas CEO instead of me, but he's still my brother. My *baby* brother, which means I've always felt this . . . I don't know, responsibility, I guess, to look after him."

I bristle a little at the *baby brother*, mostly because it's always been the basis of Fleur's arguments: as the older sibling, it's only fair this company be handed to her. But this is her pony show, not mine, so I let it slide.

"Understandable," I say instead, like I grew up with a younger sibling or for that matter any siblings at all, like before Sem, I had any idea what it was to have someone who needed me. I've been on my own since I was sixteen, when my mother's indifference and her endless string of skeevy, creepy boyfriends became too much to bear. I emptied out the shoebox where she stashed her cash and hopped a Greyhound bus to Atlanta. When she finally called three whole weeks later, it was to yell at me for stealing her money.

"Tell me what's going on with him."

"With who?"

"Thomas, of course. He's just been acting so . . . *strange*."

I look up from the menu, curious now. *Strange*, as in buying thirty-euro necklaces and leaving them on random bikes? That kind of strange?

"Strange how?" I say.

"Moody. Short-tempered and just . . . *off*. I'm not the only one who's noticed this change in him. Roland has seen it. So has Mama. We're all very worried."

I put the menu down. Well, that explains the lunch invitation, at least, along with her request I not say anything to Thomas. Thomas has been acting weird. People are worried about him. They sent her here to ask me if he's okay.

A waiter steps up to the table, but Fleur shoos him away. "He didn't tell you about all the fights with Xander, did he?"

Fight could mean a lot of things. An argument. A silly little skirmish. A knock-down, drag-out brawl. It's a word that can have a million connotations, but I don't have to ask which one Fleur is referring to, because her right hand curls into a fist.

I try to picture it: reserved, respectable Thomas, trading blows with anyone, much less Xander. The image is so ridiculous that I actually laugh. "Oh, come on. They actually *hit* each other?"

Fleur nods, her eyes wide and earnest. "Yes. More than once. I'm telling you, those two fought about *everything*. Xander's designs for a new collection of earrings. A price hike at the lab in China. Thomas's constant hovering—that's what Xander called it, hovering and that he needed to back off. One of the polishers had to actually pull them apart."

"That . . . doesn't sound like Thomas at all."

"Yes it does, Willow. Ever since the Cullinans, my brother has been carrying a lot of pent-up rage, and it doesn't help that Xander was obsessed with them. He was planning on launching a lab-grown Cullinan collection, did you know that? You should have seen Thomas's face when he found out Xander was growing matches to the Cullinan stones. He planned to use them as the centerpiece in rings, necklaces, bracelets. Like that bracelet Thomas made for you, but with a Cullinan grown in a lab."

God's gemstones, that's what Thomas called them. He could talk for days about how the Cullinans were formed, how millions of years of heat and pressure deep in the earth rearranged atoms into colorful crystal systems for his great-great-grandfather to brush off and polish. He would have never agreed to a lab-grown Cullinan collection.

"Thomas didn't mention any of this to me," I say now to Fleur, and it's not a lie. It's Xander who danced around this topic.

I want to lab-grow the shit out of that Cullinan.

Fleur gives me a wide-eyed nod. "Thomas called Xander a thief and a traitor in front of everybody. He fired him on the spot, then had the guards pat him down and escort him off the premises like some kind of criminal."

Which I happen to know that he was. Whatever stones the killer took from Xander's apartment, they weren't exactly on the books, but the Cullinans . . . Could Thomas be right? Could Xander have really pulled off the heist of the century?

"Thomas is just so volatile," she says on a sigh. "He has the whole staff walking on eggshells. They're afraid of saying something that will make him lose his temper."

Volatile? Steady, serious Thomas?

"He hasn't been getting much sleep since the Cullinans vanished, but even then. That doesn't sound like Thomas at all."

Fleur releases another sigh, a long puff of air that smells like wine and designer perfume. "So you see the change in him, too. Good. I mean, not *good*, but *you* know. We're not crazy to think there's something wrong."

"I didn't say he was volatile, Fleur. I've never seen Thomas lose his temper. Like, *ever*."

The waiter sidles up to the table for another try.

"We haven't even looked," Fleur tells him in testy Dutch. "Come back in another few minutes."

His bright smile drops off his face. "Of course. My apologies." He scurries away.

Fleur reaches for her wine. "Does Thomas have a 3D printer at home?"

Her question is so unexpected, the switch of subject so far out of left field, the only thing I can think of to say is, "A what?"

"A 3D printer. Do you have one at home, and if so, what kind?"

I think about all the devices Thomas has lining the cupboards of his study upstairs, the scales and the lights and the microscopes and a bunch of other equipment I have no idea what it's for. What does a 3D printer even look like? Is it different than a normal printer?

"I don't know. No. At least I don't think so. Why?"

"Did you know you can print virtually anything these days? Prototypes for jewelry designs, that's what we use the ones at the factory for, but the sky's the limit in terms of what you can make. Furniture, artificial teeth, chocolate bonbons, shoes, toys, dinosaur skeletons, guns."

At the last one, I laugh. "Guns are illegal in this country."

It's a common refrain among the Dutch despite regular shootings that make the news, most of them mob related. Criminals have guns, yes, but that's what makes them criminals. For a Dutch person, the American approach of fighting guns with more guns is asinine.

Fleur gives me a big-eyed, solemn nod. "Illegal to purchase, yes, but a person can still make one. It's not even that difficult. All they need is a €300 printer they buy on bol.com."

The Dutch version of Amazon.

"Dare I ask how you know this?"

"Because I saw the blueprints." She plants both arms onto the table and leans in. "They were on Thomas's desk. He downloaded them from the internet."

I stare at Fleur, and her eyes bore into mine because *this*. This is what she brought me here to tell me. Not that Thomas is losing his temper at work. Not that he exchanged blows with Xander. That he's *armed*. I picture Thomas in his office not all that far from here, seated behind his father's old desk and his grandfather's before that, printing a gun, a real, actual *gun* with a random set of blueprints he found on the internet, and the image is so ridiculous that I laugh again. He wouldn't even know how to hold the thing.

"Be serious, Fleur. Those blueprints could have belonged to anyone. Did you ask him why they were on his desk?"

"Of course. He said he found them on the printer, but he was lying. I could tell." She plunks both elbows on the table and leans over her empty plate. "Willow, why does my brother need a gun?"

Her brother, not *my husband*. Even when she's trying to manipulate me, Fleur can't help but be possessive.

"He doesn't. Are you kidding me? Thomas doesn't need a gun. And having a printout of instructions on your desk is a very different thing than holding the actual weapon in your hand. Blueprints are circumstantial evidence at best. Blueprints don't mean anything."

She leans back in the booth, shaking her head. "I know my brother, Willow, and this means something. There is something going on with him, something very serious and very wrong, and my gut says it has something to do with Xander. Thomas won't talk to me about it. But I'm hoping he'll talk to you."

He won't. I almost say the words out loud, but I swallow them down because Fleur is really serious. She really thinks Thomas is sitting behind a 3D printer somewhere, feeding the machine a file that will build him a handgun. This was her agenda all along—to tell me he's arming himself, and for what? To paint her brother as unhinged? To pry information out of me she can use in her campaign for CEO? To scare me?

"I'll try. I'll talk to Thomas tonight." I say this in lieu of what I'm really thinking, that Fleur might have an agenda here, but so do I. And my agenda has nothing to do with hers.

"Good." Fleur nods, just once, settling back in the booth with a satisfied smile. And why wouldn't she? Fleur is a Prins, and she's used to getting what she wants. "Let me know what he says, will you?"

A request, even though we both know it's not one.

There's movement in our periphery, the waiter creeping up to the table for another try.

Fleur looks up with a bright smile. "There you are! Tell us about the pasta special."

November 17th, 11:13 p.m.

THE SECOND I'M settled in my chair, Xander pops out of his, stepping to a framed black-and-white photograph on the wall. A Bastiaan Woudt, a Dutch photographer whose prints go for €10,000 and up. Xander tugs on the edge of the frame, and it swivels away from the wall. Behind it, bolted into the concrete, is a safe.

I watch as he skips the finger pad to tap in the code: 05732#, which I commit to memory. The safe beeps three times, followed by a metallic *thwunk*. He swings the door open and pulls a black velvet tray from the bottom shelf.

A black velvet tray filled with diamonds. Dozens and dozens of them, of every shape and size and color. Far more diamonds than a Prins employee should have at home, locked in a safe hidden in a wall.

With a pair of tweezers, he picks up the largest stone from the center compartment and holds it under the desk light.

"Here's the one I grew to the certification specs," he says, sinking onto the chair across from me. "Same weight, same clarity and fluorescence, same cut of course. The Cullinans were all the original Prins cut. There've been some improvements since, but this one is old-school."

I nod, but I don't have a gemologist's eye. For me, a diamond is a diamond is a diamond.

"There's a tiny bit of feathering between seven and eight, but it's not visible to the naked eye. You'd need a scope with at least 10x magnification, and even then, the inclusion is hard to find if you're not trained to look for it. This stone is virtually flawless."

"Like the one in my bracelet."

"Exactly like it. Except the one on your wrist took a billion years to make, and this one"—carefully, he settles the stone on the leather desk pad. It tips to the side, blinding white in the light—"about ten weeks."

"That's it? Only ten?"

Xander grins. "And that's not even the best part. The best part is there's no limit to how many I can grow. One or ten or ten thousand. I can grow as many as I want. As many as I can sell."

All these months I've spent wondering why a man with Xander's résumé would take this job. Why when he could work for anyone—Cartier or Van Cleef & Arpels or Chopard—he'd choose to work for the shaky House of Prins. Or launch his own firm. He's got enough names in his Rolodex to support it, models and A-list actresses and royalty who already serve as walking advertisements for his designs.

Xander could work for anyone. He could live anywhere. Why choose a struggling diamond house in Amsterdam?

He stretches an arm across the desk. “May I?”

The answer is: for this. The Cullinan on my wrist. Its lab-grown twin sitting on the desk. The dozens of diamonds locked in a hidden safe on the wall, all copies of Prins-mined stones, I’m guessing.

I flick the safety latch with a fingernail, but I don’t slide the cuff from my arm. Not yet.

“On one condition.”

PART TWO

"I never hated a man enough to
give him diamonds back."

—Zsa Zsa Gabor

RAYNA

On Friday, Xander's funeral is already in full swing by the time I arrive, a packed room of mourners sitting shoulder-to-shoulder while a man in a navy suit drones on at the podium. I slide into an open spot at the far end of the back row. A strategic spot close to the door, in case I need to make a speedy exit.

Yes, I am well aware that attending Xander's funeral falls under the category of Things That Make Me Look Guiltier, but the reasons I should pay my respects were too many to ignore. I actually *liked* Xander. I spent the night leading up to his death in his bed. I let him kiss me and give me multiple orgasms. Xander and I were connected in the most intimate of ways, even if for only a few hours. I couldn't *not* come.

It's what the killer would do, I happen to know from my many hours spent watching true-crime TV—sneak into their own victim's funeral for one last, blood-soaked finale. One final look at loved ones sniffling into their hankies, to revel in the damage he's done. To think *I did that*. I put those tears there. My gaze scans the crowd, thinner than I expected it to be after all the press surrounding Xander's death, and I wonder if the killer is one of the people in this modern and bright room, if he's thinking all those things.

I don't understand a lick of what any of the speakers are saying, a rolling parade of people at the podium while above their heads, pictures flash by on a giant screen. A skinny Xander chasing a ball down a scraggly field. Lounging on a Dutch beach packed with people. Sitting on the hood of a dusty Opel sedan in jeans and sunglasses, his shirt sleeves rolled up to reveal tanned forearms. Holding a pile of uncut gems in a palm, or peering at them through a loupe, and my heart twists for this man I barely knew. He was so handsome, and that cocky grin, he's apparently had it all his life.

My phone buzzes against my hip, and I dig it out of a pocket. A text from Lars, the second today. The first came this morning when I woke up alone—Good morning, Rayna, sign of life please. Now, another: Any beanie sightings?

I smile and tick out a reply: So far so good, thx for checking in.

It feels good to know someone is watching out for me, I think as I slide the phone back into my pocket. Even better still to know the man with the beanie didn't follow me here. I'm pretty sure he's not one of the people sitting in the rows before me, and he's not outside, either, lingering in the lot or huddled on the corner with the press. By the time I arrived, twenty minutes past the starting time, everyone but three reporters was already inside.

A tall man in a tasteful black suit and glasses steps to the podium. I take in his thick thatch of dark hair, the black, horn-rimmed glasses, and the air in my lungs turns light and tingly. This is the guy from those articles I read, Xander's partner in the lab-grown line. Thomas Prins.

He spouts off a jumble of guttural sounds I recognize as Dutch, and I can tell by the way he makes himself comfortable that it's going to be a long one. My mind and my gaze wander, to the hunched shoulders and slumped heads of the people in front of me, the slices of pale, drawn faces whenever they look to the side. I picture Xander on the shower floor, the zip tie squeezing his neck, and I shudder. These people will need therapy for the rest of their lives, and probably, so will I.

A titter goes through the crowd, and I return my attention to the podium, to the man in the dark suit. He smiles at someone in one of the front rows, then tucks a sheet of paper into the inside pocket of his jacket and makes his way back to his seat. I sit up a little straighter, following him with my gaze. The place isn't all that big, but I'm way in the back, and I don't have a good angle on the others in his row. An elderly couple, stiff-backed and regal, another well-dressed couple, two teenage girls. The Prins family, and they certainly look the part.

I'm staring at the backs of their heads, all close-clipped cuts and salon highlights, when suddenly, a ripple of motion goes down the row like a football stadium wave. One by one, backs straighten. Bodies lean over or hike up on a hip, digging cellphones out of pockets and bags. They turn to each other and exchange alarmed looks, whispering about whatever is on their screens. Some kind of news, and it doesn't look good.

My gaze sticks to one of them, the brunette seated at the far end. I see her pretty profile as she whispers to the elderly woman next to her, the delicate bones in her neck, the glittering diamonds dangling from her earlobes. I know virtually no one in this country, and yet I know her.

It's the woman from the park. The one with the cute kid and ugly dog.

And she's seated in the Prins row at Xander's funeral.

What are the odds?

Never mind. I already know.

The answer is none.

Zero.

THE FUNERAL IS still going strong when I slip out the back row and into the lobby, almost colliding with a woman with watery eyes and a severe bun. She hands me a pen and gestures to the guest book, where I scribble something illegible, then pluck my coat from the rack. Sometime while I was inside, the early afternoon clouds have melted into a bright blue sky, offering a perfect view of the press gathered at the corner. A good dozen bodies bouncing on their toes to keep warm.

I'm looking around for an alternative escape route when a familiar voice comes from just behind me. "I thought I might find you here."

I rearrange my face, making sure to park my expression firmly in neutral before I turn around. "Detective Boomsma. Hi."

Honestly, I would have preferred running into a reporter.

The detective leans back on his heels. "Funny fact. Only ten percent of murder victims die at the hands of a stranger. Family members, colleagues, friends. Lovers. Those are the more likely suspects."

"Not funny ha-ha, but I can see the point of you telling it, and I feel like this is an excellent moment for me to assure you that I'm here because Xander was a friend. I came to honor his memory, and okay, fine, maybe a little bit for myself, to give his tragedy some closure."

"I take it you didn't find any more trackers."

I shake my head. "No, but there's definitely a man following me. I've seen him twice now."

"Did you get a description?"

By now, the lobby is starting to fill with bodies anyway—servers standing ready with trays of drinks and food for the mourners, who are probably getting up and out of their seats. The detective gestures to a side door overlooking a courtyard, and it's not the worst place to talk. Open to the street but mostly concealed behind a giant weeping willow, dropping a thick waterfall of branches that hangs over the opening like a curtain. And behind that curtain, visible from the window but not from the street, are two benches, twin slabs of concrete sitting low to the ground. I zip my coat and follow the detective through the door.

Outside, the courtyard is quiet, though I can hear the reporters chatting through the branches. They're still up at the street, but they've seen the movement in the lobby, and they're getting ready, pointing their bodies and zoom lenses at the double doors. If they see us, though, it's only our feet, stepping to the benches behind the swaying curtain.

"Young," I say, taking a seat. "Early thirties or so. Tall. Light skin that's mostly white. Hair is brown, I think. Both times I saw him, he was wearing a hat. And before you ask, no, I wasn't quick-thinking enough to snap a photo, but you better believe I will next time."

"Do you remember seeing him that night with Xander? Did he maybe . . . I don't know, follow the two of you home?"

I frown. "I was drunk, and even then, how would I know? He looks like every other guy in this country. Who knows how many times he's trailed me before I noticed him."

"I'm asking because there's been another murder. A woman reported a body bobbing in the weeds behind her houseboat on the Amstel. The victim was shot through the head."

I shiver, and not just because the bench is a block of ice. Because another person is dead. Shot in a country where guns are illegal.

"And you're telling me this, why? Because the two murders are connected?"

He dips his chin, not quite a nod. "The man was a diamond trader. Up until last fall, he worked for House of Prins."

I don't have to think too long about what this means, not just that another man is dead but that yet another murder is connected to House of Prins. "I'm very sorry for that man's family, but surely now you must see that Xander's death had nothing to do with me. I just happened to be there for it."

"It certainly complicates things."

"The press over there"—I wave a hand in their general direction—"they told me I was the lead suspect."

"That's not for the press to decide, and they only said it to get a reaction. Don't give them one."

"My roommate said the same thing. But they're making it difficult for me to get through my own front door. Anytime I try to come or go, it's an ambush. My neighbors hate me."

"I'll tell the patrols to start scattering them. You said you met Xander on Tinder, correct?"

I nod. "Yes. And if you give me back my phone, I can prove it. All our messages are still on there."

He gives me a look, one that says *fat chance*, and I'm guessing he's already seen those messages. While iPhones are notoriously hard to break into, my passcode isn't just a string of random digits. Like an idiot, I used numbers that meant something to me, ones that would be familiar enough for me to remember but also predictable for anyone who knows me: my birthday, the month followed by the year.

"Who initiated contact?"

"I'm guessing you cracked the code on my phone, which means you already know it was Xander. He's the one who slid into my DMs, not the other way around."

"Okay, but who swiped first, you or him?"

I frown, wondering where this line of questioning is going. "Xander did. Why?"

"Did he ever ask you about anything personal?"

"We met on a dating app, Detective. We were getting to know each other. Of course his questions were personal."

"Let me rephrase. Did any of his questions strike you as strange?"

I pause, giving myself time to think, to remember the first flurry of messages. He asked me where I was from, what brought me to Holland, how I was liking it here so far, all pretty standard get-to-know-you fare. Later, during our date, we talked about our families, our schooling, past relationships and break-ups. All of it was personal. None of it went super deep.

"Nothing jumps out at me, why?"

"Did he talk about his work at all?"

"Barely. I knew Xander was a gemologist, but I didn't know the extent of it until after his death. Most of what I know about Xander's job I've learned since then, by searching his name online."

"So you Googled him."

"Yes. Why? What are you trying to get at here?"

"I'm trying to see if he told you anything significant, even if it didn't seem that way to you at the time."

"Like what?"

"Like if he had any reason to seek you out. For example, that you knew some people in common, or your work crossed paths somehow."

"I'm a travel writer, and not a very successful one at that. My job has literally nothing to do with diamonds."

His gaze wanders to my ringless hands, to the string of cheap beads poking out of my sleeves, to the scarf draped loosely around my neck, bare except for the gold-plate necklace I got at a boutique in the Nine Streets.

"They're fake," I say, picking the pendant up from my chest, running a finger along the tiny stones set in the three Xs, the crest for Amsterdam. "Not even good fakes. I think I paid like €39, and that's including the chain. I don't own any diamonds."

The *not anymore* piles up on my tongue, but I swallow it back down. No need to open old wounds that aren't all that old, to prompt any new questions about my past.

"Not even in your jewelry box back home?"

I shake my head, a silent no when what I'm really thinking is, *what's the point of a jewelry box when you own nothing worth putting inside?*

He pulls a black velvet bag from his inside coat pocket, wriggling a finger inside to tug out a bracelet, a complicated cuff with what's got to be hundreds of diamonds fanning out from a spectacular whopper in the center. "Then I take it this doesn't belong to you."

I laugh, because while it's true that once upon a time, Barry bought me nice things, they were nothing like this. This is the kind of piece jewelers show in private back rooms, with cameras in every corner and an armed guard blocking the door. The kind you see on auction websites, or in photographs wrapped around Princess Diana's arm.

Like the necklace Xander hung around my neck, the one that disappeared from his nightstand.

"No, that bracelet doesn't belong to me. Not in a million years would it ever belong to me." I run a finger over the biggest stone, smooth and icy under my skin. "It's stunning, though."

"We found it in Xander's desk."

I look up in surprise. "So the thief found the matching necklace in the nightstand drawer but left this piece behind? How did they miss it?"

"Could be they ran out of time, or maybe they just didn't look hard enough. It was wrapped in a cloth at the back of his desk drawer, buried under a pile of papers."

"Are the stones real?"

"Unclear. It's not that easy to determine a diamond's origins. Unless it has a laser inscription stating it's lab-grown, which these don't, it's hard for even the experts to tell. These have certification numbers, though, so I'm guessing yes."

"Well, either way, I've never seen it before, and it's definitely not mine."

He slides the bracelet into the velvet bag and tucks it back in his coat pocket. "Did Xander ever mention anything about a gun?"

"You seem to be under the impression that I knew Xander better than I did. No, he didn't mention anything about a gun. Why would he?"

"Because Xander had one, built from parts created on a 3D printer and just as deadly as a metal one, but virtually untraceable. No serial numbers, no paper trails for us to follow."

"Can printers really do that? Summon a deadly weapon out of thin air?"

"Guns, ballistic knives, grenades. They're flooding the market faster than we can stop them. Last month, a newspaper got their hands on a design for a 3D semiautomatic. You could buy the instructions along with the printer and all the materials you needed on the internet and have it shipped to your doorstep here in Holland. Nothing illegal about it until you actually hit Print."

"That's quite the loophole you've got on your hands there, but I'm still trying to figure out why you're telling me all this. Unless you think that Xander was the one who shot the guy in the Amstel."

"The gun we found in Xander's apartment hadn't been fired, but it's just as easy to print ten as it is to print one. The technology extends to other things, as well. Face masks printed from a scan of a photograph, or gloves with someone else's fingerprints. The last one's especially handy when the safe works with biometrics."

"And let me guess: Xander's opened with a fingerprint, which explains his finger, I guess, though yuck. I'm guessing that's how they got in the safe."

"There's a keypad, too, but you'd have to know the code to bypass the fingerprint. Either way, you're correct. The thief used Xander's finger to gain access."

"And now you're wondering if maybe I'm the thief. If I took the necklace and whatever diamonds were in his safe."

"It crossed my mind at first, but then I realized only an idiot would call me up, on a Sunday evening no less, to tell me about the dream she had about a safe she'd cleaned out a couple days before." He shakes his head, regarding me. "I don't know you all that well, but you don't strike me as an idiot."

"Is that a compliment? Because if so, it could use a little work."

"You didn't let me finish. There's a *but*. That picture you posted, the one of you and Xander currently circulating online, that was a dumb move."

"I know. That's why I took it down."

"It may be off your page, but it's too late to stop it from getting plastered all over the internet. Everybody who sees it knows you were in Xander's bed the morning someone murdered him and took off with his diamonds. He compared you to a Cullinan. He mentioned the stones by name. Do you know how many people are looking for the Cullinans? How much they're worth?"

"By the look on your face, I'm guessing a lot."

"The point is, people are going to be wondering if you're telling the truth about what you heard and saw. If maybe you were watching from under a bed or through the cracked door of a closet and saw something that could identify them. If maybe you were the one who emptied out that safe."

"You just told me you didn't think that."

"No, but the killer will, and he's a professional. A trained assassin who knows how to dump a body in the Amstel or get in and out of a secured building without being seen."

I stare through the branches at the bodies bustling around the parking lot, saying tearful goodbyes, dropping into cars while, just beyond, a shallow mist has gathered like steam over the grazing field.

I turn back to the detective watching me with a solemn expression. "Like the man in the baseball cap, who I'm guessing was behind the tracker since he was with me in the tram. And two days ago, someone left a note in my mailbox. A warning note."

"What did it say?"

"That if they can find me so easily, then so can he. The person who wants the necklace. They told me to watch my back, that I'm not safe."

"They're right. You're not."

"If you're trying to scare me, Detective, it's working."

"What I'm trying to do is keep you safe." He pushes to a stand, his big body towering above mine. "Be aware of your surroundings. Trust your gut. Because two people are dead, and I'd really prefer you not be the third."

WILLOW

It takes an eternity to get out of the funeral home. The rows empty out one by excruciatingly slow one, a bottleneck of fidgety people jostling for the lobby and the promise of room-temperature wine and sweaty cheese blocks on toothpicks.

I stand behind Thomas in the center aisle, pinned in the swarm of people, and my legs are still wobbly with leftover adrenaline. When the news hit our phones like a string of tiny bombs going down the row, my first thought was of Sem. That he was hurt, or worse. I was scrambling for my cell when I saw the newsflash on Thomas's screen.

> Body of diamond trader linked to House of Prins found in Amstel River.

No name, no further details, but it was enough. My heart settled, the kicks morphing into a painful churning in my gut. A dead Prins trader, another death linked to the House. Whatever is going on here, it can't be good.

I lean my face into Thomas's shoulder and whisper, "Did the article say how long he was in there?"

There being the Amstel, the wide waterway that slices through the center of Amsterdam on its way to the River IJ. Big and busy enough that it's conceivable he landed in the water months ago, that his death was a boating accident, that he drowned. Prins is one of the largest diamond houses in the city. Lots of traders work with them. Maybe this death means nothing.

Thomas shakes his head, his muscles going rigid under the lambswool of his suit jacket. Not an answer to my question but a signal for me to stop talking. People are watching. They could hear. A funeral is neither the time nor the place to talk about a second dead body.

In the lobby, we make a quick pit stop at Xander's sister, who must have no idea of the animosity between her brother and Thomas, because she accepts our condolences with a warm hug. If any of the Prins family find it awkward that we're here, pretending to mourn the man they had patted down and escorted from the building only a week ago, you'd never know it by their heartfelt offers of sympathy. If nothing else, the Prinses' manners are impeccable.

Thomas and I are the first to make it outside.

"I don't think it's one of ours," he says, scrolling through the news clips on his phone. "It must have been an independent trader, but even then, I would have known if one of them went missing."

"Maybe he wasn't missing for that long," I suggest. "Or it could have been a foreign trader."

"Still weird I haven't heard *something*, even if it was only a rumor. Traders are a tight-knit group, a lot of them from families that have been in the business for generations." He shakes his head, thumb flicking on his iPhone screen. "The media's not giving me anything but the headline."

I think back to the words I saw on Thomas's screen: *Body of diamond trader linked to House of Prins found in Amstel River. Linked* could mean anything. The cousin of a trader who works for Prins, or a transaction that happened some twenty years ago. My thoughts spin, and I can't be the only one wondering. Social media will already be lit up by now, endless rambling theories of how the two deaths are connected, a slew of armchair detectives pointing their conspiracies back to the House. To Thomas, who may or may not have a 3D-printed gun.

One of the double doors pops open and out breezes Willem, his cellphone pressed to an ear. "I'm guessing this newsflash means you won't make tee time."

Arthur, I'm assuming. Willem's golf buddy and former fraternity brother, currently head of police for Amsterdam. Willem laughs at whatever he says, then turns for the parking lot, his wool overcoat flapping in his wake. Thomas hurries after his father like an obedient duckling, leaving me alone in the courtyard.

No, not alone. There's a cluster of smokers huddled against an ivy-covered wall, the press huddled up at the street, and a low murmur of voices talking nearby. I look around for who's speaking, but I don't see anyone else.

Anna files out the door next, along with the rest of the family: Fleur and the ever-agreeable Roland, the twins looking surly and bored. Roland peels off to bum a smoke, while Fleur and Anna scurry after Willem and Thomas. The twins and I exchange a look before slowly taking up the rear.

We're halfway across the parking lot when Yara wrinkles her perfect nose. "What is that smell?"

"It's shit," Esmée says, covering hers. "Oh, God, it's poisonous. This is why I only eat organic."

Esmée is the pretty twin, her skinny limbs draped in a white-collared dress that I'm pretty sure I saw hanging in the window at Prada, and I hate to tell her, but organic sheep shit stinks, too. The pasture bordering the lot is filled with them, a long stretch of green dotted with white and black balls of fluff. While tourists come for Amsterdam's canal houses and museums and coffee shops, this right here is the real Holland—miles and miles of reclaimed farmland crisscrossed with dikes and canals to hold in the livestock. The girls are right, though; it's poisonous.

We catch up to Fleur, her thumbs tapping furiously at her phone. "I've put out a few lines," she says, I'm guessing to Thomas, but he doesn't seem to be listening. His thumbs are working his phone, too. "So far nobody knows anything."

I look around for Willem and Anna, but they must have ducked into their car, the sleek Mercedes idling at the far end of the lot.

Thomas grunts. "Wait a minute. According to the *NRC*, his body was found two days ago."

"I need a name, Thomas. I can't make a move until you give me a name." She pauses, groaning. "Oh, shit. The AP is reporting it too, a diamond trader connected to House of Prins. Dammit. I need to get back to the office."

Yara comes up behind her mother, poking Fleur in the ribs. "Can we just go? I have hockey and this is taking *forever*."

"Yeah," her twin says halfheartedly. With the dark, delicate fabric and those big eyes draped in mascara, Esmée could easily pass for sixteen, but everything else about her is still twelve. She holds her phone high and blows a big pink bubble for the camera. Snapchat, I'm guessing. The twins are both obsessed.

Fleur's answer is aimed at Thomas. "Don't just stand there. *Do* something. Call Martin, see what he knows."

Thomas frowns. He doesn't like being ordered around, least of all by his sister. "Martin deals with dozens of diamond traders every day. He would have told me if any of them had fallen into the Amstel."

"Not if this guy wasn't Dutch. Maybe Martin just assumed he flew back home."

Thomas silently concedes the point and pulls up a number on his phone. I wonder briefly who this Martin is—an employee? an industry colleague?—but Thomas is already pressing the phone to his ear. I hear his friendly greeting as he walks away, his untroubled voice as he begins the call with chitchat, and the lightheartedness in his tone scoops out the underside of my belly. Thomas can be so contrived, so overly charming when he wants to be.

Esmée tugs on her mother's arm. "Mama, please. It's *freezing*."

Yara's gaze wanders to the field, her nose crinkling in disgust. "And those sheep need a bath. At least give us the car keys so we can wait where it's warm."

Esmée hooks a finger around the strap of Fleur's Dior bag and slides it from her shoulder. "Why did you make us come to this stupid thing? We didn't even know the dead guy."

Now, finally, Fleur looks up from her phone. "Because you and your sister are next in line. The future faces of House of Prins. Because one day, this company will belong to the two of you, and it's best to learn now that this job means taking on responsibility for every single staff member, even the ones you don't like very much. It means attending a lot of functions when you'd really rather stay home, and talking to a lot of people you don't know and don't *care* to know, but still treating them like they're your new best friends anyway. Because you are a Prins and people are watching, so you might as well get used to it now."

Esmée rolls her eyes, flipping open the bag. "Jeez, Ma. You make it sound so appealing."

Fleur returns to her phone, her thumbnails tap-tap-tapping away at the screen.

I clear my throat. "What about Sem?"

Fleur looks up, letting the silence stretch. She frowns like she just noticed me standing here, four feet away. "I'm sorry, what?"

"I said, what about Sem? Sem is next in line, too."

She gives me a tight smile. "Of course he is, but Yara and Esmée are older. They'll get there first. That's all I meant by it."

I press my lips together, my gaze wandering to Thomas pacing the spot two cars just left empty. He ends the call, sliding the phone into his pants pocket as he heads back our way.

"Martin saw the newsflash, too," he says, more to Fleur than to anyone else. "He's spent the past hour calling everyone we do business with. He's just as clueless as we are."

"Still. That doesn't mean—"

"It's Frederik." Willem announces the name in a voice so commanding, even the sheep at the dike raise their heads. He shuts the door to the Mercedes with a sharp pop that echoes over the field. "The media hasn't announced it yet, but it's Frederik Albers. He's the trader they pulled from the Amstel."

His words land like a bomb in the parking lot, which by now has mostly cleared, leaving only a few dark and silent cars and the smokers up by the sidewalk. Fleur curses under her breath. Thomas looks panicked.

Frederik Albers, who Thomas fired last year, whose name police found on an invoice for a low-light video surveillance system like the one in the Prins vault, and who just a few days ago Thomas threatened to kill. We were in a private board room at Willem's private social club, but still. It doesn't look good.

That makes two. Two former employees of House of Prins, two men fired by Thomas, both dead.

"Are you absolutely certain?" Fleur asks, whirling around to face her father, now coming across the lot. On the opposite side of the Mercedes, Anna stands in the open passenger's door, watching us across its gleaming roof.

"The dental records match up," Willem says. "Arthur's men are notifying the family now."

Thomas shoves a hand in his hair, making it stick up on one side. "Fuck. *Fuck*."

Fleur thrusts a hand at the twins. "Esmée, give me the keys. Now."

Esmée stands frozen, one arm still deep in her mother's Dior. "What about hockey practice?"

"Your father will call an Uber." Fleur's stabs the air with her hand. "*Give them to me.*"

Esmée hands over the bag, then turns to where her father is still standing by the ivy-covered wall, a cigarette clamped between two fingers. "Papa!"

"The coroner hasn't filed the report yet," Willem says, "but Arthur is pretty certain Frederik's body wasn't in the water all that long. They should have a window for time of death narrowed down by the end of today."

"Did he say if it's the same killer?" Fleur asks.

Willem lifts both hands. "Methodology is not the same, but Arthur says it's possible. We'll know more after they've analyzed the bullet."

At the last word, Fleur and Thomas exchange a look. Frederik was killed with a bullet, in a country where guns are illegal but can be built by a 3D printer. I stare at Thomas, whose face has gone ashen, and my thoughts tip into something darker.

Willem starts barking orders. "Girls, get your father to take you home. Anna, you take Willow. Thomas, Fleur and I will ride with you. We'll hammer out a strategy on the way. Let's go."

And because he's still the supreme authority where House of Prins is concerned, his words set everyone in motion. The girls shriek for their father, who flicks his butt in a ditch. Anna hustles around the idling Mercedes for the driver's seat. Fleur and Willem pile into Thomas's BMW and slam the doors. Thomas follows behind, then stops halfway there, pivoting on his heels toward me. Almost like I'm an afterthought, which of course I am.

"You going to be okay?"

I nod.

"I don't know how long I'll be."

I do. News like this means Thomas won't be home anytime soon. I don't tell him that I'm used to it.

"It's fine. Do what you have to do. I'll be fine." I always am.

He gives me a brusque nod. "I promised Sem I'd be home for bedtime. Tell him I'll take him to school tomorrow instead."

"Tomorrow's Saturday."

"Tell him I'll make him breakfast, then."

My heart twists for Sem, who will be crushed. He won't understand, but I promise to tell him anyway.

Thomas watches me for another second or two, and just when I think he's about to turn to leave, he steps closer and drops a kiss on my lips instead, one that's lightning quick and perfunctory. Not a good kiss but a kiss nonetheless, and my eyes burn with the sudden shock of it, with nostalgia, along with the knowledge that this kiss wasn't for me. It was for his mother, watching from behind the windshield of her car.

And then just as suddenly he's gone, taking off at a brisk jog toward his father and sister waiting in the car. I step backward and give him plenty of room to back out, following the glow of his taillights as he swings the car around and points it to the street. I don't turn to Anna, not yet. I don't want her to see my tears.

He's pulling out when I spot her across the lot, a redhead in a giant puffy coat and black boots, pushing through a wall of willow branches. They swing behind her like a beaded curtain, long and graceful, and it's her. It's Rayna D.

"*Kom je*?" Anna says—*Are you coming?*—and her voice snaps me out of the spell. I tear my gaze away from Rayna and look at Anna behind the rolled-down window of her Mercedes, stretched out alongside me. "If we're going to beat the traffic, we need to leave now."

I look back to Rayna, still standing in front of the weeping willow. Frozen at the edge of the gravel, staring me down.

I shake my head at my mother-in-law. "Thanks, but I think I'll take the train."

RAYNA

The woman from the park stares at me with a bold, almost aggressive gaze, looking every bit the Prins. Fur-trimmed coat, knee-high suede boots, red soles peeking out from skyscraper heels. It's such a different look than the first time I saw her, barefaced and hair blowing all around, her puffy coat streaked with dog hair and mud. It took me a minute to make the connection.

She comes at me across the pavement, holding out a hand. "It's beyond time we made the official introductions, don't you think? I'm Willow Prins. Sorry I didn't introduce myself the first time."

My gaze dips to her outstretched hand, the smattering of diamonds sitting on multiple fingers. When I don't reach for it, she tucks it in the pocket of her coat.

"So why didn't you?" I ask.

She gives me a smile, one that's at the same time warm and self-deprecating. "Because what was I going to say? Hey, you're the girl who found my husband's business partner dead on the floor. Want to grab a coffee sometime?" She tucks a lock of hair behind a delicate ear, a gesture that makes her seem nervous. "That would've been weird."

"As if this isn't."

Willow laughs like I'm joking, which I'm decidedly not. It's beyond weird, standing here, outside of Xander's funeral, talking to this woman who knows who I am. My tragic connection to her family. She knew it when she sidled up to the bench I was stretching against to ask if I'd seen her dog's ball, and she knows it now.

"Did you follow me to the park?"

Her eyes go wide at the suggestion, and she gives a firm shake of her head. "No. I swear. You can ask Sem. My son. He and I go there all the time with Ollie, the dog you saw. He'll tell you that grass field is our spot." She pauses, gazing up the street her family just drove down when they left her here in a cloud of exhaust. "But when I spoke to you, I *did* know who you were. I mean, obviously. Xander was an associate of the House and a friend. I recognized you from the pictures online. I've been following this story from the beginning."

Her and everybody else on the planet. Last time I looked, that picture was still everywhere, and now there are plenty of others floating around the internet, as well. Me, pushing through the reporters outside my door, hustling down the street as they shout my name, ducking into stores and behind buildings. I'm not all that great at math, but with dozens of pictures and clips of me floating around every social media site in a country of only seventeen million, the odds are good the killer has seen me, too.

"Those people you were with," I say, "the ones who just drove off in the fancy cars . . ."

Willow glances down the empty road, then turns back with a nod. "My husband, Thomas. His parents and sister. Her family."

Pretty, privileged people, born and bred Prinses who, despite this woman's designer clothes, don't fit her somehow. The way they bustled around the parking lot, all that urgency and self-importance, the way her husband kissed her, with his arms hanging stiffly at his sides, before he raced off and left her alone. Her face as she watched him drive off, with such obvious hurt and longing. I barely know this woman, but I saw it, and yet her own husband can't.

"They seem like real gems."

Willow snorts, her dark hair moving like liquid over her shoulders. "That's one way to put it. They certainly think of themselves as the diamonds they're so proud of peddling."

"They left you here."

Willow doesn't seem all that torn up about it. She shrugs, the fur of her collar tickling her earlobes. "Diamond business. I'm used to it, unfortunately."

A sudden and icy wind blows across the lot, stirring up leaves and tugging at our hair and clothes, and Willow points to dark clouds gathering above the field. Typical Dutch weather, and why no matter the temperature, the terraces fill up the second the sun shines because heaven forbid you miss a single ray.

"I'm headed to the train station. You?"

For a second or two, I consider denying it. The station is a good fifteen-minute walk plus another twenty on the train, and I'm not sure I want to commit to that much time in this woman's company.

But those storm clouds . . . My coat has a hood, but I didn't think to bring an umbrella—always a mistake in a country with weather as fickle as this one. I'd really love to make it to the station before the sky starts dumping rain.

In the end, I just shrug. "Lead the way."

It takes her a second or two to tap in the coordinates on Google Maps, then she points us away from the sheep and back toward town.

"Listen," she says once the two of us have fallen into stride, "I'm in a weird position here. Not that any of this is about me, of course. It's about you and Xander and the tragedy you witnessed—"

"I didn't witness anything."

"You didn't see the killer? You can't identify him at all?"

"No. I slept through the whole thing."

"Still. You were there, in his penthouse when Xander was killed, which means no matter how innocent you may be of any wrongdoing, you *were* involved. Sorry to say it, but that makes you a target."

I pause to let a dusty Fiat pass by before we cross the otherwise empty street. Two-story row homes rise up on both sides, ugly yellow brick facades with lace-covered windows and overplanted front yards the size of a postage stamp. Such a far cry from the majestic buildings that line Amsterdam's canals, it feels like we're in a different country.

"The detective told me much the same, but I don't have the necklace and neither does he. It's missing, along with whatever else was in Xander's safe. I'm kind of assuming the killer has it."

"Even if that's true, what about all the other people who've seen that picture of you wearing a necklace worth half a million euros? And by now, let me tell you, plenty have. Do you know what they're thinking? I'll tell you what they're thinking, that you might be an easy way to score some diamonds."

"But I don't *have* any."

"That's actually worse." She shoots me an apologetic wince. "Sorry, but it's true. At least with diamonds in your back pocket, you'd have some leverage. Something to barter for your life."

A coiling sense of dread throbs in the pit of my stomach. All this time I've been so focused on proclaiming my innocence—I didn't hurt Xander, I didn't steal his diamonds—that I haven't allowed myself to think very hard about the implications. Say someone confronts me. Say they hold a knife to my throat or a gun to my head, then what? Willow is right. They're not going to believe I didn't swipe a diamond or two just because I say so. I would be better off with diamonds to use as leverage.

A sentiment very similar to the one in that note. *I hope for your sake you have the necklace.*

I stop dead in the center of a two-lane street. A bike zooms by, a mother with a kid of around seven or eight standing on the back rack, his hands resting lightly on her shoulders. By now, I'm used to all the precarious ways people ride their bikes in this country—without helmets and at top speeds—but a kid balancing on the back of one like he's some kind of tightrope walker is a new one for me.

But it must not be for Willow, because she doesn't so much as bat an eye. She just waits for it to pass, then steps onto the sidewalk on the other side.

"You wrote the note, didn't you?"

Willow turns around, frowning at me across the bike lane. "What note?" Her expression is practically theatric.

"The note, Willow. Oh my God, you *were* following me. It's how you knew my running route, which house I lived in, which mail slot to drop that note into. Because you've been following me around town."

"Get out of the street, Rayna."

Up at the light, a car slides into the intersection, then rolls to a stop. The driver taps his horn, three staccato beeps in quick succession. My feet stay planted to the pavement.

"What about the tracker? Was that yours, too? And the break-in?"

Her eyes go wide. "Someone broke in to your house? When?"

"Tell me."

The car honks again, longer this time, and she hustles into the street, grabs me by the wrist, and drags me to the curb.

"No, Rayna. I didn't track you. I didn't have to. But I did leave you that note."

I wrench my arm out of her grip. "How did you find me?"

"Have you Googled yourself lately? Or done an image search on the picture that's currently breaking the Dutch internet? Because you may have locked your socials down, but there are still plenty of screenshots of you, flitting around the streets of Amsterdam. Anybody who knows anything about this city can point to the exact spot on the map where they were taken, and anybody who doesn't can check the geotag. Ever heard of it? Geotags have meta-data that's specific to locations, a geographic—"

"I know what a geotag is."

The sky starts spitting water, fat, freezing raindrops that splatter the pavement, the parked cars, our clothes, and skin. The wind is picking up, too. I know what those frigid gusts mean, and so does Willow. She checks the map, then gestures for me to follow her further up the street.

"The point is, I found you in like five minutes flat."

"And the park?"

Her gaze flits away for a second or two, then lands dead on mine. "Okay, fine. I may have planted myself in your path, but I swear to you—I *swear*—it's only because I wanted to see you face-to-face. To look you in the eye and see if all those things people are saying about you online are true."

"And?"

"And I think you're telling the truth. I do. I think you are an innocent bystander in another man's tragedy, but you should know that doesn't mean you're off the hook. Xander's killer is still out there. If he didn't already know you were asleep in Xander's bed when he came through there, he does now. And I'm pretty sure he knows where you live."

An icy shiver dances down my spine. I think about the break-in, and Willow is right. I've made myself far too easy to find.

Still.

"*Why*, though?" I ask. "You don't know me. You don't know anything about me. Why do you care?"

"Because Xander worked for my husband. He was a friend." She pauses to frown. "Was he a friend? I don't know. He was self-absorbed and cared way too much about what other people thought of him, and his behavior rode the knife edge of what is socially and morally acceptable. We bickered like siblings. He drove me up an absolute tree. But he was also exceptionally kind."

A sudden sadness pings me in the center of the chest. "*So* kind. When we were texting, I mentioned in passing that I'd murder for some Nerds Gummy Clusters, and he brought a pack on the date. He got them at that store on the Leidsestraat. He hadn't even met me yet and he went to all that trouble."

Willow looks over with a smile. "That sounds exactly like something he'd do. Last year, he sent me flowers on Mother's Day after I told him I don't have the best relationship with mine. He learned sign language so he could crack jokes with my son. As annoying as his behavior could be, he made up for it in a million little ways. I'm going to miss the guy."

I nod. "Me, too."

"So anyway, after I spoke to you in the park, my curiosity morphed into concern. I wanted to make sure you understood the danger you were in. I'd hate for what happened to Xander to happen to you, too."

We walk in silence for a bit while I try to process all this. Try to process Willow tracking me down, following me around town, leaving me notes of warning simply because she was concerned for a stranger's safety. If it were the other way around, would I have done the same thing? Would I have worried for her?

Maybe. It's possible.

Because suddenly I'm thinking about the time I trailed two Americans around the Albert Heijn simply because hearing their chatter felt like home. Or when I introduced myself to some random lady on the street simply because she was holding a copy of *USA Today*. Maybe I'm lonely in my new expat life, but there's a spark of truth in Willow's words. There's something about meeting a fellow American so far from home that conjures an instant and automatic connection.

"Lemme ask you this," I say as a raindrop smacks me in the forehead. I flip up my hood and wipe it away with a sleeve. "If you were me, what would you do?"

"Hire security. But assuming you can't afford that . . ." She pauses, looking over just long enough for me to shake my head. "I don't know. Be really, really careful, I guess."

Her words echo Detective Boomsma's parting shot: *Two people are dead, and I'd really prefer you not be the third.* I think of the man in the ball cap and beanie who's found me twice now, and helplessness presses down on me like a hot, lead blanket.

Suddenly, the skies open up, dropping icy rain on our heads in a solid, soaking sheet. Willow squeals and takes off for the first shelter she sees, a café across the street with an awning just big enough to cover a sliver of sidewalk. I race behind, dodging the puddles and bikes and parked cars.

We press ourselves to the building for a second or two, shivering and watching the downpour, then Willow points a finger at the door. "Drink?"

"God, yes."

WILLOW

Everything about Rayna is a surprise. Seeing her step out from that curtain of branches outside Xander's funeral, the shock mingling with fear on her face when I told her I found her in five minutes flat, her enthusiastic yes when I asked if she wanted a drink. We've been here all of twenty minutes, and already, she's on her third glass of wine.

"I've never seen a dead person before, and Xander was . . ." She winces, her entire body giving a hard shudder. "His neck. His hand. Every time I close my eyes, I see him just . . . lying there."

I think back to the articles I've read, the gruesome descriptions of the zip tie wrapped around his neck. I don't remember reading anything about his hand.

"What happened to Xander's hand?"

She leans into the table, too tipsy to bother to lower her voice. "His finger was gone, Willow. They chopped it off, presumably to get in the safe. It worked on biometrics."

My stomach twists, and I try not to picture it. The image is too awful to even contemplate.

But also, why? Xander's safe has a fingerprint pad, yes, but it also opens with a code. Did Xander change it? Did he refuse to cough it up for the killer? A safe full of stolen lab-growns hardly seems worth losing your life trying to protect.

"I know," she says at the look on my face. "It's the stuff of nightmares. I probably should get some therapy."

I blow out a breath, leaning into the table like she does, mimicking her body language. "And you didn't hear *anything*?"

"Not a peep. I'm assuming that's what saved me, that the killer didn't know I was there."

I nod because she's not wrong. If Rayna had stumbled out of bed at the noise, if she'd followed it into the bathroom and witnessed Xander in his death throes, there would have been two funerals today, not one.

"Xander was stealing from the House, apparently. One of the Asian labs was sneaking extra diamonds into their shipments for him to sell under the table. I don't know much more than that, only that my husband fired him the night of the murder. Don't go spreading that around, by the way. The timing doesn't look great."

A smarter part of me knows that I've probably said too much, and maybe it's the wine on an otherwise empty stomach, but the words came out before I can stop them.

She gives me a look like she did in that parking lot, filled with distrust.

"It's true, Rayna, I swear, and that's not even all of it. Six months after he came on board, the Cullinans disappeared from the vault. Six months after that, he was murdered in his shower, and now a diamond trader was found in the Amstel with a bullet in his head. You see why I had to warn you, right? Xander was caught up in something bad. Something that got him killed."

My words seem to do the trick. She blinks at me, and her frown dissolves, her expression changing from wariness to resignation in a split second. She picks up her glass, then just as quickly puts it back down with a hard *thwack*. "Jesus. I sure know how to pick them, don't I? A thief and a black market criminal. I mean . . . what the hell?"

"Don't beat yourself up about it. I know what a charmer Xander could be. He fooled a lot of people, my husband included."

It's shocking, actually, how long it took for Thomas to figure this out. I knew it the second I laid eyes on the man, when he rolled up to his own welcome party in a vintage Aston Martin and a Gucci suit. The hotshot gemologist Thomas lured from abroad to save the House from itself.

"I'm not savvy, as evidenced by . . . well, my whole entire life. And sorry, but . . ." She bites the inside of her lip, regarding me over the table. "Doesn't that make you nervous?"

"Which part?"

"That there are two dead men. First Xander and now the trader. Two murders, both connected to the House of Prins. The detective told me the trader was shot in the head in the same breath he said Xander had a gun. A 3D-printed one, apparently. The detective asked me if I'd seen it."

I sit up straighter in my chair. Xander had a 3D-printed gun. Thomas had instructions for a 3D-printed gun on his desk. According to Fleur, he claimed he found the papers on the printer. Could it really be that simple?

Rayna frowns. "What?"

"It's just . . . Fleur asked me if Thomas had one. She said she found instructions on how to print a gun on Thomas's desk and asked me if I'd seen it."

"Willow, why does your husband need a gun?"

"I don't know. Why does anyone need a gun?"

"Maybe because he's scared."

"Scared the scandal will impact his precious diamond house, you mean. That's why they all ran off and left me like they did. After the newsflash about Frederik, they had to rush back to the office to do damage control." I pick up my wine, my finger tapping the glass. "And there's no gun. I've searched the house. If my husband owns one, 3D printed or otherwise, it's not under our roof."

"Still. That's an awful lot of hypothetical guns floating around in a country where they're highly illegal."

"Tell me about it." I glance at the people around us, the couple at the next table, the group of women huddled around the fireplace, the waiter carrying a loaded-down tray on his fingertips. None of them are listening, but I lean into the table anyway. "I really wish you had some of those missing diamonds."

"Me, too. Though I don't think the man in the baseball cap will see it that way. Even if—"

"Hang on." Two words ping me like a tuning fork, and I sit up straighter on my chair. "What man in the baseball cap?"

"I've seen him twice now, first in a baseball cap and the second time in a beanie. I noticed him because I'd just found a tracker in my bag and there was something about the way he was watching me, the smile he gave when I shook him off, almost like a touché. It was creepy."

"I don't know if it means anything, but Xander said a guy in a ball cap was following him, too."

Her face blanches. "I think it must mean something. Don't you?"

My skin goes warm, and I think back to what I told Xander that night—*that description could fit a million men in this country, a ball cap means nothing, stop being paranoid.*

Except it definitely means something. I nod. "I wish I didn't, but I do."

"Well, shit. Now I really wish I had some of Xander's diamonds."

"What about the necklace?"

She frowns. "What about it?"

"You really don't have it?" Her frown deepens and I quickly add, "That guy who's tracking you around town? He's assuming you do. You realize that, right?"

I don't say what I'm really thinking, that any man who would kill Xander for the diamonds in his safe wouldn't hesitate to do the same to Rayna. It's why she's still alive right now, why baseball cap man hasn't slipped a zip tie around her neck and pulled it tight just yet, because he's hoping she'll lead him to the diamonds.

"But I don't. Somebody's already searched my apartment for it. The necklace is not there. I don't have it."

She doesn't blink as she says it, doesn't look away, doesn't shift in her chair, doesn't squirm or fidget at all. The truth, then. Rayna doesn't have the necklace. This is not the greatest news for either of us.

That necklace I've been seeing all over the news. I want those diamonds too.

"You should probably find another place to stay," I say, but I don't offer up my guest room because what would I say? How would I explain it to Thomas, to Martina? I don't need either one of them analyzing my invitation, why I've chosen to bring the woman the press has positioned as Xander's killer into our home. It would summon up too many questions.

Rayna frowns. "The detective told me to stay put. He's ordered extra patrols, and he says my street has more cameras than any other in Amsterdam." She studies my face, and the lines in her forehead deepen. "You don't agree?"

I shake my head. "If I were you, I'd disappear for a while. Just until things settle."

She falls back in her chair, her expression crumpling. "I wouldn't have the slightest idea how to disappear in this country. I don't speak the language. I'm still learning how things work. And I'd need a thick wad of cash—cash that I don't have—to even try."

"The last one I can help you with. All we need is an ATM."

"Willow. I can't ask you to do that. I have no idea how I'd pay you back, or when. It would take me *years.* Though I'd probably feel better if I could get my hands on a gun."

"I can help you with that, too."

We fall silent then, the gravity of the conversation hitting us both in a warm, boozy rush. Rayna would feel better with a gun. She's an innocent bystander in all this, and now she wants a weapon, a deadly kind of protection. I think of Xander's killer tracking Rayna around town, of Willem saying that Arthur's men would *deal with her* somehow, and she definitely needs a gun.

"Let me ask you this," she says. "What does your husband think happened? Who does he think killed Xander?"

"Who the hell knows? Thomas doesn't talk to me. We're not exactly on the same page these days. I'm pretty sure he's having an affair."

Once again, the words fling themselves off my tongue before I can stop them. The wine and the warmth and Rayna watching me with that scrunched brow—it's doing something to me, and it's not like I have anyone else to say it to. The friends I've made here know me as a Prins, and they all have some kind of tie to Thomas—husbands who've known him since college days, the female halves of couples we see socially. Rayna has never met Thomas or his family, and it feels good, telling someone. Telling her.

"I don't have proof," I say, "not yet at least, but a woman knows these things."

"Do we, though? Because I sure didn't."

"Well, I do, and I'll tell you something else." My cell buzzes against the table, but I ignore it. "If there's another woman in his life, if he wants to be with her, then he needs to just come out and say it. Stop sneaking around. Stop lying about where he is and who he's with. Who he loves. Because I'm not the kind of person who can just . . . close my eyes to it. I'm not the kind of wife who can keep acting like nothing is wrong, like I haven't noticed that he's checked out. Spiritually, emotionally, mentally. That his love has just . . . drained away."

I say these things and I feel it all over again, the anger I felt when I spotted him coming out of the Conservatorium Hotel, the restless sense of urgency his betrayal has injected into my chest, my blood, my bones. I am married to a man who still comes home every night, still sleeps inches away from me in bed, still eats meals across the table and reads books beside me on the couch, still smiles and laughs and kisses me, but only when his mother is watching.

"Jesus, Willow, I'm so sorry." She backtracks with a shake of her head. "I always hated when people said that to me when my marriage imploded. *I'm sorry* implied that they pitied me, and Lord knows I was pitiful, but I didn't want their pity. Pity just pissed me off even more than I already was. But I say it now to you because what you're describing—I've been there and it's awful."

"You want to know the worst part? I kinda get it. I'm a totally different person than when we first met. I'm living in a country that is not my own, trying to express myself in a language that ties my tongue and makes it easier for me to say nothing at all. My four-year-old son has a better vocabulary than I do. Do you know how much smarter I am in English? How much funnier? Thomas has no idea. His family has no idea. They think I'm an idiot and a bore, and why wouldn't they? Of course my husband fell out of love with me. I wouldn't love me anymore, either."

She gives me a closed-lipped smile, commiseration mixed with comfort. "I'm sure that's not true."

"Which part?"

"All of it. There's a reason your husband chose you."

"You're right. There is. Because I got pregnant. Ours was a classic shotgun wedding, not that Thomas ever gave any indication he wasn't thrilled by the news. He's a better person than that. But before he chose me, like *really* chose me, he chose Sem."

At the thought of Sem, my body vibrates in my seat, my bones threatening to bust out of my skin. From the moment those two pink lines appeared on the stick, every decision I've made has been for Sem. Holding him inside, carrying him to term, keeping him alive. When people hear my story, they point to Sem as my golden ticket, and I suppose he was in a lot of ways. They think I'm a gold digger, when nothing could be further from the truth.

Rayna is quiet for a long while. "I should probably preface what I'm about to say with the fact that I'm the last person on the planet you should be listening to when it comes to relationship advice. But I've been to a lot of therapy, so I have a pretty decent idea of what a therapist would say to you right now, and that's that you can only be in charge of your half of the relationship. You can't carry the whole thing all on your own. You can't make another person participate or reciprocate. The only thing you can do is decide if you want to be with someone who isn't giving you one hundred percent."

"Thank you. But it's not that simple."

"Because of the money?"

"Because of the money, because of Sem's health, because I'm stuck here either way. But mostly because of Sem." My cell buzzes again, and this time, I glance at the screen and see I've missed multiple texts from Martina. A familiar worry pounds in my chest, and I snatch up my phone and start scrolling. "Oh, shit. Sem's not eaten all day, and now he's complaining of a headache."

"The flu?"

"Maybe, but Sem has cochlear implants. Anytime he complains of ear or head pain, it freaks me the hell out." I pull a fifty from my wallet and toss it to the table, batting away Rayna's hands as she scrambles for her wallet. "It's on me. Also, screw the train. Let's Uber back."

"Easy for you to say. You're rolling in dough."

"I have *access* to dough. Not at all the same thing. But you're right. Uber's on me, too." I pull up the app on my phone and request a black car. As soon as we're assigned a driver, I drop the phone in my bag. "Six minutes. And about that gun."

"Which one?"

"The one I can help you get."

"Oh, my God, Willow," she says, panic creeping into her voice. "I thought you were kidding. Are you serious right now? You really think I should get a *gun*?"

I stay quiet, holding her gaze, and my silence is not an answer, and yet at the same time, it is. Yes, Rayna needs a gun. Yes, I'm completely serious.

And not a gun that's like Xander's diamonds, grown with enough fire and hardness to fool people into believing it's the real thing. Only an idiot or a half ass would settle for a gun printed with plastic. Rayna needs a *real* gun, one made out of steel and that uses metal bullets.

"Okay . . . now I'm really freaked out." She drains the last of the wine from her glass and pushes to a stand. "And even if I agreed with you, which I'm still not certain I do, I wouldn't have the first idea where to get one."

"Well, let me know, because if there's one thing I've learned by becoming a Prins, it's that money opens all sorts of doors. Even illegal ones." I stand, shoving my arms into the sleeves of my coat. "Actually, especially those."

RAYNA

I spend the rest of the weekend in my sad, beige room, catching up on the work I've let slide since Xander's death put a target on my back. On Saturday, Ingrid packed a bag and fled to her parents' house, leaving me alone and my nerves jangling, my body jumping at every noise. The jarring ding of the bell from someone down on the street, the sound of footsteps coming up the stairs, a dog's incessant barking in an apartment below.

And all weekend long, Willow's words ring in my ears.

You need a gun, one that's not printed out of plastic.

After the detective told me about the second murder, after his questions shifted in tone to imply that whoever killed Xander will be coming after me next, I have to admit it's not the worst idea.

A gun, a real, metal, *highly illegal* gun. I think about her offer all weekend, but really, I don't need that long. The last straw comes Sunday evening, as I'm sorting clothes in front of the washing machine at the far end of the hall.

I'm shaking out a pile of laundry, shoving the whites into the machine when something goes flying. A flash of metal that hits the wall before it disappears under the machine. An earring? A coin? I don't have all that many of either, so I drop to my hands and knees and peer under the washer, but the hallway is too dark, the floor far too dirty. All I see is a thick field of dust bunnies.

I fetch a clothes hanger from the wardrobe in my room and use it to scoop everything out. The dust bunnies. A filthy sports sock with a hole in the toe. A million tiny pellets of what looks suspiciously like mouse droppings.

And another tracker. An identical match to the one I found in my bag.

I hold it in my palm, and it sizzles the skin because I know what it means. It means that first tracker, the one I shoved under my seat on the tram, wasn't a fluke. It wasn't dropped in my bag by accident. It's absolute, irrefutable proof that someone is following me, and I led them right to where I live.

I do a quick and frantic search through the rest of the clothing in the pile. I turn each piece inside out and give it a good shake, feeling every pocket and around every hem. Another tracker drops from the back pocket of my favorite jeans, pinging me in the toe.

I leave the laundry in a messy pile and return to my room, turning everything upside down and inside out, ransacking the place like a tornado. I peel off the bedding and flip the mattress up against the wall. I dump out drawers and move the furniture around to get underneath, running my fingers along every floorboard and crack. I roll the carpet into the hall and upend my suitcase and peer into the dark corners of the wardrobe. I shake out every book and bag and piece of clothing I own.

In the end, I find four more. One in my backpack, another in my purse, two more tucked in the pockets of my coats, including the one I wore to Xander's funeral. I line the trackers up on my dresser, thinking about how whoever is behind them got close enough to drop these things in my bags and clothing. The idea makes me dizzy with dread.

I rummage through the mess for my phone and text Willow.

Yes to what we talked about. Found more trackers in my stuff.

Within seconds, she marks the message with a !!, and another second after that, the phone rings.

"Holy shit," she says by way of hello, and I fall back onto the bed, filling her in.

"Six, Willow. Two of them in my coats, which means they know everywhere I've been since I don't know how long, including my apartment. I need that . . . *item* we talked about."

"Yes, you do." She's smart enough not to say the word out loud.

"How fast can you get one? How much?"

"Give me a day or two, and I'm guessing under a thousand."

I don't want to think about what a thousand-euro hole will do to my already tight budget, but I also can't say no. I stare at the trackers on my dresser, and this doesn't seem like the time to tighten the money belt. I need a weapon to protect myself no matter how much it costs.

"Okay. Thank you. Truly."

Willow must hear the worry in my voice because hers softens. "Don't worry about price. Pay me back whenever you can. I'll call you as soon as I've got something."

I thank her again, and we hang up.

I check the time—almost seven, then pull up the number for the detective. He's not going to like that I'm calling him after hours again, but I'm not going to make the same mistake twice. I need to get those trackers out of my house and into his hands, so he can tell me whose head I should point that gun at.

"Arie Boomsma."

"Me again. I found some more trackers. Six, to be precise. They were in my things. I have no idea how long they've been there."

"Where are you?"

"At home. They definitely know where I live."

"I'm on my way. Give me fifteen minutes." He hangs up before I can respond.

Fifteen minutes to jump out of my skin at every voice outside, at every moan and creak and door slam in the stairwell. The whole time, the detective's words scream through my head. *Two people are dead, and I'd really prefer you not be the third.*

I'd really prefer that, too.

I pace the apartment, and maybe it's the mess, or the building's slanted walls and low-lying ceilings sitting directly under the roofline, but I want to crawl out of my skin. There's only one way out of an apartment at the tippy-top of a stairwell, and it's the same way the killer would use to get in. My room, already cramped and claustrophobic, feels like a death sentence. I can't stay here another second.

A buzzer rips the air, and I squeal, checking the clock. Thirteen and a half minutes since the detective hung up on me, but there's no video on the door buzzer system, no way to see if it's the detective or one of the reporters or worse, an armed killer, and I can't stay here another second. I grab my bag and the trackers from my dresser, snatch my keys and coat from the hook, and make the long trek down the stairs.

I'm coming to the ground floor when I see him, the detective's face peering through the frosted window at the top of the door. I spot the cluster of reporters behind him, their words tumbling over each other as they jostle for a prime spot. Detective Boomsma turns and barks something sharp, and they shut up. Telling them to back off, I'm guessing.

I scurry down the last few steps and conceal myself behind the door. But they must know it's me on the other side, because the questions start up the second I crack the door.

Rayna, Rayna! Did you really spray-paint the walls of your ex-husband's home?

Take a baseball bat to his car windows?

Make a bonfire of his designer shoes and custom suits on the lawn?

Yeses across the board. His artwork, his watches and expensive clothes, the lead glass windows he imported from some stupid chateau in France, all destroyed. And screw it, I'll just say it: ruining all his most precious things felt so damn good. It felt better than sex, definitely better than any orgasm Barry had ever given me, which were mediocre and clumsy at best. It felt like payback for the things he took from me.

My pride. My future. My former best friend.

The second the detective is inside, I slam the door in their faces, but not before they can fire off one more question.

How many nights did you spend in jail for assault?

I look up, returning the detective's stare. "The answer, for the record, is zero. I spent zero nights in jail, and it wasn't assault. It was disorderly conduct. That's an important legal distinction."

"You drove your husband and his fiancée off the road. You almost killed her."

I roll my eyes. "She broke a couple of bones. She's fine."

Even now, a year and some change removed from the incident, thinking about that day still fills me with red-hot shame. Seeing her BMW pulling out of my old neighborhood, chasing them down a country road, her surprise at looking over and seeing a hysterical me alongside her, gesticulating and screaming out the passenger's window. I didn't drive them off the road. I didn't even cross the center line; it was all her. She gave a nervous jerk of the wheel and *boom*—they were in a ditch. Thank God there was an eyewitness, a farmer plowing a nearby soybean field who saw the whole thing go down from the seat of his tractor. He saved me—well, him and my tearful apology in front of a judge.

It's also why, as furious as it makes me that Barry offered Dad a job, I can't really blame him for taking it. All those charges Barry filed, the mountain of legal bills, the look on my father's face when he posted my bail. My parents don't have that kind of money. They cleaned out their retirement account for me.

"That doesn't mean you didn't do any of those things the people out there are accusing you of," Detective Boomsma says, not all that unkindly. "It only means you got lucky."

I roll my eyes. "I spent six months on a pullout in my parents' basement and in an ankle bracelet. I walked away from a seven-year marriage with nothing, not one red cent. I hardly think any of that makes me lucky."

At the far end of the hall, a door swings open to reveal the nosiest of my neighbors, an elderly woman in a housedress and slippers. She and the detective have a brief conversation, a quick back and forth of guttural gibberish, and that's when I notice the rest of him. A pair of slim-cut slacks, a navy shirt peeking out from his leather coat, boots of dark brown suede. Even his hair has been tamed, finger-raked off his head. He smells nice, too, a mix of spice and leather. Not a kid's party this time.

The neighbor shuts the door. The detective turns back to me, and I hate the pity I see on his face. I shake my head, eager to talk about something else. *Anything* else.

"Sorry if I ruined your night. Which obviously I did. Sorry."

He waves it off with a grunt. "The trackers?" he says, and I drop them into his palm. "I'll take these to the lab tonight. It may be a day or two before I know anything. You're sure these are the only ones?"

"Pretty sure. I tore my room apart. Those six are the only ones I found. Do you think that's what whoever broke in was there for, to put trackers in my things?"

"It's certainly plausible."

"I remembered something else. Xander used a key fob to work the elevator. We couldn't get to his floor without it."

"Those fobs work via radio frequency, a technology that's particularly vulnerable to hacking. You don't even need access to the actual fob; you can copy it simply by proximity, through his pants pockets, for example, by sitting next to them on the train. All you need is a cloning device, which you can buy for €17.99 on bol.com."

"So what are you saying, that the killer hijacked his fob?"

"I'm saying it's a distinct possibility." His gaze dips to my coat, wedged under an arm, and my keys, clutched in a fist. "I hope you're not planning on going anywhere."

"Better than the alternative, waiting upstairs like some kind of sitting duck."

The detective slaps a hand to the door he just came through. "After the burglary upstairs, your neighbors all know not to buzz just anyone in, and you live on one of the most well-secured streets in all of Amsterdam. There's not a store on this street that doesn't have cameras watching every car and bike and pedestrian who goes by. My colleagues and I are watching, too."

"So you'll know what my killer looked like, then. Excellent."

The detective's expression softens. "I'll order some extra patrols and put a rush on the trackers. Just . . . stay inside. Go upstairs and lock the door. Don't let anyone inside."

I bite my lip, but my heart won't settle. The thought of sitting upstairs in that tiny apartment all night alone, of pressing my ear to the door so I can hear the ambush coming for me sends an uneasy feeling churning in my stomach. It's been building for days now, ever since the break-in and now, the trackers. Do I really want to go back up there? Even with all the cameras and the detective's extra patrols, do I feel safe? The answer is a hard no.

He reaches for the latch. "I'll call you as soon as I know anything."

There's a swell of voices, more shouted questions from the reporters as he steps outside, and for once, I'm glad for them. Those assholes might be trapping me inside, but at least they're keeping everybody else out, too. I'm steeling myself for a face-off with them when I hear my neighbor's door swing open behind me.

She smiles, says something to me in rapid-fire Dutch.

I shove my arms in my coat sleeves and give her an apologetic smile. "I'm sorry. I don't speak Dutch. I don't understand."

But she must be the only Dutch person on the planet who doesn't speak even a few words of English, because she keeps going, the loose skin of her neck quivering, her arms making a swooping motion.

I may not understand the words, but I understand the gesture. "You want me to come inside?"

She bobs her head in an enthusiastic nod, her wrinkly lips forming around a word so heavily accented that it takes me a couple of seconds to recognize it as English.

Alley. The woman said alley.

I hustle down the hallway and follow her inside.

Her apartment is furnished exactly like I would have expected, with faded floors and outdated fixtures and furniture of heavy, carved oak topped with what look like mini Persian rugs, the fringe hanging down the side. Her curtains are drawn, but I can hear the reporters just outside, their voices muffled by the glass.

"*Hufters,*" she says, flapping a dismissive hand in their direction, and from her expression, I'm assuming it's something bad.

She leads me down a narrow hallway and into a galley kitchen where time has stood still. Formica table, square white wall tiles, metal countertops, an ancient water heater hanging from the wall above the sink, a relic from the time of World War II.

And at the very back of the house, a door.

I step to it and push the curtains aside, peering out the window onto a courtyard the size of a postage stamp. My gaze trails over the moss-covered tiles topped with a plastic table with two matching chairs, over a collection of potted plants and colorful garden gnomes in various poses, to a wooden gate set in the back hedge.

The alley. I had no idea, and how could I? The window in my place is set too high on the slanted wall to see anything but sky. I'd need a ladder to even open it.

"Thank you," I say, whirling around. "*Dank u wel.* You are a lifesaver. Truly. You don't have any idea how amazing this is."

The neighbor beams and shoos me outside with another surge of Dutch, and with one last wave, I take off across the backyard. Slowly, I peel the door open and peek into the alley. Except for a bike parked a few houses down, it's blissfully empty.

I step into it and disappear into the night.

WILLOW

It's weird how I can't stop thinking about Rayna.

She's the first thing I thought of when I tugged a warm and sweaty Sem out of bed and into a pair of jeans and his favorite Ajax sweatshirt, wriggling socks onto his feet so the seam lay straight across the tops of his chubby toes. I thought about her as I was spreading peanut butter on his bread or apple slice, bribing him with the promise of a gummy bear for each gooey bite. Somewhere, not all that deep inside, I know it's too much, all this worry for a woman I just met and barely know, but I can't stop thinking about her. I can't stop thinking of her face when she told me about the gun.

Xander had a gun. Thomas had instructions to print a gun. Is it the same gun, or are there two guns floating around somewhere?

It's not in the house; I know that for a fact. By now it's Sunday evening and I've searched the place more times than I'd like to count, rifled through every closet and cubby and drawer, only to come up empty-handed. No 3D-printed gun, no shopping bag containing another cheap bauble, no scribbled note or receipt. Which means exactly nothing, other than that my husband is too smart to leave a paper trail. Whatever Thomas is hiding, whatever evidence there is of his secrets, he's not brought it into the house.

"Mama?" Sem says, digging a purple crayon from the box.

Sem and I are seated on the floor in the living room, coloring Paw Patrol pictures I printed from the internet. He's already in his pajamas, already clean and ready for bed. Cartoons flash on the flat-screen, the sounds mingling with those of Martina, cleaning up in the kitchen while Ollie hovers for scraps at her feet. On the other side of the big picture window, the outside lights have been on for hours already, turning the yard into a canvas of golden yellows and bright greens, a zigzagging trail of spotlights on bushes, trees, garden statues.

I pick up a blue crayon, start in on Chase's cap. "Yes, sweetie."

"When Floppy gets to come home with me, can we take him to the American bookstore?"

At that, I exchange the crayon for my glass of wine. Floppy is the stuffed bunny his class adopted at the beginning of the school year, a classroom "pet" they get to bring home in turns. The last time Floppy came home in Sem's book bag, Ollie chewed off one of his googly eyes, and Martina had to scour the booths that line the Albert Cuyp Market until she found one that matched. I was really hoping summer break would come sooner than Floppy's next sleepover.

"Sure. But when will that be?"

"I don't know, but Mama, *luister.*" *Listen.* He waves a hand in front of my face like I so often do with him. It's how I know what he's about to say is important. "I want a Floppy for my birthday. A *real* one."

A real bunny, one that will chew the fringe off Thomas's antique carpets and leave little pellets of shit like a trail of breadcrumbs through the house. There's no way Thomas will ever agree to a bunny, and yet I'm already thinking about where to get one. The mothers at school would know, or maybe Ollie's vet. I bury my nose in my glass of wine and wonder how long it will be before Thomas notices a pet bunny. I think of him coming out of the Conservatorium, the cheap trinket he hung for her on that bike, and I wonder if Sem and I will still be living here by the time his fifth birthday rolls around.

It's a depressing thought, one that beats like a swarm of frantic bats in my chest. I look around the room, at the furniture and the paintings and the silk rug under my butt. This house, Thomas's bank account, the way being a Prins opens doors I could never have opened on my own . . . When you've got every luxury you could ever wish for, it's too easy to forget that these things are not permanent. That nothing is.

I look over at my son, the tabs on his processor strap flapping behind his ears as he colors a chunk of brown dog. Up to $100,000 a pop, that's what those little suckers cost, and yes, insurance would have paid for all that back in the States, assuming I had some. But what about all the co-pays? The years of audiological rehab and mapping appointments and speech therapies that he *still* needs? I could never have afforded that all on my own. I needed Thomas to foot those bills—I *still* do.

Ollie is the first to hear it, the buzz of Thomas coming through the door. With a startled chuff, he sprints out of the kitchen for the door, his nails slipping against the marble in the hallway. Sem's eyes go wide with delighted surprise. Thomas hasn't made it home for dinner in . . . I can't remember how long.

"Papaaaaaaa!" Sem tosses down his crayons and jumps to his feet, racing out of the room.

I'm draining my wine when I realize it's not one set of adult footsteps coming down the hall, but two. Thomas and another man, a stranger in dark pants and a fitted shirt. He pauses in the doorway, his gaze taking in the coloring pages spread across the table, me sitting cross-legged on the floor, a bouquet of colorful crayons in a fist.

The man comes across the carpet to shake my hand. "Arie Boomsma. Sorry to disturb."

My heart gives a hard kick, then rolls into a rushing gallop. Boomsma. This is the detective Rayna mentioned, the one who's been questioning her. The one she talked to at the funeral. The one who told her about the gun.

I look to Thomas, trying to catch his eye, but he's studiously avoiding mine. Sem hangs on his legs like a monkey.

I dump the crayons onto the coffee table and push to a stand, willing my voice not to shake. "Willow Prins. *Aangenaam.*" Nice to meet you.

"Let's talk in my study, where it's quieter," Thomas says, and I realize with a start that I'm included in this conversation. This man is here to question *both* of us. Thomas drapes a hand over Sem's head, nudging him onto the floor. "Martina, will you get Sem to bed, please? We need a few minutes alone with our guest."

Martina comes bustling out of the kitchen. "Of course, of course. Go." She untangles Sem from Thomas's leg and shoos us in the direction of the stairs. I avoid her questioning gaze, though I won't be able to escape it later. Martina doesn't like what this after-hours visit means, either.

Silently, Thomas leads us upstairs to his study, a moody room on the back side of the house. Ebony wood paneling, thick rugs of gunmetal gray, heavy curtains on the windows that even during the daytime keep the room as dark and cool as a cave. He flips a switch by the door, and the lamps and wall sconces flicker to life.

He waves at the matching mohair chairs in front of his desk. "Detective Boomsma found something you need to see. Something that belongs to us."

I drop into the stool. "Okay."

My husband isn't the type of person to talk in riddles, so I have a pretty good idea what he means. *Something*, as in diamonds. The detective found diamonds, they belong to us, and they're somehow connected to a murder case. An icy tingling spreads over my skin like a thin layer of frost.

The detective sinks onto the chair next to mine, tugging a velvet bag from his jacket pocket. He turns it upside down over a hand, and something shiny and heavy drops into his palm. My gasp is loud in the quiet room.

It's my bracelet, the one Thomas snapped on my wrist that night back in the fall, right before taking the call that had him racing out of our anniversary dinner. I take in the wide band, the 25.62 carats of flawless diamonds set in neat clusters, and in the very center, the giant, eleven-carat Prins-cut stone.

I stare at it hard, as if just by looking, I could make it disappear. Xander's words echo through my head, the ones he said that night back in November: *I want to grow the shit out of that Cullinan.* And then Fleur's words, more recently at lunch: *Xander was obsessed with the Cullinans. Unbeknownst to Thomas, he planned to launch a lab-grown Cullinan collection.*

"Where did you get that?"

The detective leans back in his chair, his gaze bouncing from me to Thomas. "One of my officers found it in Xander's desk drawer. It was hidden in a box of staples and covered with a pile of papers, so it seems like he made at least some attempt to conceal it. It's probably why the thief missed it, because Xander hadn't stored it in the safe."

"But *how*?" Thomas says. "My wife has worn that piece only a handful of times."

He glances at me as he says it, and I nod even though we both know it's even less than that. I've worn it exactly four times—the night he gave it to me, Anna's birthday dinner at his parents' house, a benefit gala at the Waldorf Astoria, and some cocktail party at the Amsterdam Diamond Exchange. The bracelet is not the type of thing you throw on with a pair of jeans, or to take your kid to school. It lives in the safe more often than not. And every time, it was Thomas who pulled the piece from the velvet tray, not me. Look pretty and sport the bling—that is my job as spouse of a Prins.

Detective Boomsma's gaze flickers between us, landing finally on me. "I'd like to back up a bit. What was your relationship with Xander van der Vos?"

My mouth goes dry, and I wet my lips with my tongue. "Xander worked for Thomas. That's how I knew him. So I guess you could say it was a business relationship."

"You didn't see him socially."

"I saw him at social functions that had to do with Thomas's business. Industry parties, company events, things like that."

"And outside of these business functions?"

"This area of Amsterdam is fairly insular. I run into people all the time at the gym, in the stores, at restaurants. Xander included." I pause, choosing my next words carefully. "But it was never anything planned, if that's what you're asking."

"When is the last time you talked to him?"

His words feel like a trap. I didn't count how many times Xander called me in the days before his death, but it was a lot. Someone was following him. Listening in on his calls. Moving things around in his office, his home. Tilting the picture in front of the hidden safe in his study just to mess with him. And he was convinced that person was Thomas.

The detective watches me, waiting for an answer, and I can't lie. Even if Xander managed to delete the calls from his phone, the police would have requested the records from the cellphone company by now. He will have seen my number all over Xander's call log. My gut says he already knows about the calls—and if he doesn't, he will soon.

I give myself a moment to think. "I'd have to check my call logs to be sure, but probably a day or two before his death. He called me a lot that week. He seemed like he was dealing with something, honestly. He wasn't making a lot of sense."

Across the desk, Thomas's gaze drills into mine. "Xander was calling you? You didn't tell me that."

Because you're not the only one in this marriage with secrets. Because Xander wasn't the only one doing the talking. Because I said some things, too.

I lift a casual shoulder. "You know how Xander was. He was calling to complain about you, which I told him was entirely inappropriate and futile." I turn to the detective. "I don't work at the company. I hold no sway there, but it seemed like Xander needed to vent. I figured it was best to just . . . let him."

"And you?" Detective Boomsma says, turning to Thomas. "When was the last time you spoke with Xander?"

Thomas clears his throat. "The night he died. I called him from the factory."

"What time was the call?"

"Just after midnight." Thomas's answer is immediate. He doesn't pause to think about it, doesn't hesitate even a split second. He's probably thinking the same thing I did earlier, that there's no use denying it. The detective will already know this from Xander's call logs.

"That's awfully late to be calling an employee."

"True, but there were some issues at one of the Asian labs and they needed immediate sorting out."

"What kind of issues?"

"A shipment with more diamonds than we ordered, stones that were unaccounted for on the waybill. Things like that."

The detective swings an ankle onto his knee, trying to get comfortable in a chair that was built for a man half his size. "Real diamonds?"

"Lab-grown diamonds *are* real, Detective. They are optically, chemically, and physically identical to their mined counterparts, virtually indistinguishable from the stones miners pull from the dirt. The only difference is in how they're created, by pressure deep in the earth's mantle or by a scientist in a laboratory."

"But the diamonds we're currently talking about, these 'issues' you mentioned, they were with lab-grown diamonds?" He pauses for Thomas's nod. "And you thought Xander might be behind the mistake."

"It wasn't a mistake, Detective. It was fraud. The lab was sending two, three, sometimes four or more of the same stone but only listing one on the waybill, the same stone that would make its way into our inventory. The others disappeared into Xander's pocket."

"And you know this how?"

"Because it didn't happen with just one shipment, but many, and for who knows how long. You saw where Xander lived, in a building that commands the highest prices per square meter in all of Amsterdam. He drove a custom Bentley and owned a collection of art and watches that went far, far above his pay grade. He couldn't have afforded all those things, not with what I was paying him."

"So basically, you called to accuse him."

"No." Thomas clears his throat. "I called to fire him and tell him I'd be pressing charges."

"Interesting timing." The detective leans back in his chair with a loud creak. "Xander died before you could press charges, but you also didn't file a police report."

"I have a diamond house to protect, Detective. After the Cullinan theft and now these two murders, it seems prudent to just . . . accept the loss and move on."

Detective Boomsma scratches at a cheek. "I'll have my people take a closer look at Xander's financials, but if he's behind the scam with the Asian lab like you suspect, he was likely moving money around via nontraditional methods. Cash, hawala, Bitcoin. Those diamonds and whatever money he made selling them on the black market, it's likely untraceable."

Thomas gives him a resigned nod. "Like I said, it's best to put this behind us."

"But this bracelet." The detective taps a finger to the desk, rattling the links. "Are you absolutely certain yours is in the safe?"

Thomas looks to me for the answer, and I nod, then just as quickly shake my head. "I—I can't remember the last time I opened the safe, honestly. I don't go in there all that often."

It's one of the few things my mother-in-law can't detest about me, as much as she doesn't understand my unwillingness to let Thomas drape me in diamonds. The wife of a diamond heir who doesn't love the bling? Anna finds it utterly incomprehensible at the same time she secretly admires me for my modesty—a trait the Dutch love in spades. It's hard to accuse me of being a gold digger when the only diamond I ever wear consistently is my engagement ring.

Thomas flips on the desk lamp, a fluorescent jewelers light with built-in magnifying glass. He points to the bracelet. "May I?"

With a shrug, the detective pushes it across the desk.

"I made this bracelet, Detective. I built it with my own hands. I spent five months drawing it, first on paper, then with 3D renderings, printing the wax model, casting it with metal. None of our master jewelers helped me with this piece. I did all the work myself. I selected and set every one of the hundred and twenty-three stones, including the last remaining Cullinan." He taps the center stone then flips the bracelet over, holding it under the desk light. "See here? *For my wife on the occasion of our fifth anniversary.* This is it, Detective. This is the bracelet I made for her. A one-of-a-kind piece."

I press my lips together, staying silent. Yes, Thomas did all those things. He spent all those months tinkering away on the factory floor in order to build what is undeniably a masterpiece, a stunning swirl of hundreds of flawless diamonds. The result is a piece that belongs on a princess or in a museum, sitting on a velvet pillow behind a case of bulletproof glass. Not on an arm. Certainly not on *my* arm. The bracelet is so delicate, its stones far too priceless—and Detective Boomsma was just carrying it around in his pocket. Thomas is right; it is an absolute work of art.

If only it were a work of love.

But also, I didn't miss that word—3D. Thomas has a 3D printer at work. He used it to make this bracelet, and maybe a gun.

"How did it get from your safe to Xander's desk drawer?"

Thomas shakes his head. "Impossible. None of the house staff can open the safe. Only Willow and I know the code."

"And you're sure this is the one you made and not a copy."

Thomas pulls a loupe from his top desk drawer and peers through it at the largest of the stones. The Cullinan.

"Correct GIA certification number is engraved on the girdle." Thomas looks up, meeting the detective's gaze across the desk. "Though after the ten-carat fiasco, I'm sure I don't have to tell you it proves nothing. The other stones are engraved, as well. I'd have to check the numbers against the certs to see if they match up, but I'm guessing they will, too." He looks back at the bracelet through the loupe, freezes. Frowns. "Huh. Hang on."

Detective Boomsma leans forward on his chair. "What do you see?"

"The clasp on this bracelet is different than mine. Well, not different. It's the same clasp, but it's not. I engraved the inside of the original clasp with my initials. You only see it if you know where to look." Thomas looks up from the loupe, his gaze finding mine across the desk. "Willow, check the safe, will you?"

I nod and rise from my chair, taking my time moving through the rooms and into our closet, because I already know what I'll find. The original bracelet safe and sound in the vault, sitting on a navy velvet pillow. I wriggle it off the cushion and check the inside of the clasp. Thomas's initials are engraved into the side.

I carry it back to the study and place the bracelet on the desk, sinking silently back into my chair.

Detective Boomsma lays the two pieces side by side—an identical match, and not just to my eye. To Thomas's and the detective's too.

"Just so I understand," the detective says. "The bracelet in Xander's desk drawer is a copy."

Thomas nods. "It certainly looks that way. The renderings are saved on the Prins server. They're password protected, but Xander could have gotten to them somehow."

"And the stones?"

"Lab-growns, I'm guessing, though I'd have to take both pieces to the factory to be sure. Like I told you, lab-growns are identical to mined. I can't differentiate between the two with the naked eye or even a loupe. I need sophisticated equipment, advanced screening devices. Only a trained gemologist will be able to tell which is which."

A trained gemologist like Xander. He had access to all those screening devices, too.

"But you said the stones were marked?"

"When a diamond is graded by one of the big firms, Gemological Institute of America or the International Gemological Institute for example, its certification number is engraved on the diamond's girdle. This is for the customer's protection as well as for identification purposes in the event of theft or resale." Thomas picks up the loupe and holds it to the center stone on the replica bracelet. "Same cut and shape as the Cullinan, same microscopic inclusion on the crown near the girdle, too small to see with the naked eye.

I'd need to pull up the certification specs to pinpoint any differences, but from what I can see, these stones are identical." He lowers the bracelet, pulls the loupe away from his eye. "But I'd need to put both pieces through a screening at the factory to be sure."

Detective Boomsma nods, pushing to a stand. "Then let's go."

RAYNA

The alley dumps me onto the busy Hobbemastraat, bustling with the after-dinner crowd. I take a hard left, following the tram tracks along the northern end of the Vondelpark. At the gates, I pause for a swarm of bikers, silently blessing them as they pedal by.

"Are you *insane*?" Ingrid once said after I'd told her I took a short-cut through the park on the way home from the bars. "Unless you're a junkie or a rapist, nothing good happens in the park after dark. Don't go there. It's not safe."

I wonder if she's still at her parents' house on the eastern outskirts of the city, where she spent most of the weekend, if it was maybe to get away from me. Ingrid swears she's not mad, that she doesn't blame me for bringing in the thief who took her cash, but I'm not convinced she's telling the truth. Ever since the break-in, things between us have felt off, and I don't deny feeling a little annoyed she left me there all alone, an easy target at the top of the stairs. Especially now that I found more trackers.

The bikers disappear into the shadows, and I slide my phone from my pocket, pulling up Ingrid's number.

Stay away from the apartment. I found more trackers in my things.

The text lands as delivered but not read. I watch the screen for a few more seconds, and I'm about to click my phone off when it buzzes with an incoming text.

I'm headed to Café Luxembourg on the Spui, wanna meet up for a drink?

I'm more excited than I should be at Lars's invitation, mostly because it seems that Ingrid is ignoring me. I don't blame her, and honestly, I wouldn't mind some company. Nothing happened between me and Lars that first night we met, not even a kiss on the cheek as I slid off his bike, but he seems nice enough, and his regular check-ins always make me smile. If there's ever a night that I don't want to be alone, this is it.

My thumbs tick out a reply. Is it far from the Leidseplein? Because that's where I am.

Not quite, but I'm close. Only a block or so away.

Actually, prob easier if I come to you. I'm hitting the thumbs-up emoji when the next text lands on my screen. Be there in 5. Don't talk to anyone wearing a beanie ☺

I laugh and drop my phone in my pocket, then choose the busiest, most well-lit route to the Leidseplein, trailing a cluster of Portuguese tourists too drunk to notice the random American hanging like a shadow on the edge of their group. I stick close as they cross the bridge and stumble through a covered square, skirting around the pillars and peering into the dark corners, watching for anyone who might be waiting to grab me as I pass by. At the far end, I shoot out of the colonnades and catch my breath under a street light, staring back into the darkness until I know for sure that no one's coming but more tourists. I'm not being followed.

I cross the street and take it all in. The movie theater looming over a long row of colorful restaurants and bars, the gingerbread facade of the iconic orange theater with its twin spires, the people packing the Leidseplein, the most famous square in all of Amsterdam thanks in large part to the Bulldog, the world-famous coffee shop housed somewhat ironically in a former police station.

This is the part of the city that never sleeps, where the crowds stay thick until deep in the night, people huddling under heaters on terraces and spilling out of the bars and restaurants despite the freezing cold. There's safety in numbers, I tell myself as I step into the chaos.

My phone buzzes against a hip, and I stop by a tram stand to dig it out. "Hey, Ingrid. Did you see my text?"

"Just now. Are you okay?"

"I'm fine, but don't go home. Not until the police know who the trackers belong to."

She makes a throaty sound, her voice crackling in the phone speaker. "Good luck with that. Those things are impossible to trace. Where are you? Is that a tram?"

It clangs, sending a gaggle of pedestrians scurrying away from the tracks.

"Yes, I'm on the Leidseplein. It's a madhouse."

"Smart thinking. What's your plan?"

A group of drunk tourists come tumbling out of a bar across the street, and as much as I'd love the warmth of a table inside, my best bet is a conspicuous spot on one of the terraces on the square. I check for trams and bikes and head that way.

"I'm still figuring that out, but I'm not sleeping at home tonight. You probably shouldn't, either."

I keep my gaze on the people around me on the terrace, servers with their trays full of drinks and the couple laughing at the next table and the tourists taking photographs on the edge of the square. I watch three Americans with blowouts and stiletto boots do shots at a high-top by the door, thinking they must not have gotten the memo on the weather or on Amsterdam's cobblestoned streets. Just beyond, a dark man in an army coat looks my way, his eyes hidden under a baseball cap.

A baseball cap. My heart gives a heavy, warning thud.

"Do you want to come here?" she asks. "My parents have a pullout couch."

It's a solid offer, but Ingrid's parents live all the way in Diemen, a suburb that's reachable by public transport, but the roads between here and there will be dark and deserted, and now it's starting to spit snow. The Leidseplein is surrounded by hotels. I just need a few minutes to search for one on my phone.

"Thanks," I say, keeping him in my periphery as he chats with someone, a man. They slap hands and clap backs and exchange animated, rapid-fire greetings, and it's not him. It's not the man from the tram, not the guy in the beanie paying for his shawarma. I blow out a long, relieved breath. "But I'm just going to find a hotel. The detective promised to call as soon as he knew something. Hopefully, it's just for one night. We can regroup tomorrow."

The man in the ball cap takes off up the street, and I watch until he disappears around the corner.

"Are you sure?" Ingrid says.

"I'm sure. But thank you."

"Okay, well . . . some of the hostels near there aren't so awful, and they might let you pay in cash. You'll probably still have to show an ID, but if you're lucky there won't be a paper trail."

A paper trail. I hadn't thought of that. I know from my first few nights in this country that hotels ask for a passport, which is sitting in my suitcase under the bed. Maybe they'll accept my driver's license, but they'll probably make a copy and plug the information into a computer somewhere. Let's just hope it's an old dusty desktop that's not hooked up to the internet.

"Seriously, Rayna, come here, it's not a bother. I'll text you the address."

I think about the multiple transfers I'd have to make to get to Diemen, or sliding into the back of a cab alone, and I don't know. It feels wrong somehow. A table further up the terrace erupts with laughter, and I take in the people on the packed terrace, the pedestrians swarming the square, and it's settled. I'm safer here.

"I'll send you a pin with my location as soon as I've got a place to sleep. Promise. I'll talk to you tomorrow."

At the corner, a man unchains his bike from where it's leaning against a brick building. No beanie, but he's alone, and he seems suspiciously sober. He wraps the chain around his handlebars and climbs on, his gaze skimming over mine before he pedals off, but even after he's gone, I can't quite relax. I clutch my phone and look around the square, scanning the faces. Five minutes, Lars said. I wish he'd hurry up.

I awaken my phone and Google nearby hostels, even though I'm too old to be sharing a dorm room with a bunch of smelly strangers, *way* too old to be arguing about who gets the top bunk. Hotels in the city center are expensive, though, and Ingrid is right; the last thing I need is a paper trail.

After a bit of searching, I find a two-star hostel a couple blocks away. The reviews are decent and even better, booking.com says there's a private room available for less than €100 a night. Maybe for an extra twenty, they'll believe me when I say I've lost my ID.

I look up, and that's when it happens: I spot a familiar face further down the terrace, sipping a beer. I see his chin nestled in the collar of his coat, the patch of dark hair poking out of a hat.

He reaches for his beer, and the sight of him runs through me like a shock of electricity.

It's beanie man, though the hat-du-jour is a bright red hoodie—not the most subtle choice, though it does blend in with the young crowd on the square. He hasn't seemed to notice me yet, or more likely, he's trying very hard to keep up the charade, which makes it easy for me to zoom in on his profile and snap a surreptitious shot. He sips his beer and scrolls on his phone, and I wonder if he's staring at a flashing blue dot.

Which means . . . *shit.* Did I miss a tracker? I didn't bring a bag, and it's definitely not in my pants or coat. Did he put spyware on my phone? Is there another type of tracker I haven't spotted yet in my things—something smaller maybe? Less obvious? My entire body itches at the thought, like when reports of bedbugs taking over Paris surfaced three days after I'd just returned from there.

I sit there for a long minute, thinking about what to do. The bars will be open another five, maybe six hours, which gives me time to shake this guy off, but in order to do that, I need to know how he found me.

A big body steps up to my table. Same faded jeans he wore the night we first met, same scuffed boots and beaded chains poking out of a navy sweater, same cheeky grin that drops off his face the moment I lift my face to his.

"Uh-oh," Lars says. "What's wrong?"

WILLOW

After Thomas and the detective leave, I check on Sem, sound asleep in his bed, then go downstairs to an empty kitchen. Martina is long gone, which is good since that means I don't have to see her worried face. She thinks these murders tie back to House of Prins, too. She thinks her job is in danger, and after that visit from the detective, I'm not sure how to reassure her.

I make myself a cup of chamomile tea, sit at the kitchen table, and try to think, *really* think about what it means that my bracelet was in Xander's desk drawer. Even if the Cullinan in that bracelet was a lab-grown, it's concerning that he set it in an exact replica of the bracelet. What was he planning to do, sell the bracelet on the black market? With a stone like the Cullinan as its centerpiece, he had to know the bracelet would get back to Thomas eventually. Now he knows there is a copy of the Cullinan floating around. He'll be looking for them in other places, too.

Thomas was right about one thing, though: Xander was in cahoots with the Asian lab. He told me that night at his penthouse, in the same breath he said he could grow any stone I wanted. The six-carat Prins-cut dazzler in my engagement ring, for example, or the four-carat dangly teardrops in the earrings I was wearing that night. All Xander needed was a copy of the grading certificates, which he could use to grow a match so perfect, so exact that not even my husband would see the difference. That night at his penthouse, I asked him to grow me twelve.

Twelve lab-grown diamonds that are physically, chemically, and optically identical twins to twelve of the mined diamonds Thomas gave to me. More than fifty carats in all, and that's excluding the Cullinan in the bracelet. That stone I promised to Xander.

It was sloppy of him, though, setting the lab-grown Cullinan in a replica of the bracelet, making it look like the real thing. A stone like the Cullinan isn't exactly subtle, not even if he sold it on the black market. Now all those other lab-grown stones Xander was ordering from the Asian lab and selling under the table, Thomas will be looking for those, too.

It's past two by the time headlights flash on the upstairs bedroom window, Thomas's car turning into the driveway. He parks under the giant elm and idles there for long enough I kick off the covers. He's been gone for almost seven hours now—the equivalent of an entire workday on top of the one he'd just finished—and I wonder how he's filled all those hours. If he spent them all at the factory.

I step out of bed and to the big bay window, pressing my forehead to the freezing glass. Thomas is still sitting in his car just below. I see the inky smudge that's the top of his head through the sunroof, lit up by the soft glow of a cellphone. Too far for me to see what he's seeing, but I gather from the blobs of white and green that it's WhatsApp. Thomas is messaging someone.

The interior light pops on, the door swings open, and I step back from the window before he can spot me spying. At the foot of the stairs, Ollie hears him, too. I catch his groan as he heaves himself to his feet, the excited click-click-click of his nails on the marble floor, heavy panting when Thomas comes through the door. I sink onto the edge of the bed and wait.

Thomas doesn't notice me sitting in the dark, just breezes through the bedroom for the closet. He's almost to the hallway that connects the two when I call out his name.

"Thomas."

He jumps, his whole body twitching in surprise, in shock. He whirls around, his gaze searching out mine in the dim room. "Jesus Christ, Willow. You almost gave me a heart attack."

"Long day," I say, pointing out the obvious. I have no idea what he's thinking, can't quite gauge his mood. He doesn't look happy to find me waiting up for him, but maybe it's more than that. Maybe he's just not happy, period. "You look tired."

He sighs, slumping against the wall. "Exhausted. The only thing I want is to get out of these clothes and into bed. Do you mind?" He turns for the closet before I can ask him to wait.

I push off the bed and follow him down the hallway, coming into the closet as he's stripping out of his sweater. He folds it and drops it in a drawer, then starts in on his belt while I clasp my hands tight on top of the marble island and force myself to just say it. To ask the question that has me standing here, watching him undress in a closet at 2:00 a.m., staring down the husband who won't quite meet my eyes.

"Thomas, are you having an affair?"

He whirls around, the buckle on his belt rattling. "What?"

"You heard me. Are you having an affair? Is there someone else?"

He steps out of his pants and shakes them out, holding them at the hem. "No, Willow. There's no one else."

Liar.

A shiver of something unpleasant shimmies its way down my spine. Jealousy? Panic? I push it aside and plow on.

"Then who were you out there messaging? Because I saw you in the car. You were on your phone."

"Offices are open in Asia. Those messages were for work."

It's a convenient answer, especially in light of the bracelet bombshell Detective Boomsma dropped earlier, one that doesn't feel that far off base. Thomas works seven days a week, and when he is home, he'll step away from everything—meal times with me and Sem, a rare moment relaxing on the couch, a game of catch in the backyard—to take a call or answer an email. He sleeps with his phone next to the bed, for crap's sake. Why wouldn't those messages be for work?

"And the necklace?"

He peels off his socks and tosses them in the hamper. "What necklace?" He pads to the bathroom in his boxers, and with a sigh, I follow behind.

"The one you bought at Rive Gauche."

At the last two words, Thomas experiences a full-body reaction. He stops in the middle of the bathroom, his bare back stiffening before he turns on a heel.

"You were *following* me?" The same thing Rayna said to me, only this time, I don't deny it. His tone is heavy with disbelief, with insult, and so is his expression.

"No, Thomas. *No.* You do not get to turn this around. Who did you buy the necklace for? Whose bike did you hang it on?"

A mottled shadow darkens his face like a bruise. "Jesus, Willow, seriously? You *were* following me. I can't believe this. I can't believe *you.*"

I give an angry shake of my head. "Whose bike, Thomas?"

He steps to the sink and rummages through the drawer for the toothpaste, squirting a neat line of blue goo onto his brush. "No one's. The necklace was a piece of junk. I don't know who the bike belonged to. I chose it at random."

"You chose a random person to give a cheap necklace?"

"I figured somebody would want it. It would be a shame to just throw it away."

The frugality is so very Dutch. Thomas has all the money in the world and yet he can't bear wasting a single penny.

"That makes no sense! Why buy a necklace and hang it on a rusty bike?" Frustration rises in my chest, spilling over into my voice. "If there's someone else, Thomas, if you've . . . changed your mind about me—about us—just say it. Because I'm not one of those women who tries harder when there's a challenge. I'm not attracted to someone who's not attracted to me."

Especially when I'm pretty sure you never loved me the way a man is supposed to love his wife. These are the words I can't quite force over my lips, no matter how much I need to know the answer.

It's a question I should have asked ages ago, back when his workdays first started to extend into the evenings, back when this chasm between us was still barely a crack. Before I let the hurt pile up and up and up, so high I can no longer see a way to glue us back together. Long before I decided to find solutions in a man like Xander.

But what the hell do I know about marriage? About love? What do I know about commitment? My father took off before I was born. My mother was too focused on the parade of worthless men to pay a lick of attention to me, her only child. Sixteen is an awfully early age to learn that you're barely a side note in your own parent's life, but this is the legacy of my upbringing, that I crave stability. When Thomas dropped to his knee, offering a life as a Prins and all that entails, I grabbed on with both hands—not just for me, but for Sem.

But it was my mother, with her fickle nature and endless supply of men waiting in the wings, who taught me to always have a backup plan.

Thomas flips on the water, holding his toothbrush under the stream. "No, Willow. There's no one else. I already told you. And I haven't changed my mind."

"I saw you, Thomas. Coming out of the Conservatorium."

He pauses, barely a split second, but long enough that I see it. "When? Which day? Because I'm working on a line of lab-growns exclusive to the boutique there. I'm in that building once a week, sometimes more."

"Tuesday. The day you were supposed to be in Antwerp for the conference."

"I *was* in Antwerp. I took the helicopter." He shoves the toothbrush in his mouth, speaking around the bristles. "Should I have my assistant forward the receipt?"

Yes. I sigh. Fold my arms across my chest. "And the necklace?"

"The necklace." He does a lightning-quick brush of his teeth then spits into the sink, rinsing his toothbrush and chucking it in the drawer with a huff. "The PI told me that store was a front. He said they have a back room where they deal in black market diamonds. I went there to . . . I don't know, take a look around."

It takes me a couple of seconds to switch gears and then a few more to rearrange the puzzle pieces in my head. The PI, the private investigator Thomas hired after the Cullinan theft, when the police had hit their last dead end. All those leads that led to nowhere, no closer to finding the Cullinans after months of investigation than they were when they vanished into thin air. The cops volleyed the case back to the insurance company, where it's stalled out yet again.

The insurance company is already being difficult enough, Willem said at last Sunday's supper. He was talking about Xander's death, insisting Thomas make sure it not get tied up in the theft. *The last thing we need is another reason for them to delay the payout.* Those Cullinans were insured for hundreds of millions of euros, money the family still hasn't seen.

"You thought Rive Gauche would sell you a Cullinan?" I say.

"I thought they'd sell me *something*, but the saleswoman either didn't know about the back room or she was playing me. When I said I was willing to pay for a piece with real stones, she gave me the address for a store down the street. A legit store. I know the owner."

"Maybe the saleswoman recognized you."

It's certainly possible. Asscher, Coster, Gassan, Prins. These are the names that dominate the diamond market here, and Thomas's picture is plastered at least once a week on a newspaper, a website, a social media post. Especially if it's true that Rive Gauche is selling stolen diamonds in back rooms, that saleswoman would have clocked Thomas as a Prins the second he walked through the door.

"I thought of that, too. But I'm not the only one who tried. Everybody I've sent over there has struck out, too."

"So the PI was wrong?"

"Sure looks like it. Anyway, can we talk about this tomorrow? I have a meeting at the factory at nine."

A short six hours and some change from now.

Thomas disappears down the hall, back through the closet and into the bedroom. I flick off the lights and follow behind.

He's already under the covers by the time I catch up. His glasses lie on the nightstand, next to his phone on the wireless charger, lit up with a soft green glow displaying the time. I slip into bed, and his hand finds mine under the comforter. A gesture that used to be so normal, so tender and full of love, that it now feels like punishment, a consolation prize swathed in pity. His fingers are warm and dry as they close around mine.

"I'm sorry," he says, his voice so low I have to strain to hear. "I know I've been really . . . absent lately."

Scream at me. Rip off my clothes and fuck me. Tell me you hate me and want a divorce. Anything other than this quiet desertion.

I lie here for a long moment, staring up at the dark ceiling, trying to figure out a way to say it. Instead, I land on, "If there's something you need to tell me, Thomas, please just do it. I'm a big girl. I can handle the truth."

I hate the way my voice sounds, thin and pleading, but it must do something to him because he's quiet for a long time. I hear his slow, steady breaths, feel the low hum of his muscles vibrating under the sheets. *This is it*, I think. *Here it comes.* I hold my breath, my whole body waiting.

"There's nothing to say," he says finally. "Everything's fine."

He releases my hand and rolls onto his side, and that's that. Conversation over. Whatever problems we have, not solved but left to fester. I lie here in the dark, telling myself I have every luxury I could have ever dreamed of. Diamonds. The Prins name. This palace and access to a bank account with more money than I could ever spend.

But I meant what I said to Rayna a few days ago. A wife knows when there's another woman in her husband's bed, or worse—in his head.

I stare into the dark, thinking I'll wait all night if I have to. I have absolutely nothing better to do than count my husband's exhales and wait for them to even out.

THOMAS'S BODY IS a deadweight on the mattress, his breaths regular puffs of soft air. I stare at the ceiling for fifteen minutes more, and then I lift the covers and slip out of bed.

Silently, I creep around to his side of the bed, lift his cellphone from the charger, and hurry with it into the bathroom. Thomas has never given me his passcode, has never actually handed me his phone and said those numbers out loud, but I've watched him punch them in enough times that I know what they are. I tick them in now, and the screen dissolves into a WhatsApp conversation.

At the top of the screen, a woman's name, Cécile, and I roll my eyes in the dim room. Cécile is Thomas's assistant, a drab woman with close-set eyes and hair as shapeless as her body. His secretary, how cliché.

I scroll through the texts, reading them in reverse. Good night, my love. I wish it was you I was coming home to. I don't know how much longer I can keep this up. I must see you, must see for myself that you're okay. I didn't tell him anything, I swear. I wouldn't do that to you. Please be careful. Please stay safe. I couldn't bear if what happened to Frederik happened to you, too. ILY forever, xx.

It's funny, all these months I've spent agonizing about where Thomas has been and who he's been with, I thought when the truth finally cracked open that I'd feel more. My husband is in love with another woman. He wishes it was her he was coming home to. He's not just a liar but a coward.

Even though I was expecting this—honestly, I've known it for some time now—seeing those words on Thomas's screen doesn't hurt me as much as it ignites something under my skin. A simmering fury that he doesn't have the balls to tell me, a nervous kind of energy to hold the phone in front of his face and slap him awake. I think of Thomas in the next room, snoring soundly in the bed we share, and I wonder if that's what he's dreaming about, this dirty little secret with Cécile.

My gaze snags on the words at the top of the screen. *Please be careful. Please stay safe.* He's scared Frederik's killer is still out there, that he might be coming for Cécile. It makes sense, I guess, that Thomas has latched on to this. Yet another distressed damsel for him to save, yet another wounded puppy for him to adopt. Thomas didn't walk away from his upbringing unscathed, either. He loves nothing more than feeling needed.

I stand there, the marble cool under my feet, and breathe through another wave of anger—at Thomas, but mostly at myself. For believing he meant it when he promised to take away my worries, for letting myself fall for his lies, for not being prepared for a woman like Cécile sneaking in the back door.

I leave the screen exactly how I found it, with Thomas's last text at the bottom of the chat, then sneak back into the bedroom and settle the phone back on the charger. Cécile can have my husband's lying, cheating ass—but not yet. I'm not letting him go just yet. Let him live in agony a little while longer.

I don't need Thomas. I don't need his lies and dodges and empty promises.

But those twelve diamonds Xander grew for me? The ones he stashed in his safe?

Those, I need. I need them now more than ever.

RAYNA

"He's here." I keep beanie man in my periphery and tip my head up at Lars. The clouds above his head are spitting snow again, a Van Gogh sky of messy white flecks swirling around all that glorious hair like a hologram.

"Who is? Who's here?"

I gesture to the empty chair next to me, and Lars drops into it. "See that guy in the red hoodie four tables over? That's him. That's beanie man. He followed me here."

Lars's eyeballs dart that way, but he's subtle enough not to turn his head. "You sure? He's not even paying attention to you."

Which is the whole smokescreen, and so is the friend who's joined him. Another man about his age in Nike high-tops and a puffy orange coat, chatting up the three girls at the next table. It seems innocent enough, two single men on the prowl, but my body is still on high alert.

"It's him. It's definitely him. *Dammit.*"

I feel around in my coat pockets for what must be the hundredth time, fingertips brushing against nothing but crumbs and lint. I'm not wearing a tracker, which means he must have followed me here—possible, I guess. Maybe he spotted me coming out of that alley.

A waiter drops by the table, and I know better than to not order. Even for a freezing Sunday night, these are prime seats, on the front row of the terrace and under a heater. If we don't pay for a drink, this man will chase us away.

"I'll have a water, please. Sparkling."

Lars orders a beer, and then we're both quiet as the waiter weaves through the tables toward the glass doors under the awning.

Lars watches him until he's disappeared inside. "So, what's the plan?"

I tell him about the hostel I found two blocks away, the sob story I've concocted about losing my ID, the trackers I found in my things that make it impossible to go home. "I need to get off the streets, but I can't go anywhere as long as that asshole is following me. I've got to get rid of him first."

"Say no more." He wriggles his cell from an inside pocket of his coat, punches at the screen, then presses the phone to his ear. I know when the line connects, because he spouts off a steady stream of Dutch. I have no idea what any of it means, but when he catches my eye, he winks.

"*Dank u wel*," he says finally—thank you—then hits End. He tosses the cell to the table.

"What was that about?"

"That was the police. I called to report two men, wearing an orange coat and a red hoodie, pickpocketing women on the Leidseplein. I told them to send someone immediately."

"You did not." I lean back in my chair, impressed. It's what I should have done instead of sitting here panicking. In fact, I kinda wish I'd thought of it.

A grin spreads across Lars's face. "Give it a minute or two. The cops are always near this square, especially at night."

The waiter delivers the drinks, a glass of pilsner draft for Lars and a bottle of water along with a tall glass for me, a lemon slice and a single ice cube sitting in a puddle at the bottom. I thank him and dump the water in the glass, then chink it against Lars's beer.

"Cheers," I say before taking a sip.

Lars settles into his chair, getting comfortable, stretching his legs out long. "So are you going to tell me why this guy is following you around town? Because in the absence of any explanations, I've come up with a theory or two."

"Which are?"

"Well, my first thought was that you are a spy, but then I figured you'd have to be a pretty shitty one to let yourself be chased around the streets of Amsterdam by some man who wears a hat for a disguise, and you certainly wouldn't need my help to get away from him. But then I thought maybe that was the point, that you're only playing helpless and playing me. You're not playing me, are you?"

I laugh. "Definitely not. And I'm definitely not a spy. What's your second theory?"

"That you're just a normal girl who came to Amsterdam to hang out for a little while and got herself into some trouble. You know, wrong place, wrong time, that sort of thing. It wouldn't be the first time. My city, it's kind of known for its shenanigans."

"That's pretty on the nose, actually."

He seems eager to hear more, but I stall by swirling the lemon around my glass. If Lars hasn't seen the pictures of me floating around the web, I'm not all that eager to point them out. I don't want to see his face when I tell him about Xander. I don't want it to change the way he looks at me.

Before I can work up the nerve, Lars nudges me with an elbow, and I follow his gaze to the opposite side of the square.

A police car rolls to a stop by the tram tracks. People are still everywhere, standing in tight circles around street performers, smoking cigarettes while they wait for the tram, and a police car on the Leidseplein is a common sight. Nobody seems to notice, not even when the doors swing open and two uniformed cops step out.

The officers scan the terrace, their gazes traveling over the people huddled under the heaters and at the tables, but it doesn't take them long. The orange jacket and red hoodie might as well be beacons.

"Here we go," Lars says as the cops march this way.

I reach for my water and settle in for the show.

Beanie man doesn't notice them, not until they're stepping up to his table, and even then, he looks at them as if they're interrupting, which they are. The girls at the next table suddenly seem a lot less interested in his pickup lines.

I don't understand what the cops say to him, but I understand their tone, the way the people at neighboring tables look over in alarm. The guy in the orange coat puts up a fuss, refusing their orders to stand up, to follow them away from the terrace and back toward the car. He empties out his pockets and dumps his belongings onto the table, presumably as proof. *Look, officers, no pickpockets here.*

But the cops either don't believe him or they don't care. They haul the two men out of their chairs, one cop latching on to each man's arm, and escort them away.

"Holy shit," I say, looking at Lars with a grin. "You did it. It actually worked."

"They won't keep them long. Only a few minutes if you're lucky."

A few minutes is plenty of time to disappear. I dig a twenty from the back of my phone and wedge it under my water glass, empty now but for the lemon slice and a half-melted ice cube.

"Thanks for saving my ass yet again, Lars, but I gotta go." I push up from the chair, and the sudden motion makes me lightheaded. The world tilts, and I fall back to the seat, waiting for the earth to settle.

If Lars notices there's something wrong, he doesn't let on. He settles his half-drunk beer onto the table and stuffs his hands into his coat pockets. "I realize I don't know you all that well, but you seem smart. No, not just smart. What's the word for someone who takes advantage of a situation? Like something unexpected happens and they see their chance and grab it."

"Opportunistic?" I frown. That doesn't sound very nice.

He pulls a hand from his pocket to snap in my direction, then stuffs it back in. "Opportunistic. That's right. Is that what happened, Rayna? You saw an opportunity and you took it?"

I tell myself that Lars could be talking about anything. That things often get lost in translation and this could be one of those times. Or maybe I just heard him wrong. Maybe I misunderstood. A buzzing in my brain is making it hard to think.

"What are you talking about?"

"You really don't know? Come on, Rayna. I think you do."

Something about the way he says it has my memories racing back to the night we met. Yes, he was the first to speak, but he was already standing there, trying to get the bartender's attention when I stepped up beside him, begging for a drink. When he mentioned the bar across the street, I'm the one who suggested food. I practically invited myself.

"No," I whisper. "I really don't know."

Or maybe I do. Maybe I made it easy for him.

He shifts his chair, picking it up by all four legs and turning it on the bricks. He leans closer, and I see it so clearly, the way danger flits across his expression before it disappears. "Where are the diamonds, Rayna? Tell me where they are and I'll let you go. I'll let you get back to your sad little life."

"My life's not sad." It's a stupid thing to latch on to, but I feel strangely defensive of the things I've done, all the decisions I've made that brought me to right here right now, freezing my ass off on a terrace in Amsterdam. I've done some sad things, and that includes trusting this man, but my life's not sad. "I don't know where the diamonds are. The killer took them."

"That would be very unfortunate."

I don't know what to say to that—unfortunate for who? I don't dare to ask—so I say nothing at all.

Music kicks in from nowhere. Loud, bass-led house moving closer, drowning out the noises on the street and battering in my brain like a jackhammer. An electric bike zooms down the center of the street, a portable speaker strapped to the handlebars. It weaves in and out of the tram tracks, sending the pedestrians scattering. The sounds beat in my brain as their bodies go in and out of focus. I shake my head, trying to shake the fuzziness from my vision, but it sticks like a thick fog.

"You're wasting my time," Lars says. "Tell me where the diamonds are. We don't have very long."

"Long before what?" I say, even though I already know the answer. I know from the way my tongue can't quite wrap itself around the words, the way a sudden surge of nausea pushes up from somewhere deep and gathers in a sour ball at the back of my throat. I know exactly what's happening here.

"Time to go," he says, heaving me out of my chair. The second I'm upright, the world tilts. The terrace, the square, the Bulldog across the street, it all turns upside down. I stumble to my left, almost knocking over a chair. Lars catches me, holding me up with a strong arm.

"Jeez, lady, watch out, yeah?" someone from the next table says, a Brit.

Lars clamps me to his torso. "Sorry. She's a little overserved. Come on, baby, let's get you home so you can sleep it off."

The Brit laughs. "Good luck, mate. She's sloshed."

I shake my head against Lars's shoulder as he tugs me toward the street. I'm not sloshed, and I'm definitely not okay.

I blink and I'm on a bridge. I don't remember getting here or even crossing the street, but I see the water and the bridge and Lars, tugging me into the back of a cab, and I know this feeling. I've felt it once before, my sophomore year, halfway through a Kappa Sigma party. It was the drunkest I've ever been, even though I'd only had one beer.

"No," I try to say, but it comes out like a moan.

The cabbie tosses me a dirty look and pulls away from the curb.

That motherfucker roofied me.

It's my last coherent thought before everything goes black.

WILLOW

It's midmorning when I step off the tram at the Prinsengracht bridge and walk the few short blocks through a steady rain. An excursion to get my mind off an impossible situation, to fill the empty hours while Sem is at school with something other than worry about the state of my marriage. When my alarm woke me this morning, Thomas was already gone.

The canal on my left shimmers in the freezing air, the rain slapping the water with a million tiny splashes. I huddle under my umbrella and hug the houses to my right, ancient structures that have had centuries to settle on their foundations and now lean every which way, a messy but charming jumble of step-stone facades. Dancing houses, they call the ones on the water near Central Station, and these are just as lopsided.

I stop at number 167, a wide four-story canal house of black-painted brick with white trim, twice the width of the houses on either side. The building belongs to a man named Jan Visser. The upstairs apartments he rents out for an ungodly monthly rate, but the whole ground floor is reserved for him, for a tiny apartment at the back and the rest an ancient, dusty shop filled with mirrors. Suspended from chains hanging from the ceiling, leaning in stacks against every wall, smothering every table and vertical surface. The most exquisite mirrors in all of northern Europe.

Jan's mirrors hang in castles and mansions all over the world. They hang in penthouses in New York and Tokyo and Beijing and in the villas lining the streets in Amsterdam Zuid, including Thomas's. Jan's mirror is the eighteenth-century masterpiece of gilded wood and smoky glass hanging above the side table in the hall, my favorite piece in the whole house.

But that mirror is not how I know Jan. Xander introduced us last fall, after I asked him to grow those diamonds. Jan and Xander were well acquainted with each other, because Jan knows how to make diamonds disappear.

There's no bell beside the double doors, and I know from experience not to bother with the handles because they're locked. With all those contraband stones Jan keeps buried in jars and boxes in the back room, he isn't the most trusting guy.

This is it, though, the store the PI told Thomas about in the Nine Streets, the one secretly dealing in stolen diamonds. They were off by only a couple of blocks.

I pin the umbrella handle under an arm, wriggle my cell from my pocket, and fire off a text. I'm here. Open up.

The diamonds are also the reason for the German shepherd sleeping on a tartan pillow just inside the door, though Gijs is more for form than function these days. He's almost as old as Jan, with the same questionable hearing and bum hip. I tap the glass, but Gijs doesn't lift his head.

At the back of the store there's movement, Jan shuffling from the workshop overlooking the generous backyard, his old body stooped and limping. He skirts around a giant table covered with antique pots and bowls, a row of old-school bikes, outside-sized trees in giant teak pots, and it takes him an eternity to reach the front, for him to sort through his keys. After forever, he peels opens the door.

I fold my umbrella and step inside, and Jan's face crinkles into a smile. We exchange the standard three kisses on the cheeks.

"So lovely of you to drop by, *meissie*. Coffee?" He locks the door behind me and reaches for his cane.

"Coffee would be perfect, thanks. How've you been?" I wedge my umbrella in a corner, leaving it to drip on the mat.

He makes a phlegmy sound deep in his throat, one that I take for *not so hot*, and motions me deeper into the warehouse. His pace is painfully slow—thump shuffle, thump shuffle. I make a quick pit stop at Gijs, who is panting at me in recognition but too lazy to get up from his bed, then I match my steps to Jan's.

"Bored out of my mind," he says. "Nothing is moving right now, not with two people dead and the cops everywhere. I'm sure you've heard about the raid. One of the kitschy stores around the corner that charges a hundred bucks for a perfumed candle. If you ask me, that's the real crime."

I hadn't heard about the raid, but I'm not all that surprised. If Thomas's private investigator had intel that brought him here, to the Nine Streets, the police will have had the same info. They would have followed the same trail. If Jan is smart, he's emptied his back room of everything but mirrors.

"At least it wasn't a grenade on the stoop," he says. "That would have been really bad."

I give him a wry smile, because he's not wrong. Grenades are a favorite mob calling card, left on the doorsteps of restaurants and stores as both a threat and a warning. Whenever the police or heaven forbid a passer-by stumbles upon one, they shutter the store for months.

We come into the workshop, a long space that runs along the entire back of the building, where dozens of mirrors in various states of repair lie on wheeled tables, topped with paint pots and brushes on rags. Shelves cover the far wall, lined with a disarray of supplies in antique glass jars, plaster and clay and gold leafing, agate for polishing. Jan explained the process to me once, a long lecture on the ancient techniques and products he uses to painstakingly restore the glass and frames, and I have to give it to him, his mirrors really are spectacular.

He points me to a round table by the kitchenette, then pours two steaming cups of coffee and carries them over. He sinks onto the chair across from me. "Now. Tell me what was so important that you had to see me today."

"I need a gun."

Jan huffs a breathy laugh. "You Americans and your guns. Do you even know how to shoot one?"

"Stop being difficult and just tell me where I can buy one."

"How soon you need it?"

"Quickly. Immediately." I pat the pocket of my coat, the thick wad of bills sitting inside. "I brought cash."

Jan reaches down the table for a spiral notebook, then scribbles an address on the top sheet, rips it off, and passes it to me. "Ask for Maksim. I'll let him know you're on your way. What else?"

"I'm sure you've heard about the diamonds that disappeared from Xander's safe the night he was killed."

Beyond the missing necklace, the reports have been rather vague about what kind or how many, as I'm guessing nobody but Xander knew what was in there. All those diamonds the Asian lab tucked into their legit shipments to House of Prins and intercepted by Xander, but how many stones? How many shipments? Perhaps a Cullinan or two or nine? Now that Xander's dead, there's no one to do inventory except the person who emptied the safe.

But when it comes to black market stones, Jan has his ear to the ground. He knows all the players, gets wind of who's moving which merchandise. If those diamonds from Xander's safe have made their way to the market, Jan will know where they are, who's got them.

Jan takes a noisy sip of his coffee. "Sure, I heard."

"Twelve of my diamonds were in his safe. The ones Xander grew to match these."

I tug a stack of papers from my bag and push them across the table, copies of the GIA certifications for stones in pieces Thomas has given me over the years. A pair of solitaire earrings, the stones seven carats apiece. A pendant in the shape of a pear, the diamond big and bright canary yellow. The six-carat diamond, bright and internally flawless, in my engagement ring. Another ring with a cluster of cushion and brilliant-cut diamonds arranged into an elaborate flower, with a whopping nineteen-carat total weight. This last one will be the most difficult to replicate, but I don't want to replicate any of these pieces. I only want Jan here to switch out the stones.

He looks at the papers, but he doesn't reach for them.

"Forget those stones. Those stones are history."

"Come on, Jan. I know you know where they are."

"I never said that I didn't. Only that you should forget about them."

I frown, giving a hard shake of my head. "I can't do that. My circumstances have changed these past few days. I need those diamonds."

It was the original deal I made with Xander: twelve lab-grown twins to twelve of my most valuable diamonds—a street value of a million euros combined—in exchange for the center stone in the bracelet, the last surviving Cullinan. For Xander, it was the deal of the century.

Only he never got that Cullinan and I never got my twelve diamonds. He was killed before we could make the exchange, before I could get the diamonds to Jan for him to make disappear. All those buyers of his, they're not coming to him only for the mirrors. They're coming for mirrors stuffed with diamonds then shipped off to addresses in the Middle East, Asia, South America.

Diamonds that will soon be mounted on fingers and hanging from wrists, and not resurface anytime soon on the black market.

Which means Thomas will never see my twelve switched-out stones. He'll never think to be suspicious. It's not a foolproof plan, I am well aware, but it's the only one I've got.

"I can pay." I wriggle off my engagement ring and settle it onto the desk. "Reset it with the matching lab-grown, and the middle stone is yours. Six carats, internally flawless. Want to grab a loupe?"

Jan stares at the ring for a couple of breaths, and I know I don't have to sell him on the cut or quality. Jan knows what this stone is worth. He knows it'll pay for the twelve lab-growns and then some.

"Nah. I trust you," he says finally, his gaze lifting to meet mine. "But I also like you, and as much as I want to help you out, the best way I can do that is by telling you to leave it alone. This road you're walking down, it's dangerous."

"My twelve stones are dangerous?"

"Yes. I'm sure I don't need to remind you that two men are dead. Buyers are spooked, and you should be, too."

"I'm well aware of the danger here, but I'm also desperate. My marriage . . . it's not working out."

"I'm very sorry to hear that."

"Whoever's got those twelve stones, I can offer them the same deal. The center stone for the lab-growns."

He laughs, another phlegmy bark.

"At least tell me where they are so I can—"

"You want to know where these stones are?" He taps a finger to the certificate copies, still sitting between us on the table, his fingertip a direct hit on one word in particular. "Look inside your own house."

Prins. The word is *Prins.* Look for Xander's stones inside House of Prins?

I shake my head. "I don't understand."

"Ask yourself what could have happened to Xander's stones, all those matches to Prins diamonds that sold for millions and millions of dollars. It's the same thing that happened to the Cullinans."

The Cullinans.

"What do Xander's lab-growns have to do with the Cullinans?"

"Think about it, Willow. Ask yourself who had the most to gain."

"The Cullinans are worth hundreds of millions of euros." I frown, shake my head again. "Literally *everybody* had the most to gain."

Jan smiles. "And at least three of them go by the name of Prins."

JAN'S WORDS CHASE me across town to Maksim.

Look inside your own house.

If I'm to believe Jan, those twelve stones that Xander grew to match twelve of mine, are in the same place as the nine missing Cullinans.

Think about who had the most to gain.

At least three of them go by the name of Prins.

If that's true, if one of the Prinses cleaned out the Cullinan drawer, then it really would be the heist of the century. The flagship House of Prins stones, stolen by a Prins. Claiming their precious Cullinans were lifted and collecting the insurance money while secretly keeping their diamonds. Not a theft, but an elaborate insurance scam.

I think about Thomas firing Xander only hours before he was strangled in the shower. About the dead trader with a hole in his head and the instructions for printing a 3D gun on Thomas's desk. About my husband who will do just about anything to protect his beloved House. Thomas, who, if I'm to believe Jan, may also have my twelve lab-grown diamonds.

All this time, I thought I knew who killed Xander, but now I wonder if I was wrong.

The transaction with Maksim takes place in the back room of an ethnic clothing store, and it's quick and surprisingly easy. A loaded Ukrainian pistol for less than €800, but thanks to a delay with the trams, I'm almost late picking up Sem. I make it to school just as the double doors burst open with an explosive whack, letting out a thick stream of noisy kids. They race out the doors and scatter across the concrete slabs, an army of ants in floppy hats and bright, puffy coats, running every which way. I search their faces for Sem, but there are so many little bodies, and not one of them is standing still.

But because this is the lunch break and we have to do this all over again in ninety short minutes, folks generally don't linger long. One by one, the kids peel away and head for home. The older kids to the kid-sized bikes, the younger ones hoisted onto their parent's bike seat. I stand here as the crowd thins out, frowning when I don't find Sem.

My gaze wanders down the building to the windows of his classroom. I spot his teacher, Juf Addie, behind the glass, talking to someone pint-sized—an adorable blond boy. I pull out my phone to see if I missed a text or call, but there's nothing. Maybe Sem needed to stay longer for some reason? Maybe he needed a quick pit stop at the bathroom?

I head across the schoolyard for the double doors.

Inside, the hallway is quiet, the coat hooks mostly empty except for the few kids who stay during the lunch break, the ones with working mothers and no nanny. I hear them somewhere deep inside the building, a muffled clamor of children's laughter.

At Juf Addie's room at the end of the hall, I rap a knuckle against the wood, then hang my head into the open doorway. "Hi. I'm looking for Sem."

I say it in my best Dutch. The teachers here understand English just fine, but they're a whole lot nicer when you speak to them in their native tongue.

Addie looks up with a smile. "Oh, Willow, you made it. You just missed him, though. He left about"—she glances at the clock on the far wall—"seventeen minutes ago."

Seventeen minutes is before the bell, and by a good ten minutes. Sem left school ten minutes early.

"What do you mean he left? With who? Did Martina pick him up?"

Addie frowns, a combination of confusion and worry. "Not Martina. His aunt. I don't remember her name, but she was listed in Sem's file as an emergency contact. Sem knew her. He went willingly."

His aunt. Sem only has one, but never, not once, has Fleur ever picked him up from anywhere. Not from our home for a sleepover with his cousins, definitely not from school. I'm surprised she even knows where to find him.

"Fleur?"

"Yes, Fleur. That's her name. She said you had an unexpected appointment outside the city. She was to fetch Sem and take him back to her house, so you could pick him up after. She told me not to expect him back until tomorrow."

Now I'm really confused. Fleur lives all the way in Blaricum, which means I have to go home, switch out my bike for the car, and fight traffic on the A1 there and back.

And why? What for? Fleur isn't exactly a doting aunt. She never bothered learning even the simplest of signs when Sem's world was still silent, she never asks what shows he likes or what books he reads or what subjects are his favorites at school. She didn't call to make plans. She *never* asks to spend the afternoon with her nephew. This makes no sense.

"Did I do something wrong? Was he not supposed to go with her?" Addie says, starting to look worried again. "She promised the McDonald's drive-through. Sem was very excited."

What kid wouldn't be? And Fleur is smart. She knew Sem wouldn't love the prospect of an entire afternoon with the twins treating him like the pesky baby brother. The promise of a Happy Meal was the only way she could get him out the door quickly, without complaint or pushback.

I thank Addie and rush back down the hallway and out the double doors, my skin prickling in warning. Something is not right. As I hustle across the yard to my parked bike, I hit Call for Fleur's cell. She takes her sweet time, letting it ring three full times before answering.

"Willow, what a surprise."

Fleur is in the car. I hear the zoom of wheels on asphalt, the hiss of wind rushing past. I picture Sem sitting on the back seat of her big Range Rover, and I wonder if she thought to bring a booster seat. Probably not. Fleur never wanted a third child, and she would have purged her house of all of that stuff the second it was no longer useful. Whatever booster seats she once had are long gone.

"As much as I applaud you wanting to spend time with your nephew, want to tell me what's going on?"

"I have something I'd like to discuss. In private. As soon as we hang up, I'll text you an address. Meet me there and I'll explain."

"Explain what? Am I on speaker? Sem, can you hear me?"

Even if I am on speaker, it's a crapshoot as to whether or not Sem will pick up on my voice. If Sem's busy on an iPad, for example, or focused on something outside the car windows, I could be screaming and he'd likely not notice. Sem hears when he knows to listen.

"Sem's fine. Don't worry."

"Sem. *Sem!* If you're listening, baby, say something. Say—"

"Willow." Fleur's voice cuts through mine, a harsh bark that kills the words in my throat. "You're the one who needs to listen. Watch for the text. Meet me at the address I send you. And don't mention this to Thomas. What I want to talk to you about has to do with him."

I haul a breath—to ask her what's going on, to scream another time for Sem—but it's too late. The line is already dead.

RAYNA

I wake up in my beige bedroom, and for the first second or two, I don't remember that anything is wrong. Rain patters against the tiny window above my head, little rivers of water rolling down the glass with just beyond, ominous clouds hanging low enough to touch. Winter in Holland all looks the same, impossible to tell if the sun's just risen or is about to set. It could be morning or evening or anywhere in between.

"About time you woke up."

The voice is low and oily, coming from the chair in the corner. I roll my pounding head on the pillow, and there he is. Lars.

He smiles, and last night comes back in horrible flashes.

The terrace on the Leidseplein. Beanie man and his friend getting carted away and the sparkling water that somewhere between the glass and my stomach, picked up a colorless, odorless, tasteless pill that dissolves quickly and easily in liquid.

I feel my body under the covers, and at least I'm still dressed. Still wearing the same jeans I had on last night, the same sweater over a tank top, now twisted around my middle. Even my coat and shoes are still on, though I kicked off one sneaker during the night, but at least Lars didn't rape me. That's about the best thing I can say about the situation.

I stay quiet, trying to decide how to play this. Do I act surprised to find him here? Pretend I don't know about the drugs? Neither seems like the best way to get out of this alive, so instead I opt for honesty.

"Thanks for bringing me home, I guess." My tongue is thick in my mouth, coated with something sour that makes me long for a toothbrush. The words come out mushy and hoarse. "Though you could have gone lighter on the roofie. How much of that shit did you give me?"

It didn't take me until now to figure out, though, that the first night in the basement club, me bumping into him, him feeding me shawarmas at his cousin's place around the corner . . . I might have made it easy for him, but nothing about that night was an accident.

"I need to know who was here, Rayna." He gestures to the room, the drawers and closets I emptied out, the clothes and shoes and bags I hurled everywhere. "Who tossed your stuff."

"Me. I tossed it, after I—" I roll onto my side and the movement pitches my stomach, firing a ball of bile up my throat. I hold still and breathe through the rolling nausea until it somewhat subsides. "Are you even an artist?" Lars rolls his eyes. No, not an artist, but a damn good liar. "Good job on the trackers, by the way. How many were there?"

"Trackers." Not a question, exactly, and yet somehow it is.

"Yes, trackers. I found six, and that's not including the one I left on the tram." I look to the nightstand for my phone, but it's not there. Of course it's not. "Good work, by the way. Picking just the right spot at the bar to make it seem like I came up to you and not the other way around. That couldn't have been easy, but you played it well. Though just happening to be on the same side of town as me last night was a bit obvious, don't you think? Where was the one that I missed?"

"The one what?"

"The tracker. Because I checked every piece of clothing I had on last night. I looked inside every compartment in my bag. I was certain I'd found them all."

"I wasn't tracking you. I've been *watching* you. I've had eyes on you this whole time."

The downstairs neighbor's face flashes before my eyes, her wrinkly smile as she gestured for me to come inside. "But I didn't go out the front door."

"I've lived in this city my entire life. You think I don't know every street and alleyway? I had eyes on both exits."

"Lemme guess. Beanie man and his friend in the orange coat."

Lars leans forward, resting his elbows on his knees. "Good guess. Let's hope for your sake that I'm not too late."

"I feel like this would go a lot faster if you'd stop talking in code. Too late for what?"

He waves a hand around the room, the mess. "The diamonds, Rayna. The necklace. Tell me where they are."

On the one hand, I suppose I should be relieved that whatever this is, it's only about diamonds. If Lars was a killer with a penchant for zip ties, if he thought I was witness to his crime, then he wouldn't have bothered with the roofie. He would have killed me and dumped me off that bridge instead of pouring me in a cab.

"I don't have any idea where the necklace went. I was so drunk that night, I barely remember putting it on. I don't remember anything past midnight." I pause, looking around my sad, beige bedroom. "Also, if I had that necklace, do you really think I'd be living here?"

Lars shifts his body on the creaky chair, reaching down for something small and dark and shiny on the floor. A single-shot, nine millimeter Staccato CS, compact enough to fit in his hand. He aims it at my head, and I think of Willow's words, echoes of ones she wrote in that note.

At least with diamonds in your back pocket you'd have some leverage. Something to barter for your life.

I scramble up the bed, moving as far away as possible. Barry had quite the collection once upon a time. I know what that gun can do.

"How are there so many guns in this country?"

Lars sighs. "I'm losing patience, Rayna, so I'm going to need you to listen very carefully. I want the necklace. I want the diamonds that were in Xander's safe. Tell me where you hid them."

"Nowhere! The last time I saw the necklace, it was in the nightstand drawer, and I didn't even know he had a safe, not until I dreamed about walking into his study—"

Lightning fast, he whips the covers off my legs and whacks me hard on the shin with the barrel of the gun. I squeal, the pain exploding up my leg. "So you knew the safe was in his study."

"Yes, but from the detective." I try to focus on his face and not the gun in his hand, the barrel pointed once again at my head. "Not from Xander. Not because he showed me."

"What about your roommate?"

"Ingrid?"

He rolls his eyes. "Yes, Ingrid."

"What about her?"

"Did you give the diamonds to her to sell? Tell me the truth. It's the only way you get out of this alive."

"I didn't give her anything. Ingrid works in an antique shop. She restores antique mirrors for a living. I don't understand any of this."

"Ingrid worked with Xander. She was one of his handlers."

"Handlers?"

Lars sighs, clearly irritated. "Of diamonds. Keep up. Ingrid sells diamonds on the black market. That's how they get the stones across borders, by hiding them in the mirrors."

I push up onto an elbow, my gaze wandering to the open doorway, the light from the living room creeping down the hall. I have no idea what time it is or if she's even home, but if this is true, if Ingrid worked with Xander to move his diamonds, those trackers Lars claimed not to know about are suddenly making a lot of sense.

"Where is she? I want to talk to her."

"Ingrid is a little tied up right now."

Tied up selling stolen diamonds. Does she know that Xander's diamonds are lab-growns? That they're worth only a tenth of the real thing? Does Lars? If not, it seems unwise to point this out.

I fall back to the bed and stare up at the window high on the wall, the thoughts gathering around my brain like that crowd of reporters down on the street. Ingrid worked for Xander, which means that first day when Xander swiped right, when Ingrid looked over my shoulder and said if I didn't want him then she did, she was lying. The morning after his murder when she wondered if the killer might also be a diamond thief, she was lying. All those times Ingrid pretended not to know Xander. She's been lying to me the whole time.

And then I think of another thing Ingrid said.

That necklace couldn't have been the only piece Xander had lying around. Did the killer get more?

That was Ingrid feeling me out, trying to figure out how much I knew, how much I *saw* that night in his penthouse. When I told her nothing—I knew nothing, I saw nothing—she shrugged it off, acted like she believed me. *Money is a big motivator,* she said to me that day, when all along, she was motivated by diamonds.

New questions roll in like the rumblings of a thunderstorm. Did Ingrid know what was going to happen that night? That someone would sneak into Xander's apartment and murder him for his diamonds? Ingrid told me to watch my back—why? Not out of genuine concern. What is my role in all of this?

"I'm . . . I'm a nobody. I write travel articles for online magazines. Xander was just some guy I met on Tinder."

As I say the words, I realize they're not true. Xander swiped first. He initiated contact, something Detective Boomsma questioned me about under the weeping willow at the funeral. He asked if Xander had any reason to seek me out, if our work crossed paths, or if we knew some people in common—which as it turns out, we do.

Ingrid.

Lars is still watching, still pointing the gun at my chest.

"Was it you? Did you kill Xander?"

"Now is not the time for questions, Rayna. Now is the time to tell me the truth. That night at Xander's penthouse. Did he give you anything? Did he mention any names?" Deep in a pocket, his phone begins to buzz, but he ignores it. His gaze sticks to mine.

"No, nothing." I shake my head. "I swear."

"Did someone come to the penthouse while you were there?"

"Yes. They cut off his finger and strangled him in the shower."

He grunts. "Besides the killer, I mean."

"Not that I saw. Xander received a phone call, but that's it."

"A phone call from who?" The phone stops its buzzing, then starts right back up again. Lars hikes up on a hip, wrestling a lump from his pocket. "What time?"

"Sometime around midnight, and I don't know who it was. Xander didn't say, and I didn't ask."

"You just said it was midnight. Why would someone be calling him that late?" Lars asks, but he doesn't seem to expect an answer. He's too engrossed in whatever's on the phone—*my* phone—in his hand. I crane my neck to see the name lighting up the screen, but there's no need, because he flips the phone around.

His eyes narrow into slits. "Why is Willow Prins calling your mobile?"

PART THREE

"It's hard to be a diamond in a rhinestone world."

—Dolly Parton

WILLOW

I drop the phone into my coat pocket and study the building across the street, a four-story monstrosity of sprawling yellow brick dotted with grimy windows that once upon a time, served as a warehouse for Amsterdam's lumber ports. The address Fleur texted is all the way north in the *houthavens*, a miserable spot this time of year, an area pressed up against the IJ River. An icy gale whips up hard enough to almost knock me over. I lean into it and hurry across the deserted street. Somewhere behind those ugly yellow walls, Fleur has Sem.

On the bike ride here, I had almost a half an hour to think about why my sister-in-law would lure me to a sketchy warehouse in an industrial neighborhood on the outskirts of town, in secret. I think of the lies she spun to pick Sem up from school, the lengths she went to bring him here so that I would have to fetch him, her warning not to tell Thomas.

Jan's words beat through my head. *Think who had the most to gain. At least three of them go by the name of Prins.*

But what do Sem and I have to do with any of it?

I clomp up the metal stairs and push through the plain door, then take a rickety elevator to the top floor. A bright space of exposed brick and filthy concrete, lit up by giant arched windows along the back wall. The air smells of stale dust and something animal.

There's only one way for me to go: down a single hallway with a door on either side. The first handle I try doesn't budge, but the door on the left gives way to a bright rectangular room lined with more arched windows, the glass dirty and cracked, the sun lighting up spiderwebs of fissures that stretch up into the building's eaves. At the far end, a wall of more filthy glass with what looks to be an industrial kitchen on the other side.

And Sem. He sits in his coat at a metal table, head in his hands, staring at a flickering iPad.

And just beyond him: Fleur.

She stands at the stove, pouring steaming water into two mugs and looking like she came straight from work. Dark pants and a slim-cut sweater poking out from her winter coat, a fur-lined Moncler I've never seen before. It hangs unzipped despite the temperature in here, as frigid as the air outside. I stare at Sem through the glass—*look up look up look up*—but his implants are Bluetooth enabled, and whatever he's watching is keeping his attention on the screen.

At least he doesn't look frightened. His cheeks are pink from the chill, but he seems otherwise content, engrossed in the winking cartoons.

Fleur turns my way, coming through a door at the end of the glass wall with the two mugs and a bright smile. "You're fast. Did you come by bike or tram?"

She says it in Dutch and in the same tone she'd use during a Sunday supper, cordial and light, as if this isn't kidnapping and she called me here for a friendly visit.

"Cut the crap and just tell me what we're doing here." My answer is in English, my mind far too flustered to work through a Dutch translation—not that there is a good one for *cut the crap*. Some of the best English phrases can't be translated. "Why all the subterfuge?"

"Subterfuge?" Fleur says, matching my English. "Such a fancy word for someone who didn't go to university."

It's a cheap shot, and Fleur knows it. I've never actually let on that my lack of education is a sore subject, but my sister-in-law is proficient in sensing another person's insecurities and tucking them away in a pocket until she can use them as ammunition. I blink at the insult, but that's my only external reaction.

"I'm educated enough to know that you're changing the subject."

She hands me one of the mugs, then fishes the tea bag out of her own cup, dunks it up and down a couple of times, then drops it on the floor with a splat. "Like I told you on the phone, I have something I'd like to discuss, and the old ways of doing things weren't getting me anywhere."

Like luring me to lunch so she can tell me about Thomas's gun. Like pretending she was worried about his well-being. I wonder now if any of what she told me that day was true.

"So you kidnapped my son?" I cast a lightning glance at Sem, who still hasn't noticed me yet, and I'm starting to think maybe that's a good thing. Until I know what Fleur wants, it's probably better he doesn't listen in.

"I'm not going to *hurt* him. I'm not a monster. But this does concern Sem, too." She shrugs.

"Concerns him how?"

"We'll get to that, I promise, but first I need to know I have your full and utter attention."

My hand grips the mug handle, and it's everything I can do to not hurl it, hot tea and all, at her head. When I'm sure my voice is controlled, I say, "You have a lot more than just my attention, Fleur."

She gives me a smile that might as well be an eye roll. "Do you know what it's like to grow up in a family like mine? What am I saying? Of course you don't. You and I, we are not the same. We are nowhere close."

"That's not the insult you think it is, FYI. But do go on."

It's like I didn't even speak. Fleur keeps talking right over me. "I was told which clubs to join, which schools to go to. Which friends I should surround myself with because *Your network is your net worth, Fleur. Choose wisely*. Being a Prins is a full-time job, and it started the day I was born."

"I'm sure that's true, but I don't see what that has to do with me."

"My whole, entire life, I've done every single thing my father expected of me. I studied the subjects he told me to and got the degrees he said would help me *cement Prins's role as the premier diamond house worldwide*. I graduated first in my class in high school *and* university, brought home perfect grades because my father accepted nothing less from me than to be the very best. I was back behind my desk four days after giving birth to twins—*twins*, Willow—because I was taught that nothing and no one was more important than the holy House of Prins. My birthright. My destiny. All my life, I've done everything right, while Thomas Prins can do whatever the hell he wants to do."

Ah. Understanding clicks like a light flipping on. "This is about Thomas's job."

"It's *my* job. Mine." She stabs a thumb at her chest with so much force, tea sploshes over the mug and onto the floor. "I was promised that CEO role. I'm the firstborn. It belongs to *me*."

Suddenly, it occurs to me that any woman who would take a child wouldn't hesitate to spike a cup of tea. I lean over to put my mug on the floor, keeping my eyes on Fleur and beyond, Sem still staring at the iPad. "I don't know what you expect me to do about it. I can't control Willem, or even Thomas for that matter."

"Oh, come on, Willow, you're smarter than that."

"Just a minute ago, you called me uneducated."

"Let me ask you this. What do you think Thomas sees in you?"

Fleur's jab is sharp, and it hits harder than she knows. What *does* Thomas see in me? Not that much, apparently, especially now that there's Cécile.

"God, do you remember Mama's expression when he brought you home that first time? Your hair and your accent and your clothes. Your *clothes*. You were like a caricature of yourself, the poor little Southern girl straight out of the trailer park."

It wasn't a trailer park, but it was close. A dilapidated duplex on the wrong side of town, pressed between a grocery store and a highway. It had bars on every window and jammers on every door, and every night I fell asleep to the sound of shootings and drag races and a constant hum of tires slapping the pavement.

But Fleur is right about one thing: that skirt was awful.

I lean a shoulder against the wall, knocking loose a mini avalanche of dust. "Give me at least a little credit, Fleur. No, I didn't have the kind of luxury you and Thomas do, but when I met Thomas I was making it work. I'd figured out how to take care of myself. Maybe that's what Thomas saw in me, that I'm a survivor."

"You were a *project*, Willow. Someone for Thomas to save. Something for him to design and make shiny and pretty so he can hang it on an arm and show it off to the world."

Again, Fleur is not wrong. Thomas's love isn't for the business side of the House. He doesn't really care about market trends or revenue streams unless it gives him an excuse to work with the master jewelers on the factory floor. That's the job Thomas *really* wants, sketching and coloring and casting the next House piece, making something spectacular out of heat and pressure and air.

Like the bracelet. Like the new, lab-grown line. Like Cécile.

And like me, once upon a time. Somewhere along the way, though, I lost my shine.

"Can you just get to the point?" I say because Fleur doesn't deserve my truth. She doesn't deserve to know how close she is to poking my sore spot. "Tell me why we're here."

"The point is, Willow"—she pauses to give me a sweet, closed-lipped smile—"I need you and Sem to leave."

"You lured me all the way over to the *houthavens* so you could tell us to leave?"

"Yes. Get on a plane and fly back to wherever you came from. Georgia, Florida, another Podunk town in one of those redneck states, I don't care which. Just take Semmy and go. You can file for divorce from there."

"First of all, why would I do that? How does me leaving Thomas help you get his job?"

"It doesn't. But it does ensure that my girls get everything."

Fleur's words that day at the funeral ring through my head, clear as a bell. We were standing in the parking lot, the girls eager to get back to their hockey practices and their lives. They wanted to know why they were required to attend the funeral of a man they barely knew.

Because you and your sister are next in line. The future faces of House of Prins. Because one day, this company will belong to the two of you . . .

When I pushed back, when I reminded Fleur it would also belong to Sem, she said of course it would, but her girls were older and would get there first. That was all she meant by it—or so she said. She was lying to me then, too.

"You wouldn't be completely starting over, so you know. I'm not *that* cruel." With her free hand, she tugs a bag from her pocket, a velvet Prins pouch. She gives it a little shake, rattling the contents. "Fifty stones. Not anything like what Thomas has in the vault at home, of course, but all Prins quality, all of them loupe clean. According to today's index, worth a half a million euros, give or take. That is, assuming you know where to sell them."

I don't miss the way the diamonds in the vault are Thomas's, not mine.

"And you think Thomas would be okay with that? Sem is his son. I can't just pick up and move to the other side of the world. He'd never allow it."

"He would if he knew the truth."

A chill shimmies up my spine, shooting a shiver across both shoulders. My gaze flashes to my son behind the glass. His iPad lies flat on the table, but his eyes are on me, watching the interaction between me and Fleur, and for once, I'm glad he has little interest in learning to read lips. I sign an order: *Stay there.*

Fleur steps closer, the steam from her mug rising in wispy puffs over her face. "Who is Sem's father, Willow? Do you even know?"

Yes, of course I know. He's a musician, a drummer and backup singer I met one night at Northside Tavern when Thomas and I were still in our early days. Sometimes, when Sem cries, I see Rocco's expression as he leans into the microphone, screwing up that beautiful face in order to hit the high notes. That night at the Tavern, I couldn't take my eyes off him.

"Thomas," I say, making sure to hold Fleur's gaze. "Thomas is Sem's father."

"Not according to their DNA, he's not."

I always knew this was a possibility, but honestly, I thought those first, niggling doubts would come from Thomas. I figured Thomas would wonder where Sem's hearing loss came from when more than fifty percent of cases in babies are genetic, or why Sem is left-handed when every Prins in history has used their right. I thought it would be Thomas who'd question all the differences between them, Sem's cowlick that won't obey no matter how much gel you slather on or his fat, stubby fingers when Thomas's and mine are long and thin. If he was suspicious, he never said a word.

And look, it's not like I actually *knew*. I didn't know for sure who Sem's father was, not until much, much later. By then, the drummer had moved on to some dive on the Florida panhandle, Thomas and I were married and living here, and Sem had held on for twenty-nine whole weeks. He was in neonatal intensive care at Amsterdam UMC, a purple and tiny wriggling thing under a warmer and attached to a heart monitor, and the spitting image of his father.

And at that point, what was I supposed to do? Say to Thomas, *Oops, on second thought I guess he's not yours*? I couldn't do that to him, but mostly, I couldn't do that to Sem. Sem wasn't out of the woods, not by a long shot, and my access to Dutch healthcare was dependent on my visa, and my visa was dependent on Thomas and the two of us sharing a home and a bed. If Thomas had tossed me out or worse, put me on the next westward-bound plane, it would have been a death sentence for Sem. I swallowed down the secret, and then pushed aside the nagging worries that Thomas would one day find out. I sacrificed my old life to exist in my new one—a life everyone wanted, but Sem *needed*. For Sem, being a Prins was life or death.

And no, it didn't hurt that by then, I knew the kind of wealth Sem stood to inherit. My future has only been as secure as my marriage, but as a Prins, Sem would be set up for life. The best schools, the best lineage, the best medical care for the rest of his hopefully long days. No way in hell I was walking away from all that.

Regardless, Dutch law is very clear. If Fleur shares the DNA results with Thomas and he discovers I've willfully deceived him, he can petition the court to revoke his fatherhood, and retroactively from the moment Sem was born. Thomas would no longer be Sem's father. Sem would lose his Dutch passport, his family, every single Prins privilege.

Maybe Fleur is bluffing. Maybe she doesn't have the DNA results in her back pocket, but the bigger question is, what will Thomas do? Would he hate me enough for the deception to walk away from Sem?

Thomas, who is too busy making love to Cécile to eat dinner with us or tuck his son into bed. Who wishes he was coming home to her instead of us. Before Cécile, I would have said no, Thomas would *never* turn his back on Sem, but Cécile has thrown a wrench into things. My gaze wanders to my son, to his misbehaving hair and those pudgy fingers I fear will never lengthen, and the truth is, I just don't know.

I push off the wall, my gaze returning to Fleur. "Okay, I'm listening."

RAYNA

My cellphone rings one last time in Lars's hand, then flips Willow's call to voicemail.

"What's the code?" Lars says, and he doesn't have to ask me twice. His other hand is still holding the gun, and he's aiming it at my face.

"0-2-1-9-8-8." My birth month and year, programmed in my new phone. Old habits die hard, I guess.

He ticks it in and the lock screen dissolves. "Call her back."

"And say what?"

"I don't know. See what she wants."

"Probably just to talk. Willow is a friend."

Friend might be overstating things, but I don't really have a good alternative. She's someone I talked to a couple of times, who poured me full of wine and warned me of dangers she didn't quite define, though as it turns out, she wasn't wrong. I really wish she'd been faster getting me that gun.

"She called you"—he taps a finger to the screen—"three times in a row. Seems like she wants more than just to talk."

The phone buzzes in his hand, not with another call but a voicemail hitting the system. He taps Play and puts it on speaker, and Willow's voice fills the room and my head.

Hey, Rayna, I really wish you'd pick up the phone because I need help, and I'm counting on you to get this on time. I'm standing outside a warehouse near the station, where Fleur is holding Sem. She picked him up from school and then brought him here, and she won't tell me why. I have no idea what I'm about to walk in to, only that I'm going in there to get him back. If you don't hear from me in the next twenty minutes or so, call your detective friend and give him this address: Van Diemenstraat 408. Tell him a child's life is in danger and to hurry.

There's so much to latch on to here. First of all, Fleur took Sem. She kidnapped her own nephew.

Lars leans over and grabs my sneaker from the floor, then tosses it at my head. "Let's go."

I don't have to ask where we're going, but I can't imagine what Lars thinks we'll find when we get there. Three members of the Prins family, sure, but what's he going to do, hold them for ransom in exchange for the missing diamonds? Like I tried to tell him last night, whoever has those stones is long gone.

I wriggle my sneaker onto my foot. "Okay, but can I at least pee first? And I wouldn't say no to a slice of toast."

Lars sighs, gesturing to the hall with his gun. "Toilet, but hurry."

In the bathroom, I empty my bladder and look around for anything I can use as a weapon, but toilets in this country are the size of a coat closet and there's not much here. A container of liquid hand soap, a grimy toilet brush in a plastic stand, a perpetual calendar Ingrid uses to keep track of birthdays hanging from a nail in the wall. I stash the calendar behind the toilet, then wriggle the nail from the plaster. It's two centimeters long at best, but I press the end to a finger pad and it's sharp enough to draw blood.

Lars raps on the door with the gun, two hard and metallic pops against wood that make me jump a good inch off the floor. "What's taking so long?"

"Okay, okay." I flush and drop the nail into my pocket, pushing it with a finger all the way to the bottom where it's level with the seam. "I'm coming."

I open the door to find two bodies, Lars and a stony-faced Ingrid, waiting for me in the hall.

"*You.*" I stab a finger at her face. "You put all those trackers in my stuff, didn't you? Of course you did. You had plenty of access."

"I don't know what you're talking about." She makes sure to hold my gaze when she says it, but I see all the other signs. The way she curls her hands into fists to pop her thumbs, the way her voice drifts higher than usual. Barry used to have the same tells whenever he was lying. Ingrid put those trackers in my things. She worked with Xander. Though I still don't see what my role is in their plan.

And Lars?

"So what, the two of you are working together now?"

Ingrid makes a throaty sound that says, *not a chance.*

Lars shakes his head.

"Then how did you know she was working with Xander?"

"It's my business to know everything about my targets." He grabs me by the arm and shoves me in the direction of the door. "Here's what's going to happen. The three of us are going to walk calmly and quietly down the stairs and out the front door. If you talk to anybody on the way, I'll shoot you. If you signal them or even look at them funny, I'll shoot you. Do you see where I'm going with this? One of you does anything other than walk and look straight ahead, you're both dead. Understood?"

Ingrid and I exchange a look, then bob our heads in a simultaneous nod.

"What about the reporters?" I say.

He wags my phone in the air. "You just tweeted a picture of yourself standing in line at the Rijks."

The picture was from a couple of weeks ago, and all it would take is for one of the reporters to zoom in on the tickets in my hand, and they'll see the date and time. One detail-oriented journalist to figure out they've been sent on a wild goose chase. Let's just pray one of them is smart enough to check.

"Let's go," he says, gesturing to the door with the gun. "My car is parked around the corner."

Silently, Ingrid and I file out the door and start the long trek down the stairs.

About halfway down, a door pops open at the end of the stairwell, an elderly neighbor grabbing the mail someone had dropped by his door. He greets us in Dutch, and it sounds friendly enough, but there's still a gun pointed at our backs so Ingrid and I don't look his way. We stare straight ahead and keep moving. The neighbor picks up his mail and goes back inside, closing the door with a click.

"Good girls," Lars says, sticking close to our heels.

The reporters are long gone by the time we step outside and follow Lars's directions to the left. His car is just where he said it would be, wedged between a dusty van and a tree on the next street. It's also surprisingly nice for someone who introduced himself as a starving artist, a four-door Tesla, but then again, Lars has been lying to me since the beginning.

He orders me behind the wheel and Ingrid to the passenger's seat, then drops into the back seat, scooting to the very middle. He taps the gun against our biceps, both a reminder and a warning. First mine, then Ingrid's.

"Start the car. Plug in the address. Van Diemenstraat 408."

I hit the brake and look for a button, but there's no need. The car fires up and Google Maps pops up on the screen. Ingrid enters the address, and the system spits out the route, a twisty tour along the edges of the city to the *houthavens*. A solid fifteen minutes with traffic, and I think of Willow, the gravity of the situation dragging down her voice as she tells me to call the detective. I just hope that whatever we find there, it's not too late.

I put the car in reverse and ease out of the parking spot, slamming the brakes to let a biker pass. Once he's gone, I back out and wriggle the car into Drive.

"At least tell me why," I say, sparing a glance at Ingrid while I follow the little blue line to the next corner, where it directs me to take a left. "What did you and Xander need me for? What was the plan here?"

She gives a pointed look to Lars over her shoulder, but he must want to know, too, because she turns back with a sigh. "Xander was spooked. He said someone at Prins knew what we were doing. He didn't dare to meet face-to-face anymore. He wasn't meeting with any of his people, apparently. He said we needed to find another way to communicate, another way to get the stones from him to me."

"Only Xander died before you two could use me as a mule."

Ingrid doesn't respond. She stares out the windshield and presses her lips into a tight line.

"He *didn't*? How?"

She glances over with a roll of her eyes. "He put them in a lipstick tube and dropped it in your bag for me to remove the second you got home." She twists around on the seat to face Lars. "And before you start, I don't have those diamonds. They were stolen. I'm guessing by you."

It takes me a couple of beats to catch up. Ingrid is referring to the break-in, and it was diamonds—not cash—that disappeared from her room. No wonder she clammed up as soon as the police arrived. No wonder she got so mad when I asked her if she was insured. How do you insure stolen diamonds?

The navigation dumps me onto a wider road, two lanes flanked by bike paths and separated by two sets of tram tracks. It's a lot to keep an eye on, especially when there's a gun pointed at the back of my head. I grip the steering wheel, and it's a good thing the speed limit is a snail's pace, because after Ingrid's little tidbit, my mind is spinning with more than traffic.

Ingrid, who pointed me to Tinder and helped me craft my profile. Who yanked my phone from my fingers and selected things like age, height, location, and maximum distance from the apartment we shared. Who would have told Xander all those things about me to help him zero in on my profile. Maybe he got lucky, or maybe he swiped for days. Either way, I'm guessing they also had a backup plan.

But the more pressing point is, Xander didn't want to date me. He wanted to drop diamonds in my pockets and use me to courier them to Ingrid. I think of the way he didn't take his eyes off me at the bar and later the restaurant, leaning in as he peppered me with questions about my work, my travels, my life. He laughed at my jokes, made me feel funny and interesting. He made me feel beautiful. It was a classic case of love bombing, but Xander didn't like me, he was *manipulating* me.

A biker comes out of nowhere, swerving over the line as it merges into the thick stream of bicycles pedaling next to us in the bike lane. I see it in my periphery and overcorrect, almost sideswiping a tram in the process.

"Watch out!" Lars shouts from the back seat, and I slam the brakes, both from the volume and the pressure of holding the car steady between moving objects on both sides. Ingrid squeals and grabs the door handle.

"I've never driven in Holland before, okay?" I say, my gaze flitting from tram to bike to the Opel riding its brakes in front of me. "How do you people do this? Your streets are like a freaking obstacle course."

The light flips to red and I hit the brakes again, breathing a sigh of relief at the chance to regroup. I slow to a stop behind the Opel,

Ingrid's earlier words bubbling up in my head. She said that she and Xander wanted to use me to communicate. "Communicate how? What, did Xander drop a note for you in my bag?"

"No, on your Instagram."

I think back to his flurry of likes on pictures going back months. But there was only one he commented on, the shot of me in front of the butterfly mural in Nashville. Nice wings, he wrote. Next time you go to Music City #ImIn.

And then there was Ingrid, commenting on every picture I posted, fragments of run-on English that felt random and often a little confusing. I brushed it off to her clunky language skills, but now I'm thinking of the comment she posted on the picture of me in that necklace, three fire emojis followed by words I didn't understand at the time: #readywhenyouare.

He's in. She's ready when he is. I'm a fucking idiot.

By now we're on the north side of town, where the iconic facades of stair-step rooflines with white piping have fallen away into something grittier. Big modern buildings dingy with soot, a maze of dark bridges and tunnels. The navigation system points us down one where passenger trains rumble overhead, the tracks leading to and from Central Station. We come out the other side into an area that looks nothing like the Amsterdam I'm used to seeing. Spacious. Modern and bright. A mix of new homes and old industrial warehouses, plenty of water and sky.

A couple more turns, and Lars shoves his upper body in the space between us, the gun resting on the console. "Find a parking spot. It's just up there."

He juts the gun at an ugly square building of yellow brick. I find a spot a hundred meters further down and squeeze the Tesla in. Lars orders us to sit tight while he pulls up the parking app on his phone and pays for an hour's time, and the absurdity hits me. A criminal who's afraid of a parking ticket.

Ingrid swivels around in her seat, a rush of vehement Dutch I take to be a plea for him to let her go. He points the gun at her forehead, and she shuts up.

He swings the barrel to mine. "You know the rules."

I shift on the seat, and the flimsy nail in my pocket pokes me in the thigh. I've brought a nail to a gun fight. I nod.

"Then let's go."

With no other choice, Ingrid and I clamber out of the car and let Lars march us inside.

WILLOW

"Those fifty stones." My gaze dips to the bag in Fleur's hand, a deep velvet Prins pouch. Not the twelve diamonds I wanted Jan to help me find, but possibly even better. "How do I know they're not lab-growns?"

"Because I'm Fleur Prins. Because my entire reputation, my life, my *destiny* is dealing in mined diamonds. Not those second-rate imposters grown in a lab."

"Except if you're the type of person who'd run a DNA test on my son, whom you essentially kidnapped from school, then I'd imagine you're also the type to screw me over with fifty carats of imposter stones grown to the exact same weight and cut and color of certified Prins stones, including the cert number engraved on the girdle."

It's what Xander would have done, what he *had* done with the twelve stones I asked him to grow. Twelve identical twins, engraved with the certification numbers of the original mined Prins, and voilà—no one suspects a thing. Xander's the one who taught me that trick. As long as Jan makes sure the original mined diamonds are long gone, no one will bother with having them tested.

Fleur's face doesn't change, but her silence is telling.

I fold my arms across my chest. "Those stones are not worth half a million dollars. They're not worth anything close."

She drops the velvet pouch back into her pocket. "Fine. So you're smarter than I gave you credit for, but let's not forget you're the one with the problem here. Not me."

"I don't know, Fleur. It seems to me that your problem might be even bigger than mine. Because what happens when people start figuring out what Xander was doing? Growing copies of Prins stones that were so good that not even you or Thomas would know the difference, not unless you put the stone through a diamond detector, and even then . . ." I shrug just like Xander did that night in his penthouse, quick and nonchalant. "Lab-growns make it through the machines designed to identify all the time, don't they? Especially when the buyer doesn't know to have them tested."

I have to admit, it was a pretty genius scheme. Growing and polishing stones to be replicas of certified Prins stones, essentially creating two identical diamonds—one "real" and one "fake," but who switched the stones? Was it the jeweler? The diamond trader? The polisher or any of the other half-dozen people who handled the stone along the way? The price of the fraud falls on the consumer—or if they're smart, their insurance. Like that couple in Blaricum with the ten-carat solitaire. By the time they figured out the stones had been switched, the offender was long gone, and so was the mined diamond.

Fleur regards me with squinty eyes. "You have enough to worry about. Why don't you let me worry about the House? Prins is *my* company, or it will be as soon as you go back to wherever you came from."

"How does this work? You think Thomas will be so devastated he'll—what? Give up? Shrug his shoulders and hand you the reins? That doesn't make any sense."

"He will, once the board finds out what Xander was doing. Thomas is the one who introduced the lab-grown line. He was the one who hired Xander. This is all on him."

"Except it's not, is it? You knew about Xander's scheme all along, didn't you? And you were fine with it, because you hoped it would be Thomas's downfall. You were hoping it would change your father's mind."

"And it will. It has. He's already in talks with the board about replacing him."

This is news to me, and I'm betting it would be for Thomas, too, if he were here. Automatically, my heart squeezes for him until I remember Cécile. Cécile who is sucking up all his love and attention instead of him giving it to me or Sem.

"It never made any sense anyway, Papa appointing Thomas. My brother never wanted to be CEO. He was always more interested in the design side of the business, always busy with his pretty drawings. Rings. Pendants. Your bracelet. He spends more time on the floor with the designers and polishers than he does worrying about profit and loss margins. Do you know he almost flunked out of Nyenrode? Papa had to hire a whole team of tutors. He had to pull some very expensive strings to drag him through six long years of school, and even then, Thomas doesn't know what EBITDA means. He doesn't have a clue! I can't imagine what Papa was thinking."

I stay silent. No matter what my opinion of my sister-in-law is, Fleur is right; it never made any sense for Willem to pass her over to appoint Thomas CEO, especially if even a scrap of what she just said is true. She's always been so much better suited for the role than her brother. Why not hand her the reins?

Ask yourself who had the most to gain.

I think of Willem at last Sunday's supper, his impatience that the insurance company was dragging their feet. His strict orders that Thomas tie himself into knots to ensure Xander's murder stayed separate from the Cullinan theft in the press, the constant discussion of company business despite his retirement. Willem is still very much in charge, both of the family and the House.

A clueless and distracted CEO would be mighty handy if, say, you never wanted to retire in the first place.

Or if you wanted to sneak contraband diamonds into shipments from Asian labs. Or if you shut your eyes to something that would torpedo your brother's job as CEO—no. Not just shut your eyes. Fleur is more proactive than that.

Fleur, who wants Thomas's job more than anything. Who never makes a move without thinking twelve steps ahead. Since when did Fleur ever sit back and play a passive role? Since when was she ever not in control? She wouldn't just sit back and watch her brother fail. She would help him crash and burn. Fleur, who isn't above kidnapping a little boy so that her twins would inherit *everything*.

"Fleur, what did you do?"

She opens her mouth to answer, but it's a deeper voice that rips the air.

"Sorry to disturb, ladies, but which one of you has my diamonds?"

RAYNA

Willow and Fleur whirl around, and their twin masks of surprise would be comical if there weren't a loaded gun pointed at my chest. They take in Lars and the weapon in his hand, the way he's positioned himself so he can cover all of us at the same time. Ingrid and me huddled in our winter coats a few feet away, Willow and Fleur in theirs just beyond. None of us move, but Fleur is the first to recover.

"Who are you? Why are you here?" Her voice is all Prins haughtiness and bravado, her question directed at Lars and Ingrid but not at me. Her eyes brush right over mine and keep going. "This is a private meeting. I'm going to have to ask you to leave."

Before any of us can answer, Willow's gaze finds mine across the dusty space. "You got my message."

She's standing by one of the arched windows by the exposed brick wall, her face lit up with dingy sun streaming through from outside, a beacon for the emotions simmering there: surprise, shock, determination. Her son, Sem, sits like a statue behind a wall of filthy glass.

Not a question, but I nod anyway.

"Did you do what I asked?"

Call the detective. Tell him a child's life is in danger and to hurry.

I don't think Sem has spotted the gun in Lars's fist just yet, but he knows enough to be afraid. His eyes are wide, the skin of his mouth stretched tight. Half hidden behind the flap of her coat,

Willow signs words he must understand, because his gaze sticks to her hand while hers sticks to mine.

I look lightning quick to Lars and shake my head, hoping she gets the message behind the gesture. No, I didn't call the detective. I didn't get the chance. No one is coming to save us, and perhaps even more pressing, no one but us knows we're here.

"Well, I did." Willow hooks a thumb in the chain strap of her Chanel bag, hanging from a shoulder. "I did what you asked."

I nod because I understand, too. This is not Willow, one-upping me. This is her, telling me a secret packed in our mutual gaze. Willow has the gun we talked about. It's in her bag. I just pray she knows how to use it.

Lars has had enough of our back and forth. He raises the gun, stretching his arm long so she's staring down the barrel. "Stop fucking around and give me my diamonds."

This is the place where Willow is supposed to look shocked. Where she says something like, *What are you talking about? What diamonds?*

But that's not what she says at all.

"You already got your diamonds."

It shouldn't sting as much as it does, the realization that Willow lied—or at the very least, concealed her involvement here. Despite what I said to Lars earlier, the two of us are not friends. She owes me nothing, not even an explanation. I tell myself I shouldn't care.

And yet . . .

And yet.

She meets my gaze, only for a second or two before it flits away.

Lars cocks his head and scowls. "You think I'd be standing here right now if I had those stones? When I said you'd never see my face again, I meant it."

"And yet here you are." If I didn't know better, I'd say Willow sounds annoyed.

"Uh, *yeah*." Lars's eyes go wide. "That's because they weren't there. The safe you said would be stuffed with stones was empty. Somebody cleaned it out before I got there."

Willow flips the clasp on the front of her bag, a move she disguises behind a subtle shift to her right. "Nice try, but I'm not buying it."

"What, you think I'm lying? I'm telling you, somebody else got there first. They took the diamonds you swore would be there."

"I swore nothing."

"Hang on, hang on." Fleur holds up both hands, her gaze bounces between them. "You know him? She knows you?"

"Yes, Willow knows me," Lars says at the same time Willow says, "No," but I don't know why she bothers. All this talk about diamonds, the cleaned-out safe, the accusations of lying. By now we've all figured out that Lars isn't exactly a stranger.

"I'm the guy she hired to kill Xander."

Lars's words fall like a bomb into the room.

I gasp as Willow gives a hard shake of her head. "No. *No.* I didn't hire you to *kill* him. I hired you to clean out his safe."

Fleur takes a step to the side, putting some distance between them. "You hired a *hit man*?"

"I just told you, I hired a *thief* who as it turns out is also a murderer. I never said to *kill* Xander. I gave him the safe code and said he could have everything in there, and that's it. I *definitely* didn't tell him to cut off Xander's finger and strangle him with a zip tie. That's all on Lars."

Fleur makes a face, and I know she's picturing it, too, Xander dead and bloody on the floor. For his sake, I just hope he was dead by the time Lars pulled out the knife. I hope he was at least spared that agony.

Next to me, Ingrid releases a long, weary breath. "Do I really need to be here for this? I'm already late for work."

"Shut up," Lars barks, turning to Ingrid just long enough for Willow to sign something to her son, a rapid-fire movement of her hands that I don't understand, but Sem does. He gives her a slow, solemn nod. Ingrid sees it, too, but she doesn't let on. She gathers her teddy bear coat snug around her neck and mumbles something in Dutch, her breath sending curls of condensation into the frigid air.

Lars aims his gun back at Willow. "Listen to me, hear what I'm telling you. Xander was already dead when I got there. His safe was already empty. I saw the body and I got the hell out of there."

"Is this some kind of trick? Because I already paid you plenty. As I recall, twenty thousand euros."

"C'mon, Willow. You and I both know the diamonds were the real incentive."

"What diamonds?" Fleur says, turning to Willow. "You promised this guy diamonds?"

"The diamonds that were in Xander's safe!" Willow says, as much to Fleur as to Lars. She shifts her body another step to the right, and I see where she's going, why she keeps creeping further into the room. She's aiming for the spot between Sem and Lars's gun so she can plant her body between the two.

The only problem is, she's doing more than putting herself in the path of a bullet. She's dragging Lars's gaze to the wall of glass. Step by step, little by little. Another meter or two, and it'll be hard not to notice the little boy sitting behind it.

"Why, though?" Fleur whirls to face Lars, not willing to let it go. "*Why* did she hire you to steal the contents of Xander's safe? What did she tell you was in there?"

Fleur is not the only one here who doesn't understand. Willow hired Lars to creep through Xander's apartment, to search the rooms one by one until he found the safe, which Lars claims was empty. So . . . what? He murdered Xander out of fury? For revenge? I don't understand *any* of this.

"Did you know I was there? Did you see me sleeping?"

It's like I didn't even speak. My words don't register with Lars, with anyone. They're all too focused on the missing diamonds, the empty safe.

Ingrid lets loose another sigh. "Can I just go? Seriously. This has nothing to do with me."

It's too many questions coming at Lars at the same time, and from too many people. He swipes an arm through the air, poking the gun first at Ingrid, then me. "You two, shut up."

Fleur is next: "Lady, I don't fucking know. Willow wanted those diamonds gone. She paid me to make them disappear. It's not my job to ask why."

And then, finally, he aims his words and weapon at Willow. "A safe stuffed with diamonds, that's what I was promised."

"Not by me! I never promised you that."

"Twelve diamonds worth a million, assuming you know where to sell them, plus an eleven-and-three-quarter-carat, internally flawless, original Prins-cut diamond that will net you millions—plural." He glances at Fleur, lifting a single shoulder. "Probably not a direct quote, but you get the gist."

"Eleven and three-quarter carats," Fleur says, her voice flat. She turns to Willow, watching her through squinted eyes. "Internally flawless. Original Prins cut."

"The Cullinan is in the vault at home. Ask Thomas. We just saw it."

"And the other twelve stones?"

Willow juts a thumb in Lars's direction; her other hand reaches under the flap of her Chanel bag. "You're going to believe this guy? Honestly, Fleur. I thought you were smarter than that."

Willow has a point. Lars is a thief. An admitted criminal who doesn't seem all that opposed to murder. It's not all that far of a stretch to think he's a liar, too.

But also, there's this: What are the chances? Two thieves, both sneaking past locked doors and security cameras to break into Xander's penthouse on the same day, likely only minutes apart. I don't believe Lars's story, either.

But Fleur seems to. She glares at her sister-in-law, her fingers brushing over a lump in her coat pocket, tapping whatever's in there until it makes a muted chinking sound. "Yes, I believe him, because I know the kind of stones Xander was peddling. I know he was growing matches and switching them out."

Willow arches a plucked brow. "How, because you were helping him?"

"Helping him? You think *I* was helping him?"

Willow's hand fishes around in the bottom of her bag, and what's taking her so long? Also, what's her plan here—to shoot Lars through her Chanel bag? To whip out the gun and take him by surprise? I try to catch her eye, but Willow keeps her focus on Fleur.

"There's no way Xander could have gotten away with it for this long, not without help from someone inside the House. How else would he have known which stones to copy? Which diamonds were headed for jewelers in on the scheme? If anyone found out what Xander was doing, if consumers found out the rock they paid hundreds of thousands of euros for was worth only a tenth of that, it would be the end of the lab-grown line. Thomas's pet project, destroyed. I can't believe I didn't think of it sooner."

Fleur laughs, a harsh, angry sound. "What about the twelve diamonds in Xander's safe? Tell us about those, Willow. What were you planning to do with them?"

Lars scowls, running his free hand over his chin. "What do you mean, *grow a match*? A match to what?"

"Xander would have needed copies of the certs," Willow says, ignoring everyone but Fleur. "He could have requested them from the grading institutes, but not without raising suspicion. But you could. You could get him those certs, and then he could use them as blueprints to grow stones with the exact same weights, exact same measurements and colors, exact same crystals or clouds or feathers in the exact same spots."

Willow is yelling now, two bright spots glowing on her cheeks, same as Fleur's.

Fleur fills her lungs and yells right back, "What about you? *You* had Xander grow a copy of the Cullinan, and for what? What were you planning to do with it, Willow, and what are those other twelve—"

"OH MY GOD ENOUGH." Ingrid's shriek is loud enough to pierce an eardrum. An icy wind pushes through the cracks in the arched windows on the wall, rattling the glass enough to rain dirt and mortar onto the floor, but otherwise the room is silent.

"You're both right," she says. "Fleur told Xander which diamonds to copy and which traders and jewelers would be willing to switch out the stones for a cut. The mined stones he gave to me, to move on the black market. Willow asked him to grow copies of twelve Prins stones, that rock on her finger, the Cullinan, a whole bunch of others. But Xander got spooked. He was convinced someone was on to him. I'm guessing that's why she hired Lars to get those stones out of Xander's safe, before he did something *really* crazy and told her husband what Willow was planning with those twelve rocks."

"Which was?" Lars says, but Willow doesn't have to answer. The rest of us already know.

We all know that none of that jewelry Willow is wearing, the ring and the studs in her ears and whatever else is under all those layers of cashmere and lambswool, belongs to her. Same with the money. She told me as much that day in the café. *I have access to dough. Not at all the same thing as having it.* I think of her face when she told me about her husband's affair, her worries about what would happen to her son, to his health, once she no longer has access to a Prins bank account. Willow's plans for Xander's lab-growns were the same as his: to set them in the pieces her husband gave her, to switch them out for the original, mined stones. Twelve flawless Prins diamonds for her to sell, and nobody but her and Xander would know the difference. Not unless they put the stones through a machine, and even then, why would they suspect anything? Lab-grown diamonds look, feel, and sparkle exactly like their mined counterparts. Honestly, it's kind of brilliant.

The answer clicks in Lars's mind, too. "Fakes? You sent me there for *fakes*?"

"Lab-grown diamonds aren't fake. They're exactly like mined diamonds in composition and fire and sparkle. They're still worth a lot of money, especially that copy of the Cullinan. Maybe not millions plural, but still a big nu—"

"They're fucking fakes!" he says, cutting her off. "I don't want lab-grown diamonds. I want the real thing. I want what you owe me, you bitch." When she doesn't respond, he raises the gun and stalks forward, four long strides until it's pressed against her forehead.

"Here." Willow tugs her hand from her bag and wriggles the ring from her finger, holding it out to Lars. "That middle stone is very valuable. I'd give you more, but these and the earrings are all I'm wearing." She gives him those, too, then shoves up her sleeves to show him her empty wrists, tugs her coat away from her naked neck.

Lars drops the pieces in his pocket, then swivels the barrel to Fleur. "Now you."

It takes Fleur a full sixty seconds to peel it all off. Multiple rings, the marble-sized solitaires in her ears, a couple of bracelets and glittery pendants tangled in chains around her neck. "This is it. There's no more."

Lars is gearing up for a protest when it happens. His gaze drifts over Willow's shoulder and locks on the little body sitting stock-still behind the glass, staring at his mother's right hand. Willow takes a big step to her right, a human wall smack into the path between them, but it's too late. Lars has already seen.

His face spreads into a smile and he lowers the gun, tucking it behind his big body. "Hey, kid. Come here. Your mom and I want to talk to you."

WILLOW

I stare at the man I've seen only one time before, on the edge of a shabby park on the south side of town, and the fury that floods through me is hot and clean and pure—next to my love for Sem, the purest thing I've ever felt. Lars grins at my son through the glass, and my fingers tingle where they touch the gun. I want to shoot this man. If he so much as touches my son, I won't hesitate. I'll shoot him, and I won't miss.

"Hey, kid, come here!" He shouts it this time.

"Leave him alone," I say, and in a voice that is not my own. My jaw clenches so tight it hurts. This is the man on the other end of the texts, and while I can shrug off his threats when they're aimed at me, pointing his attention and the gun at my son has black spots clouding my vision. "Leave my son alone."

Lars tries again, this time in Dutch. "*Hé, jongen. Kom hier—nú.*" Come here *now*.

Sem doesn't move. Nothing. Not even a blink. He keeps his eyes on my hand and his butt in the chair, no indication at all that he heard. And he probably didn't. Earlier I told him to look at nothing but my hand, and so far he hasn't.

Good boy, I sign, and this time I don't try to hide it. *Stay.*

Lars turns back to me with a frustrated grunt. "What, is he deaf or something?"

"Yes. Those things on his head are the processors for his cochlear implants, but he still misses a lot. He hears you, but only when he knows to listen." I sign another order, this time with both hands. *Listen only to my hands. Not to what I say with my mouth.*

Without looking up to meet my gaze, Sem dips his chin in a solemn nod.

"What did you say?"

"I told him not to worry. I said that everything's okay." A lie I pray is the truth.

"Tell him to get over here. Tell him we're going for a ride."

My heart hammers in my chest, my palms going slick with sweat despite the freezing air. Not a chance in hell my son is getting in Lars's car. I managed to get the magazine seated with one hand, but the gun is not loaded. For that I need both hands.

"A ride where?"

"First your house, then hers." Lars stabs his gun in Fleur's direction. Two Prinses; two vaults full of diamonds.

But the fifth generation heirs of a diamond house have learned a thing of two in the last hundred-plus years. Like how to safeguard their stones with multiple levels of security, for example, by programming a code that opens the vault at the same time it sets off a silent alarm at the police station. Not that Lars will ever get that close. I only need a second or two to whip the gun out and pull back the slide, and then I will shoot that asshole through the heart.

"Tell your kid to come here." He swings his own gun to Sem. Pointing it at his little head. "*Tell. Him.*"

"Okay, okay. Come, Semmy," I say, signing through the glass. "It's okay. You can come."

I tell him more, too—to come straight to me, to not look anywhere else but at my hands.

Slowly, Sem slides from the chair. Leaves the iPad flashing cartoons and moves to the open doorway at the end of the wall. He peers around the corner, his gaze zeroing in on my hands.

I sign it once more: *When I sign run, go as fast as you can down the stairs. Not the elevator but the stairs. Wait for me outside.*

Lars shoots me a furious scowl. "What's wrong with him? Does he talk?"

I nod, motioning my son to come straight to me. He scurries over, and I tuck him behind my body, holding him there with both hands. It's what I was trying to do earlier, become a human shield, before Lars spotted him over my shoulder.

"At least let them go," I say, gesturing to Rayna and Jan's blonde apprentice—Astrid? Ingrid? I don't remember her name but I also don't really care. It's Rayna I'm concerned about. I need to get her out of here so she can do what I asked and call the detective. "They have nothing to do with this."

Lars laughs, a dark, angry sound. "Not a chance in hell, lady. I'm not *that* stupid."

The blonde spouts off a stream of vehement Dutch, promises she won't tell, that she'll keep her mouth closed, but Rayna keeps her gaze trained on me. She tilts her head to the side, and I can see the questions swirling in her pupils, questions she knows better than to ask out loud. Questions like: *Where's the gun? Why haven't you pulled it out yet?* I stare back with what I hope is an unambiguous answer: *Soon. Be ready.*

"Yo, kid." Lars leans down, propping a hand on his knee as he shouts at the side of Sem's head. "You're not going to give me any trouble, are you? Look at me when I talk to you."

If Sem hears anything, he doesn't respond. He just buries his face in my back.

"I'll give you everything in the safe. Just leave Sem out of it."

"Sem. Nice Dutch name. Hey, Sem. *Sem.*"

Nothing. No response. My fingers tingle with adrenaline, with determination. Two seconds. That's all I need.

Lars straightens. "I thought you said he could hear."

I spread my feet, make my body a bigger shield. "He can, normally. The batteries in his implants must be low. They—"

Lars lurches forward before I can finish, before I can react with more than a blink of surprise. He grabs Sem by the collar and gives a mighty tug. Sem squeals, his fists gripping at the fabric of my coat, his cries for help clawing at my heart.

But Lars is too quick and too strong. He wrenches Sem loose and drags him into the air, pinning him to his chest with one steely arm.

With his other, he holds the gun.

"Lars, please." My eyes fill with tears, and so do Sem's. His mouth opens in a silent wail. "*Please.* I'll give you anything you want."

I stare at my son, at the twin streams of tears rolling down his cheeks, and Lars might as well have shoved his fist through my chest and ripped out my heart. My hand wanders to my bag, one finger ducking under the flap. "Point the gun away from my son. Aim it at me instead."

"Not until I get my diamonds."

"Here." Fleur tugs the velvet bag from her pocket, pries loose the strings, and pours the stones into a palm. "Fifty carats. You can have all of them in exchange for Sem."

Lars's cheeks flush red with fury. "Are you fucking kidding me? You've had those in your pocket this whole time?"

"They're yours. Put Sem down and come get them."

"How do I know they're real and not fakes grown in a lab?"

"Because I'm Fleur Prins," she says, the same proud speech she gave to me only a few minutes earlier. "Because mined diamonds are my life, my *destiny.* I detest those second-rate imposters as much as you do."

Lars's fingers tighten on the gun, the barrel still dangerously close to Sem's skin, but the diamonds are doing their job. Lars is distracted enough not to notice when I reach a hand into my bag, or the way Rayna has crept up behind me. My fingers making contact with cold, smooth metal . . .

"Here." Fleur wriggles her fingers so the diamonds bounce around her palm, and Lars is like Xander when he saw the Cullinan on my wrist: blinded by the fire and sparkle. "They're yours. You can have all of them, just put Sem down."

As usual, Fleur has thought this through. She waits until his grip has loosened a little on Sem to do it, to toss all those fifty carats up into the air. She hurls them high in the direction of one of the arched windows, directing them into a ray of milky sunlight. The stones spin in the gleam, shooting colorful rainbows onto the exposed brick, the dusty floor, our clothes. It works like a charm. Lars sees nothing but diamonds.

He doesn't notice when I whip the gun from my bag and tuck it in the folds of my coat.

He doesn't see Rayna step up behind me, how the gun slides from my hand into hers, the way my hand comes away empty.

He doesn't see how Fleur skitters backward, getting into position.

The diamonds hit the floor and scatter, cutting lines in the dirt and dust. Lars dumps a wriggling Sem onto the ground and dives after them. He goes for the biggest ones first, snatching them up before chasing after the next, all in one fluid movement, and I don't think about what will happen if Rayna doesn't know how to use that gun. The only thing I see is Sem.

I snatch him off the floor with shaking hands and hug him to my chest while he sobs and sobs. "I've got you," I say, pressing my lips to his processor. "You're fine. I've got you. You're safe. Everything's fine."

I say it over and over until he hears me, until he understands the words and believes them, until his little body turns limp and shuddering in my arms.

Right up until he hears the shot.

RAYNA

It's only thirteen minutes before the cops arrive, but we pack as much as we can into those thirteen minutes. Fleur sits us down at the table behind the glass—me on the stool at the far end, Willow next to me with a sniffling Sem clinging to her chest—and walks us through what happens next.

"Here we go," she says as heavy boots clatter up the stairs. "Just tell them what we talked about and everything will be fine."

Easy for her to say. Fleur is a Prins, and it's not like Willow and I were given much of a choice. We were fed our scripts and swallowed them whole, too traumatized to come up with a believable alternative or even think through the scenarios that would end in the detective not slapping on handcuffs. Willow gives me an encouraging nod, and I nod back even though . . . holy shit. I am so not prepared for this.

Detective Boomsma is the first to appear, trailed by a half dozen cops and more behind them still on the stairs. He takes his time as he moves across the space, pausing to study the dust tracks on the floor, the big arched window minus its pane, the carnage four stories below. I made the mistake of looking out that same window, so I know the horror of what's down there. Lars, his eyes open and mouth agape, lying on a messy pool of blood and brains, glass shards glittering like diamonds all around.

At least Sem didn't see that part. Willow kept him far, far away from that window, and she made sure he didn't see anything that happened right after it, either. She slipped his processors into her pocket the second that shot rang out, and she kept his face buried in her coat. From the moment Lars went sailing through the window, Sem didn't hear or see a thing, which means he can't be a witness.

Neither can Ingrid. She vanished right around the time that Lars did, when gravity tugged him to the ground. I think of his face just before it disappeared from view, and a shudder runs down my spine.

Detective Boomsma peels away from the other officers and makes his way slowly to the kitchen, pausing in the doorway to fiddle with his phone. I register his familiar frame as he moves to the table, the long limbs and hardened eyes as he tosses his phone to the table. On the screen, Voice Memos is recording everything.

"Tell me what happened. In English, please."

That last bit is for me, I know, not so much so that I can understand, but more so I can dispute any stories that stray from the truth—which I most definitely won't be doing. This is Fleur's show, and I'm happy to let her take the lead.

In a calm, controlled voice, she spouts off the tale we agreed to for the detective, a short and dirty summary of the events that led to a man falling four stories to his death. I watch the detective's face the whole time, and I can't tell if he thinks it's the most cockamamie story he's ever heard, or the most brilliant.

When she's done, Detective Boomsma sits silently for a few seconds, staring out the window Lars busted through only moments before, blinking at the blue sky and clouds as if trying to put them together, all these puzzle pieces that are not quite seamless.

Finally, he turns back to the table.

"So let me get this straight. Lars found Rayna and forced her here at gunpoint. On the way, he ordered her to summon Willow, who just happened to be having lunch with Sem and Fleur and a bag of fifty lab-grown diamonds in her pocket."

The three of us give him a simultaneous nod.

"And what's Lars's connection to Rayna again?"

"Lars killed Xander," Fleur says. "He knew about the diamonds and went there to steal them. But he didn't realize Rayna was asleep in the bedroom until he saw it on the news. He tracked her down because he thought she could help him get more."

This isn't exactly true. Lars denied killing anyone, but he'd already proven to be a thief and a liar; why not a murderer, too? He didn't seem all that torn up about Xander's death, only that someone else got to his precious diamonds first—unless he was lying about that, too. It seemed like a good bet to blame Lars for everything, and as Fleur pointed out in those thirteen minutes, he isn't exactly able to dispute that.

"The diamonds from Xander's safe."

"I assume so, yes. Lars didn't define which diamonds or how many." Fleur shifts in her chair, crossing and uncrossing her legs. "All I know is that when Willow and I got here, he held us at gunpoint because he wanted more."

"I see," the detective says, eyeing me. "How did he know you could summon Willow?"

This is one point Fleur didn't think to cover, and I suffer through a flash of red-hot panic before I manage to stitch together an answer. "I'm not entirely sure, but I'm guessing because he was the one tracking me."

It's a bit of a gamble, insinuating that the trackers were planted by Lars and not Ingrid, but I'm counting on Ingrid being smart enough to have masked her identity when she plunked down the money to buy them. She even said it at one point, that trackers are notoriously hard to trace. Either way, Ingrid won't be calling up the detective anytime soon to dispute my story, and it certainly makes sense that the trackers could have belonged to Lars. The detective motions for me to keep going.

"Lars said he'd been watching me for a while. It's possible he saw me with Willow on the day of Xander's funeral. We had drinks near the station. We took the same train back to Amsterdam. If he was tailing me that day, he would have seen us together."

"Tell me again how the victim fell through the window."

"Lars charged me," Fleur says, sounding annoyed to have to repeat herself. "He wanted the diamonds, and there was a scuffle. Surely you can't expect me not to fight back."

I don't have time to explain the nuances of the Dutch legal system, Fleur said to me in these thirteen minutes, *but in my country you can't take a hockey stick to a criminal's head and expect to get away with it. Self-defense is allowed, but it must be in proportion to the attack, and you must use a lesser form of violence whenever possible. Shoving a man out a fourth-story window is not a lesser form of violence.*

But Lars had a gun, I argued.

Yes, but so did you.

After that I shut up. This is Fleur's kingdom; the rest of us are simply living in it.

The detective purses his lips. "A scuffle."

Fleur nods.

"Between you and a man twice your size."

She nods again. "I pushed him off me. He lost his footing. The next thing I knew he . . ." She cringes, flapping a hand in the general direction of the window.

Stick as close as possible to the truth, Fleur said over and over in those thirteen minutes. *People will swallow a lie when it's concealed in truth.*

The detective looks to Willow and me, and we back Fleur up with another nod.

"But you're the one who called Rayna," he says to Willow. "You had her number."

"Yes. We exchanged numbers that day on the train. Fleur was a few minutes late for our lunch, so I called Rayna to catch up."

Willow is the one who pointed out a potential flaw in this part of the story. If the detective looks into the call logs, he'll see that it wasn't a call but a voicemail. One I've already deleted from my phone, though I'm assuming it's still floating around somewhere for the detective to pluck from a virtual cloud. Fleur swears she can make the voicemail disappear, but we didn't have time to discuss the details.

"And the guns?"

Plural. One still clutched in Lars's fist down on the docks, the other lying on the floor where I flung it after shooting out that arched window. It wasn't all that difficult to dream up that part of the story—that when Fleur tossed the diamonds into the air, when Lars dove for them, the second gun dropped out of his pocket. Lars was so distracted by the sparkle, he didn't even notice, but I did. I picked up the gun and *boom*.

"I didn't know the gun was going to shoot. I thought you had to pull back on the little hook thing first." I wriggle my thumb like it's working a hammer, which the striker-fired handgun Willow handed me doesn't have. I racked the slide and fired in one smooth motion, and I hit my target dead on. The detective was right about Americans and their guns. I've been shooting paper plates in the backyard since I was seven. "I guess it's a good thing the bullet hit the glass, and not a person."

Detective Boomsma's expression stays carefully blank. "I guess it is."

Honestly, Fleur and I couldn't have coordinated any better if we'd spent days hammering out a plan. The second Lars went after those stones, our eyes met across the dust-filled space. She saw Willow's gun in my hand. I saw the sun break through the clouds through the arched window, lighting up Lars's back as he plucked diamonds out of the dirt. I aimed and Fleur charged. The bullet shattered the glass at the same time Lars's body sailed through it, all that fabulous hair flying, floating against a bright blue sky. A beautiful, choreographed dance, and Fleur and I didn't have to say a word.

"A couple of plot holes, though," the detective says, and I have to work hard to keep my face straight. *Plot holes.* We had thirteen minutes to stitch together this story; of *course* there are plot holes. I stare at the detective and tell myself to breathe.

He pokes up a thumb. "First of all, Lars didn't murder Xander. A Polish man did, a known contract killer with a penchant for strangling his victims with zip ties. He was seen in Amsterdam the day before Xander's murder, and the next morning on a bridge crossing the Amstel, upstream from where the body was found. By the time we made the connection to the murders, the assassin was long gone."

Fleur frowns. "Contract for who? Who was this assassin working for?"

The detective turns his death stare on her. "I was hoping you could tell me."

"Me? I'm not the detective in this scenario. You are."

"Maybe it'll help if I tell you that Polish police have reported a huge influx of diamonds hitting the black market there. Uncertified. Untraceable. We're operating under the assumption that it's how the assassin was paid, with diamonds."

That shuts Fleur up. She shakes her head, and I see it then—the tiniest flash of a realization before she blinks it away. A contract killer, paid in diamonds. Hired by someone she knows, someone close.

Meanwhile I'm thinking: *What are the odds?* A contract killer creeping through the penthouse mere minutes before Lars did, murdering Xander with a zip tie while I slept in the next room, using his sawed-off finger to empty the safe down the hall. Two thieves, two close brushes with death while I was unconscious.

I know the bedroom was dark. I know I didn't make a peep. But wouldn't a diamond thief look in every cabinet and drawer and nightstand? Wouldn't a trained killer think to sweep all the rooms for potential witnesses?

Or maybe this, too, is one of the detective's plot holes. Maybe I'll never know why the killer missed me, but for now, I only know it's too much. Information overload. I can't keep straight what I'm supposed to know and not know. *Stick to the story*, Fleur insisted over and over, *and I'm telling you, no one but us will know.* I clamp my mouth shut, too terrified to say another word.

Because I'm not going to be the one to let slip what really happened here. I'm not going to accidentally admit that we're on the hook for larceny, possession of an illegal weapon, conspiracy to murder, *murder,* and probably a bunch of other charges we haven't even thought of yet. This story we're spinning is both a cover and a pact: if one of us goes down, we all do. Lying to a police officer is the least of our worries.

Fleur sighs, and she arranges her expression into something softer. "Detective, I know you're doing your job here, but can we continue this conversation tomorrow? As you can see, my nephew is traumatized, and honestly, so am I. I would very much like to get home to my family."

The detective stares at the back of Sem's head, and I can practically hear him turning our story over in his mind, looking for cracks where the pieces don't quite line up—and there have got to be plenty. There's no way we've thought of all the things that could trip us up in those thirteen panicked minutes. Yet again, Fleur is right; we need to get out of here, to regroup and go over things with a calmer, less hurried mind. We need more time to sort through the facts, pick at the evidence, weave the loose ends into our reality.

I see it on his face, his decision to let us go for now settling in. "I'll want to talk to you again. All three of you. Separately."

The last word is both a weapon and a warning. This isn't over, only a reprieve. The detective wants to talk to us separately.

"Of course. I'll have my attorney reach out first thing tomorrow." Fleur rises from her chair, and the rest of us follow suit.

We file down the stairs and out of the building, and it's all I can do not to sprint to Fleur's car, parked a block away, a dark Range Rover with leather seats as soft as butter. She starts the engine and cranks up the heat, flicking the buttons for the seat warmers, pressing the gas pedal until the air in the vents turns warm. And all the time, none of us says a word.

"Papa will call Arthur," Fleur says finally, her voice loud in the quiet space. She nods at me in the front seat next to her, at Willow and Sem huddled behind. "He'll push him to close the investigation for the House's sake. Arthur will do it for Papa."

"The police chief," Willow offers up before I can ask. She reaches around Sem for the seat belt and gives it a generous tug. "The two of them are friends."

Willow's father-in-law is friends with the police chief. Of course he is.

Still.

"But what if—"

"Papa will handle it."

"Okay, but the detective won't—"

"Papa will handle it."

She says it with so much vehemence, so much conviction, that I don't waste any more breath arguing back. I don't know Fleur very well, but I know her type. She's the female version of Barry, all arrogance and blustery entitlement, and why wouldn't she be? Fleur is a Prins. Her father is friends with the chief of police. If he says

Arthur will close the investigation before the detective can crack open our lies, then he'll close the investigation. Period, end of story.

Fleur shoves the car into Drive and pulls into traffic, and I sink into the warm leather of her passenger's seat, watching the scenery fly by. Maybe it's because she's telling me what I want to hear, or maybe I was with Barry long enough to believe in the Prins power of persuasion, but for the first time in what feels like months, I take a breath big enough to reach the bottom of my lungs.

It's good to be a Prins, even if only by association.

WILLOW

I'm seated on my favorite couch in the sunroom, waiting for Thomas to get home. Martina is gone, sent home early so I can have this moment with him alone, even though I'm not—alone, that is. The floorboards creak above my head; Rayna and Sem playing in his room upstairs. She and I haven't talked about what happened yet, but I saw the way she looked at me at the *houthavens*. Rayna is angry, but not angry enough that she refused my offer to stay here tonight. I need to make amends with her, but first I need to talk to Thomas.

Outside, it's getting dark, the bottom of the sky glowing orange with the sun's last gasp. I look out over the pretty backyard, the relentlessly blustery wind shaking the trees and the tiny lumps of dirt that in a few weeks I know will be crocus buds, and it hits me then. I'm going to miss this place. I'm going to miss this house and this view and Martina bustling around the kitchen.

But I'm not going to miss being a Prins.

On the other side of the house, the front door swings open and shut, followed by a familiar thud, Thomas's briefcase hitting the foyer floor. It's followed by the chink of metal in the china bowl where he always drops his keys. He comes down the polished marble tiles, the same tiles he and hundreds of other men have walked down for more than a hundred years.

"Willow?"

"In the sunroom."

When I called him earlier to tell him what happened at the *houthavens*, I repeated the same story we told the detective. He was too traumatized by Sem facing down a gun to notice all the plot holes or ask why his sister had a bag of fifty diamonds, but I know those questions are coming at some point. What I don't yet know is how much I'm prepared to tell him.

On the carpet by my feet, Ollie is traumatized, too, or at least he senses my own trauma, the way my body is still vibrating with residual fear. He sits up straighter at the sounds of Thomas in the hallway, but his body stays glued to my legs. He hasn't left my side since Sem and I got home, now a couple of hours ago.

Thomas appears in his coat and scarf, looking around the room for Sem. When he doesn't find him, his eyebrows draw together in a tight pucker.

"Sem's upstairs." I point to the ceiling, where the floorboards creak above my head. "He's fine. Playing video games with Rayna up in his room. I told her she could stay the night. She's keeping him busy so we can talk."

Thomas nods. He hasn't met Rayna yet, but he knows what she did for me and Sem. He collapses on the opposite end of the couch, the tails of his coat bunching up on the cushion beneath him, and looks at me across the approaching darkness. He's only a few feet away, but there's so much distance between us. Too much for us to bridge.

"I want a divorce."

"What?" His gaze whips to mine, and he genuinely seems unable to comprehend, but it's an act. Just because he doesn't have the balls to say those words out loud doesn't mean he disagrees. His hands are tight claws on his knees.

"A divorce, Thomas. And not just because of Cécile. Because you never should have married me in the first place."

He doesn't deny either, which is a surprise at the same time it's not. Deep in his heart, Thomas knows whatever we had has lost steam. I was supposed to be a fun little diversion on his business trips through Atlanta. He was supposed to be an occasional holiday from the monotony of my life, a sex-filled all-inclusive stay in his suite at the St. Regis. Thomas and I, we've never been some great love story. We've both known this for a while now.

He lets his head fall back, staring up at the ceiling for the span of a few breaths. "I'll give you a divorce. I'll give you anything you want. Just please." His voice breaks on the last word, and he pauses to pull himself together. "Please don't take Sem back to the States."

This is the place where I could make my demands. Where despite the prenup I willingly signed, I could pressure him to buy me a house down the street, fill it with fancy furniture, cover all the utilities and bills—and knowing Thomas, he'd agree. Fleur wasn't that far off when she called me Thomas's pet project, someone for him to pluck out of poverty and mold into something pretty enough to belong on his arm. But he never would have bothered if it hadn't been for Sem.

"I don't want anything from you, Thomas, except for you to be the best, most loving father you can be for our son. Sem is a Prins. He belongs here, in Amsterdam, with *both* his parents."

Relief smooths out his brow. "So you're staying?"

I nod. "I'm staying."

He gives me a silent but searing look, and something passes between us that I can't quite put into words. Gratitude, certainly, but also regret, resignation, a jumble of emotion between two people who never should have gotten married in the first place. He reaches out his hand, and I drop mine into it.

"I'm staying."

Even if one day down the line, the suspicions start to niggle in Thomas like they did his sister. If a month or a year or a decade from now, Thomas decides to pluck a hair from Sem's head or drop his toothbrush into a plastic bag and send it off to a lab. Call me delusional, but I really don't think Thomas will ever do that. I don't think he'll take that chance. It's his sister I worry about.

He gives my hand a squeeze then releases me to wriggle out of his coat. "I guess the good news is, I'll be a much more present father now that I'm unemployed. I handed my resignation to the board today."

"You quit the House? Why?"

"Come on, Willow. You know why." He tosses his coat over the armrest and relaxes into the couch. "I never wanted the CEO role. Fleur is right; I'm not cut out for it. Especially after the events of today, it just seems pointless to spend all day doing something that makes me so miserable. I'd have been much better suited on the creative team with the designers and marketing staff. It's where I wanted to be all along, where I always thought I was headed."

I think of the bracelet in the vault upstairs, all the details and thought he put into the piece, even if the sentiment was lacking. Thomas is right; creative would be a much better fit. If jewelry design is what he wants to do, the other houses will be fighting over him, a Prins, heading up the design department.

"Good for you. How did your father take it?"

"Not well. He yelled. A *lot*. As usual, he's only worried about the optics of a Prins walking away from the House. Fleur, however." He shrugs. "I'm sure she's popping open a bottle right about now."

I'm sure she is. The big corner office, the title of CEO. The House of Prins at her fingertips.

Even though, deep inside her heart, she knows she's not truly in charge, not as long as Willem is alive. I saw her face when Detective Boomsma said the Polish contract killer was paid with diamonds, the way it went white with shock. The diamond payment was news to Fleur, and it led to the same conclusion I came to: that her father has been keeping her in the dark about some things, too.

Willem, who saw the lab-growns coming from a mile away and read the writing on the wall. Who watched all the other big houses cave like the pearl titans once did, after a couple of Japanese assholes figured out how to seed their own pearls and took a blowtorch to the prices. Who uses his children like chess pieces, bending them to his will, moving them around to suit his needs.

Five generations of House of Prins, a multibillion dollar house of cards, and it's about to fall. Maybe not immediately, but at some point in the not-too-distant future. Willem knows he can't stop the industry from toppling, but he can safeguard his fortune, preserve the Prins family legacy for generations to come. Willem is ruthless that way.

Look in your own house. Jan's words, beating inside me on repeat. *Look in your own house look in your own house look in your own house.*

I sat in that freezing, dusty kitchen, listening to Fleur spinning a story for the detective, and it occurred to me she's just as much a pawn as Thomas. Better trained, perhaps, and definitely more willing, but a pawn nonetheless. That diamond payment may have been a surprise, but I watched the realization sink in her head at the same time it did in mine.

The answers came to me like a flash in that freezing metal chair, Sem clinging to my chest like a monkey. All the little puzzle pieces that never quite added up, never made much sense, they all clicked into place. For Fleur, but also for me.

"About the Cullinans," I say. Unlike Thomas and Fleur, I'm not that easy of a pawn. "I think I know where they are."

WE COME INTO his parents' living room a half hour later, and Thomas was right. There's an open bottle of Cristal in a crystal ice bucket on the side table and a triumphant Fleur holding a half-full flute. She raises it at her younger brother, and by her and Roland's smug expressions, you'd never know she'd spent most of the past year playing second string.

"Did you change your mind? Because it's too late. I just got off an emergency Zoom with the board. You've already been replaced."

Anna twists around on the couch to face her son, and her pleasant smile dissolves. "Thomas, for goodness sake, this isn't a barn. Give your coat to one of the staff."

He ignores her orders, skirting around the furniture to where his father is seated, in his usual wingback chair in front of the roaring fireplace. A glass of brown liquid is clutched in a hand, and this is definitely a celebration. I sink onto a chair at the edge of the room and watch. This is Thomas's show, and I'm happy to let him have the starring role.

"I want out."

"Out?" Anna huffs an annoyed sigh. "Darling, you just got here. Sit down. I'll get someone to pour you a drink."

"Mama, please. This is House business. It doesn't concern you."

At that, Anna clamps her glossy lips together. As wife of a Prins, she knows her place. Look pretty and sport the bling. Another reason why I won't miss this family.

Thomas turns back to his father. "I want you to buy me out. Sem, too. My son and I want nothing to do with House of Prins."

Fleur laughs, a condescending tinkle. "Thanks for your faith in me, little brother, but that would be a very stupid move. Even for you."

"Stupid and impossible," Willem says. "Our stocks hold value, but they're not made of cash. Profits are constantly being reinvested in the company, not sitting in a bank account somewhere. We don't have that much money liquid. We don't have anywhere close."

"Papa's right, which you would know if you'd paid even the slightest attention in business school," Fleur says, crossing her legs. "Just because a company is worth, say, a hundred million euros doesn't mean we can get our hands on that much cash. The House is not an ATM. Don't be ridiculous. We're not going to buy you out."

On the couch across from her, Roland rolls his eyes in support.

Thomas points a finger at his sister's face. "Fleur, and it pleases me more than you will ever know to say this, but fuck you. Fuck you, and you're wrong."

"Which part?"

"All of it. The insurance company closed the case. They're transferring the money next week, which means House of Prins is about to be flush with cash. More than enough to buy me and Sem out, and you *will* buy us out because of these."

Thomas fishes three lumps from his pants pocket and tosses them onto the coffee table like dice. Three flawless, knuckle-sized stones. One third of the missing Cullinans.

Someone gasps. Roland, I think.

Fleur and Willem are glaringly silent.

Anna settles her drink onto a side table. "Sweetheart, are those what I think they are?"

She sounds genuinely puzzled, and I wonder if it's because Willem has ordered her to play innocent for Thomas's sake. To keep both her children in the fold.

Thomas ignores her, focusing instead on his father. "And before you think about finding a new hiding spot for yours, you should know that I'll take this to the media. *De Telegraaf. Financiële Dagblad. NRC* and all the rest, the international papers, too. I'll tell them you helped Xander and Frederik steal the Cullinans from the vault and had them both silenced, because that's what happened here, isn't it? You hired a Polish contract killer, and you paid him in diamonds."

Willem doesn't shake his head, doesn't nod, doesn't blink, doesn't open his mouth. This haughty veneer he wears like a shield, this stiff back and practiced nonresponse, and I knew it. Willem is the master manipulator behind *everything.*

"What about you?" Thomas says, turning to Fleur. "What's your role in all this? Did you know the Cullinans were in the mirrors?"

Roland turns to his wife with a frown. "The Cullinans are in the mirror? Which mirror?"

The mirrors Willem gave us this past Christmas, the three antique masterpieces Jan so lovingly restored. One for Thomas, one for Fleur. The third is hanging in this very room, on the wall above Willem's wing chair, in the place of prestige above the fireplace.

Back at the house, when Thomas and I pulled his away from the wall and peered at the backing, we spotted a tiny slit in the plaster. A compartment at the bottom of the frame of swirling ivy and gilded flowers, a pocket just big enough for three big-ass stones. Once Thomas got over the shock of holding three of the missing Cullinans in his hand, he said he was surprised they gave him his fair share. So am I, honestly.

Fleur stares into her champagne glass, her feckless husband sitting next to her, and I can practically hear the gears churning. I smell the smoke as she peels back the layers. The hired killer paid in diamonds. The Cullinans in the mirror. I see the moment she arrives at the truth, comes to the humiliating conclusion that there's more than one puppet in this room, more than one pawn in her father's complexly plotted play. Willem's face is unreadable, but not Fleur's. He didn't tell her about the Cullinans, either.

Which makes me wonder what Willem's plan was here. What would have happened to those stones if Thomas and I never figured this out? What would have happened if, one day, we'd tired of the mirrors? If we'd sold them or tossed them in the trash?

Or maybe it doesn't matter. Maybe Willem thinks like many people in the diamond industry do, that their glory days are coming to an end. Maybe not tomorrow, but the end is coming. As Xander loved to say, lab-grown diamonds are a seismic shift in the industry, and prices the cartel has kept artificially high for decades are about to crumble. And it's not like Willem can sell the Cullinans anytime soon, maybe ever. Maybe he thought the insurance money was a surefire way to save the House.

I look up, and he's watching me from across the room, an open, unabashed stare that admits but also challenges. *So what?* his face says. *I know what you did, too.* The diamonds Xander grew for me, what I was planning to do with them. But Willem's crimes trump mine by a million, trillion miles.

The Prins family, coming full circle. The giant diamond that was once upon a time pilfered by Willem's great-great grandfather from a Praetorian mine and smuggled back to Holland, cut into pieces and stolen again a hundred-plus years later—*poof*—from the Prins vault. Only this time, for hundreds of millions of euros' worth of insurance.

For a Prins, everything begins and ends, always, with the Cullinans.

"This is what's going to happen," Thomas says, scooping the three Cullinans into a palm. "I've already hired Sebastian's team at Oaklins to give us an accurate valuation of the House. Fleur said a hundred million. I'm thinking that's probably on the low end, but Sebastian will be able to tell us for sure. Normally, these things take three weeks, but Sebastian said he could do it in two. Oaklins is world class. They'll give us a fair price."

He pauses for their response, but it doesn't come. The room falls into silence. The only sound is the muted clanging of the staff, bustling around in the kitchen.

Thomas lifts both hands in the air at his sides, turning to Fleur, "Congratulations, I guess. You and the twins will inherit the whole thing. Sem and I don't want any part in it."

Fleur pops off the couch. "You know he's not even yours, right? Sem is not your son."

Her words fall into the room like a grenade, sucking up all the air, and a surge of something sour rises in my chest like nausea. Every head in the place swings to me, all but Thomas's. He stands there like a statue, glaring at his sister with such obvious hatred that the breath catches in my throat.

"It's true! *Tell* him, Willow." She waves an arm in his direction, and champagne sloshes over the side of her glass and lands on the silk carpet with a splat. "Tell Thomas that Sem doesn't belong to him."

I stay quiet, because how do I explain that it's true and it isn't? I think about Thomas's face when I told him about the pregnancy, the way he dropped to his knees and kissed my stomach, the way he immediately started making plans. No hesitation. No questioning if there was any possibility this baby couldn't be his. I wasn't certain a baby would give us enough steam to sustain a marriage, but Thomas was. From the very beginning, Thomas was sure enough for both of us.

So they don't share some of the same DNA. Does that make their love for each other any less real? Does that make it impossible for them to be father and son? I look at Thomas, and I pray the answer is no.

"I had him tested," Fleur says, not letting it go. "Sem is not a Prins. He doesn't have so much as an ounce of Prins blood in him."

Thomas barks a laugh, a thick, meaty sound. "Thank God. I wish I could say the same."

THOMAS AND I are quiet on the short drive home. I sit in the soft leather of his passenger's seat and watch the familiar scenery flash by, the stately villas of the Apollolaan, the empty playground at Sem's school, and the angry, icy waters of the canal, the shops and restaurants with their glowing windows and signs, the bikers weaving in and out of traffic, and the people out walking their dogs. Sometime in the past few hours, the rain and the clouds have blown off. The night is clear, the lights and the sky twinkling.

It's true what I said earlier, that I don't want to leave Amsterdam. No matter what Thomas does next, I want to stay here, to live here with Sem. I want our answer to the question *Where are you from?* to be *Amsterdam*. This place is home, and it's not like I have a better one in the States to return to. I belong here, as does Sem.

In the driveway, Thomas rolls to a stop in his usual spot, and my mind tracks back to me standing in the bedroom window upstairs, watching him text Cécile through the sunroof. Only yesterday, which is something of a shock. It feels like a lifetime ago.

I twist on my seat to face him, taking in his handsome profile in the dark. "How long have you known?"

It's the piece I'd missed before, back at his parents' house. The fury on his face when he looked at his sister, the betrayal—it was all directed at her. None of it was for me. He didn't even glance my way because he knew. Thomas already knew.

His hands are still gripping the wheel, but they're more relaxed now, not strangling it like they were his knees the first time we talked about Sem tonight. As awful as things were at his parents' house, as shocking as Fleur's bombshell was for me, Thomas had a different response: relief. Or maybe he's like me, relieved that the awful secret is finally out in the open.

"Since Sem was a baby. And I didn't *know* know. Unlike my horrible sister, I never had him tested."

"Why didn't you say something?"

"Because what was I going to say? *Hey, this kid I've fallen head over heels in love with isn't mine, so please don't move with him to the other side of the planet.* You have no idea, Willow. For the past four years, I've lived in absolute terror."

Understanding settles over me slowly, then all at once, like watching a building implode and knowing it's about to fall seconds before it hits the ground.

All this time, I thought Thomas didn't have the balls to ask me for a divorce, that he was too chicken to say that awful word out loud, to put those wheels in motion.

But that's not why.

It's because he was terrified of the consequences. He was terrified that I was holding the secret of Sem's paternity in my back pocket to use as a bargaining chip or worse, that I would be like the kids at Sem's school and take my toys and go home, back to the States. That I would blurt out the truth and snatch away his parental rights out of anger or spite. I think of the way his voice broke when he begged me not to move Sem to the US. Thomas thought a divorce meant I'd be divorcing him of Sem.

"I've been terrified, too, FYI. Of you finding out and hating me for it, then disowning us both. I can live with your hatred of me, but I couldn't bear Sem's heartbreak, or to watch him suffer because he needs a medical treatment that I can't afford on my own."

"I would never let that happen. *Never.* I won't abandon either of you. I love Sem more than anything, and I love you for making me a father. I just wish I could have loved you better."

I reach across the console and take his hand. "See? You're already Sem's father in every way that counts, and a much better parent than any of ours have ever been. At some point, we'll have to talk about how to handle this with Sem, but for now, just know that Sem loves you. He needs you in his life, and so do I."

He lifts my hand to his lips and drops a kiss on my knuckles. "Thank you."

"Sem wants a bunny for his birthday, by the way. A real one."

"Then I guess we're getting a bunny."

Thomas says it so instantly, so effortlessly, that *we* ringing in my ear, and that's when I know we'll be okay. Thomas and I will figure out how to share our son, how to make sure he is happy and healthy and loved. We will unwind the bonds that tie us together, all but the most important one, and we'll be better parents for it. I take back what I said before, about Thomas and me not being a great love story. Ours is the greatest love story of all because it gave us Sem.

I think about him sleeping upstairs, his soft little sighs as his lungs rise and fall with breath, about Rayna in the guest room across the hall, still reeling from Xander and Lars and the lies I told that put her life in danger, about the amends I need to make and the truths I need to tell, to Rayna but also to Thomas. He deserves to know the truth. All of it.

I unwind my hand from his and tip my head at the house. "Come on. I want you to meet my new friend, Rayna."

★ ★ ★ ★ ★

ACKNOWLEDGMENTS

I was barely out of college when I shoved all my worldly belongings into a couple of suitcases and moved to the Netherlands. I learned the language, I made new friends, I built a life I learned to love, and none of it was easy. All the frustrations Rayna and Willow feel about finding their way in a foreign land were mine at one time, but I also share their enchantment for this place that all these years later I still call home. Amsterdam is loud and it's crowded and the weather can be a little iffy, but there's no place I'd rather be. Beyond its beauty, there's something magical about this city, and I hope I've given a glimpse of that here. All that goes to say, this book has been a long time coming.

Thanks to agent Nikki Terpilowski for reading an earlier, crappier version and pointing the way. To editors Gabriella Mongelli, Kate Studer, and Tracy Wilson for your help shaping the manuscript into a book, and to Annie Chagnot for swooping in at the eleventh hour and finishing the job. Erika Imranyi, thanks for all the juggling behind the scenes; I know it was tricky.

To everyone at Park Row Books for inviting me into your home and working so tirelessly on my behalf. Emer Flounders and Sophie James, thank you for your publicity genius.

To my Killer Author Club cohosts, Heather Gudenkauf and Kaira Rouda; thanks for making Tuesday nights my favorite of the week. To Vanessa Lillie and Cate Holahan, I'm so blessed to be on this Young Rich Widows ride with you two; as Camille would say, "We got this, sugar." And to all those other authors happy to lend an ear or talk me off a ledge—you know who you are—thank you for making such a solitary business feel a lot less lonely. I can't imagine doing this without you.

To my family and friends, thank you for showing up at endless book launches; I know there are a lot of them. To my parents, Bob and Diane, for being my biggest fans. To Ewoud, Evan, and Isabella, you three are my most cherished love story.

And finally to you, the reader of this book, and to all the generous Bookstagrammers, BookTokkers, bloggers, reviewers, booksellers, and librarians, *dank jullie wel* for coming with me on this fictional tour of Amsterdam. If you haven't already, I hope you get to see the city for real one day very soon.